"I REMEMBER BABYLON" by Arthur C. Clarke —Communication satellites had seemed like the perfect way to send forth messages of peace and understanding till someone found a way to transmit a far deadlier and more terrifying vision. . . .

"MIND PARTNER" by Christopher Anvil—He had taken on a mission to shut down a new and seemingly unstoppable "drug" ring. But how could he defeat these elusive enemies when he was no longer sure whose life he was living?

"THE HANDLER" by Damon Knight—Pete was everyone's best friend, the life of the party, a total success—but you had to know how to handle him. . . .

"THE VOICES OF TIME" by J. G. Ballard—Is this how the universe will end, not with a bang but a. . . .

These are just some of the futures you'll find in—

ISAAC ASIMOV PRESENTS THE GREAT SF STORIES:

Watch for these exciting DAW anthologies:

ASIMOV PRESENTS THE GREAT SF STORIES
  Classics of short fiction from the Golden Age through today.
  Edited by Isaac Asimov and Martin H. Greenberg.

THE ANNUAL WORLD'S BEST SF
  The finest stories of the current year.
  Edited by Donald A. Wollheim with Arthur W. Saha.

THE YEAR'S BEST HORROR STORIES
  The finest terror stories of the current year.
  Edited by Karl Edward Wagner.

SWORD AND SORCERESS
  Original tales of fantasy and adventure with female protagonists.
  Edited by Marion Zimmer Bradley.

ISAAC ASIMOV

PRESENTS

THE GREAT SF STORIES

#22

(1959)

EDITED BY ISAAC ASIMOV AND MARTIN H. GREENBERG

DAW BOOKS, INC.

DONALD A. WOLLHEIM, FOUNDER

375 Hudson Street, New York, NY 10014

**ELIZABETH R. WOLLHEIM
SHEILA E. GILBERT
PUBLISHERS**

Cover art by Angus McKie.

DAW Book Collectors No. 842.

First Printing, February 1991

1 2 3 4 5 6 7 8 9

DAW TRADEMARK REGISTERED
U.S. PAT. OFF. AND FOREIGN COUNTRIES
—MARCA REGISTRADA,
DAW HECHO EN U.S.A.

PRINTED IN THE U.S.A.

ACKNOWLEDGMENTS

CONTENTS

INTRODUCTION

The first year of the new decade was full of important events, not all of them pleasant. Ninety-two Blacks were killed in a police massacre at Sharpeville in South Africa, a catalyst for the freedom struggle in that sad land. In the U.S., the "sit-in" movement for civil rights surged as Blacks occupied lunch counters in Greensboro, North Carolina. In 1960 Fidel Castro took Cuba closer to the Soviet Union and began to expropriate American companies on the island. The Belgian Congo received its independence, but United Nations forces had to be sent to restore order in the aftermath of freedom. The French detonated their first atomic bomb as the nuclear club reached four.

Princess Margaret (remember her?) wed Tony Armstrong-Jones as differences between the Peoples Republic of China and the Soviet Union became public knowledge.

Gary Francis Powers and his U-2 spy plane were shot down over the U.S.S.R.; President Eisenhower at first denied, then admitted that we were overflying the Soviet Union—Khrushchev canceled a scheduled summit meeting. John F. Kennedy and Vice President Richard Nixon won the Democratic and Republican nominations for President, and Kennedy won the election in November by 112,000 votes, possibly cast by "dead" voters from Chicago.

The Nazi in charge of the extermination of the Jewish population of Europe, Adolf Eichmann, was seized by Israeli agents in Argentina and flown to Israel for trial.

Broadway had a great year in 1960 with the opening of *Becket*, *The Fantasticks*, *Bye, Bye Birdie*, *An Evening With Mike Nichols and Elaine May*, *Camelot*, *Irma La Douce*, Lillian Hellman's *Toys in the Attic*, and Tammy Grimes as *The Unsinkable Molly Brown*. In sports, Pete Runnels of the Red Sox and Dick Groat of the Pirates led the majors in hitting, while Ernie Banks led in homers with 41. Pittsburgh took the World Series from the Yankees in seven games. The American Football League debuted while Pete Rozelle became Commissioner of the National Football League. Jim Brown of Marty's Cleveland Browns led the NFL in rushing, Ray Berry of the Colts was the leading receiver, and Mike Ditka of the University of Pittsburgh was an All-America end. The 1960 Olympics in Rome saw Wilma Rudolph and Cassius Clay (later Muhammad Ali) win gold medals as Rafer Johnson won a brilliant victory in the decathlon. Floyd Patterson kayoed Ingemar Johansson to retake the heavyweight boxing crown, but the Packers lost the NFL Championship game to the Eagles. Venetian Way with Willie Hartack aboard won the Kentucky Derby.

In 1960 the Nobel Prize for Medicine and Physiology went to Burnett and Medawar for their research in acquired immunity, a subject which would come to dominate medical concerns in the 1980s. Theodore Maiman invented the laser, while in space, the first communications satellite (Echo I) and the first weather satellite (Tiros I) were successfully launched.

Top films of the year included *The Magnificent Seven*, *Last Year at Marienbad*, Billy Wilder's *The Apartment*, *Exodus*, *Elmer Gantry*, Kirk Douglas as *Spartacus*, *Never On Sunday*, and Alfred Hitchcock's great *Psycho*, with Anthony Perkins as Norman Bates. Elizabeth Taylor won Best Actress honors for *Butterfield 8*. Harold Schonberg became music critic for *The New York Times* in 1960, while Jasper Johns painted "Light Bulb," Willem de Kooning painted "A Tree In Naples," and Louise Nevelson sculpted "Sky Cathedral."

Tragedies of the year included the destruction of Ebbets Field and the divorce of one of America's favorite couples, Lucille Ball and Desi Arnaz. On the other hand, the first oral contraceptive appeared in 1960, along with the first felt-tip pen and Librium, which tended to balance things out. In the world of books (their world, not ours) notable titles included *The Loneliness Of The Long Distance Runner* by Allan Sillitoe, *The Rise And Fall Of The Third Reich* by William L. Shirer, *Rabbit, Run* by John Updike, *Growing Up Absurd* by Paul Goodman, *To Kill A Mockingbird* by Harper Lee, *The Chapman Report* by Irving Wallace, *The Conscience Of A Conservative* by Barry Goldwater, *The Sot-Weed Factor* by John Barth, *The Stages Of Economic Growth* by Eugene Rostow, *Hawaii* by James Michener, *Into The Stone And Other Poems* by James Dickey, *Love And Death In The American Novel* by Leslie Fiedler, *Advise And Consent* by Allen

Drury, *The End Of Ideology* by Daniel Bell, and *The Magician Of Lublin* by Isaac Bashevis Singer (the other Isaac).

The top three shows on the tube, *Gunsmoke*, *Wagon Train*, and *Have Gun Will Travel*, were all Westerns; debut shows included *The Bob Newhart Show*, *Route 66*, *The Andy Griffith Show*, *My Three Sons*, and *The Flinstones*, but on the other hand, *Howdy Doody* bit the dust after more than 2,000 episodes. However, the best television of the year was the Debate between Kennedy and Nixon, which many maintain won the Presidency for the Senator from Massachusetts (along with the zombie voters of Chicago).

The world of music was enriched by such gems as "The Twist," Jimmy Jones' great "Handy Man," Sam Cooke's "Chain Gang," Ray Charles' "Georgia On my Mind," the unforgettable "Itsy Bitsy Teenie Weenie Yellow Polka Dot Bikini," and the King's "Are You Lonesome To-Night." Not to mention Lukas Foss' *Time Cycle* and Milton Babbitt's *Three Movements for Orchestra*. A smart and creative guy named Berry Gordy started Motown Records.

Death took Mack Sennett, Oscar Hammerstein II, Aneurin Bevan, Margaret Sullivan, Boris Pasternak, Aly Khan, Clark Gable, Emily Post, Albert Camus, and Richard Wright.

Mel Brooks was Mel Brooks.

In the real world the magazines continued to experience difficulties as the much underrated *Fantastic Universe* went out of business in March, followed a month later by *Future Science Fiction*.

The paperback explosion continued, as did the publication of at least some hardcover science fiction—the most important novel of the year in book form was *A*

INTRODUCTION

Canticle For Leibowitz, published by Lippincott. Other noteworthy books included the novels *Drunkard's Walk* by Frederik Pohl, *Rogue Moon* by Algis Budrys, *The Tomorrow People* by Judith Merril, *The Genetic General* by Gordon R. Dickson, *And Then The Town Took Off* by Richard Wilson, *Venus Plus X* by Theodore Sturgeon, the wonderful *The High Crusade* by Poul Anderson, which gets my vote as the best novel of 1960, and the startling *Flesh* by Philip José Farmer.

It was an even better year for anthologies and collections, most especially *Strange Relations* by Philip José Farmer, *A Decade Of Fantasy And Science Fiction* edited by Robert P. Mills, *Galaxies Like Grains Of Sand* by Brian W. Aldiss, *The Science-Fictional Sherlock Holmes*, edited by The Council of Four, *The Worlds Of Clifford Simak*, *13 Great Stories Of Science Fiction* and *Six Great Short Science Fiction* novels, both edited by the great Groff Conklin, *Guardians Of Time* by Poul Anderson, and *Out of Bounds* by Judith Merril.

One of the most important books of 1960 was non-fiction—Kingsley Amis' *New Maps Of Hell*, the first important (and largely laudatory) discussion of the sf field by someone from the outside. It was one of the first indications that science fiction would be taken seriously by the outside world. At the same time Thomas D. Clareson started *Extrapolation* (a journal that is still going strong as a publication of The Science Fiction Research Association) as the Newsletter of the Conference on Science Fiction of the Modern Language Association.

In the real world, two more important people made their maiden voyages into reality; in January—R. A. Lafferty with "Day of the Glacier"; and in February—

Ben Bova with "A Long Way Back." *Astounding Science Fiction* changed its name to *Astounding Science Fact & Fiction* on its way to becoming *Analog*.

On television, we were treated to the BBC's productions of Nigel Kneale's *The Quatermass Experiment*, *Quatermass II*, and *Quatermass And The Pit*. Fantastic films of the year included Gore Vidal's *Visit To a Small Planet*, the awful *The Atomic Submarine*, the beautiful Susan Cabot as *The Wasp Woman*, *The Electronic Monster*, the Japanese *Battle In Outer Space*, *Dinosaurus*, *12 To The Moon*, the excellent *Village Of The Damned*, Sir Arthur Conan Doyle's *The Lost World*, H. G. Wells' *The Time Machine*, *Beyond The Time Barrier*, *The Two Faces Of Dr. Jekyll*, the lonely *Last Woman On Earth*, and *Man In The Moon*.

The Family gathered in Pittsburgh for the 18th World Science Fiction Convention—Pittcon. Hugo Awards (for work in the previous year) went to *Starship Troopers* by Robert A. Heinlein, "Flowers for Algernon" by Daniel Keyes, THE TWILIGHT ZONE, *The Magazine Of Fantasy And Science Fiction,* Ed Emshwiller, and a Special Award to Hugo Gernsback as "The Father of Magazine Science Fiction."

Let us travel back to that honored year of 1960 and enjoy the best stories that the real world bequeathed to us.

MARIANA

BY FRITZ LEIBER (1911–   )

FANTASTIC
FEBRUARY

Fritz Leiber (for a brief while he was known as Fritz Leiber, Jr.) is the distinguished winner of both The World Fantasy Award for lifetime accomplishment, conferred by the World Fantasy Convention, and the lifetime achievement Grand Master Nebula of the Science Fiction Writers of America, evidence of his enormous talent. He was still writing a monthly column for Locus in the 1990s.

Fritz has graced the pages of this series often, and it is a pleasure to welcome him back with "Mariana," a story that Philip K. Dick would have been proud to have written. His most recent collection is the massive The Leiber Chronicles (1990) edited by yours truly, one of the most pleasurable "tasks" I've ever been lucky enough to be assigned. (MHG)

"Solipsism" comes from Latin words meaning "one's self alone." Almost any thinking individual must go through some phase where he wonders what is "real."

15

Fritz Leiber

All we know is what we sense, but how trustworthy are our sensations? Is all an illusion? Can we know anything at all for certain other than ourselves and our thoughts?

The point is made chillingly at the end of Mark Twain's "The Mysterious Stranger." It is to be found in Robert A. Heinlein's classic "They." It is a question that has no answer and cannot be solved. Those who play with solipsism must usually abandon it at last and simply go on with their lives.

And now you are ready for "Mariana." (IA)

Mariana had been living in the big villa and hating the tall pine trees around it for what seemed like an eternity when she found the secret panel in the master control panel of the house.

The secret panel was simply a narrow blank of aluminum—she'd thought of it as room for more switches if they ever needed any, perish the thought!—between the air-conditioning controls and the gravity controls. Above the switches for the three-dimensional TV but below those for the robot butler and maids.

Jonathan had told her not to fool with the master control panel while he was in the city, because she would wreck anything electrical, so when the secret panel came loose under her aimlessly questing fingers and fell to the solid rock floor of the patio with a musical *twing* her first reaction was fear.

Then she saw it was only a small blank oblong of sheet aluminum that had fallen and that in the space it had covered was a column of six little switches. Only the top one was identified. Tiny glowing letters beside it spelled TREES and it was on.

* * *

When Jonathan got home from the city that evening she gathered her courage and told him about it. He was neither particularly angry nor impressed.

"Of course there's a switch for the trees," he informed her deflatingly, motioning the robot butler to cut his steak. "Didn't you know they were radio trees? I didn't want to wait twenty-five years for them and they couldn't grow in this rock anyway. A station in the city broadcasts a master pine tree and sets like ours pick it up and project it around homes. It's vulgar but convenient."

After a bit she asked timidly, "Jonathan, are the radio pine trees ghostly as you drive through them?"

"Of course not! They're solid as this house and the rock under it—to the eye and to the touch too. A person could even climb them. If you ever stirred outside you'd know these things. The city station transmits pulses of alternating matter at sixty cycles a second. The science of it is over your head."

She ventured one more question: "Why did they have the tree switch covered up?"

"So you wouldn't monkey with it—same as the fine controls on the TV. And so you wouldn't get ideas and start changing the trees. It would unsettle *me*, let me tell you, to come home to oaks one day and birches the next. I like consistency and I like pines." He looked at them out of the dining-room picture window and grunted with satisfaction.

She had been meaning to tell him about hating the pines, but that discouraged her and she dropped the topic.

About noon the next day, however, she went to the secret panel and switched off the pine trees and quickly turned around to watch them.

At first nothing happened and she was beginning to think that Jonathan was wrong again, as he so often was though would never admit, but then they began to waver and specks of pale green light churned across them and then they faded and were gone, leaving behind only an intolerably bright single point of light— just as when the TV is switched off. The star hovered motionless for what seemed a long time, then backed away and raced off toward the horizon.

Now that the pine trees were out of the way Mariana could see the real landscape. It was flat gray rock, endless miles of it, exactly the same as the rock on which the house was set and which formed the floor of the patio. It was the same in every direction. One black two-lane road drove straight across it— nothing more.

She disliked the view almost at once—it was dreadfully lonely and depressing. She switched the gravity to moon-normal and danced about dreamily, floating over the middle-of-the-room bookshelves and the grand piano and even having the robot maids dance with her, but it did not cheer her. About two o'clock she went to switch on the pine trees again, as she had intended to do in any case before Jonathan came home and was furious.

However, she found there had been changes in the column of six little switches. The TREES switch no longer had its glowing name. She remembered that it had been the top one, but the top one would not turn on again. She tried to force it from "off" to "on" but it would not move.

All the rest of the afternoon she sat on the steps outside the front door watching the black two-lane road. Never a car or a person came into view until

Jonathan's tan roadster appeared, seeming at first to hang motionless in the distance and then to move only like a microscopic snail although she knew he always drove at top speed—it was one of the reasons she would never get in the car with him.

Jonathan was not as furious as she had feared. "Your own damn fault for meddling with it," he said curtly. "Now we'll have to get a man out here. Dammit, I hate to eat supper looking at nothing but those rocks! Bad enough driving through them twice a day."

She asked him haltingly about the barrenness of the landscape and the absence of neighbors.

"Well, you wanted to live *way out*," he told her. "You wouldn't ever have known about it if you hadn't turned off the trees."

"There's one other thing I've got to bother you with Jonathan," she said. "Now the second switch—the one next below—has got a name that glows. It just says HOUSE. It's turned on—I haven't touched it! Do you suppose . . ."

"I want to look at this," he said, bounding up from the couch and slamming his martini-on-the-rocks tumbler down on the tray of the robot maid so that she rattled. "I bought this house as solid, but there are swindles. Ordinarily I'd spot a broadcast style in a flash, but they just might have slipped me a job relayed from some other planet or solar system. Fine thing if me and fifty other multi-megabuck men were spotted around in identical houses, each thinking his was unique."

"But if the house is based on rock like it is . . ."

"That would just make it easier for them to pull the trick, you dumb bunny!"

They reached the master control panel. "There it is," she said helpfully, jabbing out a finger . . . and hit the HOUSE switch.

For a moment nothing happened, then a white churning ran across the ceiling, the walls and furniture started to swell and bubble like cold lava, and then they were alone on a rock table big as three tennis courts. Even the master control panel was gone. The only thing that was left was a slender rod coming out of the gray stone at their feet and bearing at the top, like some mechanistic fruit, a small block with the six switches—that and an intolerably bright star hanging in the air where the master bedroom had been.

Mariana pushed frantically at the HOUSE switch, but it was unlabelled now and locked in the "off" position, although she threw her weight at it stiff-armed.

The upstairs sped off like an incendiary bullet, but its last flashbulb glare showed her Jonathan's face set in lines of fury. He lifted his hands like talons.

"You little idiot!" he screamed, coming at her.

"No Jonathan, no!" she wailed, backing off, but he kept coming.

She realized that the block of switches had broken off in her hands. The third switch had a glowing name now: JONATHAN. She flipped it.

As his fingers dug into her bare shoulders they seemed to turn to foam rubber, then to air. His face and gray flannel suit seethed iridescently, like a leprous ghost's, then melted and ran. His star, smaller than that of the house but much closer, seared her eyes. When she opened them again there was nothing at all left of the star or Jonathan but a dancing dark after-image like a black tennis ball.

*   *   *

MARIANA

She was alone on an infinite flat rock plain under the cloudless, star-specked sky.

The fourth switch had its glowing name now: STARS.

It was almost dawn by her radium-dialed wristwatch and she was thoroughly chilled, when she finally decided to switch off the stars. She did not want to do it—in their slow wheeling across the sky they were the last sign of orderly reality—but it seemed the only move she could make.

She wondered what the fifth switch would say. ROCKS? AIR? or even. . . ?

She switched off the stars.

The Milky Way, arching in all its unalterable glory, began to churn, its component stars darting about like midges. Soon only one remained, brighter even than Sirius or Venus—until it jerked back, fading, and darted to infinity.

The fifth switch said DOCTOR and it was not on but off.

An inexplicable terror welled up in Mariana. She did not even want to touch the fifth switch. She set the block of switches down on the rock and backed away from it.

But she dared not go far in the starless dark. She huddled down and waited for dawn. From time to time she looked at her watch dial and at the night-light glow of the switch-label a dozen yards away.

It seemed to be growing much colder.

She read her watch dial. It was two hours past sunrise. She remembered they had taught her in third grade that the sun was just one more star.

She went back and sat down beside the block of switches and picked it up with a shudder and flipped the fifth switch.

The rock grew soft and crisply fragrant under her and lapped up over her legs and then slowly turned white.

She was sitting in a hospital bed in a small blue room with a white pin-stripe.

A sweet, mechanical voice came out of the wall, saying, "You have interrupted the wish-fulfilment therapy by your own decision. If you now recognize your sick depression and are willing to accept help, the doctor will come to you. If not, you are at liberty to return to the wish-fulfilment therapy and pursue it to its ultimate conclusion."

Mariana looked down. She still had the block of switches in her hands and the fifth switch read DOCTOR.

The wall said, "I assume from your silence that you will accept treatment. The doctor will be with you immediately."

The inexplicable terror returned to Mariana with compulsive intensity.

She switched off the doctor.

She was back in the starless dark. The rocks had grown very much colder. She could feel icy feathers falling on her face—snow.

She lifted the block of switches and saw, to her unutterable relief, that the sixth and last switch now read, in tiny glowing letters: MARIANA.

THE DAY THE ICICLE WORKS CLOSED

BY FREDERIK POHL (1919–   )

GALAXY
FEBRUARY

As Isaac points out below, avarice is certainly a central concern in Fred Pohl's writings, especially his stories and novels from the 1950s and early 1960s. 1960 was a good year for him, a year that saw the publication of his novel Drunkard's Walk, *his first solo novel since 1957's* Slave Ship. *In addition, he published a fine collection,* The Man Who Ate The World, *which contained such stellar examples of the production-consumption process as "The Wizards of Pung's Corners" and "The Waging of the Peace" (1958 and 1959), not to mention the incredible title novella.*

"The Day the Icicle Works Closed" is vintage Pohl, full of greed and power-seeking. (MHG)

It is possible, sometimes, to try to play the game of reducing a complex piece of literature to a single word or phrase. Thus, Alexandre Dumas's The Count of Monte Cristo *can be distilled to "Revenge"; his* The Three Musketeers *to "Friendship."*

We might do the same, perhaps, to the general corpus of a person's writings. For instance, I like to think that if all my fiction were lumped together and boiled down, you would end with the word "Reason." At least I tend to solve the problems raised in my stories by a long-drawn-out battle of competing rationalisms.

I don't know whether this can be done for everyone, but it seems to me that Fred Pohl has a clear enemy that runs through much of his major fiction, since his (and Kornbluth's) classic "Gravy Planet." That is "Greed." As, for instance, consider this story. (IA)

I

The wind was cold, pink snow was falling and Milo Pulcher had holes in his shoes. He trudged through the pink-gray slush across the square from the courthouse to the jail. The turnkey was drinking coffee out of a vinyl container. "Expecting you," he grunted. "Which one you want to see first?"

Pulcher sat down, grateful for the warmth. "It doesn't matter. Say, what kind of kids are they?"

The turnkey shrugged.

"I mean, do they give you any trouble?"

"How could they give me trouble? If they don't clean their cells they don't eat. What else they do makes no difference to me."

Pulcher took the letter from Judge Pegrim out of his pocket, and examined the list of his new clients. Avery Foltis, Walter Hopgood, Jimmy Lasser, Sam Schlesterman, Bourke Smith, Madeleine Gaultry. None of the names meant anything to him. "I'll take Foltis," he guessed, and followed the turnkey to a cell.

THE DAY THE ICICLE WORKS CLOSED

The Foltis boy was homely, pimply and belligerent. "Cripes," he growled shrilly, "are you the best they can do for me?"

Pulcher took his time answering. The boy was not very lovable; but, he reminded himself, there was a fifty-dollar retainer from the county for each one of these defendants, and conditions being what they were Pulcher could easily grow to love three hundred dollars. "Don't give me a hard time," he said amiably. "I may not be the best lawyer in the Galaxy, but I'm the one you've got."

"Cripes."

"All right, all right. Tell me what happened, will you? All I know is that you're accused of conspiracy to commit a felony, specifically an act of kidnaping a minor child."

"Yeah, that's it," the boy agreed. "You want to know what happened?" He bounced to his feet, then began acting out his story. "We were starving to death, see?" Arms clutched pathetically around his belly. "The Icicle Works closed down. Cripes, I walked the streets nearly a year, looking for something to do. Anything." Marching in place. "I even rented out for a while, but—that didn't work out." He scowled and fingered his pimply face. Pulcher nodded. Even a body-renter had to have some qualifications. The most important one was a good-looking, disease-free, strong and agile physique. "So we got together and decided, the hell, there was money to be made hooking old Swinburne's son. So—I guess we talked too much. They caught us." He gripped his wrists, like manacles.

Pulcher asked a few more questions, and then interviewed two of the other boys. He learned nothing he

25

hadn't already known. The six youngsters had planned a reasonably competent kidnapping, and talked about it where they could be heard, and if there was any hope of getting them off it did not make itself visible to their court-appointed attorney.

Pulcher left the jail abruptly and went up the street to see Charley Dickon.

The committeeman was watching a three-way wrestling match on a flickery old TV set. "How'd it go, Milo," he greeted the lawyer, keeping his eyes on the wrestling.

Pulcher said, "I'm not going to get them off, Charley."

"Oh? Too bad." Dickon looked away from the set for the first time. "Why not?"

"They admitted the whole thing. Handwriting made the Hopgood boy on the ransom note. They all had fingerprints and cell-types all over the place. And besides, they talked too much."

Dickon said with a spark of interest, "What about Tim Lasser's son?"

"Sorry." The committeeman looked thoughtful. "I can't help it, Charley," the lawyer protested. The kids hadn't been even routinely careful. When they planned to kidnap the son of the mayor they had talked it over, quite loudly, in a juke joint. The waitress habitually taped everything that went on in her booths. Pulcher suspected a thriving blackmail business, but that didn't change the fact that there was enough on tape to show premeditation. They had picked the mayor's son up at school. He had come with them perfectly willingly— the girl, Madeleine Gaultry, had been a babysitter for him. The boy was only three years old, but he couldn't miss an easy identification like that. And there was more: the ransom note had been sent special delivery, and young Foltis had asked the post-office clerk to put the postage on instead of using the automatic meter. The clerk remembered the pimply face very well indeed.

The committeeman sat politely while Pulcher explained, though it was obvious that most of his attention was on the snowy TV screen. "Well, Milo, that's the way it goes. Anyway, you got a fast three hundred, hey? And that reminds me."

Pulcher's guard went up.

"Here," said the committeeman, rummaging through his desk. He brought out a couple of pale green tickets. "You ought to get out and meet some more people. The Party's having its annual Chester A. Arthur Day Dinner next week. Bring your girl."

"I don't have a girl."

"Oh, you'll find one. Fifteen dollars per," explained the committeeman, handing over the tickets. Pulcher sighed and paid. Well, that was what kept the wheels oiled. And Dickon had suggested his name to Judge Pegrim. Thirty dollars out of three hundred still left him a better week's pay than he had had since the Icicle Works folded.

The committeeman carefully folded the bills into his pocket, Pulcher watching gloomily. Dickon was looking prosperous, all right. There was easily a couple of thousand in that wad. Pulcher supposed that Dickon had been caught along with everybody else on the planet when the Icicle Works folded. Nearly everybody owned stock in it, and certainly Charley Dickon, whose politician brain got him a piece of nearly every

27

major enterprise on Altair Nine—a big clump of stock in the Tourist Agency, a sizable share of the Mining Syndicate—certainly he would have had at least a few thousand in the Icicle Works. But it hadn't hurt him much. He said, "None of my business, but why don't you take that girl?"

"Madeleine Gaultry? She's in jail."

"Get her out. Here." He tossed over a bondsman's card. Pulcher pocketed it with a scowl. That would cost another forty bucks anyway, he estimated; the bondsman would naturally be one of Dickon's club members.

Pulcher noticed that Dickon was looking strangely puzzled. "What's the matter?"

"Like I say, it's none of my business. But I don't get it. You and the girl have a fight?"

"Fight? I don't even know her."

"She said you did."

"Me? No. I don't know any Madeleine Gaultry— Wait a minute! Is that her married name? Did she used to be at the Icicle Works?"

Dickon nodded. "Didn't you see her?"

"I didn't get to the women's wing. I—" Pulcher stood up, oddly flustered. "Say I'd better run along, Charley. This bondsman, he's open now? Well—" He stopped babbling and left.

Madeleine Gaultry! Only her name had been Madeleine Cossett. It was funny that she should turn up now—in jail and, Pulcher abruptly realized, likely to stay there indefinitely. But he put that thought out of his mind; first he wanted to see her.

The snow was turning lavender now.

Pink snow, green snow, lavender snow—any color

THE DAY THE ICICLE WORKS CLOSED

of the pastel rainbow. It was nothing unusual. That
was what had made Altair Nine worth colonizing in
the first place.

Now, of course, it was only a way of getting your
feet wet.

Pulcher waited impatiently at the turnkey's office
while he shambled over to the women's wing and,
slowly, returned with the girl. They looked at each
other. She didn't speak. Pulcher opened his mouth,
closed it, and silently took her by the elbow. He
steered her out of the jail and hailed a cab. That was
an extravagance, but he didn't care.

Madeleine shrank into a corner of the cab, looking
at him out of blue eyes that were large and shadowed.
She wasn't hostile, she wasn't afraid. She was only
remote.

"Hungry?" She nodded. Pulcher gave the cab driver
the name of a restaurant. Another extravagance, but
he didn't mind the prospect of cutting down on lunches
for a few weeks. He had had enough practice at it.

A year before this girl had been the prettiest secretary in the pool at the Icicle Works. He dated her half
a dozen times. There was a company rule against it,
but the first time it was a kind of schoolboy's prank,
breaking the headmaster's regulations, and the other
times it was a driving need. Then—

Then came the Gumpert Process.

That was the killer, the Gumpert Process. Whoever
Gumpert was. All anybody at the Icicle Works knew
was that someone named Gumpert (back on Earth,
one rumor said; another said he was a colonist in the
Sirian system) had come up with a cheap, practical
method of synthesizing the rainbow antibiotic molds
that floated free in Altair Nine's air, coloring its pre-

cipitation and, more important, providing a priceless export commodity. A whole Galaxy had depended on those rainbow molds, shipped in frozen suspensions to every inhabited planet by Altamycin, Inc.—the proper name for what everyone on Altair Nine called the Icicle Works.

When the Gumpert Process came along, suddenly the demand vanished.

Worse, the jobs vanished. Pulcher had been on the corporation's legal staff, with an office of his own and a faint hint of a vice-presidency, some day. He was out. The stenos in the pool, all but two or three of the five hundred who once had got out the correspondence and the bills, they were out. The shipping clerks in the warehouse were out, the pumphands at the settling tanks were out, the freezer attendants were out. Everyone was out. The plant closed down. There were more than fifty tons of frozen antibiotics in storage and, though there might still be a faint trickle of orders from old-fashioned diehards around the Galaxy (backwoods country doctors who didn't believe in the new-fangled synthetics, experimenters who wanted to run comparative tests), the shipments already en route would much more than satisfy them. Fifty tons? Once the Icicle Works had shipped three hundred tons a day—physical transport, electronic rockets that took years to cover the distance between stars. The boom was over. And of course, on a one-industry planet, everything else was over too.

Pulcher took the girl by the arm and swept her into the restaurant. "Eat," he ordered. "I know what jail food is like." He sat down, firmly determined to say nothing until she had finished.

*   *   *

But he couldn't.

Long before she was ready for coffee he burst out, "Why, Madeleine? Why would you get into something like this?"

She looked at him but did not answer.

"What about your husband?" He didn't want to ask it, but he had to. That had been the biggest blow of all the unpleasant blows that had struck him after the Icicle Works closed. Just as he was getting a law practice going—not on any big scale but, through Charley Dickon and the Party, a small, steady hand-out of political favors that would make it possible for him to pretend he was still an attorney—the gossip reached him that Madeleine Cossett had married.

The girl pushed her plate away. "He emigrated."

Pulcher digested that slowly. Emigrated? That was the dream of every Niner since the Works closed down, of course. But it was only a dream. Physical transport between the stars was ungodly expensive. More, it was ungodly slow. Ten years would get you to Dell, the thin-aired planet of a chilly little red dwarf. The nearest *good* planet was thirty years away.

What it all added up to was that emigrating was almost like dying. If one member of a married couple emigrated, it meant the end of the marriage. . . . "We got a divorce," said Madeleine, nodding. "There wasn't enough money for both of us to go, and Jon was unhappier here than I was."

She took out a cigarette and let him light it. "You don't want to ask me about Jon, do you? But you want to know. All right. Jon was an artist. He was in the advertising department at the Works, but that was just temporary. He was going to do something big.

31

Then the bottom dropped out for him, just as it did for all of us. Well, Milo, I didn't hear from you."

Pulcher protested, "It wouldn't have been *fair* for me to see you when I didn't have a job or anything."

"Of course you'd think that. It's wrong. But I couldn't find you to tell you it was wrong, and then Jon was very persistent. He was tall, curly-haired, he has a baby's face—do you know, he only shaved twice a week. Well, I married him. It lasted three months. Then he just had to get away." She leaned forward earnestly. "Don't think he was just a bum, Milo! He really was quite a good artist. But we didn't have enough money for paints, even, and then it seems that the colors are all wrong here. Jon explained it. In order to paint landscapes that sell you have to be on a planet with Earth-type colors; they're all the vogue. And there's too much altamycin in the clouds here."

Pulcher said stiffly, "I see." But he didn't, really. There was at least one unexplained part. If there hadn't been enough money for paint, then where had the money come from for a starship ticket, physical transport? It meant at least ten thousand dollars. There just was no way to raise ten thousand dollars on Altair Nine, not without taking a rather extreme step. . . .

The girl wasn't looking at him.

Her eyes were fixed on a table across the restaurant, a table with a loud, drunken party. It was only lunch time, but they had a three-o'clock-in-the-morning air about them. They were *stinking*. There were four of them, two men and two women; and their physical bodies were those of young, healthy, quite good-looking, perfectly normal Niners. The appearance of the physical bodies was entirely irrelevant, though, because

32

they were tourists. Around the neck of each of them was a bright golden choker with a glowing red signal-jewel in the middle. It was the mark of the Tourist Agency; the sign that the bodies were rented.

Milo Pulcher looked away quickly. His eyes stopped on the white face of the girl, and abruptly he knew how she had raised the money to send Jon to another star.

II

Pulcher found the girl a room and left her there. It was not what he wanted. What he wanted was to spend the evening with her and to go on spending time with her, until time came to an end: but there was the matter of her trial.

Twenty-four hours ago he had got the letter notifying him that the court had appointed him attorney for six suspected kidnappers and looked on it as a fast fee, no work to speak of, no hope for success. He would lose the case, certainly. Well, what of it?

But now he wanted to win!

It meant some fast, hard work if he was to have even a chance—and at best, he admitted to himself, the chance would not be good. Still, he wasn't going to give up without a try.

The snow stopped as he located the home of Jimmy Lasser's parents. It was a sporting-goods shop, not far from the main Tourist Agency; it had a window full of guns and boots and scuba gear. He walked in, tinkling a bell as he opened the door.

"Mr. Lasser?" A plump little man, leaning back in a chair by the door, got slowly up, looking him over.

"In back," he said shortly.

He led Pulcher behind the store, to a three-room apartment. The living room was comfortable enough, but for some reason it seemed unbalanced. One side was somehow heavier than the other. He noticed the nap of the rug, still flattened out where something heavy had been, something rectangular and large, about the size of a Tri-V electronic entertainment unit. "Repossessed," said Lasser shortly. "Sit down. Dickon called you a minute ago."

"Oh?" It had to be something important. Dickon wouldn't have tracked him down for any trivial matter.

"Don't know what he wanted, but he said you weren't to leave till he called back. Sit down. May'll bring you a cup of tea."

Pulcher chatted with them for a minute, while the woman fussed over a teapot and a plate of soft cookies. He was trying to get the feel of the home. He could understand Madeleine Gaultry's desperation, he could understand the Foltis boy, a misfit in society anywhere. What about Jimmy Lasser?

The elder Lassers were both pushing sixty. They were first-generation Niners, off an Earth colonizing ship. They hadn't been born on Earth of course—the trip took nearly a hundred years, physical transport. They had been born in transit, had married on the ship. As the ship had reached maximum population level shortly after they were born, they were allowed to have no children until they landed. At that time they were all of forty. May Lasser said suddenly, "Please help our boy, Mr. Pulcher! It's isn't Jimmy's fault. He got in with a bad crowd. You know how it is: no work, nothing for a boy to do."

"I'll do my best." But it was funny, Pulcher thought, how it was always "the crowd" that was bad. It was never Jimmy—and never Avery, never Sam, never Walter. Pulcher sorted out the five boys and remembered Jimmy: nineteen years old, quite colorless, polite, not very interested. What had struck the lawyer about him was only surprise that this rabbity boy should have had the enterprise to get into a criminal conspiracy in the first place.

"He's a good boy," said May Lasser pathetically. "That trouble with the parked cars two years ago wasn't his fault. He got a fine job right after that, you know. Ask his probation officer. Then the Icicle Works closed. . . ." She poured more tea, slopping it over the side of the cup. "Oh, sorry! But— But when he went to the unemployment office, Mr. Pulcher, do you know what they said to him?"

"I know."

"They asked him would he take a job if offered," she hurried on, unheeding. "A *job*. As if I didn't know what they meant by a 'job'! They meant *renting*." She plumped the teapot down on the table and began to weep. "Mr. Pulcher, I wouldn't let him rent if I died for it! There isn't anything in the Bible that says you can let someone else use your body and not be responsible for what it does! You know what tourists do! 'If thy right hand offend thee, cut it off.' It doesn't say, unless somebody else is using it. Mr. Pulcher, renting is a *sin*!"

"May." Mr. Lasser put his teacup down and looked directly at Pulcher. "What about it, Pulcher? Can you get Jimmy off?"

The attorney reflected. He hadn't known about Jimmy Lasser's probation before, and that was a bad sign. If the county prosecutor was holding out on information of that sort, it meant he wasn't willing to cooperate. Probably he would be trying for a conviction with maximum sentence. Of course, he didn't have to tell a defense attorney anything about the previous criminal records of his clients. But in a juvenile case, where all parties were usually willing to go easy on the defendants, it was customary. . . . "I don't know, Mr. Lasser. I'll do the best I can."

"Damn right you will!" barked Lasser. "Dickon tell you who I am? I was committeeman here before him, you know. So get busy. Pull strings. Dickon will back you, or I'll know why!"

Pulcher managed to control himself. "I'll do the best I can. I already told you that. If you want strings pulled, you'd better talk to Dickon yourself. I only know law. I don't know anything about politics."

The atmosphere was becoming unpleasant. Pulcher was glad to hear the ringing of the phone in the store outside. May Lasser answered it and said: "For you, Mr. Pulcher. Charley Dickon."

Pulcher gratefully picked up the phone. Dickon's rich, political voice said sorrowfully, "Milo? Listen, I been talking to Judge Pegrim's secretary. He isn't gonna let the kids off with a slap on the wrist. There's a lot of heat from the mayor's office."

Pulcher protested desperately: "But the Swinburne kid wasn't hurt! He got better care with Madeleine than he was getting at home."

"I know, Milo," the committeeman agreed, "but that's the way she lies. So what I wanted to say to you, Milo, is don't knock yourself out on this one because you aren't going to win it."

"But—" Pulcher suddenly became aware of the Lassers just behind him. "But I think I can get an acquittal," he said, entirely out of hope, knowing that it wasn't true.

Dickon chuckled. "You got Lasser breathing down your neck? Sure, Milo. But you want my advice you'll take a quick hearing, let them get sentenced and then try for executive clemency in a couple months. I'll help you get it. And that's another five hundred or so for you, see?" The committeeman was being persuasive; it was a habit of his. "Don't worry about Lasser. I guess he's been telling you what a power he is in politics here. Forget it. And, say, tell him I notice he hasn't got his tickets for the Chester A. Arthur Day Dinner yet. You pick up the dough from him, will you? I'll mail him the tickets. No—hold on, don't ask him. Just tell him what I said." The connection went dead.

Pulcher stood holding a dead phone, conscious of Lasser standing right behind him. "So long, Charley," he said, paused, nodded into space and said, "So long," again.

Then the attorney turned about to deliver the committeeman's message about that most important subject, the tickets to the Chester A. Arthur Day Dinner. Lasser grumbled, "Damn Dickon, he's into you for one thing after another. Where's he think I'm going to get thirty bucks?"

"Tim. Please." His wife touched his arm.

Lasser hesitated. "Oh, all right. But you better get Jimmy off, hear?"

Pulcher got away at last and hurried out into the cold, slushy street.

At the corner he caught a glimpse of something palely glowing overhead and stopped, transfixed. A huge skytrout was swimming purposefully down the avenue. It was a monster, twelve feet long at least and more than two feet thick at the middle; it would easily go eighteen, nineteen ounces, the sort of lunker that sportsmen hiked clear across the Dismal Hills to bag. Pulcher had never in his life seen one that size. In fact, he could only remember seeing one or two fingerlings swim over inhabited areas.

It gave him a cold, worried feeling.

The skyfish were about the only tourist attraction Altair Nine had left to offer. From all over the Galaxy sportsmen came to shoot them, with their great porous flesh filled with bubbles of hydrogen, real biological Zeppelins that did not fly in the air but swam it. Before human colonists arrived, they had been Altair Nine's highest form of life. They were so easy to destroy with gunfire that they had almost been exterminated in the inhabited sections; only in the high, cold hills had a few survived. And now. . . .

Were even the fish aware that Altair Nine was becoming a ghost planet?

The next morning Pulcher phoned Madeleine but didn't have breakfast with her, though he wanted to very much.

He put in the whole day working on the case. In the morning he visited the families and friends of the accused boys; in the afternoon he followed a few hunches.

From the families he learned nothing. The stories were all about the same. The youngest boy was Foltis, only seventeen; the oldest was Hopgood at twenty-six. They all had lost their jobs, most of them at the Icicle Works, saw no future, and wanted off-planet. Well, physical transport meant a minimum of ten thousand dollars, and not one of them had a chance in the worlds of getting that much money in any legitimate way.

Mayor Swinburne was a rich man, and his three-year-old son was the apple of his eye. It must have been an irresistible temptation to try to collect ransom money, Pulcher realized. The mayor could certainly afford it, and once the money was collected and they were aboard a starship it would be almost impossible for the law to pursue them.

Pulcher managed to piece together the way the thing had started. The boys all lived in the same neighborhood, the neighborhood where Madeleine and Jon Gaultry had had a little apartment. They had seen Madeleine walking with the mayor's son—she had had a part-time job, now and then, taking care of him. The only part of the thing that was hard to believe was that Madeleine had been willing to take part in the scheme, once the boys approached her.

But Milo, remembering the expression on the girl's face as she looked at the tourists, decided that wasn't so strange after all.

For Madeleine had rented.

Physical transport was expensive and eternally slow.

But there was a faster way for a man to travel from planet to planet—practically instantaneous, from one end of the Galaxy to the other. The pattern of the mind is electronic in nature. It can be taped, and it can be broadcast on an electromagnetic frequency. What was more, like any electromagnetic signal, it could be used to modulate an ultrawave carrier. The result: Instantaneous transmission of personality, anywhere in the civilized Galaxy.

The only problem was that there had to be a receiver. The naked ghost of a man, stripped of flesh and juices, was no more than the countless radio and TV waves that passed through everyone all the time. The transmitted personality had to be given form. There were mechanical receivers, of course—computerlike affairs with mercury memory cells where a man's intelligence could be received, and could be made to activate robot bodies. But that wasn't *fun*. The tourist trade was built on *fun*. Live bodies were needed to satisfy the customers. No one wanted to spend the price of a fishing broadcast to Altair Nine in order to find himself pursuing the quarry in some clanking tractor with photocell eyes and solenoid muscles. A body was wanted, even a rather attractive body; a body which would be firm where the tourist's own, perhaps, was flabby, healthy where the tourist's own had wheezed. Having such a body, there were other sports to enjoy than fishing.

Oh, the laws were strict about misuse of rented bodies.

But the tourist trade was the only flourishing industry left on Altair Nine. The laws remained strict, but they remained unenforced.

Pulcher checked in with Charley Dickon. "I found out why Madeleine got into this thing. She rented. Signed a long-term lease with the Tourist Agency and got a big advance on her earnings."

Dickon shook his head sadly. "What people will do for money," he commented.

"It wasn't for her! She gave it to her husband, so he could get a ticket to someplace off-world." Pulcher got up, turned around and kicked his chair as hard as he could. Renting was bad enough for a man. For a woman it was—

"Take it easy," Dickon suggested, grinning. "So she figured she could buy her way out of the contract with the money from Swinburne?"

"Wouldn't you do the same?"

"Oh, I don't know, Milo. Renting's not so bad."

"The hell it isn't!"

"All right. The hell it isn't. But you ought to realize, Milo," the committeeman said stiffly, "that if it wasn't for the tourist trade we'd all be in trouble. Don't knock the Tourist Agency. They're doing a perfectly decent job."

"Then why won't they let me see the records?"

The committeeman's eyes narrowed and he sat up straighter.

"I tried," said Pulcher. "I got them to show me Madeleine's lease agreement, but I had to threaten them with a court order. Why? Then I tried to find out a little more about the Agency itself—incorporation papers, names of shareholders and so on. They wouldn't give me a thing. Why?"

Dickon said, after a second, "I could ask you that too, Milo. Why did you want to know?"

Pulcher said seriously, "I have to make a case any way I can, Charley. They're all dead on the evidence. They're guilty. But every one of them went into this kidnapping stunt in order to stay away from renting. Maybe I can't get Judge Pegrim to listen to that kind of evidence, but maybe I can. It's my only chance. If I can show that renting is a form of cruel and unusual punishment—if I can find something wrong in it, something that isn't allowed in its charter, then I have a chance. Not a good chance. But a chance. And there's got to be something wrong, Charley, because otherwise why would they be so secretive?"

Dickon said heavily, "You're getting in pretty deep, Milo. . . . Ever occur to you you're going about this the wrong way?"

"Wrong how?"

"What can the incorporation papers show you? You want to find out what renting's like. It seems to me the only way that makes sense is to try it yourself."

"Rent? Me?" Pulcher was shocked.

The committeeman shrugged. "Well, I got a lot to do," he said, and escorted Pulcher to the door.

The lawyer walked sullenly away. Rent? Him? But he had to admit that it made a certain amount of sense. . . .

He made a private decision. He would do what he could to get Madeleine and the others out of trouble. *Completely* out of trouble. But if, in the course of trying the case, he couldn't magic up some way of getting her out of the lease agreement as well as getting an acquittal, he would make damn sure that he didn't get the acquittal.

Jail wasn't so bad; renting, for Madeleine Gaultry, was considerably worse.

III

Pulcher marched into the unemployment office the next morning with an air of determination far exceeding what he really felt. Talk about loyalty to a client! But he had spent the whole night brooding about it, and Dickon had been right.

The clerk blinked at him and wheezed: "Gee, you're

Mr. Pulcher, aren't you? I never thought I'd see *you* here. Things pretty slow?"

Pulcher's uncertainty made him belligerent. "I want to rent my body," he barked. "Am I in the right place or not?"

"Well, sure, Mr. Pulcher. I mean, you're not, if it's voluntary, but it's been so long since they had a voluntary that it don't make much difference, you know. I mean, I can handle it for you. Wait a minute." He turned away, hesitated, glanced at Pulcher and said, "I better use the other phone."

He was gone only a minute. He came back with a look of determined embarrassment. "Mr. Pulcher. Look. I thought I better call Charley Dickon. He isn't in his office. Why don't you wait until I can clear it with him?"

Pulcher said grimly. "It's already cleared with him."

The clerk hesitated. "But— Oh. All right," he said miserably, scribbling on a pad. "Right across the street. Oh, and tell them you're a volunteer. I don't know if that will make them leave the cuffs off you, but at least it'll give them a laugh." He chuckled.

Pulcher took the slip of paper and walked sternly across the street to the Tourist Rental Agency, Procurement Office, observing without pleasure that there were bars on the windows. A husky guard at the door straightened up as he approached and said genially, "All right, sonny. It isn't going to be as bad as you think. Just gimme your wrists a minute."

"Wait," said Pulcher quickly, putting his hands behind him. "You won't need the handcuffs for me. I'm a volunteer."

The guard said dangerously, "Don't kid with me,

sonny." Then he took a closer look. "Hey, I know you. You're the lawyer. I saw you at the Primary Dance." He scratched his ear. He said doubtfully, "Well, maybe you are a volunteer. Go on in." But as Pulcher strutted past he felt a heavy hand on his shoulder and, click, click his wrists were circled with steel. He whirled furiously. "No hard feelings," boomed the guard cheerfully. "It costs a lot of dough to get you ready, that's all. They don't want you changing your mind when they give you the squeeze, see?"

"The squeeze—? All right," said Pulcher, and turned away again. The squeeze. It didn't sound so good, at that. But he had a little too much pride left to ask the guard for details. Anyway, it couldn't be *too* bad, he was sure. Wasn't he? After all, it wasn't the same as being executed. . . .

An hour and a half later he wasn't so sure.

They had stripped him, weighed him, fluorographed him, taken samples of his blood, saliva, urine and spinal fluid; they had thumped his chest and listened to the strangled pounding of the arteries in his arm.

"All right, you pass," said a fortyish blonde in a stained nurse's uniform. "You're lucky today, openings all over. You can take your pick—mining, sailing, anything you like. What'll it be?"

"What?"

"While you're *renting*. What's the matter with you? You got to be doing something while your body's rented, you know. Of course, you can have the tank if you want to. But they mostly don't like that. You're conscious the whole time, you know."

Pulcher said honestly: "I don't know what you're talking about," But then he remembered. While a person's body was rented out there was the problem of what to do with his own mind and personality. It couldn't stay in the body. It had to go somewhere else. "The tank" was a storage device, only that and nothing more; the displaced mind was held in a sort of pickling vat of transistors and cells until its own body could be returned to it. He remembered a client of his boss', while he was still clerking, who had spent eight weeks in the tank and had then come out to commit a murder. No. Not the tank. He said, coughing, "What else is there?"

The nurse said impatiently, "Golly, whatever you want, I guess. They've got a big call for miners operating the deep gas generators right now, if you want that. It's pretty hot, is all. They burn the coal into gas, and of course you're right in the middle of it. But I don't think you feel much. Not *too* much. I don't know about sailing or rocketing, because you have to have some experience for that. There might be something with the taxi company, but I ought to tell you usually the renters don't want that, because the live drivers don't like seeing the machines running cabs. Sometimes if they see a machine-cab they tip it over. Naturally, if there's any damage to the host machine it's risky for you."

Pulcher said faintly, "I'll try mining."

He went out of the room in a daze, a small bleached towel around his middle his only garment and hardly aware of that. His own clothes had been whisked away and checked long ago. The tourist who would shortly wear his body would pick his own clothes; the haberdashery was one of the more profitable subsidiaries of the Tourist Agency.

Then he snapped out of his daze as he discovered what was meant by "the squeeze."

A pair of husky experts lifted him onto a slab, whisked away the towel, unlocked and tossed away the handcuffs. While one pinned him down firmly at the shoulders, the other began to turn viselike wheels that moved molded forms down upon him. It was like a sectional sarcophagus closing in on him. Pulcher had an instant childhood recollection of some story or other—the walls closing in, the victim inexorably squeezed to death. He yelled, "Hey, hold it! What are you doing?"

The man at his head, bored, said, "Oh, don't worry. This your first time? We got to keep you still, you know. Scanning's close work."

"But—"

"Now shut up and relax," the man said reasonably. "If you wiggle when the tracer's scanning you you could get your whole personality messed up. Not only that, we might damage the body an' then the Agency'd have a suit on its hands, see? Tourists don't like damaged bodies. . . . Come on, Vince. Get the legs lined up so I can do the head."

"But—" said Pulcher again, and then, with effort, relaxed. It was only for twenty-four hours, after all. He could stand anything for twenty-four hours, and he had been careful to sign up for only that long. "Go ahead," he said. "It's only for twenty-four hours."

"What? Oh, sure, friend. Lights out, now; have a pleasant dream."

And something soft but quite firm came down over his face.

He heard a muffled sound of voices. Then there was a quick ripping feeling, as though he had been plucked out of some sticky surrounding medium.

THE DAY THE ICICLE WORKS CLOSED

Then it *hurt*.

Pulcher screamed. It didn't accomplish anything, he no longer had a voice to scream with.

Funny, he had always thought of mining as something that was carried on underground. He was under *water*. There wasn't any doubt of it. He could see vagrant eddies of sand moving in a current; he could see real fish, not the hydrogen Zeppelins of the air; he could see bubbles, arising from some source of the sand at his feet— No! Not at his feet. He didn't have feet. He had tracks.

A great steel bug swam up in front of him and said raspingly, "All right, you there, let's go." Funny again. He didn't hear the voice with ears—he didn't have ears, and there was no stereophonic sense—but he did, somehow, hear. It seemed to be speaking inside his brain. Radio? Sonar? "Come on!" growled the bug.

Experimentally Pulcher tried to talk. "Watch it!" squeaked a thin little voice, and a tiny, many-treaded steel beetle squirmed out from under his tracks. It paused to rear back and look at him. "Dope!" it chattered scathingly. A bright flame erupted from its snout as it squirmed away.

The big bug rasped, "Go on, follow the burner, Mac." Pulcher thought of walking, rather desperately. Yes. Something was happening. He lurched and moved. "Oh, God," sighed the steel bug, hanging beside him, watching with critical attention. "This your first time? I figured. They *always* give me the new ones to break in. Look, that burner—the little thing that just went down the cline, Mac! That's a burner. It's going to burn the hard rock out of a new shaft. You follow it and pull the sludge out. With your *buckets*, Mac."

Pulcher gamely started his treads and lurchingly followed the little burner. All around him, visible through the churned, silty water, he caught glimpses of other machines working. There were big ones and little ones, some with great elephantine flexible steel trunks that sucked silt and mud away, some with wasp's stingers that planted charges of explosive, some like himself with buckets for hauling and scooping out pits. The mine, whatever sort of mine it was to be, was only a bare scratched-out beginning on the sea floor as yet. It took him—an hour? a minute? he had no means of telling time—to learn the rudiments of operating his new steel body.

Then it became boring.

Also it became painful. The first scoops of sandy grime he carried out of the new pit made his buckets tingle. The tingle became a pain, the pain an ache, the ache a blazing agony. He stopped. Something was wrong. They couldn't expect him to go on like this! "Hey, Mac. Get busy, will you?"

"But it *hurts*."

"Goddamighty, Mac, it's *supposed* to hurt. How else would you be able to feel when you hit something hard? You want to break your buckets on me, Mac?" Pulcher gritted his—not-teeth, squared his—not-shoulders, and went back to digging. Ultimately the pain became, through habit, bearable. It didn't become less. It just became bearable.

It was boring, except when once he did strike a harder rock than his phospher-bronze buckets could handle, and had to slither back out of the way while the burner chopped it up for him. But that was the only break in the monotony. Otherwise the work was strictly routine. It gave him plenty of time to think.

THE DAY THE ICICLE WORKS CLOSED

This was not altogether a boon.

I wonder, he thought with a drowned clash of buckets, I wonder what my body is doing now.

Perhaps the tenant who now occupied his body was a businessman, Pulcher thought prayerfully. A man who had had to come to Altair Nine quickly, on urgent business—get a contract signed, make a trading deal, arrange an interstellar loan. That wouldn't be so bad! A businessman would not damage a rented property. No. At the worst, a businessman might drink one or two cocktails too many, perhaps eat an indigestible lunch. All right. So when—in surely only a few hours now—Pulcher resumed his body, the worst he could expect would be a hangover or dyspepsia. Well, what of that? An aspirin. A dash of bicarb.

But maybe the tourist would not be a businessman.

Pulcher flailed the coarse sand with his buckets and thought apprehensively: He might be a sportsman. Still, even that wouldn't be so bad. The tourist might walk his body up and down a few dozen mountains, perhaps even sleep it out in the open overnight. There might be a cold, possibly even pneumonia. Of course, there might also be an accident—tourists did fall off the Dismal Hills; there could be a broken leg. But that was not *too* bad, it was only a matter of a few days rest, a little medical attention.

But maybe, Pulcher thought grayly, ignoring the teeming agony of his buckets, maybe the tenant will be something worse.

He had heard queer, smutty stories about female tenants who rented male bodies. It was against the law. But you kept hearing the stories. He had heard of men who wanted to experiment with drugs, with drink, with—with a thousand secret, sordid lusts of the flesh.

All of them were unpleasant. And yet in a rented body, where the ultimate price of dissipation would be borne by someone else, who might not try one of them? For there was no physical consequence to the practitioner. If Mrs. Lasser was right, perhaps there was not even a consequence in the hereafter.

Twenty-four hours had never passed so slowly.

The suction hoses squabbled with the burners. The scoops quarreled with the dynamiters. All the animate submarine mining machines constantly irritably snapped at each other. But the work was getting done.

It seemed to be a lot of work to accomplish in one twenty-four hour day, Pulcher thought seriously. The pit was down two hundred yards now, and braced. New wet-setting concrete pourers were already laying a floor. Shimmery little spiderlike machines whose limbs held chemical testing equipment were sniffing every load of sludge that came out now for richness of ore. The mine was nearly ready to start producing.

After a time Pulcher began to understand the short tempers of the machines. None of the minds in these machines were able to forget that, up topside, their bodies were going about unknown errands, risking unguessed dangers. At any given moment that concrete pourer's body, for instance, might be dying . . . might be acquiring a disease . . . might be stretched out in narcotic stupor, or might gayly be risking dismemberment in a violent sport. Naturally tempers were touchy.

There was no such thing as rest, as coffee-breaks or sleep for the machines; they kept going. Pulcher, when finally he remembered that he had had a purpose in coming here, it was not merely some punishment that had come blindly to him for a forgotten sin, began to try to analyse his own feelings and to guess at the feelings of the others.

The whole thing seemed unnecessarily *mean*. Pulcher understood quite clearly why anyone who had had the experience of renting would never want to do it again. But why did it have to be so unpleasant? Surely, at least, conditions for the renter-mind in a machine-body could be made more bearable; the tactile sensations could be reduced from pain to some more supportable feeling without enough loss of sensation to jeopardize the desired ends.

He wondered wistfully if Madeleine had once occupied this particular machine.

Then he wondered how many of the dynamiters and diggers were female, how many male. It seemed somehow wrong that their gleaming stainless-steel or phosphor-bronze exteriors should give no hint of age or sex. There ought to be some lighter work for women, he thought idly, and then realized that the thought was nonsense. What difference did it make? You could work your buckets off, and when you got back topside you'd be healthy and rested—

And then he had a quick, dizzying qualm, as he realized that that thought would be the thought in the mind of the tourist now occupying his own body.

Pulcher licked his—not-lips and attacked the sand with his buckets more viciously than before.

"All right, Mac."

The familiar steel bug was back beside him. "Come on, back to the barn," it scolded. "You think I want to have to haul you back? Time's up. Get the tracks back in the parking lot."

Never was an order so gladly obeyed.

But the overseer had cut it rather fine. Pulcher had

just reached the parking space, had not quite turned his clanking steel frame around when, *rip*, the tearing and the pain hit him. . . .

And he found himself struggling against the enfolded soft shroud that they called "the squeeze."

"Relax, friend," soothed a distant voice. Abruptly the pressure was removed from his face and the voice came nearer. "There you are. Have a nice dream?"

Pulcher kicked the rubbery material off his legs. He sat up.

"Ouch!" he said suddenly, and rubbed his eye.

The man by his head looked down at him and grinned. "Some shiner. Must've been a good party." He was stripping the sections of rubbery gripping material off him as he talked. "You're lucky. I've seen them come back in here with legs broken, teeth out, even bullet holes. Friend, you wouldn't believe me if I told you. 'Specially the girls." He handed Pulcher another bleached towel. "All right, you're through here. Don't worry about the eye, friend. That's easy two, three days old already. Another day or two and you won't even notice it."

"Hey!" Pulcher cried suddenly. "What do you mean, two or three days? How long was I down there?"

The man glanced boredly at the green-tabbed card on Pulcher's wrist. "Let's see, this is Thursday. Six days."

"But I only signed up for twenty-four hours!"

"Sure you did. *Plus* emergency overcalls, naturally. What do you think, friend, the Agency's going to evict some big-spending tourist just because you want your body back in twenty-four hours? Can't do it. You can see that. The Agency'd lose a fortune that way." Unceremoniously Pulcher was hoisted to his feet and escorted to the door. "If only these jokers would read

52

the fine print," the first man was saying mournfully to his helper as Pulcher left. "Oh, well. If they had any brains they wouldn't rent in the first place—then what would me and you do for jobs?"

The closing door swallowed their laughter.

Six days! Pulcher raced through medical check-out, clothes redemption, payoff at the cashier's window. "Hurry, please," he kept saying, "can't you please hurry?" He couldn't wait to get to a phone.

But he had a pretty good idea already what the phone call would tell him. Five extra days! No wonder it had seemed so long down there, while up in the city time had passed along.

He found a phone at last and quickly dialed the private number of Judge Pegrim's office. The judge wouldn't be there, but that was the way Pulcher wanted it. He got Pegrim's secretary. "Miss Kish? This is Milo Pulcher."

Her voice was cold. "So *there* you are. Where have you been? The judge was *furious*."

"I—" He despaired of explaining it to her; he could hardly explain it to himself. "I'll tell you later, Miss Kish. Please. Where does the kidnap case stand now?"

"Why, the hearing was yesterday. Since we couldn't locate you, the judge had to appoint another attorney. Naturally. After all, Mr. Pulcher, an attorney is supposed to be in court when his clients are—"

"I know that, Miss Kish. What happened?"

"It was open and shut. They all pleaded *non vult*—it was over in twenty minutes. It was the only thing to do on the evidence, you see. They'll be sentenced this afternoon—around three o'clock, I'd say. *If* you're interested."

IV

It was snowing again, blue this time.

Pulcher paid the cab driver and ran up the steps of the courthouse. As he reached for the door he caught sight of three airfish solemnly swimming around the corner of the building toward him. Even in his hurry he paused to glance at them.

It was past three, but the judge had not yet entered the courtroom. There were no spectators, but the six defendants were already in their seats, a bailiff lounging next to them. Counsel's table was occupied by—Pulcher squinted—oh, by Donley. Pulcher knew the other lawyer slightly. He was a youngster, with good political connections—that explained the court's appointing him for the fee when Pulcher didn't show up—but without much to recommend him otherwise.

Madeleine Gaultry looked up as Pulcher approached, then looked away. One of the boys caught sight of him, scowled, whispered to the others. Their collective expressions were enough to sear his spirit.

Pulcher sat at the table beside Donley. "Hello. Mind if I join you?"

Donley twisted his head. "Oh, hello, Charley. Sure. I didn't expect to see you here." He laughed. "Say, that eye's pretty bad. I guess—"

He stopped.

Something happened in Donley's face. The young baby-fat cheeks became harder, older, more worried-looking. Donley clamped his lips shut.

Pulcher was puzzled. "What's the matter? Are you wondering where I was?"

Donley said stiffly, "Well, you can't blame me for that."

"I couldn't help it, Donley. I was trying to gather evidence—not that that helps much now. I found one thing out, though. Even a lawyer can goof in reading a contract. Did you know the Tourist Agency has the right to retain a body for up to forty-five days, regardless of the original agreement? It's in their contract. I was lucky, I guess. They only kept me five."

Donley's face did not relax. "That's interesting," he said noncommittally.

The man's attitude was most peculiar. Pulcher could understand being needled by Donley—could even understand this coldness if it had been from someone else—but it wasn't like Donley to take mere negligence so seriously.

But before he could try to pin down exactly what was wrong the other lawyer stood up. "On your feet, Pulcher," he said in a stage whisper. "Here comes the judge!"

Pulcher jumped up.

He could feel Judge Pegrim's eyes rake over him. They scratched like diamond-tipped drills. In an ordinarily political, reasonably corrupt community, Judge Pegrim was one man who took his job seriously and expected the same from those around him. "Mr. Pulcher," he purred. "We're honored to have you with us."

Pulcher began an explanation but the judge waved it away. "Mr. Pulcher, you know that an attorney is an officer of the court? And, as such, is expected to know his duties—and to fulfill them?"

"Well, Your Honor. I thought I was fulfilling them. I—"

"I'll discuss it with you at another time, Mr. Pulcher," the judge said. "Right now we have a rather disagreeable task to get through. Bailiff! Let's get started."

It was all over in ten minutes. Donley made a couple of routine motions, but there was no question about what would happen. It happened. Each of the defendants drew a ten-year sentence. The judge pronounced it distastefully, adjourned the court and left. He did not look at Milo Pulcher.

Pulcher tried for a moment to catch Madeleine's eye. Then he succeeded. Shaken, he turned away, bumping into Donley. "I don't understand it," he mumbled.

"What don't you understand?"

"Well, don't you think that's a pretty stiff sentence?"

Donley shrugged. He wasn't very interested. Pulcher scanned the masklike young face. There was no sympathy there. It was funny, in a way. This was a face of flint; the plight of six young people, doomed to spend a decade each of their lives in prison, did not move him at all. Pulcher said dispiritedly, "I think I'll go see Charley Dickon."

"Do that," said Donley curtly, and turned away.

But Pulcher couldn't find Charley Dickon.

He wasn't at his office, wasn't at the club. "Nope," said the garrulous retired police lieutenant who was the club president—and who used the club headquarters as a checker salon. "I haven't seen Charley in a couple of days. Be at the dinner tonight, though. You'll see him there." It wasn't a question, whether Pulcher would be at the dinner or not; Pop Craig knew he would. After all, Charley had passed the word out. *Everybody* would be there.

Pulcher went back to his apartment.

It was the first time he had surveyed his body since reclaiming it. The bathroom mirror told him that he had a gorgeous shiner indeed. Also certain twinges made him strip and examine his back. It looked, he thought gloomily, staring over his shoulder into the mirror, as though whoever had rented his body had had a perfectly marvelous time. He made a mental note to get a complete checkup some day soon, just in case. Then he showered, shaved, talcumed around the black eye without much success, and dressed.

He sat down, poured himself a drink and promptly forgot it was there. He was thinking. Something was trying to reach the surface of his mind. Something perfectly obvious, which he all the same couldn't quite put his finger on. It was rather annoying.

He found himself drowsily thinking of airfish.

Damn, he thought grouchily, his body's late tenant hadn't even troubled to give it a decent night's sleep! But he didn't want to sleep, not now. It was still only early evening. He supposed the Chester A. Arthur Day Dinner was still a must, but there were hours yet before that. . . .

He got up, poured the untasted drink into the sink and set out. There was one thing he could try to help Madeleine. It probably wouldn't work. But nothing else would either, so that was no reason for not trying it.

The mayor's mansion was ablaze with light; something was going on.

Pulcher trudged up the long, circling driveway in slush that kept splattering his ankles. He tapped gingerly on the door.

The butler took his name doubtfully, and isolated Pulcher in a contagion-free sitting room while he went off to see if the mayor would care to admit such a person. He came back looking incredulous. The mayor would.

Mayor Swinburne was a healthy, lean man of medium height, showing only by his thinning hair that he was in his middle forties. Pulcher said, "Mr. Mayor, I guess you know who I am. I represent the six kids who were accused of kidnapping your son."

"Not accused, Mr. Pulcher. Convicted. And I didn't know you still represented them."

"I see you know the score. All right. Maybe, in a legal sense, I don't represent them any more. But I'd like to make some representations on their behalf to you tonight—entirely unofficially." He gave the mayor a crisply worded, brief outline of what had happened in the case, how he had rented, what he had found as a renter, why he had missed the hearing. "You see, sir, the Tourist Agency doesn't give its renters even ordinary courtesy. They're just bodies, nothing else. I can't blame anybody who did *anything* to avoid it."

The mayor said dangerously, "Mr. Pulcher, I don't have to remind you that what's left of our economy depends heavily on the Tourist Agency for income. Also that some of our finest citizens are among its shareholders."

"Including yourself, Mr. Mayor. Right." Pulcher nodded. "But the management may not be reflecting your wishes. I'll go farther. I think, sir, that every contract the Tourist Agency holds with a renter ought to be voided as against public policy. Renting out your body for a purpose which well may be in violation of law—which, going by experience, nine times out of ten *does* involved a violation of law—is the same thing as contracting to perform any other illegal act. The contract simply cannot be enforced. The common law gives us a great many precedents on this point, and—"

"Please, Mr. Pulcher. I'm not a judge. If you feel so strongly, why not take it to court?"

Pulcher sank back into his chair, deflated. "There isn't time," he admitted. "And besides, it's too late for that to help the six persons I'm interested in. They've already been driven into an even more illegal act, in order to escape renting. I'm only trying to explain it to you, sir, because you are the only hope. You can pardon them."

The mayor's face turned beet red. "Executive clemency, from *me*? For *them*?"

"They didn't hurt your boy."

"No, they did not," the mayor agreed. "And I'm sure that Mrs. Gaultry, at least, would not willingly have done so. But can you say the same of the others? Could she have prevented it?" He stood up. "I'm sorry, Mr. Pulcher. The answer is no. Now you must excuse me."

Pulcher hesitated, then accepted the dismissal. There wasn't anything else to do.

He walked somberly down the hall toward the entrance, hardly noticing that guests were beginning to arrive. Apparently the mayor was offering cocktails to a select few. He recognized some of the faces—Lew Yoder, the County Tax Assessor, for one; probably the mayor was having some of the whiter-collared politicians in for drinks before making the obligatory appearance at Dickon's fund-raising dinner. Pulcher looked up long enough to nod grayly at Yoder and walked on.

"Charley Dickon! What the devil are you doing here like that?"

Pulcher jerked upright. Dickon here? He looked around.

But Dickon was not in sight. Only Yoder was coming down the corridor toward him; oddly, Yoder was looking straight at him! And it had been Yoder's voice.

Yoder's face froze.

The expression on Yoder's face was an odd one but not unfamiliar to Milo Pulcher. He had seen it once before that day. It was the identical expression he had seen on the face of that young punk who had replaced him in court, Donley.

Yoder said awkwardly, "Oh, Milo, it's you. Hello. I, uh, thought you were Charley Dickon."

Pulcher felt the hairs at the back of his neck tingle. Something was odd here. Very odd. "It's a perfectly natural mistake," he said. "I'm six feet tall and Charley's five feet three. I'm thirty-one years old. He's fifty. I'm dark and he's almost bald. I don't know how anybody ever tells us apart anyway."

"What the devil are you talking about?" Yoder blustered.

Pulcher looked at him thoughtfully for a second.

"You're lucky," he admitted. "I'm not sure I know. But I hope to find out."

V

Some things never change. Across the entrance to The New Metropolitan Cafe & Men's Grille a long scarlet banner carried the words:

VOTE THE STRAIGHT TICKET

THE DAY THE ICICLE WORKS CLOSED

Big poster portraits of the mayor and Committeeman Dickon flanked the door itself. A squat little soundtruck parked outside the door blared ancient marches of the sort that political conventions had suffered through for more than two centuries back on Earth. It was an absolutely conventional political fund-raising dinner; it would have the absolutely conventional embalmed roast beef, the one conventionally free watery Manhattan at each place, and the conventionally boring after-dinner speeches. (Except for one.) Milo Pulcher, stamping about in the slush outside the entrance, looked up at the constellations visible from Altair Nine and wondered if those same stars were looking down on just such another thousand dinners all over the Galaxy. Politics went on, wherever you were. The constellations would be different, of course; the Squirrel and the Nut were all local stars and would have no shape at all from any other system. But—

He caught sight of the tall thin figure he was waiting for and stepped out into the stream of small-time political workers, ignoring their greetings. "Judge, I'm glad you came."

Judge Pegrim said frostily, "I gave you my word, Milo. But you've got a lot to answer to me for if this is a false alarm. I don't ordinarily attend partisan political affairs."

"It isn't an ordinary affair, Judge." Pulcher conducted him into the room and sat him at the table he had prepared. Once it had held place cards for four election-board workers from the warehouse district, who now buzzed from table to table angrily; Pulcher had filched their cards. The judge was grumbling:

"It doesn't comport well with the bench to attend this sort of thing, Milo. I don't like it."

"I know, Judge. You're an honest man. That's why I wanted you here."

"Mmm." Pulcher left him before the *Mmm* could develop into a question. He had fended off enough questions since the thoughtful half hour he had spent pacing back and forth in front of the mayor's mansion. He didn't want to fend off any more. As he skirted the tables, heading for the private room where he had left his special guests, Charley Dickon caught his arm.

"Hey, Milo! I see you got the judge out. Good boy! He's just what we needed to make this dinner complete."

"You have no idea how complete," said Pulcher pleasantly, and walked away. He didn't look back. There was another fine potential question-source; and the committeeman's would be even more difficult to answer than the judge's. Besides, he wanted to see Madeleine.

The girl and her five accomplices were where he had left them. The private bar where they were sitting was never used for affairs like this. You couldn't see the floor from it. Still, you could hear well enough, and that was more important.

The boys were showing nervousness in their separate ways. Although they had been convicted hardly more than a day, had been sentenced only a few hours, they had fallen quickly into the convict habit. Being out on bail so abruptly was a surprise. They hadn't expected it. It made them nervous. Young Foltis was jittering about, muttering to himself. The Hopgood boy was slumped despondently in a corner, blowing smoke rings. Jimmy Lasser was making a castle out of sugar cubes.

Only Madeleine was relaxed.

As Pulcher came in she looked up calmly. "Is everything all right?" He crossed his fingers and nodded. "Don't worry," she said. Pulcher blinked. *Don't worry.* It should have been he who was saying that to her, not the other way around. It came to him that there was only one possible reason for her calm confidence.

She trusted him.

But he couldn't stay. The ballroom was full now, and irritable banquet waiters were crashing plates down in front of the loyal Party workers. He had a couple of last-minute things to attend to. He carefully avoided the eye of Judge Pegrim, militantly alone at the table by the speaker's dais, and walked quickly across the room to Jimmy Lasser's father. He said without preamble: "Do you want to help your son?"

Tim Lasser snarled, "You cheap shyster! You wouldn't even show up for the trial! Where do you get the nerve to ask me a question like that?"

"Shut up. I asked you something."

Lasser hesitated, then read something in Pulcher's eyes. "Well, of course I do," he grumbled.

"Then tell me something. It won't sound important. But it is. How many rifles did you sell in the past year?"

Lasser looked puzzled, but he said, "Not many. Maybe half a dozen. Business is lousy all over, you know, since the Icicle Works closed."

"And in a normal year?"

"Oh, three or four hundred. It's a big tourist item. You see, they need cold-shot rifles for hunting the fish. A regular bullet'll set them on fire—touches off the hydrogen. I'm the only sporting-goods merchant in town that carries them, and—say, what does that have to do with Jimmy?"

Pulcher took a deep breath. "Stick around and you'll find out. Meanwhile, think about what you just told me. If rifles are a tourist item, why did closing the Icicle Works hurt your sales?" He left.

But not quickly enough. Charley Dickon scuttled over and clutched his arm, his face furious. "Hey, Milo, what the hell! I just heard from Sam Apfel—the bondsman—that you got that whole bunch out of jail again on bail. How come?"

"They're my clients, Charley."

"Don't give me that! How'd you get them out when they're convicted, anyway?"

"I'm going to appeal the case," Pulcher said gently.

"You don't have a leg to stand on. Why would Pegrim grant bail anyhow?"

Pulcher pointed to Judge Pegrim's solitary table. "Ask him," he invited, and broke away.

He was burning a great many bridges behind him, he knew. It was an exhilarating feeling. Chancy but tingly; he decided he liked it. There was just one job to do. As soon as he was clear of the scowling but stopped committeeman, he walked by a circular route to the dais. Dickon was walking back to his table, turned away from the dais; Pulcher's chance would never be better. "Hello, Pop," he said.

Pop Craig looked up over his glasses. "Oh, Milo. I've been going over the list. You think I got everybody? Charley wanted me to introduce all the block captains and anybody else important. You know anybody important that ain't on this list?"

"That's what I wanted to tell you, Pop. Charley said for you to give me a few minutes. I want to say a few words."

THE DAY THE ICICLE WORKS CLOSED

Craig said agitatedly, "Aw, Milo, if you make a speech they're all gonna want to make speeches! What do you want to make a speech for? You're no candidate."

Pulcher winked mysteriously. "What about next year?" he asked archly, with a lying inference.

"Oh. Oh-*ho*." Pop Craig nodded and returned to his list, mumbling. "Well. In *that* case, I guess I can fit you in after the block captains, or maybe after the man from the sheriff's office—" But Pulcher wasn't listening. Pulcher was already on his way back to the little private bar.

Man had conquered all of space within nearly fifty light years of dull, yellow old Sol, but out in that main ballroom political hacks were talking of long-dead presidents of almost forgotten countries centuries in the past. Pulcher was content to listen—to allow the sounds to vibrate his eardrums, at least, for the words made little sense to him. If, indeed, there was any content of sense to a political speech in the first place. But they were soothing.

Also they kept his six fledglings from bothering him with questions. Madeleine sat quietly by his shoulder, quite relaxed still and smelling faintly, pleasantly, of some floral aroma. It was, all in all, as pleasant a place to be as Pulcher could remember in his recent past. It was too bad that he would have to go out of it soon. . . .

Very soon.

The featured guest had droned through hìs platitudes. The visiting celebrities had said their few words each. Pop Craig's voluminous old voice took over again. "And now I wanta introduce some of the fine Party workers from our local districts. There's Keith Ciccarelli from the Hillside area. Keith, stand up and take a bow!" Dutiful applause. "And here's Mary Beth Whitehurst, head of the Women's Club from Riverview!" Dutiful applause—and a whistle. Surely the whistle was sardonic; Mary Beth was fat and would never again see fifty. There were more names.

Pulcher felt it coming the moment before Pop Craig reached his own name. He was on his way to the dais even before Craig droned out: "That fine young attorney and loyal Party man—the kind of young fellow our Party needs—Milo Pulcher!"

Dutiful applause again. That was habit, but Pulcher felt the whispering question that fluttered around the room.

He didn't give the question a chance to grow. He glanced once at the five hundred loyal Party faces staring up at him and began to speak. "Mr. President. Mr. Mayor. Justice Pegrim. Honored guests. Ladies and gentlemen." That was protocol. He paused. "What I have to say to you tonight is in the way of a compliment. It's a surprise for an old friend, sitting right here. That old friend is—Charley Dickon." He threw the name at them. It was a special political sort of delivery; a tone of voice that commanded: *Clap now.* They clapped. That was important, because it made it difficult for Charley to think of an excuse to interrupt him—as soon as Charley realized he ought to, which would be shortly.

"Way out here, on the bleak frontier of interstellar space, we live isolated lives, ladies and gentlemen." There were whispers, he could hear them. The words were more or less right, but he didn't have the right political accent; the audience knew there was something wrong. The true politician would have said: *This fine, growing frontier in the midst of interstellar space's greatest constellations.* He couldn't help it; he would have to rely on velocity now to get him through. "How isolated, we sometimes need to reflect. We have trade relations through the Icicle Works—now closed. We have tourists in both directions, through the Tourist Agency. We have ultrawave messages— also through the Tourist Agency. And that's about all.

"That's a very thin link, ladies and gentlemen. *Very* thin. And I'm here to tell you tonight that it would be even thinner if it weren't for my old friend there—yes, Committeeman Charley Dickon!" He punched the name again, and got the applause—but it was puzzled and died away early.

"The fact of the matter, ladies and gentlemen, is that just about every tourist that's come to Altair Nine this past year is the personal responsibility of Charley Dickon. Who have these tourists been? They haven't been businessmen—there's no business. They haven't been hunters. Ask Phil Lasser, over there; he hasn't sold enough fishing equipment to put in your eye. Ask yourselves, for that matter. How many of you have seen airfish right over the city? Do you know why? Because they aren't being hunted any more! There aren't any tourists to hunt them."

The time had come to give it to them straight. "The fact of the matter, ladies and gentlemen, is that the tourists we've had haven't been tourists at all. They've been natives, from right here on Altair Nine. Some of them are right in this room! I know that, because I rented myself for a few days—and do you know who took my body? Why, Charley did. Charley himself!" He was watching Lew Yoder out of the corner of his eye. The assessor's face turned gray; he seemed to shrink. Pulcher enjoyed the sight, though. After all, he had a certain debt to Lew Yoder; it was Yoder's slip of the tongue that had finally started him thinking on the right track. He went on hastily: "And what it all adds up to, ladies and gentlemen, is that Charley Dickon, and a handful of his friends in high places—most of them right here in this room—have cut off communication between Altair Nine and the rest of the Galaxy!"

That did it.

There were yells, and the loudest yell came from Charley Dickon. "Throw him out! Arrest him! Craig, get the sergeant-at-arms! I say I don't have to sit here and listen to this maniac!"

"And I say you do," boomed the cold courtroom voice of Judge Pegrim. The judge stood up. "Go on, Pulcher!" he ordered. "I came here tonight to hear what you have to say. It may be wrong. It may be right. I propose to hear all of it before I make up my mind."

Thank heaven for the cold old judge! Pulcher cut right in before Dickon could find a new point of attack; there wasn't much left to say anyway. "The story is simple, ladies and gentlemen. The Icicle Works was the most profitable corporation in the Galaxy. We all know that. Probably everybody in this room had a couple of shares of stock. Dickon had plenty.

"But he wanted more. And he didn't want to pay for them. So he used his connection with the Tourist Agency to cut off communication between Nine and the rest of the Galaxy. He spread the word that Altamycin was worthless now because some fictitious character had invented a cheap new substitute. He closed down the Icicle Works. And for the last twelve months he's been picking up stock for a penny on the dollar, while the rest of us starve and the Altamycin the rest of the Galaxy needs stays right here on Altair Nine and—"

He stopped, not because he had run out of words but

because no one could hear them any longer. The noises the crowd was making were no longer puzzled; they were ferocious. It figured. Apart from Dickon's immediate gang of manipulators, there was hardly a man in the room who hadn't taken a serious loss in the past year.

It was time for the police to come rushing in, as per the phone call Judge Pegrim had made, protestingly, when Pulcher urged him to the dinner. They did—just barely in time. They weren't needed to arrest Dickon so much; but they were indispensable for keeping him from being lynched.

Hours later, escorting Madeleine home, Milo was still bubbling over. "I was worried about the mayor! I couldn't make up my mind whether he was in it with Charley or not. I'm glad he wasn't, because he said he owed me a favor, and I told him how he could pay it. Executive clemency. The six of you will be free in the morning."

Madeleine said sleepily, "I'm free enough now."

"And the Tourist Agency won't be able to enforce those contracts any more. I talked it over with Judge Pegrim. He wouldn't give me an official statement, but he said—Madeleine, you're not listening."

She yawned. "It's been an exhausting day, Milo," she apologized. "Anyway, you can tell me all about that later. We'll have plenty of time."

"Years and years," he promised. "Years and—" They stopped talking. The mechanical cab-driver, sneaking around through back streets to avoid the resentment of displaced live drivers, glanced over its condenser cells at them and chuckled, making tiny sparks in the night.

THE FELLOW WHO MARRIED THE MAXILL GIRL

BY WARD MOORE (1903–1978)

THE MAGAZINE OF FANTASY AND SCIENCE FICTION
FEBRUARY

Ward Moore was among other things, a chicken farmer from New Jersey who will always be remembered as the author of Bring The Jubilee, *(1953) one of the three or four finest alternate history novels ever written. What is often forgotten about this novel is the fact that it was published by Farrar Straus (now Farrar, Straus & Giroux) one of the elite publishers in the United States and therefore (it being the 1950s) one without a science fiction line. The fame of this book has overshadowed his other excellent novels, which include* Greener Than You Think *(1947), still one of my favorite disaster stories,* Joyleg *(with Avram Davidson, 1962),* and Caduceus Wild *(1978).*

But a greater injustice is that Ward Moore never had a collection of his shorter fiction published, because he produced a number of outstanding works, most notably "Adjustment" *(1957),* "Frank Merriwell in the White House" *(1973),* "Lot" *and* "Lot's Daughter" *(1953*

THE FELLOW WHO MARRIED THE MAXILL GIRL

and 1954), and the story you are about to read. He deserves better. (MHG)

Ever since H. G. Wells' The War of the Worlds, *it has been fashionable to look upon people from other worlds as automatically dangerous; as unreasoning enemies of Earth and its people. In countless stories they have come here to wreak insensate damage. My thought has always been that this is an example of "projection." We expect extraterrestrial intelligences to behave as Earthmen do when they encounter a strange civilization; we expect them to play the Mongols to western Europe; and Europeans to Africa and America.*

It's not necessarily so and sometimes we can unbend to the point where an alien creature may be something other than a ravening monster, as in the motion picture, E.T. *Or consider* "The Fellow Who Married The Maxill Girl." *(IA)*

After a couple of weeks Nan began to understand him a little. Nan was the third oldest Maxill girl. The wild one, they called her in Henryton, not forgetting they had said the same of Gladys and later Muriel; Gladys now high in the Eastern Star, and Muriel, married to Henryton's leading hardware and furniture dealer— Muriel, mother of the sweetest twins in Evarts County. But they said it of Nan with more assurance.

Everyone knew Maxill had bought the old Jameson place, eighty of the most worthless acres ever to break a farmer's heart, the year after Cal Coolidge became President, because he—Malcolm Maxill that is, not Mr. Coolidge—wanted an out-of-the-way location for a still. Naturally they looked for his six kids, all girls, to run wild with such a background. Not that Henryton, or Evarts County either, for that matter, upheld Prohibition or admired Andrew Volstead. But buying a so-called half-pint now and then (striking a blow for liberty, the more robust males called it, a trifle shamefacedly) was one thing, and condoning moonshining and bootlegging in their midst was something else again.

Of course moonshining was in the past now. Prohibition had been dead for two years, and people wondered more how Maxill was going to make a living from his worthless land than over his morals. But Nan had been seen necking in automobiles (a Velie and a Rickenbacker) with different boys, and heavens knew on how many unobserved occasions she'd done the same, and honestly, commented Henryton—not to say Evarts County—maybe the juvenile authorities should be notified, because Nan was still underage. Besides, she had a mean, sullen look, defiant and rebellious, that showed she needed a strong hand.

No one thought of going to her father. Everybody knew he kept a loaded shotgun handy (gossips said that was how Muriel—empty chatter—those *lovely* twins) and had run more than one nosy character off his place. Henryton people tended to mind their own business—they had plenty to think about with the Depression—so talk of the authorities, remained just talk. Still, it isolated Nan Maxill more than ever and encouraged her wildness.

He—the fellow; they hadn't any other name for him for a long time; all the Maxills knew who was meant when one of them used the pronoun—was found by Josey in the south pasture, which hadn't been a pasture for years and years, just a hummocky, lumpy expanse of weeds and obstinate brush. Josey was eleven and shy, a birthmark down the left side of her face was complicated from time to time by almost every possible affliction of the skin, so that she had begun hiding from strangers at the age of seven and never found reason to break the pattern.

She hadn't hidden from him. All her natural childish curiosity about people, long suppressed, overwhelmed by their greedy inquisitiveness over her blemishes, seemed stirred by the sight of him. Though, as everyone said afterward, he didn't really look different. He was oddly dressed, but Henryton had seen boys from Spokane or San Francisco who dressed even more oddly, and his complexion had a peculiar vitality and sheen and at the same time a delicacy which contrasted with those of the farmers accustomed to sun all day, or those who hid in shadowed stores or offices to earn dollars.

"Who're you?" asked Josey. "'My dad don't like fellers snooping around. What's your name? Maybe you better get out; he's got a gun and *believe* me he can use it. What's that stuff you're wearing? Looks like it was your skin, only blue, not something sewed at all. I can sew real good myself; it relaxes me, so I'll probably never be a delinquent. You're not deaf and dumb, are you, Mister? There's a man in Henryton's deaf, dumb *and* blind. People buy pencils from him and drop pennies and nickels in his hat. Say, why don't you say something? My dad'll sure run you off. That's a funny kind of humming. Can you whistle? There's a piece they got a record of in school—I can whistle the whole thing. It's called *Flight of the Bum-*

73

blebee. Want to hear me? Like this . . . Gee, you don't need to look so miserable. I guess you just don't like music. That's too bad. I thought when you were humming like that—the way you are now too, and I think it sounds real nice even if you don't like my whistle—you must like music. All us Maxills do. My Dad can play the fiddle better than anybody. . . ."

She told Nan later (because Nan had been the sister who had most to do with taking care of her) he hadn't seemed just not to understand, like a Mexican or something, but acted as though he wouldn't have caught on even if he'd known the meaning of every single word. He came close, still humming, though a different tune if you could call it that; it was more like snatches of odd melodies. He put his hands—she didn't notice them particularly then—very gently on her face. The touch made her feel good.

He walked with her to the house—it seemed right and natural—with his arm lightly around her shoulder. "He don't talk," she told Nan; "he don't even whistle or sing. Just hums, sort of. Suppose Dad'll run him off. Maybe he's hungry."

"Your face—" began Nan, then swallowed and looked from the child to him. She was in bad humor, frowning, ready to ask what he wanted or tell him sharply to be off. "Go wash your face," she ordered Josey, staring after her as she obediently took down the enameled basin and filled it. The muscles in Nan's cheek relaxed. "Come in," she said to him; "there's a hot apple pie."

He stood there, humming, making no move, smiling pleasantly. Involuntarily she smiled back, though she had been in a mood and the shock of Josey's face was still in her mind. It was hard to tell his age; he didn't look as though he shaved, but there was no adolescent down, and his eyes had mature assurance. She puzzled over the strangely light color; darkandhandsome had always been an indivisible word to her, yet she thought them and the pale hair quite exciting.

"Come in," she repeated; "there's a hot apple pie."

He looked at her, the kitchen behind her, at the unpromising acres over his shoulder. You might have thought he'd never seen such ordinary sights before. She took his sleeve—the feel of it sent prickles through her thumb and fingers as though she'd touched something live instead of inert, touched silk expecting cotton, metal anticipating wood—and pulled him through the door. He didn't hold back or, once inside, seem ill at ease. He merely acted—strange. As though he didn't know a chair was for sitting on or a spoon was for cutting the flaky crust and scooping up the juicy, sticky, dripping filling, or even that the pie was for putting in the mouth, tasting, chewing, swallowing, eating. The horrid thought of mental deficiency crossed her mind, to be dismissed by the sight of him, so unequivocally whole and invulnerable. Still . . .

Josey ran to her. "Nan, Nan—I looked in the mirror! Look at me. My face!"

Nan nodded, swallowing again, glancing swiftly at him and away. "It must have been that last prescription. Or else you're just growing out of it, baby."

"The—the *thing*! It's lighter. Faded."

The birthmark, angry and purple, had receded in size and color. The skin around it was clear and vibrant. Nan put her fingers wonderingly on the smooth cheek and stooped to kiss her sister. "I'm so happy."

He sat there, humming again. Oh, what a silly, Nan thought cheerfully. "Here," she said, in the manner of one addressing an idiot or a foreigner. "Eat. See. Like this. Eat."

Obediently he put the guided spoon of pie into his mouth. She was relieved when he disposed of it normally; she had been afraid she might have to direct each spoonful. At least he didn't have to be fed like a baby. She hesitated a fraction of a second before pouring a glass of milk, feeling small for doing so. She wasn't mean—none of the Maxills were; their faults usually sprang from an excess of generosity—but the cow was drying up, she was a hard one to breed, her father wasn't much of a hand with animals anyway, and the kids needed the milk, to say nothing of the butter Nan preferred to lard for baking. But it would be shameful to grudge—

He had put the glass to his lips, evidently more at home with methods of drinking than of eating, and taken a single sip before sputtering, choking and spitting. Nan was furious, equally at the waste and the manners, until she noticed his hands for the first time. They were strong-looking, perhaps longer than ordinary. On each there was a thumb and three fingers. The three fingers were widely spaced; there was no sign of deformity or amputation. He was simply eight-instead of ten-fingered.

Nan Maxill was a softhearted girl. She had never drowned a kitten or trapped a mouse in her life. She forgot her annoyance instantly. "Oh, poor man!" she exclaimed.

There was no question he must stay and her father must be cozened into allowing it. Ordinary decency—

contrary to Maxill custom—demanded hospitality. And if they let him go, her unsatisfied curiosity would torment her for years. On his part he showed no inclination to leave, continuing to examine each object and person with interest. His humming wasn't monotonous, or tiresome. Though it sounded like no music she had ever heard, it was agreeable enough for her to try to imitate it. She found it deceptively complicated and hard—almost impossible for her to reproduce.

His reaction was enthusiastic surprise. He hummed, she hummed, he hummed back joyously. Briefly the Maxill kitchen echoed a strange, unearthly duet. Then—at least so it seemed to Nan—he was demanding more, far more, than she was able to give. His tones soared away on subtle scales she couldn't possibly follow. She fell silent; after a questioning interval, so did he.

Malcolm Maxill came home in ill-humor. He worked for his son-in-law during the winter and for a month or so in summer; his natural irritation at this undignified role was not lessened by the hardware merchant's insinuations that this employment was in the manner of family charity: who else in Evarts County would hire an ex-bootlegger? Maxill looked to the day he could sell the farm—it was clear of mortgages since it would have been inconvenient in his former profession to have bankers scrutinizing his affairs—and work for himself again. But even good farms were hard to sell in times like these and there were no offers on the eighty acres. More to give an impression to an unlikely prospective buyer that the place had potentialities than in hope of profit, he kept the cow, some pigs and chickens, planted twenty acres or so each spring to corn it never paid to harvest, and looked with disgust on the decayed orchard which was good only for firewood—for which he couldn't get back the cost of cutting.

He stared belligerently at the fellow. "What do you want around here?"

The stranger hummed. Nan and Josey started, explaining at the same time. Jessie and Janet begged, "Oh, Daddy, please."

"All right, all right," growled their father. "Let him stay a couple of days if you're all so hot about it. I suppose at least he can do the chores for his board and maybe cut down a few of those old apple trees. Can you milk?" he asked the fellow. "Huh; forgot he's a dummy. O.K. come along; soon find out whether you can or not."

The girls went with them, Nan carrying the milkpail and tactfully guiding the stranger. Sherry, the cow, was fenced out rather than fenced in: she had the run of the farm except for the cornfield and the scrubby kitchen garden. She was not bedded down in the barn in summer; she was milked wherever she was found. Half-Jersey, half-Guernsey, (and half anybody's guess, Malcolm Maxill said sourly), her milk was rich with cream but it had been too long since she last freshened and the neighboring bulls had never earned their stud fee, though their owners didn't return it when she failed to calve.

Maxill set the pail under Sherry's udder. "Go ahead," he urged, "let's see you milk her." The fellow just stood there, looking interested, humming. "Wouldn't you know it? Can't milk." He squatted down disgustedly, gave a perfunctory brush of his hand against the dangling teats, and began pulling the milk, squit, squit, shish, down into the pail.

The fellow reached out his four-fingered hand and stroked the cow's flank. City man or not, at least he wasn't scared of animals. Of course Sherry wasn't balky or mean; she hardly ever kicked over the pail or swished her tail real hard in the milker's eyes. Still it took confidence (or ignorance) to walk around her left side and touch the bag from which Maxill was drawing, slish, slish, slish, the evening milk.

Nan knew her father was no farmer and that a real one would be milking Sherry only once a day by now, drying her up, since she yielded little more than three quarts. But Maxill knew you were supposed to milk a cow twice a day, just as he knew how long to let mash ferment and he was no chemist either. He went by rules.

"Be darned," exclaimed Maxill, who seldom swore in front of his children. "That's the most she's given in months and I ain't stripped her yet."

The cow's unexpected bounty put him in good humor; he didn't seem to mind slopping the pigs nor the stranger's helplessness at throwing scratch to the chickens. (The girls usually did this anyway; Maxill's presence was a formality to impress the fellow with the scope and responsibility of the chores.) He ate what Nan had cooked with cheerful appetite, remarking jovially that the dummy would be cheap to feed since he didn't touch meat, butter or milk, only bread, vegetables and water.

Maxill's jollity led him to tune up his fiddle—only Josey and Nan noted the stranger's anguish—and run through *Birmingham Jail*, *Beautiful Doll*, and *Dar-*

danella. Maxill played by ear, contemptuous of those who had to read notes. Josey whistled (after an apologetic glance), Jessie played her mouth-organ, Janet performed expertly with comb and toilet-paper. "You'd think," grunted Maxill, "with his humming he could give us a tune himself. How about it?" And he offered the fiddle.

The fellow looked at the fiddle as though it were explosive. He put it down on the table as fast as he could and backed away. Nan grieved at this evidence of mental deficiency; Jessie and Janet giggled; Malcolm twirled his finger at his temple; even Josey smiled ruefully.

Then the fiddle began playing. Not playing really, because the bow lay unmoving beside it and the strings didn't vibrate. But music came out of the sound holes, uncertainly at first, then with swelling assurance. It resembled the fellow's humming except that it was infinitely more complicated and moving. . . .

Next morning Maxill took the fellow down to the orchard, the girls tagging along. They weren't going to miss the possibility of more miracles, though now everyone had had a chance to think things over, the Maxills weren't so sure they'd actually heard the fiddle, or if they had, that it hadn't been by some perfectly explicable trick or illusion. Still, if he could seem to make it play without touching it, maybe he could do similar things with the ax.

Maxill hacked at a dead limb. The ax bounded back from the wood. The tree was not diseased or rotten, just old and neglected. Most of the branches were dead but sap still ran in the trunk, as shown by a few boughs on which a handful of fruit had set, and there was new growth on the tips. Like the rest of the orchard, the tree wasn't worth saving. The ax swung again; the branch broke off. Maxill nodded and handed the ax to the fellow.

The fellow hummed, looked at Maxill, the girls, the ax. He dropped the tool and walked over to the tree, fingering the rough bark of the corns, the gnarly outcrop of the roots, the leaves and twigs over his head. Nan halfway expected the tree to rearrange itself into cordwood, neatly split and stacked. Nothing happened, nothing at all.

"Yah! Dummy can't milk, slop pigs, feed chickens or cut wood. If it cost anything to feed him he wouldn't be worth his keep. All he can do is hum and play tricks."

"We'll do the chores this morning," Nan offered tactfully. They did them most mornings, and evenings too, but it was a convention that their father did all the man's work and left them free to concentrate on feminine pursuits. Thoughtful girls, they saved his face.

Nan couldn't believe there was nothing irrevocably wrong with the fellow. He used his eight fingers as dexterously as anyone used ten; more so, it seemed. He wouldn't feed the pigs, but he caught on fast to gathering eggs, reaching under the hens without disturbing them at all. He couldn't milk but he stood by Sherry's side while Nan did. The cow's production was still up; there was a lot more than yesterday morning.

After the chores he returned to the orchard—without the ax. Nan sent Josey to see what he was up to. "He's going to every tree on the place," Josey reported;

"just looking at them and touching them. Not doing anything useful. And you know what? He eats grass and weeds."

"Chews on them, you mean."

"No, I don't. He eats them, honest. Handfuls. And he touched my—the thing on my face. I ran right away to look in the mirror, and you can hardly see it in the shade."

"I'm glad it's fading," said Nan. "Only don't be disappointed if it comes back. It's nothing to worry about. And I'm sure his touching you had nothing to do with it. Just coincidence."

It took the fellow three days to go through the orchard, fooling around with every one of the old trees. By the end of the third day Sherry was giving two full gallons of milk, they were gathering more eggs than usual in the season when laying normally fell off, and Josey's birthmark had practically disappeared, even in full sunlight. Malcolm Maxill grumbled at the fellow's uselessness but he never said straight out that he had to move on, so everything was all right.

After the orchard (the girls went, separately and collectively, to see what he was doing; they returned no wiser) he started on the cornfield. Maxill had planted late, not merely from lack of enthusiasm for husbandry but, possessing no tractor or plow, he had to wait till those who hired out their rigs finished their own sowing. The ground had been dry; the seed had taken overlong to swell and germinate; when the tender gray-green sheaves spiraled through the hard earth, the hot sun had scorched and warped them. While the neighboring fields were already in pale tassel, his dwarfed rows barely revealed the beginning of stunted spikes.

THE FELLOW WHO MARRIED THE MAXILL GIRL

The fellow took even longer with the corn than the orchard. By now Nan realized his humming wasn't tunes at all, just his way of talking. It was a little disheartening, making him seem more alien than ever. If he'd been Italian or Portugee she could have learned the language; if he'd been a Chinaman she could have found out how to eat with chopsticks. A man who spoke notes instead of words was a problem for a girl.

Just the same, after a couple of weeks she began to understand him a little. By this time they were getting four gallons a day from the cow, more eggs than they ever had in early spring, and Josey's complexion was like a baby's. Maxill brought home a radio someone traded in at his son-in-law's store and they had fun getting all sorts of distant stations. When the fellow came close and they weren't tuned in, it played the same kind of music the fiddle had the first night. They were getting used to it now; it didn't seem so strange or even—Malcolm Maxill's words—so long-haired. It made them feel better, stronger, kinder, more loving.

She understood—what? That he was not as other men, born in places with familiar names, speaking familiar speech, doing things in customary ways? All this she knew already. The humming told her where he came from and how; it was no more comprehensible and relevant afterward than before. Another planet, another star, another galaxy—what were these concepts to Nan Maxill, the disciplinary problem of Henryton Union High, who had read novels in her science class? His name, as near as she could translate the hum, was Ash; what did it matter if he was born on Alpha Centauri, Mars, or an unnamed earth a billion light-years off?

He was humble, conscious of inferiority. He could do none of the things in which his race was so proficient. Not for him were abstract problems insoluble by electronic brains, philosophical speculation reaching either to lunacy or enlightenment, the invention of new means to create or transmute matter. He was, so he admitted and her heart filled the gaps her intellect failed to bridge, a throwback, an atavism, a creature unable to catch the progress of his kind. In a world of science, of synthetic foods and telekinesis, of final divorce from the elementary processes of nature, he had been born a farmer.

He could make things grow—in a civilization where that talent was no longer useful. He could combat sickness—in a race that had developed congenital immunity to disease. His gifts were those his species had once needed; they had outgrown the need a million generations back.

He did not pour out his confusion to Nan in a single steady flow. Only as he acquired words and she began to distinguish between his tones did their communication reach toward comprehension. Even when he was thoroughly proficient in her language and she could use his crudely, there remained so much beyond her grasp. He explained patiently over and over the technique of controlling sounds without directly touching the instrument as he had done with the fiddle and radio; she could not follow him. What he had done to Josey's face might as well have been expounded in Sanskrit.

It was still more impossible for her to envision the

ways in which Ash was inferior to his fellows. That his humming—any music he produced—so beguiling and ethereal to her, was only a dissonance, a childish babble, a lisping, stuttering cacophony, was preposterous. Spaceships she could imagine, but not instantaneous transmission of unharmed living matter through a void millions of parsecs across.

While they learned from each other the corn ripened. This was no crop to plow under or let blacken with mildew in the field. The blighted sheaves now stood head-high, the broad leaves sickling gracefully downward, exposing and protecting the two ears on every stalk. And what ears they were! Twice as long and twice as fat as any grown in Evarts County within memory, full of perfect kernels right to the bluntly rounded tips, without a single dry or wormy row. The county agricultural agent, hearing rumors, drove over to scotch them; he walked through the field for hours, shaking his head, mumbling to himself, pinching his arm. Maxill sold the crop for a price that was unbelievable, even with the check in his hand.

The meager scattering of fruit ripened. Since the coming of Ash, the trees had sent forth new wood at a great rate. Young leaves hid the scars of age: the dead wood thrusting jaggedly, nakedly upward, the still-living but sterile boughs. Under the lush foliage the girls discovered the fruit. Ash's touch had been too late for the cherries, apricots, plums, early peaches, though those trees were flourishing in their new growth with abundant promise for the coming year. But the apples, pears and winter peaches were more astonishing than the corn.

There were few; nothing could have added new

blossoms, fertilized them, or set the fruit, but the few were enormous. The apples were large as cantaloupes, the pears twice the size of normal pears, the peaches bigger than any peach could be. (Maxill exhibited specimens at the County Fair and swept all the first prizes.) They were so huge everyone assumed they must be mealy and tasteless, easily spoiled. Juice spurted from them at the bite, their flesh was firm and tangy, their taste and plumpness kept through the winter.

Nan Maxill faced the problem. Ash was properly a gift to all the people of the world. There was none who couldn't learn from him; all would benefit by what they learned. Scientists could understand what she couldn't; piece together the hints of matters above Ash's own head. The impetus he could give to technology would make the fifteenth and nineteenth centuries seem stagnant periods. Musicians and philologists could be pushed to amazing discoveries. Farmers could benefit most of all. Under his guidance dead sands and unused spaces would be rich with food; many if not all wars might be avoided. To keep him on the farm in Evarts County would be cheating humanity.

Against all this what could she set? The prosperity of the Maxills? Her growing attachment to Ash? The threat of her father selling the farm—easy enough now—and seeing the money spent until they were worse off than ever? She would have been stupid or foolish not to have considered these things. But the picture that pushed all others aside was that of Ash on the rack, victim of polite, incredulous inquisitors.

They wouldn't believe a word he said. They'd find

the most convincing reasons for disregarding the evidence of the corn, the fruit, the untouched fiddle. They would subject him to psychiatric tests: intelligence, co-ordination, memory; physical tests—every possible prying and prodding. Where was he born, what was his full name, who were his father and mother? Unbelieving, refusing to believe, but so politely, gently, insistently: Yes, yes of course, we understand; but try and think back, Mr. Uh Er Ash. Try to recall your childhood. . . .

And when they finally realized, it would be worse, not better. Now this force, Mr. Ash—try to remember how. . . . This equation; surely you can. . . . We know you practice telekinesis, just show us. . . . Again, please. . . . Again, please. . . . About healing sores, please explain. . . . Let's go through that revival of dying plant life once more. . . . Now about this ultrachromatic scale. . . . Now this, now that.

Or suppose it wasn't that way at all? Suppose the peril to Ash wasn't the apelike human greed for information but the tigerish human fear and hate of the stranger? Arrest for illegal entry or whatever they wanted to call it, speeches in Congress, uproar in newspapers and over the air. Spy, saboteur, alien agent. (How do we know what he's done to what he grows? Maybe anybody who eats it will go crazy or not be able to have babies.) There were no means of deporting Ash; this didn't mean he couldn't be gotten rid of by those terrified of an invasion of which he was the forerunner. Trials, legal condemnation, protective custody, lynchers . . .

Uncovering Ash meant disaster. Two hundred years earlier or later he could bring salvation. Not now. In this age of fear, the revelation of his existence would be an irreparable mistake. Nan knew her father wouldn't be anxious to tell who was responsible for his crops; Gladys and Muriel knew nothing except that they had a hired man who was somewhat peculiar; anyway they wouldn't call themselves to the attention of Evarts County in any controversial light. The younger kids could be trusted to follow the example of their father and sisters. Besides, she was the only one in whom Ash had confided.

That winter Maxill bought two more cows. Ancient, dry and bony, destined for the butcher's where they would have brought very little. Under Ash's care they rejuvenated from day to day, their ribs vanished beneath flesh, their eyes brightened. The small, slack bags emerged, rounded, swelled, and eventually hung as full of milk as though they had just calved.

"What I want to know is, why can't we do as much for the pigs?" he demanded of Nan, ignoring, as always except when it suited him, Ash's presence. "Hogs are way down; I could get me some bred sows cheap. He could work his hocus-pocus—I can just see what litters they'd have."

"It isn't hocus-pocus. Ash just knows more about these things than we do. And he won't do anything to help killing," Nan explained. "He won't eat meat or eggs or milk himself—"

"He did something to make the hens lay more. And look at the milk we're getting."

"The more the hens lay the farther they are from the ax. The same goes for the cows. You notice nothing's improved the young cockerels. Maybe it isn't that he won't; maybe he can't do anything to get animals ready to be eaten. Ask him."

THE FELLOW WHO MARRIED THE MAXILL GIRL

The seed catalogues began coming. Maxill had never bothered with the truck garden beyond having it plowed for the girls to sow and tend. This year he treated each pamphlet like a love letter, gloating over the orange-icicle carrots, impudent radishes, well-born heads of lettuce on the glistening covers. Nan intercepted his rhapsody of cabbages bigger than pumpkins, watermelons too heavy for a man to lift unaided, succulent tomatoes weighing three pounds or more apiece.

And Ash was content. For the first time Nan felt the double-edged anger of women toward both exploiter and exploited. Ash ought to have some self-respect, some ambition. He oughtn't be satisfied puttering around an old farm. With his abilities and the assurance of a superior among primitives he could be just about anything he wanted. But of course all he wanted was to be a farmer.

Maxill couldn't wait for the ground to be ready. While it was still too wet he had it plowed. Badly and at extra cost. He planted every inch of the fifty-odd available acres, to the carefully concealed amusement of his neighbors who knew the seed would rot.

Nan asked Ash, "Can you control whatever it is you do?"

"I can't make pear trees bear cucumbers or a grapevine have potatoes on its roots."

"I mean, everything doesn't have to be extra big, does it? Can you fix it so the corn is only a little bigger than usual?"

"Why?"

Nan Maxill knew the shame of treason, as she tried to explain.

"You're using words I don't know," said Ash. "Please

define: jealousy, envy, foreigner, competition, furious, suspicion and—well, begin with those."

She did the best she could. It wasn't good enough.
It wasn't nearly good enough. Nan, who had been
outraged at Ash's banishment, began to see how one
too far behind or too far ahead might become intolera-
ble. She could only guess what Ash represented to his
people—a reminder of things better forgotten, a hint
that they weren't so advanced as they thought when
such a one could still be born to them—but she knew
what he was on earth in the year 1937: a reproach and
a condemnation.

Spring winds snapped the dead wood on the fruit
trees, pruning them as efficiently as a man with saw,
shears and snips. The orchard could not be mistaken
for a young one, the massive trunks and tall tops
showed how long they had been rooted, but it was
unquestionably a healthy one. The buds filled and
opened, some with red-tipped unspoiled leaves, others
with soft, powdery, uncountable blossoms. The shade
they cast was so dense no weeds grew between the
trees.

Not so in the fields. Whatever Ash had done to the
soil also affected the windblown seeds lighting in and
between the furrows. They came up so thickly that
stem grew next to stem, roots tangled inextricably,
heads rose taller and taller, reaching for unimpeded
sunlight. Unless you got down on hands and knees the
tiny green pencils were invisible under the network of
weeds.

"Anyways," said Malcolm Maxill, "the darned things
came up instead of rotting; that's going to make some
of the characters around here look pretty sick. I'll

have a crop two-three weeks ahead of the rest. Depression's over for the Maxills. Know what? We'll have to cultivate like heck to get rid of the weeds; I'm going to get us a tractor on time. Then we won't have to hire our plowing next year. Suppose he can learn to run a tractor?"

"He can," said Nan, ignoring Ash's presence as completely as her father. "But he won't."

"Why won't he?"

"He doesn't like machinery."

Maxill looked disgusted. "I suppose he'd be happy with a horse or a mule."

"Maybe. He still wouldn't turn the weeds under."

"Why the dickens not?"

"I've told you before, Father. He won't have anything to do with killing."

"Weeds?"

"Anything. There's no use arguing; that's the way he is."

"Darn poor way if you ask me." But he bought the tractor and many attachments for it, cultivating the corn, sweating and swearing (when the girls were out of earshot); cursing Ash who did no more about the farm than walk around touching things. Was that a way to earn a grown man's keep?

Nan was afraid he might have a stroke when he found out the mammoth products of the year before were not to be duplicated. The orchard bore beyond all expectation or reason, not a cherry, plum or apricot was undersized, misshapen or bird-pecked. No blossom fell infertile, no hard green nubbin withered and dropped, no set fruit failed to mature. Branches bent almost to the ground under the weight of their loads; breezes twitched leaves aside to uncover briefly a pomologist's dream. Maxill was no more pleased than by the corn.

"Sacrificing quality for quantity," he growled. "Bring the top market price? Sure. I was counting on twice that."

Nan Maxill realized how much she herself had changed, or been changed, since the fellow came.

Her father seemed to her now like a petulant child, going into a tantrum because something he wanted—something she saw wasn't good for him—was denied. The boys she used to go out with were gluttonous infants, gurgling and slobbering their fatuous desires. The people of Henryton, of Evarts County, of—no, she corrected herself—people; people were juvenile, adolescent. News on the radio was of wars in China and Spain, massacre and bestialities in Germany, cruelties and self-defeat all over the world.

Had she unconsciously acquired Ash's viewpoint? He had no viewpoint, passed no judgments. He accepted what was all around him as he accepted what she told him: reflectively, curiously, puzzledly, but without revulsion. She had taken the attitude she thought *ought* to be his, unable to reach his detachment as he was unable to reach that of those who had exiled him here, as one who cannot distinguish between apes would put a gorilla and chimpanzee in the zoo cage.

As primitive characteristics were sloughed off, a price was paid for their loss. Ash's people had exchanged his ability to make things grow for a compensatory ability to create by photosynthesis and other processes. If Ash had lost the savage ability to despise and hate, had he also lost the mitigating ability to love?

Because she wanted Ash to love her.

They were married in January, which some thought odd, but the season suited Nan who wanted a "regular" wedding and at the same time a quiet one. She had expected her father's assent at least; Ash had made him prosperous in two short years; their marriage would be insurance that he would continue to do so. But Maxill's bank account, his big car, the new respect Henryton—including his son-in-law—gave him, had inflated his ideas. "Who is the fellow anyway?" he demanded. "Where'd he come from originally? What's his background?"

"Does all that matter? He's good and gentle and kind, where he came from or who his parents were doesn't change that."

"Oh, doesn't it? Maybe there's bad blood in him. Bound to come out. And he's a cripple and not right in the head besides. Why, he couldn't talk like anybody else at first. Sure it matters: you want kids who turn out idiots with the wrong number of fingers? Maybe criminals too?"

Nan neither smiled at his passion for respectability nor reminded him that her children would have a moonshiner and bootlegger for a grandfather. "Ash is no criminal."

Ash was no criminal, but what of other dangers? Not just children with the wrong number of fingers or differences she knew nothing of (she'd never dare let Ash be examined by a doctor for fear of what anatomical or functional differences might be revealed), but perhaps no children at all. Beings so different might well have sterile union. Or no carnal union at all. Perhaps no bond deeper than that of a man for a cat or horse. Nan didn't pretend for a second it wouldn't matter. It mattered terribly, every last perilous possibility. She was still determined to marry him.

Maxill shook his head. "There's another thing—he hasn't even got a name."

"We'll give him ours," said Nan. "We'll say he's a second cousin or something."

"Hell we will!" her father exploded. "A freak like that—"

"All right. We'll elope then, and get a place of our own. It won't be hard when anyone sees what Ash can do. And we won't have to have good land." She left it at that, giving him plenty of time to think over all the implications. He gave in. Grudgingly, angrily. But he gave in.

Ash had never gone into Henryton or showed himself except the few times he'd helped Maxill pay back a debt of work. Still everyone knew there was some sort of hired man on the farm. Gladys and Muriel knew him to nod to and that was about all; they were skeptically astonished to learn he was a remote relative "from back East" and still more amazed to hear he was marrying Nan. They thought she could do better. Then they remembered her reputation; maybe they should be glad the fellow was doing right. They counted the months and were shocked when a year and a half went by before Ash Maxill junior was born.

Nan had counted the months too. Some of her fears had been quickly dispelled, others persisted. She feared to look closely at her son, and the fear was not mitigated by Ash's expression of aloof interest nor the doctor's and nurses' over-bright cheeriness. Her insides settled back into place as she delicately touched the tiny nose, unbelievably perfect ears, rounded head. Then she reached to lift the wrapping blanket—

"Uh . . . uhh . . . Mrs. Maxill, uh . . ."

She knew of course even before she saw them, and a great wave of defiance flowed through her. The little dimpled hands, the little rectangular feet—eight fingers, eight toes.

She wanted to shout, It's not an impediment, you idiots! Why do you need five fingers when four will do the same things more easily and skillfully, and do things no five-fingered hand will do? It wasn't physical weakness which kept her quiet—she was a strong, healthy girl and the birth had not been complicated— but the knowledge that she must hide the child's superiority as she hid Ash's lest the ordinary ones turn on them both. She hid her face. Let them think it was anguish.

She felt a curious sympathy for her father. Malcolm Maxill was triumphant; his dire prophecies had been fulfilled; he could not restrain his gratification. At the same time it was his grandson—his flesh and blood— who was deformed. Short of betraying Ash's secret she had no way of reassuring him and even this might not console him. More than likely he would take Ash's banishment as further proof of undesirability; he did not try to hide his increasing animosity.

"You'd think," said Nan, "you'd injured him instead of doing all you have."

Ash smiled and ran his hand lightly over her shoulder. It still surprised her slightly that someone without anger, envy or hate should be capable of humor and tenderness.

"Do you expect him to be grateful?" he asked. "Have you forgotten all you told me about how people act? Anyway, I didn't do it for your father but for the sake of doing it."

"Just the same, now the baby is here, we ought to have a regular agreement. Either a share in the farm or else wages—good wages."

She knew his look of grave and honest interest so well. "Why? We have all we can eat. Your clothes wear out but your father gives you money for new ones, and the baby's too. Why—"

"Why don't your clothes wear out or get dirty?" she interrupted irrelevantly.

He shook his head. "I don't know. I told you I didn't understand these things. Until I came here I never heard of fabrics which weren't everwearing and self-cleaning."

"Anyway it doesn't matter. We ought to be independent."

He shook his head. "Why?"

Malcolm Maxill used some of the money from the bountiful crop of 1940 to buy the adjoining farm. He was indisputably a big man in Evarts County now. Three laborers worked the two farms; the house had been remodeled; a truck, two cars and a station wagon stood in the new garage beside all the shining machinery. The banker in Henryton listened deferentially when he spoke; Muriel's husband asked his advice.

Nan saw how it chafed him to be tied to farming, beholden to Ash. When he left on the long trip to Los Angeles she knew he was trying to end his dependence, searching for a deal to put him in a business where his shrewdness, money, energy, not Ash's gifts, would make the profit. Maxill wasn't mean; if he sold the land she was sure he'd settle with Ash for enough so they could get a place of their own.

A freeway accident intervened: Malcolm Maxill was killed instantly. There was no will. The estate was divided amicably enough, Gladys and Muriel waiving practically all their share in return for Nan's taking full responsibility for the three younger girls. Ash was quite content to leave arrangements—which he regarded with the detached interest an Anglican bishop might take in a voodoo mask—to her. He clearly didn't grasp the importance of possessions and power.

He had to register for the draft but as a father in an essential occupation there was little danger of being called up; anyway he would never pass a medical examination with eight fingers. The war sent farm prices up and up; Gladys went to Washington to work for the government; Josey married a sailor home on leave.

Harvests continued bountiful. Nan noted with pleasure how other farmers came to Ash for advice and help. Since he couldn't convey his knowledge to her despite partial communication in his own tongue there was no use trying with others. He never refused his aid; he simply limited it to visiting the poor growth, sick animal or doubtful field, talking platitudes from agricultural bulletins while his hands were busy. Afterward, so naturally that they were only amazed at the wisdom of the trite advice, the beasts recovered, the crop flourished, the sterile ground bore.

Her faint fear of little Ash's hands becoming a handicap after all was dissipated. He could grasp, clutch, hold, manipulate, throw better than any other child of his age. (Some years later he became the best pitcher Evarts County had ever known; he had a facing curve no opposing batter ever caught onto.) Without precocity he talked early; he learned his father's speech so well he eventually outdistanced Nan; she listened with maternal and wifely complacency as they hummed subtleties beyond her understanding.

Jessie, who took a commercial course, got a job as her brother-in-law's secretary; Janet went East to study archaeology. After V-J Day, price-controls went off; the Maxills made more and more money. Ash stopped planting corn on the old farm. Part of the acreage he put into a new orchard, on the rest he sowed a hybrid grass of his own breeding which yielded a grain higher in protein than wheat. Young Ash was a joy; yet after seven years he remained an only child. "Why?" she asked.

"You want more children?"

"Naturally I do. Don't you?"

"It's still hard for me to understand your people's obsession with security. Security of position, ancestry or posterity. How is it possible to differentiate so jealously between one child and another because of a biological relation or the lack of it?"

For the first time Nan felt him alien. "I want *my* children."

But she had no more. The lack saddened without embittering her; she remembered how she had been bent on marrying Ash even with the chance of no children at all. And she had been right: without Ash the farm would have been worthless; her father, a whining, querulous, churlish failure; she would have married the first boy who asked her after she tired of necking in cars, and would have had a husband as incapable of helping her grow and bloom as her father had been incapable with his barren acres. Even if she had known there would be no young Ash, she would still have chosen the same way.

It troubled her that Ash was unable to teach his son his farming skill. It destroyed a dream of Nan's: Ash's secret made him vulnerable; young Ash, with no secret to be extracted, could have worked his miracles for humanity without fear.

"Why can't he learn? He understands you better than I ever will."

"He may understand too much. He may have advanced beyond me. Remember, I'm a throwback, with faculties no longer needed by my people. Sports rarely breed true; he may be closer to them in some ways than I."

"Then . . . then he should be able to do some of the marvelous things they can do."

"I don't think it works that way. There's some kind of equation—not a mechanical leveling off, but compensatory gains and losses. I can't teach him even the simple sort of telekinesis I can do. But he can heal flesh better than I."

So a new dream supplanted the old: young Ash as a doctor, curing the diseases mankind suffered. But the boy, happy enough to exorcise warts from a playmate's hands or mend a broken bone by running his fingers over the flesh outside, wanted no such future. The overriding interest of his life was machinery. At six he had rehabilitated an old bicycle each Maxill girl had used in turn until it was worn beyond repair.

Beyond any repair except young Ash's, that is. At eight he restored decrepit alarm clocks to service, at ten he could fix the tractor as well or better than the Henryton garage. Nan supposed she ought to be happy about a son who might be a great engineer or inventor; unfortunately she thought the world of freeways and nuclear weapons less desirable than the one she had known as a girl—Prohibition and Depression or not.

Could she be aging? She was just over forty; the fine lines on her face, the slight raising of the veins on her hands were far less noticeable than the same signs on girls—women—five or six years younger. Yet when she looked at Ash's smooth cheeks, unchanged since the day Josey brought him in from the south pasture, she had a qualm of apprehension.

"How old are you?" she asked him. "How old are you really?"

"As old and as young as you are."

"No," she persisted. "That's a figure of speech or a way of thinking. I want to know."

"How can I put it in terms of earth years—of revolutions around this sun by this planet? It wouldn't make sense even if I knew the mathematics involved and could translate one measurement into another. Look at it this way: wheat is old at six months, an oak is young at fifty years."

"Are you immortal?"

"No more than you. I'll die just as you will."

"But you don't grow any older."

"I don't get sick either. My body isn't subject to weakness and decay the way my remote ancestors' were. But I was born, therefore I must die."

THE FELLOW WHO MARRIED THE MAXILL GIRL

"You'll still look young when I'm an old woman. Ash . . ."

Ah, she thought, it's well enough for you to talk. What people say doesn't bother you; you aren't concerned with ridicule or malice. I'd call you inhuman if I didn't love you. Every superhuman carries the suggestion of inhumanity with it. Yes, yes—we're all selfish, mean, petty, grasping, cruel, nasty. Are we condemned for not seeing over our heads, for not being able to view ourselves with the judicial attachment of a million generations hence? I suppose we are. But it must be a self-condemnation, not an admonition, not even the example of a superior being.

She could not regret marrying Ash; she would not have changed anything. Except the one pitiful little resentment against aging while he didn't. No acquired wisdom, no thoughtful contemplation could reconcile her to the idea, could prevent her shuddering at the imagined looks, questions, snickers at a woman of fifty, sixty, seventy, married to a boy apparently in his twenties. Suppose young Ash had inherited his father's impervious constitution, as he seemed to have? She saw, despite the painful ludicrousness of it, her aged self peering from one to the other, unable to tell instantly which was the husband and which the son.

In her distress, and her soreness that she should be distressed, she drew off from the others, spoke little, spent hours away from the house, wandering in a not unpleasant abdication of thought and feeling. So, in the hot, sunny stillness of an August afternoon, she heard the music.

She knew immediately. There was no mistaking its relation to Ash's humming and its even closer kinship to the polyphony he drew from the radio. For a vanishing instant she thought, heart-beatingly, that young Ash—but this was far far beyond fumbling experiment. It could only come from someone—something—as far ahead of Ash as he was of her.

She listened, shocked, anguished, exhaled. There was nothing to see except the distant mountains, the cloudless sky, ripe fields, straight road, groups of slender trees, scrabbly knots of wild berries, untrammeled weeds. Nothing hovered overhead, no stranger in unearthly clothes strolled from behind the nearest hillock. Yet she had no doubt. She hurried back to the house and found Ash. "They are looking for you."

"I know. I've known for days."

"Why? What do they want?"

He did not answer directly. "Nan, do you think I've completely failed to fit into this life?"

She was genuinely astonished. "Failed! You've brought life, wisdom, health, goodness to everything you've touched. How can you talk of failing?"

"Because, after all . . . I haven't become one of you."

"Add, 'Thank God.' You've done much more than become one of us. You've changed the face and spirit of everything around here. The land and those who live off it are better because of you. You changed me from a silly girl to—to whatever I am. You fathered young Ash. Don't ask me if a spoonful of sugar sweetens the ocean—let me believe it makes it that much less salt."

"But you are unhappy."

She shrugged. "Happiness is for those satisfied with what they have and want nothing more."

He asked, "And what do you want?"

"A world where I wouldn't have to hide you," she answered fiercely. "A world you and young Ash and his children and grandchildren could better without inviting suspicion and envy. A world outraged—not happy—with bickering, distrust, animosity and terror. I think you've brought such a world a little closer to becoming."

He said abruptly, "They want me back."

She heard the four words without comprehension; they conveyed no message to her. She searched his face as though the expression would enlighten her. "What did you say?"

"They want me back," he repeated. "They need me."

"But that's outrageous! First they send you to this savage world, then they decide they've made a mistake and whistle for you to come back."

"It isn't like that," protested Ash. "They didn't force me; I didn't have to accept the suggestion. Everyone agreed, on the basis of the very little we knew, that the people and society here (if either existed) would most likely be closer to the epoch I would naturally have fitted than the one into which I was born. I needn't have come; having come, I could have returned."

"Force! What do you call the pressure of 'everyone agreed' if not force? And it was for your own good too. That excuse for wickedness must prevail from one end of the universe to the other. I wonder if your people are really less barbarian than mine."

He refused to argue, to defend the beings who threatened—if vainly—the life she led with her husband and son, the minute good Ash was doing in Evarts County, the hope that he could do more and on a larger scale. Ash in his humility thought them superior to him; she had never questioned this till now. But suppose their evolution had not been toward better than the development Ash represented, but worse—a subtle degeneracy? Suppose in gaining the abilities so awesome to Ash they had lost some of his probity and uprightness, reverting to a morality no higher—little higher, she amended in all honesty—than that of the earth in the year 1960?

"Of course you won't go?"

"They need me."

"So do I. So does young Ash."

He smiled tenderly at her. "I will not weigh the need of millions, nor the need of love and comfort, against the need for life. Such judgments lead only to self-justification, cruelty disguised as mercy, and destruction for the sake of rebuilding."

"Then you won't go?"

"Not unless you tell me to."

Next day she walked through the orchard, recalling again its desolate condition before Ash came, Josey's face, her own unsettled heart. She walked through the new orchard where the young trees flourished without a twisted limb or fruitless branch. She walked through the new farm, never so hopeless as the homeplace, yet abused, exploited, ravaged. The fields were fair and green, the pasture lush and succulent. She came to the spot where she had been the day before and the music filled her ears and mind.

THE FELLOW WHO MARRIED THE MAXILL GIRL

Fiercely she tried to recapture her reasoning, her indictment. The music did not plead, cajole, argue with her. It was itself, outside such utility. Yet it was not proud or inexorable; removed from her only in space and time and growth; not in fundamental humanity. It was far beyond the simple components of communication she had learned from Ash, yet it was not utterly and entirely outside her understanding.

She listened for a long time—hours, it seemed. Then she went to the house. Ash put his arms around her and again, as so often, she was amazed how he could be loving without a tincture of brutality. "Oh, Ash," she cried. "Oh, Ash!"

Later she said, "Will you come back?"

"I hope so," he answered gravely.

"When—when will you go?"

"As soon as everything is taken care of. There won't be much; you have always attended to the business matters." He smiled; Ash had never touched money or signed a paper. "I'll take the train from Henryton; everyone will think I've gone East. After a while you can say I've been kept by family affairs. Perhaps you and the boy will leave after a few months, presumably to join me."

"No. I'll stay here."

"People will think—"

"Let them," she said defiantly. "Let them."

"I can find you anywhere, you know, if I can come back."

"You won't come back. If you do you'll find me here."

*   *   *

She had no difficulties with the harvest. As Ash said, she had taken care of the business end since her father's death. Hands were always eager to work at the Maxill's; produce merchants bid against each other for the crop. But next year?

She and the land could wither together without a husband's care. The lines on her face would deepen, her hair would gray, her mouth sag. The trees would die little by little, the fruit grow sparser, less and less perfect. The corn would come up more irregularly year by year, sickly, prey to parasites; stunted, gnarled, poor. Finally so little would grow it wouldn't pay to plant the fields. Then the orchards would turn into dead wood, the hardier weeds take over, the land become waste. And she . . .

She knew she was hearing the sounds, the music, only in her imagination. But the illusion was so strong, so very strong, she thought for the moment she could distinguish Ash's own tones, his message to her, so dear, so intimate, so reassuring. . . .

"Yes," she said aloud. "Yes, of course."

Because at last she understood. In the winter she would walk all over the land. She would pick up the hard clods from the ground and warm them in her fingers. In the spring she would plunge her arms into the sacks of seed, deeply, to the elbows, over and over. She would touch the growing shoots, the budding trees; she would walk over the land, giving herself over to it.

It would not be as though Ash were still there. It could never be like that. But the earth would be rich; the plants and trees would flourish. The cherries, apricots, plums, apples and pears would not be as many or so fine as they had been, nor the corn so even and tall. But they would grow, and her hands would make them grow. Her five-fingered hands.

Ash would not have come for nothing.

MINE OWN WAYS

BY RICHARD MCKENNA (1913–1964)

THE MAGAZINE OF FANTASY AND SCIENCE FICTION
FEBRUARY

Richard McKenna was the author of the superb novel The Sand Pebbles *(1962), which was made into a notable film starring Steve McQueen. It was unfortunately his only novel, since he died at the height of his literary powers.*

In the science fiction and fantasy field he is well remembered for his wonderful, kind, and gentle stories, many of which can be found in the collection Casey Agonistes And Other Science Fiction And Fantasy Stories *(1973). The title story won a Nebula Award in 1966. Damon Knight did much to further his work, and several of his finest stories (he was a natural storyteller) can be found in volumes of* Orbit.

The Sand Pebbles *reflected Mr. McKenna's more than twenty years' service in the U.S. Navy, years during which he published little fiction. Anthropological themes figure prominently in his sf, especially in the above mentioned story, "Hunter, Come Home" (1963)*

MINE OWN WAYS

"The Secret Place" (1966), and "Fiddler's Green" (1967). His is another (alas) example of what might have been. (MHG)

It is hard to understand cultural differences. When one civilization meets another, each is liable to consider the other as primitive, backward, even insane. Imagine how surprising it must be if you have lived all your life among people who speak a single language, to encounter people who make incomprehensible noises and yet manage to communicate anyway. The Greeks called all people who didn't speak Greek as "ba-ba-ba-" people because the sounds they made seemed meaningless syllables. In this way, the non-Greeks became "barbaroi," which became "barbarians" to us.

We tend to think of "barbarians" not merely as people speaking a strange language, but as people who are uncivilized. The Italians called the northern kingdoms "barbarian" and the Chinese called Europeans generally "barbarian" and so on. We also call them "savages" if they seem lacking in civilized amenities. The word is from the Latin for "backwoodsmen" but it has come to mean "unreasonably cruel."

If we ever explore other worlds, think of all the very strange "barbarians" and "savages" we will find and how difficult it would be to try to understand their ways. (IA)

Walter Cordice was plump and aging and he liked a quiet life. On what he'd thought was the last day of his field job before retirement to New Zealand, he looked at his wife in the spy screen and was dismayed.

Life had not been at all quiet while he and Leo Brumm and Jim Andries had been building the hyperspace relay on Planet Robadur—they had their wives

along and they'd had to live and work hidden under
solid rock high on a high mountain. That was because
the Robadurians were asymbolic and vulnerable to
culture shock, and the Institute of Man, which had
jurisdiction over hominid planets, forbade all contact
with the natives. Even after they'd built her the lodge
in a nearby peak, Martha was bored. Cordice had
been glad when he and Andries had gone into Tau
rapport with the communications relay unit.

That had been two months of peaceful isolation
during which the unit's Tau circuits copied certain
neural patterns in the men to make itself half sentient
and capable of electronic telepathy. It was good and
quiet. Now they were finished, ready to seal the station and take their pretaped escape capsule back to
Earth, only anthropologists from the Institute of Man
would ever visit Robadur again.

And Walter Cordice stood in the wrecked lodge and
the picture on the illicit spy screen belted him with
dismay.

Robadurians were not symbol users. They simply
couldn't have raided the lodge. But the screen showed
Martha and Willa Brumm and Allie Andries sitting
bound to stakes at a forest edge. Martha's blue dress
and tight red curls were unruffled. She sat with her
stumpy legs extended primly together and her hard,
plump pout said she was grimly not believing what she
saw either.

Near a stream, across a green meadow starred yellow with flowers, naked and bearded Robadurians dug
a pit with sharp sticks. Others piled dry branches.
They were tall fellows, lump-muscled under sparse
fur, with low foreheads and muzzle jaws. One, in a

devil mask of twigs and feathers, seemed an overseer. Beside Martha, pert, dark little Allie Andries cried quietly. Willa was straining her white arms against the cords. They knew they were in trouble, all right.

Cordice turned from the screen, avoiding the eyes of Leo Brumm and Jim Andries. In their tan coveralls against the silver-and-scarlet decor they seemed as out of place as the dead Robadurian youth at their feet. Leo's chubby, pleasant face looked stricken. Jim Andries scowled. He was a big, loose-jointed man with bold angular features and black hair. They were young and junior and Cordice knew they were mutely demanding his decision.

Decision. He wouldn't retire at stat-8 now, he'd be lucky to keep stat-7. But he'd just come out of rapport, and so far he was clear and the law was clear too, very clear: you minimized culture shock at whatever cost to yourself. But abandon *Martha?* He looked down at the Robadurian youth. The smooth ivory skin was free of blue hair except on the crushed skull. He felt his face burn.

"Our wives bathed him and shaved him and made him a pet?" His voice shook slightly. "Leo . . . Leo . . ."

"My fault, sir. I built 'em the spy screen and went to rescue the boy," Leo said. "I didn't want to disturb you and Jim in rapport." He was a chunky, blond young man and he was quite pale now. "They—well, I take all the blame, sir."

"The Institute of Man will fix blame," Cordice said.

My fault, he thought. For bringing Martha against my better judgment. But Leo's violation of the spy-screen ethic did lead directly to illicit contact and—*this mess!* Leo was young, they'd be lenient with him. All right, his fault. Cordice made his voice crisp.

"We minimize," he said. "Slag the lodge, get over and seal up the station, capsule home to Earth and report this."

Jim really scowled. "I love my wife, Cordice, whatever you think of yours," he said. "I'm getting Allie out of there if I have to culture-shock those blue apes to death with a flame jet."

"You'll do what I say, Andries! You and your wife signed a pledge and a waiver, remember?" Cordice tried to stare him down. "The law says she's not worth risking the extinction of a whole species that may someday become human."

"Damn the law, she's worth it to me!" Jim said. "Cordice, those blue apes are human now. How else could they raid up here, kill this boy, carry off the women?" He spat. "We'll drop you to seal the station, keep your hands clean. Leo and I'll get the women."

Cordice drooped his eyes. Damn his insolence! Still . . . Leo could testify Andries forced it . . . he'd still be clear. . . .

"I'll go along, to ensure minimizing," he said. "Under protest—Leo, you're witness to that. But slag this lodge right now!"

Minutes later Leo hovered the flyer outside while Cordice played the flame jet on the rock face. Rock steamed, spilled away, fused and sank into a bubbling, smoking cavity. Under it the dead youth, with his smooth, muscular limbs, was only a smear of carbon. Cordice felt better.

Half an hour later, lower on the same mountain, Leo hovered the flyer above the meadow. The Robadurians all ran wildly into the forest and Jim didn't need to use the flame jet. Leo grounded and the men piled out and Cordice felt his stomach relax. They ran toward the women. Allie Andries was smiling but Martha was shouting something from an angry face. As he stopped to untie Martha the blue horde came back out of the forest. They came yelling and leaping and slashing with wet, leafy branches and the sharp smell. . . .

Cordice came out of it sick with the awareness that he was tied to a stake like an animal and that it was his life, not his career, he had to save now. He feigned sleep and peered from eyecorners. Martha looked haggard and angry and he dreaded facing her. He couldn't see the others, except Allie Andries and she was smiling faintly—at Jim, no doubt.

Those two kids must escape, Cordice thought.

He must have been unconscious quite a while because sunset flamed in red and gold downvalley and the pit looked finished. It was elliptical, perhaps thirty feet long and three deep. Robadurians were still mounding black earth along the sides and others were piling brush into a circumscribed thicket, roughly triangular. They chattered, but Cordice knew it was only a mood-sharing noise. That was what made it so horrible. They were asymbolic, without speech and prior to good and evil, a natural force like falling water. He couldn't threaten, bribe, or even plead. Despite his snub nose and full lips he could present an impressive face—at home on Earth. But not to such as these.

Beside the pit the devil masker stood like a tall sentry. Abruptly he turned and strode toward Cordice, trailing his wooden spear. Cordice tensed and felt a scream shape itself in him. Then the devil towered lean and muscular above him. He had no little finger on his spear hand. Keen gray eyes peered down through feathers and twigs.

"Cordice, you fool, why did you bring the women?" the devil asked in fluent English. "Now all your lives are forfeit."

The scream collapsed in a grateful gasp. With speech Cordice felt armed again, almost free. But Martha spoke first.

"Men need women to inspire them and give them courage!" she said. "Walto! Tell him who you are! Make him let us go!"

Walto meant she was angry. In affection she called him *Wally Toes*. But as usual she was right. He firmed his jowls and turned a cool stat-7 stare on the devil mask.

"Look here, if you know our speech you must know we never land on a hominid planet," he said pleasantly. "There are plenty of other planets. For technical reasons we had to do a job here. It's done. We have stores and tools to leave behind." He laughed easily. "Take them and let us go. You'll never see another of us."

The devil shook his head. "It's not what we might see, it's what your women have already seen," he said. "They know a holy secret and the god Robadur demands your deaths."

Cordice paled but spoke smoothly. "I and Andries have been out of touch with the others for two months. I don't know any secret. While we were isolated Brumm built the women a spy screen and rescued that boy—"

"Who was forfeit to Robadur. Robadur eats his children."

"Arthur was being *tortured* when he broke free and ran," Martha said. "I saw *you* there!"

"On your strictly unethical spy screen."

"Why not? You're only brute animals!"

The devil pressed his spear to her throat.

"Shut up or I'll spear you now!" he said. Martha's eyes blazed defiance.

"No! *Quiet*, Martha!" Cordice choked. His front collapsed. "Brumm did it all. Kill him and let us *go!*" He twisted in his bonds.

Leo spoke from behind. "Yes, I did it. Take me and let them go." His voice was high and shaky too.

"No! Oh please no!" That was Willa, sobbing.

"Stop that!" Jim Andries roared. "All of us or none! Listen, you behind the feathers, I know your secret. You're a renegade playing god among the asymbolics. But we're here on clearance from the Institute of Man and they'll come looking for us. Your game's up. Let us go and you'll only be charged with causing culture shock."

The devil grounded his spear and cocked his head. Robadurians around the pit stood up to watch. Martha shrilled into the hush.

"My own brother is with the Institute of Man!"

"I told you shut up!" The devil slapped her with his spear butt. "I know your brother. Tom Brennan would kill you himself, to keep the secret."

"*What* secret, Featherface? That you're a god?" Jim asked.

"The secret that man created himself and what man has done, man can undo," the devil said. "I'm not Robadur, Andries, but I'm sealed to him from the Institute of Man. The Institute will cover for your deaths. It's done the same on hundreds of other homi-nid planets, to keep the secret."

"Roland Krebs! *Rollo!* You struck a lady—"

Like a snake striking, the spear leaped to her throat. She strained her head back and said "Ah . . . ah . . . ah . . . " her face suddenly white and her eyes unbelieving.

"Don't hurt her!" Cordice screamed. "We'll *swear* to forget, if you let us go!"

The devil withdrew his spear and laughed. "Swear on what, Cordice? Your honor? Your soul?" He spat. "What man has done, man can undo. You're the living proof!"

"We'll swear by Robadur," Cordice pleaded.

The devil looked off into the sunset. "You know, you might. You just might," he said thoughtfully. "We seal a class of boys to Light Robadur tonight; you could go with them." He turned back. "You're the leader, Andries. What about it?"

"What's it amount to?" Jim asked.

"It's a ritual that turns animals into humans," the devil said. "There are certain ordeals to eliminate the animals. If you're really men you'll be all right."

"What about the women?" Jim's voice was edgy.

"They have no souls. Robadur will hold you to account for them."

"You have great faith in Robadur," Jim said.

"Not faith, Andries, a scientist's knowledge as hard as your own," the devil said. "If you put a Robadurian into a barbering machine he wouldn't need faith to get a haircut. Well, a living ritual is a kind of psychic machine. You'll see."

"All right, we agree," Jim said. "But we'll want our wives unhurt. Understand that, Featherface?"

MINE OWN WAYS

The devil didn't answer. He shouted and natives swarmed around the stakes. Hands untied Cordice and jerked him erect and his heart was pounding so hard he felt dizzy.

"Don't let them hurt you, Wally Toes!"

Fleetingly in Martha's shattered face he saw the ghost of the girl he had married thirty years ago. She had a touch of the living beauty that lighted the face Allie Andries turned on Jim. Cordice said goodbye to the ghost, numb with fear.

Cordice slogged up the dark ravine like a wounded bull. He knew the priests chasing him would spear him like the hunted animal he was unless he reached sanctuary by a sacred pool somewhere ahead. Long since Jim and Leo and the terrified Robadurian youths had gone ahead of him. Stones cut his feet and thorns ripped his skin. Leo and Jim were to blame and they were young and they'd live. He was innocent and he was old and he'd die. Not fair. Let them die too. His lungs flamed with agony and at the base of a steep cascade his knees gave way.

Die here. Not fair. He heard the priests coming and his back muscles crawled with terror. Die fighting. He scrabbled in the water for a stone. Face to the spears. He cringed lower.

Jim and Leo came back down the cascade and helped him up it. "Find your guts, Cordice!" Jim said. They jerked him along, panting and swearing, until the ravine widened to make a still pool under a towering rock crowned red with the last of sunset. Twenty-odd Robadurian youths huddled whimpering on a stony slope at the left. Then priests came roaring and after that Cordice took it in flashes.

He had a guardian devil, a monstrous priest with clay in white bars across his chest. White Bar and others drove him up the slope, threw him spread-eagled on his back, and staked down his wrists and ankles with wisps of grass. They placed a pebble on his chest. He tried to remember that these were symbolic restraints and that White Bar would kill him if he broke the grass or dislodged the pebble. Downslope a native boy screamed and broke his bonds and priests smashed his skull. Cordice shuddered and lay very quiet. But when they pushed the thorn through in front of his left Achilles tendon he gasped and drew up his leg. The pebble tumbled off and White Bar's club crashed down beside his head and he died.

He woke aching and cold under starlight and knew he had only fainted. White Bar sat shadowy beside him on an outcrop, club across hairy knees. Downslope the native boys sang a quavering tone song without formed words. They were mood-sharing, expressing sorrow and fearful wonder. I could almost sing with them, Cordice thought. The pebble was on his chest again and he could feel the grass at his wrists and ankles. A stone dug into his back and he shifted position very carefully so as not to disturb the symbols. Nearby but not in view Jim and Leo began to talk in low voices.

Damn them, Cordice thought. They'll live and I'll die. I'm dying now. Why suffer pain and indignity and die anyway? I'll just sit up and let White Bar end it for me. But first—

"Leo," he said.

"Mr. Cordice! Thank heaven! We thought—how do you feel, sir?"

"Bad, Leo—wanted to say—a fine job here. Your name's in for stat-3. Wanted to say—this all my fault. Sorry."

"No, sir," Leo said. "You were in rapport, how could you—"

"Before that. When I let Martha come and so couldn't make you juniors leave your wives behind." Cordice paused. "I owe—Martha made me, in a way, Leo."

Her pride, he thought. Her finer feelings. Her instant certainty of rightness that bolstered his own moral indecision. So she ruled him.

"I know," Leo said. "Willa's proud and ambitious for me, too."

Martha worked on Willa, Cordice thought. Hinted she could help Leo's career. So she got her spy screen. Well, he *had* been grading Leo much higher than Jim. Martha didn't like Allie's and Jim's attitude.

"I'm going to die, boys," Cordice said. "Will you forgive me?"

"No," Jim said. "You're woman-whipped to a helpless nothing, Cordice. Forgive yourself, if you can."

"Look here, Andries, I'll remember that," Cordice said.

"I'm taking Allie to a frontier planet," Jim said. "We'll never see a hairless slug like you again."

Leo murmured a protest. I'll live to get even with Andries, Cordice thought. Damn his insolence! His heel throbbed and the stone still gouged his short ribs. He shifted carefully and it felt better. He hummed the native boys' song deep in his throat and that helped too. He began to doze. If I live I'll grow my body hair again, he thought.

* * *

Jim's voice woke him: Cordice! Lie quiet, now! He opened his eyes to hairy legs all around him and toothed beast faces in torchlight roaring a song and White Bar with club poised trembling-ready and no little finger on his right hand. The song roared over Cordice like thunder, and sparks like tongues of fire rained down to sear his body. He whimpered and twitched but did not dislodge the stone on his chest. The party moved on. Downslope a boy screamed and club thuds silenced him. And again, and Cordice felt sorry for the boys.

"Damn it all, that really hurt!" Jim said.

"This was the ordeal that boy Arthur failed, only he got away," Leo said. "Mrs. Cordice kept him on the screen until I could rescue him."

"How'd he act?" Jim asked.

"Trusted me, right off. Willa said he was very affectionate and they taught him all kinds of tricks. But never speech—he got wild when they tried to make him talk, Willa told me."

I'm affectionate. I know all kinds of tricks, Cordice thought. Downslope the torches went out and the priests were singing with the boys. White Bar, seated again beside Cordice on the outcrop, sang softly too. It was a new song of formed words and it disturbed Cordice. Then he heard footsteps behind his head and Jim spoke harshly.

"Hello, Featherface, we're still around," Jim said. Mrs. Cordice called you a name. *Krebs*, wasn't it? Just who in hell are you?"

"Roland Krebs. I'm an anthropologist," the devil's voice said. "I almost married Martha once, but she began calling me *Rollo* just in time."

MINE OWN WAYS

That guy? Cordice opened his mouth, then closed it. Damn him. He'd pretend a faint, try not to hear.

"You can't share the next phase of the ritual and it's your great loss," Krebs said. "Now each boy is learning the name that he will claim for his own in the last phase, if he survives. The men have a crude language and the boys long ago picked up the words like parrots. Now, as they sing with the priests, the words come alive in them."

"How do you mean?" Jim asked.

"Just that. The words assort together and for the first time *mean*. That's the Robadurian creation myth they're singing." Krebs lowered his voice. "They're not here now like you are, Andries. They're present in the immediacy of all their senses at the primal creation of their human world."

"Our loss? Yes . . . our great loss." Jim sounded bemused.

"Yes. For a long time words have been only a sickness in our kind," Krebs said. "But ideas can still assort and mean. Take this thought: we've found hominids on thousands of planets, but none more than barely entered on the symbol-using stage. Paleontology proves native hominids have been stuck on the threshold of evolving human minds for as long as two hundred million years. But on Earth our own symbol-using minds evolved in about three hundred thousand years."

"Does mind evolve?" Jim asked softly.

"Brain evolves, like fins change to feet," Krebs said. "The hominids can't evolve a central nervous system adequate for symbols. But on Earth, in no time at all, something worked a structural change in one animal's central nervous system greater than the gross, outward change from reptile to mammal."

"I'm an engineer," Jim said. "The zoologists know what worked it."

"Zoologists always felt natural selection couldn't have worked it so fast," Krebs said. "What we've learned on the hominid planets proves it can't. Natural selection might take half a billion years. *Our* fathers took a short cut."

"All right," Jim said. "All right. Our fathers were their own selective factor, in rituals like this one. They were animals and they bred themselves into men. Is that what you want me to say?"

"I want you to feel a little of what the boys feel now," Krebs said. "Yes. Our fathers invented ritual as an artificial extension of instinct. They invented a ritual to detect and conserve all mutations in a human direction and eliminate regressions toward the animal norm. They devised ordeals in which normal animal instinctive behavior meant death and only those able to sin against instinct could survive to be human and father the next generation." His voice shook slightly. "Think on that, Andries! Human and animal brothers born of the same mother and the animals killed at puberty when they failed certain ordeals only human minds could bear."

"Yes. Our secret. Our *real* secret." Jim's voice shook too. "Cain killing Abel through ten thousand generations. That created *me*."

Cordice shivered and the rock gouged his short ribs.

"Dark Robadur's sin is Light Robadur's grace and the two are one," Krebs said. "You know, the Institute has made a science of myth. Dark Robadur is the species personality, instinct personified. Light Robadur is the human potential of these people. He binds Dark Robadur with symbols and coerces him with ritual. He does it in love, to make his people human."

"In love and fear and pain and death," Jim said.

"In pain and death. Those who died tonight were animals. Those who die tomorrow will be failed humans who know they die," Krebs said. "But hear their song."

"I hear it. I know how they feel and thank you for that, Krebs," Jim said. "And it's only the boys?"

"Yes, the girls will get half their chromosomes from their fathers. They will get all the effect of the selection except that portion on the peculiarly male Y-chromosome," Krebs said. "They will remain without guilt, sealed to Dark Robadur. It will make a psychic difference."

"Ah. And you Institute people *start* these rituals on the hominid planets, make them self-continuing, like kindling a fire already laid," Jim said slowly. "Culture shock is a lie."

"It's no lie, but it does make a useful smokescreen."

"Ah, Krebs, thank you. Krebs—" Jim lowered his voice and Cordice strained to hear. "—would you say Light Robadur might be a *transhuman* potential?"

"I hope he may go on to become so," Krebs said. "Now you know the full measure of our treason. And now I'll leave you."

His footsteps died away. Leo spoke for the first time.

"Jim, I'm scared. I don't like this. Is this ritual going to make *us* transhuman? What does that mean?"

"We can't know. Would you ask an ape what *human* means?" Jim said. "Our fathers bred themselves through a difference in kind. Then they stopped, but they didn't have to. I hope one of these hominid planets will breed on through the human to another difference in kind." He laughed. "That possibility is the secret we have to keep."

"I don't like it. I don't want to be transhuman," Leo said. "Mr. Cordice! Mr. Cordice, what do you think?"

Cordice didn't answer. Why let that damned Andries insult him again? Besides, he didn't know what to think.

"He's fainted or dead, poor fat old bastard," Jim said. "Leo, all this ritual is doing to you is forcing you to prove your human manhood, just like the boys have to. We have our manhood now only by accident of fertilization."

"I don't like it," Leo said. "That transhuman stuff. It's . . . immoral."

"It's a hundred thousand years away yet," Jim said. "But I like it. What I don't like is to think that the history of galactic life is going to head up and halt forever in the likes of old Wally Toes there."

"He's not so bad," Leo said. "I hope he's still alive."

I am, God damn you both! Cordice thought. They stopped talking.

Downslope the priests' voices faded and the boys sang their worded creation song alone. White Bar went away. The sky paled above the great rock and bright planets climbed to view. Cordice felt feverish. He lapsed into a half-dream.

He saw a fanned network of golden lines. Nodes thickened to become fish, lizards and men. A voice whispered: *All life is a continuum in time. Son to*

*father, the germ worldline runs back unbroken to the
primordial ocean. For you life bowed to sex and death.
For you it gasped sharp air with feeble lungs. For you it
bore the pain of gravity in bones too weak to bear it.
Ten thousand of your hairy fathers, each in his turn,
won through this test of pain and terror to make you a
man.*

Why?

I don't know why.

Are you a man?

What is a man? I'm a man by definition. By natural
right. By accident of fertilization. What else is a man?"

*Two billion years beat against you like surf, Walter
Cordice. The twenty thousand fists of your hairy fathers
thunder on you as a door. Open the way or be shattered.*

I don't know the way. I lost the way.

Through dream mists he fled his hairy fathers. But
they in him preserved intact the dry wisps that bound
him terribly with the tensile strength of meaning. They
steadied the pebble that crushed him under the
mountainweight of symbol. All the time he knew it.

By noon of the clouded day thirst was the greater
agony. Cordice scarcely heard the popping noises made
by the insects that fed on his crusted blood and serum.
But he heard every plash and ripple of the priest-
guarded water downslope. Heard too, once and again,
the death of boys whose animal thirst overpowered
their precarious new bondage to the symbol. Only
those who can remember what the grass wisps *mean*
survive, Cordice thought. Poor damned kids! To be
able to suffer and sin against instinct is to live and be
human.

Jim's and Leo's voices faded in and out of his fever

dreams. His back was numb now, where the rock dug into it.

Rose of sunset crowned the great rock above the pool when White Bar prodded Cordice downslope with his club. Cordice limped and rubbed his back and every joint and muscle of his misused body ached and clamored for water. Jim and Leo looked well. Cordice scowled silence at their greetings. I'll die without their damned pity, he thought. He moved apart from them into the group of native boys standing by the rock-edged pool. Their thin lips twitched and their flat nostrils flared and snuffled at the water smell. Cordice snuffled too. He saw Krebs, still masked in twigs and feathers, come through the rank of priests and talk to Jim.

"You'll all be thrown into the water, Andries. For the boys, Dark Robadur must swim the body to the bank or they drown. Light Robadur must prevent the body from drinking or they get clubbed. The two must co-act. Understand?"

Jim nodded and Krebs turned back to the priests. These kids can't do it, Cordice thought. I can't myself. He shook the arm of the boy beside him and looked into the frightened brown eyes. *Don't drink*, he tried to say, but his throat was too gummed for speech. He smiled and nodded and pinched his lips together with his fingers. The boy smiled and pinched his own lips. Then all the boys were doing it. Cordice felt a strange feeling wash through him. It was like love. It was as if they were all his children.

Then wetness cooled his body and his face. He dogpaddled and bit his tongue to keep from gulping. White Bar jerked him up the bank again and behind him he heard the terrible cries and the club thuds. Tears stung his eyes.

Then he was limping and stumbling down the dark ravine. At steep places the native youths held his arms and helped him. They came through screening willows and he saw a fire near the brush-walled pit. The three women stood there. They looked all right. Cordice went with the boys toward the pit.

"Wally Toes! Don't let them hurt you!" Martha cried.

"Shut up!" Cordice yelled. The yell tore his gummed throat.

The boys faced outward and danced in a circle around the pit. The priests danced the opposite way in a larger circle and faced inward. There was ten feet of annular space between the rings. The priests howled and flung their arms. Cordice was very tired. His heel hurt and his back felt humped. Each time they passed, White Bar howled and pointed at him. He saw Martha every time he passed the firelit area. A priest jumped across and pulled the boy next to Cordice into the space between the rings. Cordice had to dance on away, but he heard screams and club thuds. When he came round again he saw them toss a limp body between the dancers into the pit.

They took more boys and made them kneel and did something to them. If the boys couldn't stand it, they killed them. Even if they did stand it, the priests threw them afterward into the pit. I've got to stand it, Cordice thought. If I don't, they'll kill me. Then White Bar howled and leaped and had him.

Threw him to his knees.

Held his right hand on a flat stone.

Pulled aside the little finger.

Bruising it off with a fist ax! Can't STAND it!

Outrage exploded in screaming pain. Hidden strength leaped roaring to almost-action. Then his hairy fathers came and made him be quiet and he stood it. White Bar chewed through the tendons with his teeth and when the finger was off and the stump seared with an ember the priests threw Cordice into the pit.

He felt other bodies thump beside him and his hairy fathers came very near. All around him they grinned and whispered: *You ARE a man. Your way is open.* He felt good, sure and peaceful and strong in a way he had never felt before. He wanted to hold the feeling and he tried not to hear Jim's voice calling him for fear he would lose it. But he had to, so he opened his eyes and got to his feet. Leo and Jim grinned at him.

"I knew you'd make it, old timer, and I'm glad," Jim said.

Cordice still had the feeling. He grinned and clasped bloody hands with his friends. All around the pit above their heads the piled brush crackled and leaped redly with flame.

Beyond the fire the priests began singing and Cordice could see them dancing in fantastic leaps. The living native boys struggled free of the dead ones and stood up. He counted fourteen. Smoke blew across the pit and the air was thick and suffocating. It was very hot and they all kept coughing and shifting and turning.

Outside the singing stopped and someone shouted a word. One native boy raised his arms and hunted back and forth along the pit edge. He went close and recoiled again.

"They called his name," Jim said. "Now he has to go through the fire to claim it. Now he has to break Dark Robadur's most holy *Thou shalt not.*"

Again the shout. Twice the boy stepped up and twice recoiled. His eyes rolled and he looked at Cordice without seeing him. His face was wild with animal fire-fear.

Leo was crying. "They can't see out there. Let's push him," he said.

"No," Cordice said.

He felt a Presence over the pit. It was anxious and sorrowful. It was familiar and strange and expected and very right. His hairy fathers were no part of it, but they greeted it and spoke through him.

"Robadur, Robadur, give him strength to pass," Cordice prayed.

A third shout. The boy went up and through the flame in one great leap. Vast, world-lifting joy swirled and thundered through the Presence.

"Jim, do you feel it?" Cordice asked.

"I feel it," Jim said. He was crying too.

The next boy tried and fell back. He stood rigid in the silence after the third shout. It was a terrible silence. His hair was singed off and his face was blackened and his lips were skinned back over strong white teeth. His eyes stared and they were not human now and they were very sad.

"I've *got* to help him," Leo said.

Jim and Cordice held Leo back. The boy dropped suddenly to all fours. He burrowed under the dead boys who didn't have names either. Vast sorrow infolded and dropped through the Presence. Cordice wept.

Boy after boy went through. Their feet knocked a dark gap in the flaming wall. Then the voice called *Walter Cordice!*

Cordice went up and through the dark gap and the fire was almost gone there and it was easy.

He went directly to Martha. All her bright hardness and pout were gone and she wore the ghost face. It gleamed as softly radiant as the face of little Allie Andries, who still waited for Jim. Cordice drew Martha off into the shadows and they held each other without talking in words. They watched as the others came out and then priests used long poles to push the flaming wall into the pit. They watched the fire die down and they didn't talk and the dancers went away and Cordice felt the Presence go away too, insensibly. But something was left.

"I love you, Martha," he said.

They both knew he had the power to say that word and the right to have a woman.

Then another long time and when he looked up again the flyer was there. Willa and Allie stood beside it in dim firelight and Krebs was coming toward him.

"Come along, Cordice. I'll dress that hand for you," Krebs said.

"I'll wait by the fire, Walter," Martha said.

Cordice followed Krebs into the forest. His nervous strength was leaving him and his legs felt rubbery. He hurt all over and he needed water, but he still felt good. They came to where light gleamed through a hut of interlaced branches. Leo and Jim were already dressed and standing inside by a rough table and chest. Almost at once the plastigel soothed Cordice's cuts and blisters. He dressed and drank sparingly from the cup of water Jim handed him.

"Well, men—" he said. They all laughed.

Krebs was pulling away the twigs and feathers of his

mask. Under it he had the same prognathous face as the Robadurian priests. It wasn't ugly at all.

"Cordice, I suppose you know they can regenerate that finger for you back on Earth," he said. He combed three fingers through his beard. "Biofield therapists work wonders, these days."

"I won't bother," Cordice said. "When do we swear our oath? I can swear now."

"No need," Krebs said. "You're sealed to Robadur now. You'll keep the secret."

"I would have anyway," Jim said.

Krebs nodded. "Yes. You were always a man."

They shook hands around and said goodbye. Cordice led the way to the flyer. He walked hard on his left heel to feel the pain and he knew that it is no small thing, to be a man.

MAKE MINE ... HOMOGENIZED

BY RICK RAPHAEL (1919–   )

ASTOUNDING SCIENCE FICTION
APRIL

Rick Raphael worked as a newspaper copy editor and radio news editor in Idaho before serving as Press Secretary to Senator Frank Church from 1965–1969; he then spent a decade as an executive with J. C. Penney. As a science fiction writer, he is best known for his two collections of linked novellas—Code Three (1965) and The Thirst Quenchers (1965, but never published in the United States). The former is one of the best accounts of an American future dominated by automobiles and an incredible highway system—only John Jakes' On Wheels rivals it on this subject. The Thirst Quenchers is one of only a few attempts in sf to deal in detail with the problems coping with overpopulation. He has also published two thrillers—The Defector (1980) and The President Must Die (1981).

"Make Mine . . . Homogenized" is reprinted here for the first time since its magazine appearance thirty years ago—another find by Barry Malzberg—thanks again, Barry. (MHG)

The late, great John W. Campbell, Jr. had an ambivalent attitude toward science. He admired it unstintingly, but he also thought that scientists tended to become hardened into accepting whatever the current modes of thought might be and to resist changing them. He simply loved stories in which scientists were faced with something completely crazy and had to go equally crazy trying to explain it.

It is almost impossible to write such a story without being humorous about it. I know. I wrote "Pate de Foie Gras" for John Campbell in 1956 about a goose that laid golden eggs. Here Rick Raphael tickled Campbell's funny bone, and ours, with an even more outrageous situation. (IA)

"Shoo," Hetty Thompson cried, waving her battered old felt hat at the clucking cluster of hens eddying around her legs as she plowed through the flock towards the chicken house. "Scat. You, Solomon," she called out, directing her words at the bobbing comb of the big rooster strutting at the edge of the mob. "Don't just stand there like a satisfied cowhand after a night in Reno. Get these noisy females outta my way." She batted at the hens and they scattered with angry squawks of protest.

Hetty paused in the doorway of the chicken house to allow her eyes to become accustomed to the cool gloom after the bright glare of the ranch yard. She could feel the first trickles of sweat forming under the man's shirt she was wearing as the hot, early morning Nevada sun beat down on her back in the doorway.

Moving carefully but quickly through the nests, she reached and groped for the eggs she knew would be found in the scattered straw. As she placed each find carefully in the bucket she carried, her lips moved in a soundless count. When she had finished, she straightened up and left the chicken house, her face reflecting minor irritation.

Again the hens swirled about her, hoping for the handfuls of cracked corn she usually tossed to them. On the other side of the yard Solomon stepped majestically along the edge of the vegetable garden, never crossing the hoed line separating garden from yard.

"You'd better stay over there, you no-account Lothario," Hetty growled. "Five eggs short this morning and all you do is act like you were just the business agent for this bunch of fugitives from a dumpling pot." Solomon cocked his head and stared Hetty down. She paused at the foot of the backporch steps and threw the rooster a final remark. "You don't do any better than this you're liable to wind up in that pot yourself." Solomon gave a scornful cluck. "Better still, I'll get me a young rooster in here and take over your job." Solomon let out a squawk and took out at a dead run, herding three hens before him towards the chicken house.

With a satisfied smile of triumph, Hetty climbed the steps and crossed to the kitchen door. She turned and looked back across the yard towards the barn and corrals.

"Barneeeeey," Hetty yelled. "Ain't you finished with that milking yet?"

"Comin' now, Miz Thompson," came the reply from the barn. Hetty let the screen door slam behind her as she walked into the kitchen and placed the bucket of eggs on the big work table. She had her arm up to wipe her moist forehead on the sleeve of her shirt when she spotted the golden egg lying in the middle of the others in the galvanized bucket.

She froze in the arm-lifted position for several seconds, staring at the dully glowing egg. Then she slowly reached out and picked it up. It was slightly heavier than a regular egg, but for the dull, gold-bronze metallic appearance of the shell, looked just like any of the other twenty-odd eggs in the bucket. She was still holding it in the palm of her hand when the kitchen door again slammed and the handy man limped into the room. He carried two pails of milk across the kitchen and set them down near the sink.

"Whatcha lookin' at, Miz Thompson?" Barney Hatfield asked.

Hetty frowned at the egg in her hand without answering. Barney limped around the side of the table for a closer look. Sunlight streaming through the kitchen windows glinted on the shell of the odd egg. Barney's eyes grew round. "Now ain't that something," he whispered in awe.

Hetty started as though someone had snapped their fingers in front of her staring eyes. Her normal look of practical dubiousness returned.

"Huh," she snorted. "Even had me fooled for a second. Something wrong with this egg but it sure is shootin' ain't gold. One of them fool hens must of been pecking in the fertilizer storeroom and got herself an overdose of some of them minerals in that stuff.

"What are you staring at, you old fool," she glared at Barney. "It ain't gold." Hetty laid the egg at one side of the table. She walked to the sink and took a clean, two-gallon milk can from the drainboard and set it in the sink to fill it from the pails of rich, frothy milk Barney had brought in the pails.

"Sally come fresh this morning, Miz Thompson," he said. "Got herself a real fine little bull calf."

Hetty looked at the two pails of milk. "Well, where's the rest of the milk, then?"

"That's Queenie's milk," Barney said. "Sally's is still out on the porch."

"Well bring it in before the sun clabbers it."

"Can't," Barney said.

Hetty swung around and glared at him. "What do you mean, you can't? You suddenly come down with the glanders?"

"No'm, it's just that Sally's milk ain't no good," he replied.

A frown spread over Hetty's face as she hoisted one of the milk pails and began pouring into the can in the sink. "What's wrong with it, Barney? Sally seem sick or something?" she asked.

Barney scratched his head. "I don't rightly know, Miz Thompson. That milk looks all right, or at least, almost all right. It's kinda thin and don't have no foam like you'd expect milk to have. But mostly, it sure don't smell right and it danged well don't taste right.

"*Phooey,*" he made a face at the memory of the taste. "I stuck my finger in it when it looked kinda queer, and took a taste. It shore tasted lousy."

"You probably been currying that mangey old horse of yours before you went to milking," Hetty snorted, "and tasted his cancerous old hide on your fingers. I've told you for the last time to wash your hands before you go to milking them cows. I didn't pay no eighteen hundred dollars for that prize, registered Guernsey just to have you give her bag fever with your dirty hands."

"That ain't so, Miz Thompson," Barney cried indignantly. "I did too, wash my hands. Good, too. I wuzn't near my horse this morning. That milk just weren't no good."

Hetty finished pouring the milk into the cans and after putting the cans in the refrigerator, wiped her hands on her jeans and went out onto the porch, Barney trailing behind her. She bent over and sniffed at the two milk pails setting beside the door. *"Whew,"* she exclaimed, "it sure does smell funny. Hand me that dipper, Barney."

Barney reached for a dipper hanging on a nail beside the kitchen door. Hetty dipped out a small quantity of the milk, sipped, straightened up with a jerk and spewed the milk out into the yard. "Yaawwwk," she spluttered, "that tastes worse 'n Diesel oil."

She stirred distastfully at the swirling, flat-looking liquid in the pails and then turned back to the kitchen. "I never saw the like of it," she exclaimed. "Chickens come out with some kind or sorry-looking egg and now, in the same morning, an eighteen hundred dollar registered, fresh Guernsey gives out hogwash instead of milk." She stared thoughtfully across the yard at the distant mountains, now shimmering in the hot, midmorning sun. "Guess we could swill the hogs with that milk, rather'n throw it out, Barney. I never seen anything them Durocs wouldn't eat. When you get ready to put the other swill in the cooker, toss that milk in with it and cook it up for the hogs."

Hetty went back into her kitchen and Barney turned

and limped across the yard to the tractor shed. He pulled the brim of his sweat-stained Stetson over his eyes and squinted south over the heat-dancing sage and sparse grasslands of Circle T range. Dust devils were pirouetting in the hazy distance towards the mountains forming a corridor leading to the ranch. A dirt road led out of the yard and crossed an oiled county road about five miles south of the ranch. The county road was now the only link the Circle T had to the cattle shipping pens at Carson City. The dirt road arrowed south across the range but fifteen miles from the ranch, a six-strand, new, barbed-wire fence cut the road. A white metal sign with raised letters proclaimed "Road Closed. U. S. Government Military Reservation. Restricted Area. Danger—Peligre. Keep Out."

The taut bands of wire stretched east and west of the road for more than twenty miles in each direction, with duplicates of the metal sign hung on the fence every five hundred yards. Then the wires turned south for nearly a hundred miles, etching in skin-blistering, sun-heated strands, the outlines of the Nevada atomic testing grounds at Frenchman's Flat.

When the wire first went up, Hetty and her ranching neighbors had screamed to high heaven and high congressmen about the loss of the road and range. The fence stayed up. Now they had gotten used to the idea and had even grown blasé about the frequent nuclear blasts that rattled the desert floor sixty miles from ground zero.

Barney built a fire under the big, smoke-blackened cauldron Hetty used for cooking the hog swill. Dale Hamilton, the county agent, had given Hetty a long talk on the dangers of feeding the pigs, raw, uncooked and possibly contaminated, garbage. When Hamilton got graphic about what happened to people who ate pork from such hogs, Hetty turned politely green and had Barney set up the cooking cauldron.

After dumping the kitchen slops into the pot, Barney hiked back across the yard to get the two pails of bad milk.

Hetty was sitting at the kitchen table, putting the eggs into plastic refrigerator dishes when the hog slop exploded in a whooshing roar, followed a split second later by an even louder blast that rocked the ranch buildings. The eggs flew across the room as the lid of the slop cauldron came whistling through the kitchen window in a blizzard of flying glass and buried itself, edgewise, in the wall over the stove. Hetty slammed backwards headfirst into a heap of shattered eggs. A torrent of broken plaster, and crockery fragments rained on her stunned figure. Through dazed eyes, she saw a column of purple-reddish fire rising from the yard.

A woman who has been thrown twenty-three times from a pitching bronco and kicked five times in the process, doesn't stay dazed long. Pawing dripping egg yokes and plaster from her face, Hetty Thompson struggled to her feet and staggered to the kitchen door.

"Barneeey," she bawled, "you all right?"

The column of weird-colored flame had quickly died and only a few flickering pieces of wood from the cauldron fire burned in scattered spots about the yard. Of the cauldron, there wasn't a sign.

"Barney," she cried anxiously, "where are you?"

"Here I am, Miz Thompson." Barney's blackened face peered around the corner of the tractor shed. "You O.K., Miz Thompson?"

"What in thunderation happened?" Hetty called out. "You try to build a fire with dynamite for kindling?"

Shaken but otherwise unharmed, Barney painfully limped over to the ranch house porch.

"Don't ask me what happened, m'am," he said. "I just poured that milk into the slop pot and then put the lid back on and walked off. I heered this big *'whoosh'* and turned around in time to see the lid fly off and the kettle begin to tip into the fire and then there was one helluva blast. It knocked me clean under the tractor shed." He fumbled in his pocket for a cigarette and shakily lighted it.

Hetty peered out over the yard and then looking up, gasped. Perched like a rakish derby hat on the arm of the towering pump windmill was the slop cauldron. "Well I'll be . . ." Hetty Thompson said.

"You sure you didn't pour gas on that fire to make it burn faster, Barney Hatfield?" she barked at the handy man.

"No siree," Barney declaimed loudly, "there weren't no gas anywhere near that fire. Only thing I poured out was that there bad milk." He paused and scratched his head. "Reckon that funny milk coulda done that, Miz Thompson? There ain't no gas made what'll blow up nor burn so funny as that did."

Hetty snorted. "Whoever heard of milk blowing up, you old idiot?" A look of doubt spread. "You put all that milk in there?"

"No'm, just the one bucket." Barney pointed to the other pail beside the kitchen door, now half-empty and standing in a pool of liquid sloshed out by the blast wave. Hetty studied the milk pail for a minute and then resolutely picked it up and walked out into the yard.

"Only one way to find out," she said. "Get me a tin can, Barney."

She poured about two tablespoons of the milk into the bottom of the can while Barney collected a small pile of kindling. Removing the milk pail to a safe distance, Hetty lighted the little pile of kindling, set the tin can atop the burning wood and scooted several yards away to join Barney who had been watching from afar. In less than a minute a booming *whoosh* sent a miniature column of purple, gaseous flame spouting from the can. "Well whadda you know about that?" Hetty exclaimed wonderingly.

The can had flown off the fire a few feet but didn't explode. Hetty went back to the milk pail and collecting less than a teaspoon full in the water dipper, walked to the fire. Standing as far back as she could and still reach over the flames, she carefully sprinkled a few drops of the liquid directly into the fire and then jumped back. Miniature balls of purple flame erupted from the fire before she could move. Pieces of flaming kindling flew in all directions and one slammed Barney across the back of the neck and sent a shower of sparks down his back.

The handy man let out a yowl of pain and leaped for the watering trough beside the corral, smoke trailing behind him. Hetty thoughtfully surveyed the scene of her experiment from beneath raised eyebrows. Then she grunted with satisfaction, picked up the remaining milk in the pail and went back to the ranch house. Barney climbed drippingly from the horse trough.

The kitchen was a mess. Splattered eggs were over everything and broken glass, crockery and plaster covered the floor, table and counters. Only one egg remained unbroken. That was the golden egg. Hetty picked it up and shook it. There was a faint sensation of something moving inside the tough, metallic-looking shell. It shook almost as a normal egg might, but not quite. Hetty set the strange object on a shelf and turned to the task of cleaning up.

Johnny Culpepper, the ranch's other full-time hand and Hetty's assistant manager, drove the pickup into the yard just before noon. He parked in the shade of the huge cottonwood tree beside the house and bounced out with an armload of mail and newspapers. Inside the kitchen door, he dumped the mail on the sideboard and started to toss his hat on a wall hook when he noticed the condition of the room. Hetty was dishing out fragrant, warmed-over stew into three lunch dishes on the table. She had cleaned up the worst of the mess and changed into a fresh shirt and jeans. Her iron-gray hair was pulled back in a still-damp knot at the back after a hasty scrubbing to get out the gooey mixture of eggs and plaster.

"Holy smoke, Hetty," Johnny said. "What happened here? Your pressure kettle blow up?" His eyes widened when he saw the lid of the slop cauldron still embedded in the wall over the stove. His gaze tracked back and took in the shattered window.

"Had an accident," Hetty said matter-of-factly, putting the last dishes on the table. "Tell you about it when we eat. Now you go wash up and call Barney. I want you to put some new glass in that window this afternoon and get that danged lid outta the wall."

Curious and puzzled, Johnny washed at the kitchen sink and then walked to the door to shout for Barney. On the other side of the yard, Barney released the pump windmill clutch. While Johnny watched from the porch, the weight of the heavy slop cauldron slowly turned the big windmill and as the arm adorned by the kettle rotated downward, the cast-iron pot slipped off and fell to the hard-packed ground with a booming clang.

"Well, for the luvva Pete," Johnny said in amazement. "Hey, Barney, time to eat. C'mon in."

Barney trudged across the yard and limped into the kitchen to wash. They sat down to the table. "Now just what have you two been up to," Johnny demanded as they attacked the food-laden dishes.

Between mouthfuls, the two older people gave him a rundown on the morning's mishaps. The more Johnny heard, the wilder it sounded. Johnny had been a part of the Circle T since he was ten years old. That was the year Hetty jerked him out of the hands of a Carson City policeman who had been in the process of hauling the ragged and dirty youngster to the station house for swiping a box of cookies from a grocery store. Johnny's mother was dead and his father, once the town's best mechanic, had turned into the town's best drunk.

During the times his father slept one off, either in the shack the man and boy occupied at the edge of town, or in the local lockup, Johnny ran wild.

Hetty took the boy to the ranch for two reasons. Mainly it was the empty ache in her heart since the death of Big Jim Thompson a year earlier following a ranch tractor accident that had crushed his chest. The other was her well-hidden disappointment that she had been childless. Hetty's bluff, weathered features would never admit to loneliness or heartache. Beneath the surface, all the warmth and love she had went out to the scared but belligerent youngster. But she never let much affection show through until Johnny had become part of her life. Johnny's father died the following winter after pneumonia brought on by a night of lying drunk in the cold shack during a blizzard. It was accepted without legal formality around the county that Johnny automatically became Hetty's boy.

She cuffed and comforted him into a gawky-happy adolescence, pushed him through high school and then, at eighteen, sent him off to the University of California at Davis to learn what the pundits of the United States Department of Agriculture had to say about animal husbandry and ranch management.

When Hetty and Barney had finished their recitation, Johnny wore a look of frank disbelief. "If I didn't know you two better, I'd say you both been belting the bourbon bottle while I was gone. But this I've got to see."

They finished lunch and, after Hetty stacked the dishes in the sink, trooped out to the porch where Johnny went through the same examination of the milk. Again, a little fire was built in the open safety of the yard and a few drops of the liquid used to produce the same technicolored, combustive effects.

"Well, what do you know," Johnny exclaimed, "a four hundred octane Guernsey cow!"

Johnny kicked out the fire and carried the milk pail to the tractor shed. He parked the milk on a work-bench and gathered up an armful of tools to repair the blast-torn kitchen. He started to leave but when the milk bucket caught his eye, he unloaded the tools and fished around under the workbench for an empty five-gallon gasoline can. He poured the remaining milk into the closed gasoline can and replaced the cap.

Then he took his tools and a pane of glass from an overhead rack and headed for the house.

Hetty came into the kitchen as he was prying at the cauldron lid in the wall.

"You're going to make a worse mess before you're through," she said, "so I'll just let you finish and then clean up the whole mess afterwards. I got other things to do anyway."

She jammed a man's old felt hat on her head and left the house. Barney was unloading the last of the supplies Johnny had brought from Carson in the truck. Hetty shielded her eyes against the metallic glare of the afternoon sun. "Gettin' pretty dry, Barney. Throw some salt blocks in the pickup and I'll run them down to the south pasture and see if the pumps need to be turned on.

"And you might get that wind pump going in case we get a little breeze later this afternoon. But in any case, better run the yard pump for an hour or so and get some water up into the tank. I'll be back as soon as I take a ride through the pasture. I want to see how that Angus yearling is coming that I picked out for house beef."

A few minutes later, Hetty in the pickup disappeared behind a hot swirl of yellow dust. Barney ambled to the cool pump house beneath the towering windmill. An electric motor, powered either from the REA line or from direct current stored in a bank of wet cell batteries, bulked large in the small shed. To the left, a small, gasoline-driven generator supplied standby power if no wind was blowing to turn the arm-driven generator or if the lines happened to be down, as was often the case in the winter.

Barney threw the switch to start the pump motor.

Nothing happened. He reached for the light switch to test the single bulb hanging from a cord to the ceiling. Same nothing. Muttering darkly to himself, he changed the pump engine leads to DC current and closed the switch to the battery bank. The engine squeaked and whined slowly but when Barney threw in the clutch to drive the pump, it stopped and just hummed faintly. Then he opened the AC fuse box.

Johnny had freed the cauldron lid and was knocking out bits of broken glass from the kitchen window frame before putting in the new glass when Barney limped into the room.

"That pot busted the pump house 'lectric line, Johnny, when it went sailing," he said. "Miz Thompson wants to pump up some water and on top of that, the batteries are down. You got time to fix the line?"

Johnny paused and surveyed the kitchen. "I'm going to be working here for another hour anyway so Hetty can clean up when she gets back. Why don't you fire up the gasoline kicker for now and I'll fix the line when I get through here," he said.

"O.K.," Barney nodded and turned to leave. "Oh, forgot to ask you. Miz Thompson tell you about the egg?"

"What egg?" Johnny asked.

"The gold one."

Johnny grinned. "Sure, and I saw the goose when I came in. And you're Jack and the windmill is your beanstalk. Go climb it, Barney and cut out the fairy tales."

"Naw, Johnny," Barney protested, "I ain't kidding. Miz Thompson got a gold egg from the hens this morning. At least, it looks kinda like gold but she says it ain't. See, here it is." He reached into the cupboard where Hetty had placed the odd egg. He walked over and handed it to Johnny who was sitting on the sink drain counter to work on the shattered window.

The younger man turned the egg over in his hand. "It sure feels funny. Wonder what the inside looks like?" He banged the egg gently against the edge of the drain board. When it didn't crack, he slammed it harder, but then realizing that if it did break suddenly, it would squish onto the floor, he put the egg on the counter and tapped it with his hammer.

The shell split and a clear liquid poured out on to the drain board, thin and clear, not glutenous like a normal egg white. A small, reddish ball, obviously the yoke, rolled across the board, fell into the sink and broke into powdery fragments. A faint etherlike odor arose from the mess.

"I guess Miz Thompson was right," Barney said. "She said that hen musta been pecking in the fertilizer chemicals. Never seen no egg like that before."

"Yeh," Johnny said puzzledly. "Well, so much for that." He tossed the golden shell to one side and turned back to his glass work. Barney left for the pumphouse.

Inside the pumphouse, Barney opened the gasoline tank and poked a stick down to test the fuel level. The stick came out almost dry. With another string of mutterings, he limped across the yard to the tractor shed for a gas can. Back in the pumphouse, he poured the engine tank full, set the gas can aside and then, after priming the carburetor, yanked on the starter pull rope. The engine caught with a spluttering roar and began racing madly. Barney lunged for the throttle and cut it back to idle, but even then, the engine was running at near full speed. Then Barney noticed the white fluid running down the side of the engine tank and dripping from the spout of the gasoline can. He grinned broadly, cut in the pump clutch and hurriedly limped across the yard to the kitchen.

"Hey, Johnny," he called, "did you put that milk o' Sally's into a gas can?"

Johnny leaned through the open kitchen window. "Yeh, why?"

"Well, I just filled the kicker with it by accident, and man, you orter hear that engine run," Barney exclaimed. "Come see."

Johnny swung his legs through the window and dropped lightly to the yard. The two men were halfway across the yard from the pumphouse when a loud explosion ripped the building. Parts of the pump engine flew through the thin walls like shrapnel. A billowing cloud of purple smoke welled out of the ruptured building as Johnny and Barney flattened themselves against the hot, packed earth. Flames licked up from the pump shed. The men ran for the horse trough and grabbing pails of water, raced for the pumphouse. The fire had just started onto the wooden walls of the building and a few splashes of water doused the flames.

They eyed the ruins of the gasoline engine. "Holy cow," Johnny exclaimed, "that stuff blew the engine right apart." He gazed up at the holes in the pumphouse roof. "Blew the cylinders and head right out the roof. Holy cow!"

Barney was pawing at the pump and electric motor. "Didn't seem to hurt the pump none. Guess we better get that 'lectric line fixed though, now that we ain't got no more gas engine."

The two men went to work on the pump motor. The broken line outside the building was spliced and twenty minutes later, Johnny threw the AC switch. The big, electric motor spun into action and settled into a workmanlike hum. The overhead light dimmed briefly when the pump load was thrown on and then the slip-slap sound of the pump filled the shed. They watched and listened for a couple of minutes. Assured that the pump was working satisfactorily, they left the wrecked pumphouse.

Johnny was carrying the gasoline can of milk. "Good thing you set this off to one side where it didn't get hit and go off," he said. "The way this stuff reacts, we'd be without a pump, engine, or windmill if it had.

"Barney, be a good guy and finish putting in that glass for me will you? I've got the frame all ready to putty. I've got me some fiddlin' and figurin' to do."

Johnny angled off to the tractor and tool shed and disappeared inside. Barney limped into the kitchen and went to work on the window glass. From the tractor shed came the sounds of an engine spluttering, racing, backfiring and then, just idling.

When Hetty drove back into the ranch yard an hour or so later, Johnny was rodeoing the farm tractor around the yard like a teen-ager, his face split in a wide grin. She parked the truck under the tree as Johnny drove the tractor alongside and gunned the engine, still grinning.

"What in tarnation is this all about?" Hetty asked as she climbed down from the pickup.

"Know what this tractor's running on?" Johnny shouted over the noise of the engine.

"Of course I do, you young idiot," she exclaimed. "It's gasoline."

"Wrong," Johnny yelled triumphantly. "It's running on Sally's milk!"

The next morning, Johnny had mixed up two hundred gallons of Sally's Fuel and had the pickup, tractor, cattle truck and his 1958 Ford and Hetty's '59 Chevrolet station wagon all purring on the mixture.

Mixing it was a simple process after he experimented and found the right proportions. One quart of pure Sally's milk to one hundred gallons of water. He had used the two remaining quarts in the gasoline can to make the mixture but by morning, Sally had graced the ranch with five more gallons of the pure concentrate. Johnny carefully stored the concentrated milk in a scoured fifty-five gallon gasoline drum in the tool shed.

"We've hit a gold mine," he told Hetty exultantly. "We're never going to have to buy gasoline again. On top of that, at the rate Sally's turning this stuff out, we can start selling it in a couple of weeks and make a fortune."

That same morning, Hetty collected three more of the golden eggs.

"Set 'em on the shelf," Johnny said, "and when we go into town next time I'll have Dale look at them and maybe tell us what those hens have been into. I'll probably go into town again Saturday for the mail."

But when Saturday came, Johnny was hobbling around the ranch on a wrenched ankle, suffered when his horse stumbled in a gopher hole and tossed him.

"You stay off that leg," Hetty ordered. "I'll go into town for the mail. Them girls can just struggle along without your romancing this week." Johnny made a wry face but obeyed orders.

"Barneeey," Hetty bawled, "bring me a quarter of beef outta the cooler." Barney stuck his head out of the barn and nodded. "I been promising some good beef to Judge Hatcher for a month of Sundays now," Hetty said to Johnny.

"If you're going to stop by the courthouse, how about taking those crazy eggs of yours into the county agent's office and leave them there for analysis," Johnny suggested. He hobbled into the kitchen to get the golden eggs.

Barney arrived with the chilled quarter of beef wrapped in burlap. He tossed it in the bed of the pickup and threw more sacks over it to keep it cool under the broiling, midmorning sun. Johnny came out with the eggs in a light cardboard box stuffed with crumpled newspapers. He wedged the box against the side of beef in the forward corner of the truck bed. "One more thing, Hetty," he said. "I've got a half drum of drain oil in the tractor shed that I've been meaning to trade in for some gearbox lube that Willy Simons said he'd let me have. Can you drop it off at his station and pick up the grease?"

"Throw it on," Hetty said, "while I go change into some town clothes."

Johnny started to hobble down the porch steps when Barney stopped him. "I'll get it boy, you stay off that ankle." Barney climbed into the pickup and drove it around to the tractor shed. He spotted two oil drums in the gloomy shed. He tilted the nearest one and felt liquid slosh near the halfway mark, then rolled it out the door. Barney heaved it into the truck bed, stood it on end against the cab and drove the pickup back to the ranch house door as Hetty came out wearing clean jeans and a bright, flowered blouse. Her gray hair was tucked in a neat bun beneath a blocked Stetson hat.

She climbed into the truck, waved to the two men and drove out the yard. As she bumped over the cattle guard at the gate, the wooden plug that Johnny had jury-rigged to cork the gasoline drum with its twenty-gallon load of pure Sally's milk, bounced out.

A small geyser of white fluid shot out of the drum as she hit another bump and then the pickup went jolting down the ranch road, little splashes of Sally's milk sloshing out with each bump and forming a pool on the bottom of the truck. When Hetty cowboyed onto the county road, the drum tipped dangerously and then bounced back onto its base. This time a fountain of milk geysered out and splashed heavily into the box of golden eggs. Hetty drove on.

But not for long.

With a ranch woman's disregard for watching the road, Hetty constantly scanned the nearby range lands where small bands of her cherished black Angus grazed. She prided herself on the fact that despite her sixty years, her eyes were still sharp enough to spot a worm-ridden cow at a thousand yards.

Two miles after she turned onto the county road, which ran through Circle T range land, her roving gaze took in a cow and calf on a hillside a few hundred yards south of the road. Hetty slowed the pickup to fifty miles an hour and squinted into the sun. She grunted with satisfaction and slammed on the brakes. The truck swerved and skidded to a halt at the left side of the deserted road. Hetty leaped from the truck and began a fast walk up the hillside for a closer look at the cow and calf.

She never heard the dull thump of the milk drum tipping onto the edge of the truck bed. Hetty topped the hill and walked slowly towards the cow and calf that were now edging away from her. As she eased down the far side of the hill out of sight of the pickup, a steady stream of Sally's milk was engulfing the box of golden eggs. A minute later, the reduced contents caused the drum to shift and slip. It fell onto the eggs, cracking a half dozen.

The earth split open and the world around Hetty erupted in a roaring inferno of purple-red fire and ear-shattering sound. The rolling concussion swept Hetty from her feet and tumbled her into a drywash gully at the base of the hill. The gully saved her life as the sky-splitting shock wave rolled over her. Stunned and deafened, she flattened herself under a slight overhang.

The rolling blast rocked ranches and towns for more than one hundred miles and the ground wave triggered the seismographs at the University of California nearly two hundred miles away and at UCLA, four hundred miles distant. Tracking and testing instruments went wild along the entire length of the AEC atomic test grounds, a mere sixty miles south of the smoking, gaping hole that marked the end of the Circle T pickup truck.

In a direct line, the ranch house was about eight miles from the explosion.

Johnny was lounging in Hetty's favorite rocking chair on the wide back verandah, lighting a cigarette and Barney was perched on the porch railing when the sky was blotted out by the dazzling violet light of the blast. They were blinking in frozen amazement when the shock wave smashed into the ranch, flattening the flimsier buildings and buckling the side and roof of the steel-braced barn. Every window on the place blew out in a storm of deadly glass shards. The rolling ground wave in the wake of the shock blast, rocked and bounced the solid, timber and adobe main house.

The concussion hit Johnny like a fist, pinwheeling him backwards in the rocker against the wall of the house. It caught Barney like a sack of sodden rags and flung him atop the dazed and semiconscious younger man.

The first frightened screams of the horses in the barns and corrals were mingling with the bawling of the heifers in the calf pens when the sound of the explosion caught up with the devastation of the shock and ground waves.

Like the reverberation of a thousand massed cannon firing at once, the soul-searing sound rumbled out of the desert and boiled with almost tangible density into the shattered ranch yard. It flattened the feebly-stirring men on the porch and then thundered on in a tidal wave of noise.

Barney moaned and rolled off the tangle of porch rocker and stunned youth beneath him. Johnny lay dazed another second or two and then began struggling to his feet.

"Hetty," he croaked, pointing wildly to the south where a massive, dirty column of purple smoke and fire rose skyward like the stem of a monstrous and malignant toadstool. "Hetty's out there."

He stumbled from the porch and broke into a staggering run to the pile of broken planks that seconds ago had been the tractor shed. As he crossed the yard, a great gust of wind whipped back from the north, pumping clouds of dry, dusty earth before it. The force of the wind almost knocked the bruised and shaken Johnny from his feet once again as it swept back over the ranch, in the direction of the great pillar of purple smoke.

"Implosion," Johnny's mind registered.

He tore at the stack of loose boards leaning against the station wagon, flinging them fiercely aside in his frantic efforts to free the vehicle. Barney limped up to join him and a minute later they had cleared a way into the wagon. Johnny squeezed into the front seat and drove it back from under more leaning boards. Three of the side windows were smashed but the windshield was intact except for a small, starred crack in the safety glass. Clear of the debris, Barney opened the opposite door and slid in beside Johnny. Dirt spun from beneath the wheels of the car as he slammed his foot to the floor and raced towards the smoke column that now towered more than a mile and a half into the air.

Beneath her protective overhang, Hetty stirred and moaned feebly. Twin rivulets of dark blood trickled from her nostrils. Thick dust was settling on the area and she coughed and gasped for breath.

On the opposite side of the hill, a vast, torn crater, nearly a hundred feet across and six to ten feet deep, smoked like a stirring volcano and gave off a strange, pungent odor of ether.

Johnny Culpepper's dramatic charge to the rescue was no more dramatic than the reaction in a dozen other places in Nevada and California. Particularly sixty miles south where a small army of military and scientific men were preparing for an atomic underground shot when the Circle T pickup vanished.

The shock wave rippled across the desert floor, flowed around the mountains and funneled into Frenchman's Flat, setting off every shock-measuring instrument. Then came the ground wave, rolling through the earth like a gopher through a garden. Ditto for ground-wave measuring devices. Lastly, the sound boomed onto the startled scientists and soldiers like the pounding of great timpani under the vaulted dome of the burning sky.

On mountain top observation posts, technicians turned unbelieving eyes north to the burgeoning pillar of smoke and dust, then yelped and swung optical and electronic instruments to bear on the fantastic column.

In less than fifteen minutes, the test under preparation had been canceled, all equipment secured and the first assault waves of scientists, soldiers, intelligence and security men were racing north behind white-suited and sealed radiation detection teams cradling Geiger counters in their arms like submachine guns. Telephone lines were jammed with calls from Atomic Energy Commission field officials reporting the phenomena to Washington and calling for aid from West Coast and New Mexico AEC bases. Jet fighters at Nellis Air Force base near Las Vegas, were scrambled and roared north over the ground vehicles to report visual conditions near the purple pillar of power.

The Associated Press office in San Francisco had just received word of the quake recorded by the seismograph at Berkeley when a staffer on the other side of the desk answered a call from the AP stringer in Carson City, reporting the blast and mighty cloud in the desert sky. One fast look at the map showed that the explosion was well north of the AEC testing ground limits. The Carson City stringer was ordered to get out to the scene on the double and hold the fort while reinforcements of staffers and photographers were flown from 'Frisco.

Before any of the official or civil agencies had swung into action, the Circle T station wagon had rocketed off the ranch road and turned onto the oiled, county highway leading both to Carson City—and the now-expanding but less dense column of smoke.

Johnny hunched over the wheel and peered through the thickening pall of smoke and dust, reluctant to ease off his breakneck speed but knowing that they had to find Hetty—if she were alive. Neither man had said a word since the wagon raced from the ranch yard.

There was no valid reason to associate the explosion with Hetty, yet instinctively and naggingly, Johnny knew that somehow Hetty was involved. Barney, still ignorant of his error of the oil drums, just clung to his seat and prayed for the best.

The dust was almost too thick to see, forcing Johnny to slow the station wagon as they penetrated deeper into the base of the smoke column. Hiding under his frantic concern for Hetty was the half-formed thought that the whole thing was an atomic explosion and that he and Barney were heading into sure radiation deaths. His logic nudged at the thought and said, "If it were atomic, you started dying back on the porch, so might as well play the hand out."

A puff of wind swirled the dust up away from the road as the station wagon came up to the smoking crater. Johnny slammed on the brakes and he and Barney jumped from the car to stand, awe-struck, at the edge of the hole.

The dust-deadened air muffled Johnny's sobbing exclamation:

"Dear God!"

They walked slowly around the ragged edges of the crater. Barney bent down and picked a tiny metallic fragment from the pavement. He stared at it and then tapped Johnny on the arm and handed it to him, wordlessly. It was a twisted piece of body steel, bright at its torn edges and coated with the scarlet enamel that had been the color of the Circle T pickup.

Johnny's eyes filled with tears and he shoved the little scrap of metal in his pocket. "Let's see what else we can find, Barney." The two men began working a slow search of the area in ever-widening circles from the crater that led them finally up and over the top of the little hill to the south of the road.

Fifteen minutes later they found Hetty and ten minutes after that, the wiry, resilient ranchwoman was sitting between them on the seat of the station wagon, explaining how she happened to be clear of the pickup when the blast occurred.

The suspicion that had been growing in Johnny's mind, now brought into the open by his relief at finding Hetty alive and virtually unhurt, bloomed into full flower.

"Barney," Johnny asked softly, "which oil drum did you put in the back of the pickup?"

The facts were falling into place like the pieces of a jigsaw puzzle when the Carson City reporter, leading a caravan of cars and emergency vehicles from town by a good ten minutes and beating the AEC and military teams by twenty minutes, found the Circle T trio sitting in the station wagon at the lip of the now faintly smoldering crater.

A half hour later, the AP man in San Francisco picked up the phone.

"I've just come back from that explosion," the Carson City stringer said. The AP man put his hand over the phone and called across the desk. "Get ready for a '95' first lead blast."

"O.K.," the San Francisco desk man said, "let's have it." He tucked the phone between chin and shoulder and poised over his typewriter.

"Well, there's a crater more than one hundred feet across and ten feet deep," the Carson City stringer dutifully recounted. "The scene is on County Road 38, about forty miles east of here and the blast rocked Carson City and caused extensive breakage for miles around."

"What caused it," the AP desk man asked as he pounded out a lead.

"A lady at the scene said her milk and eggs blew up," the Carson City stringer said.

Ten miles south, the leading AEC disaster truck stopped behind the six-strand fence blocking the range road. Two men with wire cutters, jumped from the truck and snipped the twanging wires. The metal "Keep Out" sign banged to the ground and was kicked aside. The truck rolled through the gap and the men swung aboard. Behind them was a curtain of dust rising sluggishly in the hot sky, marking the long convoy of other official vehicles pressing hard on the trail of the emergency truck.

When the range road cut across the county highway, the driver paused long enough to see that the heaviest smoke concentrations from the unknown blast lay to the west. He swung left onto the oiled road and barreled westward. In less than a mile, he spied the flashing red light of a State trooper's car parked in the center of the road. The scene looked like a combination of the San Francisco quake and the Los Angeles county fair.

Dozens of cars, trucks, two fire engines and a Good Humor man were scattered around the open range land on both sides of the vast crater still smoldering in the road. A film of purple dust covered the immediate area and still hung in the air, coating cars and people. Scores of men, women and children lined the rim of the crater, gawking into the smoky pit, while other scores roamed aimlessly around the nearby hill and desert.

A young sheriff's deputy standing beside the State trooper's car raised his hand to halt the AEC disaster van. The truck stopped and the white-suited radiation team leaped from the vehicle, counters in hand, racing for the crater.

"Back," the chief of the squad yelled at the top of his lungs. "Everybody get back. This area is radiation contaminated. Hurry!"

There was a second of stunned comprehension and then a mad, pandemonic scrambling of persons and cars, bumping and jockeying to flee. The radiation team fanned out around the crater, fumbling at the level scales on their counters when the instruments failed to indicate anything more than normal background count.

MAKE MINE . . . HOMOGENIZED

All of the vehicles had pulled back to safety—all except a slightly battered station wagon still parked a yard or two from the eastern edge of the crater.

The radiation squad leader ran over to the wagon. Three people, two men and a dirty, disheveled and bloody-nosed older woman, sat in the front seat munching Good Humor bars.

"Didn't you hear me?" the AEC man yelled. "Get outta here. This area's hot. Radioactive. Dangerous. GET MOVING!"

The woman leaned out the window and patted the radiation expert soothingly on the shoulder.

"Shucks, sonny, no need to get this excited over a little spilt milk."

"Milk," the AEC man yelped, purpling. "Milk! I said this is a hot area; it's loaded with radiation. Look at this—" He pointed to the meter on his counter, then stopped, gawked at the instrument and shook it. And stared again. The meter flicked placidly along at the barely-above-normal background level count.

"Hey, Jack," one of the other white-suited men on the far side of the crater called, "this hole doesn't register a thing."

The squad chief stared incredulously at his counter and banged it against the side of the station wagon. Still the needle held in the normal zone. He banged it harder and suddenly the needle dropped to zero as Hetty and her ranch hands peered over the AEC man's shoulder at the dial.

"Now ain't that a shame," Barney said sympathetically. "You done broke it."

The rest of the disaster squad, helmets off in the blazing sun and lead-coated suits unfastened, drifted back to the squad leader at the Circle T station wagon. A mile east, the rest of the AEC convoy had arrived and halted in a huge fan of vehicles, parked a safe distance from the crater. A line of more white-suited detection experts moved cautiously forward.

With a stunned look, the first squad leader turned and walked slowly down the road towards the approaching line. He stopped once and looked back at the gaping hole, down at his useless counter, shook his head and continued on to meet the advancing units.

By nightfall, new strands of barbed wire reflected the last rays of the red Nevada sun. Armed military policemen and AEC security police in powder-blue battle jackets, patrolled the fences around the county road crater. And around the fence that now enclosed the immediate vicinity of the Circle T ranch buildings. Floodlights bathed the wire and cast an eerie glow over the mass of packed cars and persons jammed outside the fence. A small helicopter sat off to the right of the impromptu parking lot and an NBC newscaster gave the world a verbal description of the scene while he tried to talk above the snorting of the gas-powered generator that was supplying the Associated Press radio-telephone link to San Francisco.

Black AEC vans and dun colored military vehicles raced to and from the ranch headquarters, pausing to be cleared by the sentries guarding the main gates.

The AP log recorded one hundred eighteen major daily papers using the AP story that afternoon and the following morning:

CARSON CITY, NEV., May 12 (AP)—A kiloton eggnog rocked the scientific world this morning.

"On a Nevada ranch, forty miles east of here,

MAKE MINE . . . HOMOGENIZED

60-year-old Mehatibel Thompson is milking a cow that gives milk more powerful than an atomic bomb. Her chickens are laying the triggering mechanisms.

"This the world learned today when an earth-shaking explosion rocked . . ."

Inside the Circle T ranch house, Hetty, bathed and cleaned and only slightly the worse for her experiences, was hustling about the kitchen throwing together a hasty meal. Johnny and Barney had swept up a huge pile of broken glass, crockery and dirt and Hetty had salvaged what dishes remained unshattered by the blast.

She weaved through a dozen men grouped around the kitchen table, some in military or security police garb, three of them wearing the uniform of the atomic scientist in the field—bright Hawaiian sports shirts, dark glasses, blue denims and sneakers. Johnny and Barney huddled against the kitchen drainboard out of the main stream of traffic. The final editions of the San Francisco *Call-Bulletin*, Oakland *Tribune*, Los Angeles *Herald-Express* and the Carson City *Appeal* were spread out on the table. Hetty pushed them aside to put down dishes.

The glaring black headlines stared up at her. "Dairy Detonation Devastates Desert," the alliterative *Chronicle* banner read; "Bossy's Blast Rocks Bay Area," said the *Trib;* "Atomic Butter-And-Egg Blast Jars LA," the somewhat inaccurate *Herald-Ex* proclaimed; "Thompson Ranch Scene of Explosion," the *Appeal* stated, hewing to solid facts.

"Mrs. Thompson," the oldest of the scientists said, "won't you please put down those dishes for a few

163

minutes and give us the straight story. All afternoon long it's been one thing or another with you and all we've been able to get out of you is this crazy milk-egg routine."

"Time enough to talk after we've all had a bite to eat," Hetty said, juggling a platter of steaks and a huge bowl of mashed potatoes to the table. "Now we've all had a hard day and we can all stand to get on the outside of some solid food. I ain't had a bite to eat since this morning and I guess you boys haven't had much either. And since you've seemed to have made yourselves to home here, then by golly, you're going to sit down and eat with us.

"Besides," she added over her shoulder as she went back to the stove for vegetables and bread, "me 'n Johnny have already told you what story there is to tell. That's all there is to it."

She put more platters on the now-heaping table and then went around the table pouring coffee from the big ranch pot. "All right, you men sit down now and dig in," she ordered.

"Mrs. Thompson," an Army major with a heavy brush mustache said, "we didn't come here to eat. We came for information."

Hetty shoved back a stray wisp of hair and glared at the man.

"Now you listen to me, you young whippersnapper. I didn't invite you, but since you're here, you'll do me the goodness of being a mite more polite," she snapped.

The major winced and glanced at the senior scientist. The older man raised his eyes expressively and shrugged. He moved to the table and sat down. There was a general scuffling of chairs and the rest of the group took places around the big table. Johnny and Barney took their usual flanking positions beside Hetty at the head of the board.

Hetty took her seat and looked around the table with a pleased smile. "Now that's more like it."

She bowed her head and, after a startled glance, the strangers followed suit.

"We thank Thee, dear Lord," Hetty said quietly, "for this food which we are about to eat and for all Your help to us this day. It's been a little rough in spots but I reckon You've got Your reasons for all of it. Seein' as how tomorrow is Your day anyway, we ask that it be just a mite quieter. Amen."

The satisfying clatter of chinaware and silver and polite muttered requests for more potatoes and gravy filled the kitchen for the next quarter of an hour as the hungry men went to work on the prime Circle T yearling beef.

After his second steak, third helping of potatoes and gravy and fourth cup of coffee, the senior scientist contentedly shoved back from the table. Hetty was polishing the last dabs of gravy from her plate with a scrap of bread. The scientist pulled a pipe and tobacco pouch from his pocket.

"With your permission, m'am," he asked his hostess. Hetty grinned. "For heaven's sake, fire it up, sonny. Big Jim—that was my husband—used to say that no meal could be said properly finished unless it had been smoked into position for digestion."

Several of the other men at the table followed suit with pipes, cigars and cigarettes. Hetty smiled benignly around the table and turned to the senior scientist.

"What did you say your name was, sonny?" she asked.

"Dr. Floyd Peterson, Mrs. Thompson," he replied, "and at forty-six years of age, I deeply thank you for that 'sonny.' "

He reached for the stack of newspapers on the floor beside his chair and pushing back his plate, laid them on the table.

"Now, Mrs. Thompson, let's get down to facts," he rapped the headlines with a knuckle. "You have played hell with our schedule and I've got to have the answers soon before I have the full atomic commission and a congressional investigation breathing down my neck.

"What did you use to make that junior grade earthquake?"

"Why, I've already told you more'n a dozen times, sonny," Hetty replied. "It must of been the combination of them queer eggs and Sally's milk."

The brush-mustached major sipping his coffee, spluttered and choked. Beside him, the head of the AEC security force at Frenchman's Flat leaned forward.

"Mrs. Thompson, I don't know what your motives are but until I find out, I'm deeply thankful that you gave those news hounds this . . . this, butter and egg business," he said.

"Milk and eggs," Hetty corrected him mildly.

"Well, milk and eggs, then. But the time has ended for playing games. We must know what caused that explosion and you and Mr. Culpepper and Mr. Hatfield," he nodded to Johnny and Barney sitting beside Hetty, "are the only ones who can tell us."

"Already told you," Hetty repeated. Johnny hid a grin.

MAKE MINE . . . HOMOGENIZED

"Look, Mrs. Thompson," Dr. Peterson said loudly and with ill-concealed exasperation, "you created and set off an explosive force that dwarfed every test we've made at Frenchman's Flat in four years. The force of your explosive was apparently greater than that of a fair-sized atomic device and only our Pacific tests— and those of the Russians—have been any greater. Yet within a half hour or forty-five minutes after the blast there wasn't a trace of radiation at ground level, no aerial radiation and not one report of upper atmosphere contamination or fallout within a thousand miles.

"Mrs. Thompson, I appeal to your patriotism. Your friends, your country, the free people of the world, need this invention of yours."

Hetty's eyes grew wide and then her features set in a mold of firm determination. Shoving back her chair and raising to stand stiffly erect and with chin thrust forward, she was every inch the True Pioneer Woman of the West.

"I never thought of that," she said solemnly. "By golly, if my country needs this like that, then by golly, my country's going to have it."

The officials leaned forward in anticipation.

"You can have Sally's Cloverdale Marathon III and I don't want one cent for her, either. And you can take the hens, too."

There was a stunned silence and then the Army major strangled on a mouthful of coffee; the security man turned beet red in the face and Dr. Peterson's jaw bounced off his breastbone. Johnny, unable to hold back an explosion of laughter, dashed for the back porch and collapsed.

*   *   *

The kitchen door slammed and Dr. Peterson stamped out on to the porch, pipe clamped between clenched teeth, his face black with anger and frustration. He ignored Johnny who was standing beside the rail wiping tears from his eyes. Culpepper recovered himself and walked over to the irate physicist.

"Dr. Peterson you're a man of science," Johnny said, "and a scientist is supposed to be willing to accept a fact and then, possibly determine the causes behind the fact after he recognizes what he sees. Isn't that so?"

"Now, look here," Peterson angrily swung around to face Johnny. "I've taken all I intend to take from you people with your idiotic story. I don't intend to . . ."

Johnny took the older man by the elbow and gently but firmly propelled him from the porch towards the barn. "I don't intend to either insult your intelligence, Dr. Peterson, or attempt to explain what has happened here. But I do intend to show you what we know."

Bright floodlights illuminated the yard and a crew of soldiers were stringing telephone wires from the guarded front gate across the open space to the ranch house. Beyond the new barbed wire fence, there was an excited stir and rush for the wire as a sharp-eyed newsman spotted Johnny and the scientist crossing the yard. The two men ignored the shouted requests for more up-to-the-minute information as they walked into the barn. Johnny switched on the lights.

The lowing of the two prize Guernseys in the stalls at the right of the door changed to loud, plaintive bawling as the lights came on. Both cows were obviously in pain from their swollen and unmilked udders.

"Seeing is believing, Doc?" Johnny asked, pointing to the cows.

"Seeing what?" Peterson snapped.

"I knew we were going to have some tall explaining to do when you fellows took over here," Johnny said, "and, of course, I don't blame you one bit. That was some blast Hetty set off out there."

"You don't know," Dr. Peterson murmured fearfully, "you just don't know."

"So," Johnny continued, "I deliberately didn't milk these cows, so that you could see for yourself that we aren't lying. Now, mind you, I don't have the foggiest idea WHY this is happening, but I'm going to show you at least, WHAT happened."

He picked up a pair of milk buckets from a rack beside the door and walked towards the cow stalls, Peterson trailing. "This," Johnny said, pointing to the larger of the two animals, "is Queenie. Her milk is just about as fine as you can get from a champion milk producing line. And this," he reached over and patted the flank of the other cow, "is Sally's Cloverdale Marathon III. She's young and up to now has given good but not spectacular quantities or qualities of milk. She's from the same blood line as Queenie. Sally had dried up from her first calf and we bred her again and on Wednesday she came fresh. Only it isn't milk that she's been giving. Watch!"

Kicking a milking stool into position, he placed a bucket under Queenie's distended bag and began squirting the rich, foaming milk into the pail with a steady, fast and even rhythm. When he had finished, he set the two full buckets with their thick heads of milk foam, outside the stall and brought two more clean, empty buckets. He moved to the side of the impatient

Sally. As Peterson watched, Johnny filled the buckets with the same, flat, oily-looking white fluid that Sally had been producing since Wednesday. The scientist began to show mild interest.

Johnny finished, stripped the cow, and then carried the pails out and set them down beside the first two.

"O.K., now look them over yourself," he told Peterson.

The scientist peered into the buckets. Johnny handed him a ladle.

"Look, Culpepper," Peterson said, "I'm a physicist, not a farmer or an agricultural expert. How do you expect me to know what milk is supposed to do? Until I was fifteen years old, I thought the milk came out of one of those spigots and the cream out of another."

"Stir it," Johnny ordered. The scientist took the ladle angrily and poked at the milk in Queenie's buckets.

"Taste it," Johnny said. Peterson glared at the younger man and then took a careful sip of the milk. Some of the froth clung to his lips and he licked it off. "Tastes like milk to me," he said.

"Smell it," Johnny ordered. Peterson sniffed.

"O.K., now do the same things to the other buckets."

Peterson swished the ladle through the buckets containing Sally's milk. The white liquid swirled sluggishly and oillike. He bent over and smelled and made a grimace.

"Go on," Johnny demanded, "taste it."

Peterson took a tiny sip, tasted and then spat.

"All right," he said, "I'm now convinced that there's something different about this milk. I'm not saying anything is wrong with it because I wouldn't know. All I'm admitting is that it is different. So what?"

170

"Come on," Johnny took the ladle from him. He carried the buckets of Queenie's milk into the cooler room and dumped them in a small pasteurizer.

Then carrying the two pails of Sally's milk, Johnny and the physicist left the barn and went to the shattered remains of the tractor shed.

Fumbling under wrecked and overturned tables and workbenches, Johnny found an old and rusted pie tin.

Placing the tin in the middle of the open spaces of the yard, he turned to Peterson. "Now you take that pail of milk and pour a little into the pan. Not much, now, just about enough to cover the bottom or a little more." He again handed the ladle to Peterson.

The scientist dipped out a small quantity of the white fluid and carefully poured it into the pie plate.

"That's enough," Johnny cautioned. "Now let's set these buckets a good long ways from here." He picked up the buckets and carried them to the back porch. He vanished into the kitchen.

By this time, the strange antics of the two men had attracted the attention of the clamoring newsmen outside the fence and they jammed against the wire, shouting pleas for an interview or information. The network television camera crews trained their own high-powered lights into the yard to add to the brilliance of the military lights and began recording the scene. Dr. Peterson glared angrily at the mob and turned as Johnny rejoined him. "Culpepper, are you trying to make a fool of me?" he hissed.

"Got a match?" Johnny queried, ignoring the question. The pipe-smoking scientist pulled out a handful of kitchen matches. Johnny produced a glass fish casting rod with a small wad of cloth tied to the weighted hook. Leading Peterson back across the yard about fifty feet, Johnny handed the rag to Peterson.

"Smell it," he said. "I put a little kerosene on it so it would burn when it goes through the air." Peterson nodded.

"You much of a fisherman?" Johnny asked.

"I can drop a fly on a floating chip at fifty yards," the physicist said proudly. Johnny handed him the rod and reel. "O.K., Doc, light up your rag and then let's see you drop it in that pie plate."

While TV cameras hummed and dozens of still photographers pointed telescopic lenses and prayed for enough light, Dr. Peterson ignited the little wad of cloth. He peered behind to check for obstructions and then, with the wrist-flicking motion of the devoted and expert fisherman, made his cast. The tiny torch made a blurred, whipping streak of light and dropped unerringly into the pie plate in the middle of the yard.

The photographers had all the light they needed!

The night turned violet as a violent ball of purple fire reared and boiled into the darkened sky. The flash bathed the entire ranch headquarters and the packed cars and throngs outside the fence in the strange brilliance. The heat struck the dumbfounded scientist and young rancher like the suddenly-opened door of a blast furnace.

It was over in a second as the fire surged and then winked out. The sudden darkness blinded them despite the unchanged power of the television and military floodlights still focused on the yard. Pandemonium erupted from the ranks of newsmen and photographers who had witnessed the dazzling demonstration.

Peterson stared in awe at the slightly smoking and

warped pie tin. "Well, cut out my tongue and call me Oppenheimer," he exclaimed.

"That was just the milk," Johnny said. "You know of a good safe place we could try it out with one of those eggs? I'd be afraid to test 'em anywhere around here after what happened to Hetty this morning."

An hour later, a military helicopter chewed its way into the night, carrying three gallons of Sally's milk from the ranch to Nellis AFB where a jet stood ready to relay the sealed cannister to the AEC laboratories at Albuquerque.

In the ranch house living room Peterson had set up headquarters and an Army field telephone switchboard was in operation across the room.

An AEC security man was running the board. Hetty had decided that one earthquake a day was enough and had gone to bed. Barney, bewildered but happily pleased at so much company, sat on the edge of a chair and avidly watched and listened, not understanding a thing he saw or heard. At the back of the room, Johnny hunched over Big Jim Thompson's roll-top desk, working up a list of supplies he would need to repair the damages from the week's growing list of explosions.

Peterson and three of his staff members were in lengthy consultation at a big table in the middle of the room. The Army field phone at Peterson's elbow jangled.

Across the room, the switchboard operator swung around and called: "It's the commissioner, Dr. Peterson. I just got through to him." Peterson picked up the phone.

"John," he shouted into the instrument, "Peterson here. Where have you been?" Tinny, audible squawks came from the phone and Peterson held it away from his ear.

"Yes, I know all about it," he said. "Yes . . . yes . . . yes. I know you've had a time with the papers. Yes, I heard the radio. Yes, John, I know it sounds pretty ridiculous. What? Get up to the ranch and find out. Where do you think I'm calling from?"

The squawking rattled the receiver and Peterson winced.

"Look, commissioner," he broke in, "I can't put a stop to those stories. What? I said I can't put a stop to the stories for one reason. They're true."

The only sound that came from the phone was the steady hum of the line.

"Are you there, John?" Peterson asked. There was an indistinct mumble from Washington. "Now listen carefully, John. What I need out here just as quickly as you can round them up and get them aboard a plane is the best team of biogeneticists in the country.

"What? No, I don't need a team of psychiatrists, commissioner. I am perfectly normal." Peterson paused. "I think!"

He talked with his chief for another fifteen minutes. At two other telephones around the big table, his chief deputy and the senior security officer of the task force handled a half dozen calls during Peterson's lengthy conversation. When Peterson hung up, the machinery was in motion gathering the nation's top biochemists, animal geneticists, agricultural and animal husbandry experts and a baker's dozen of other assorted -ists, ready to package and ship them by plane and train to the main AEC facility at Frenchman's Flat and to the Circle T.

Peterson sighed gustily as he laid down the phone and reached for his pipe. Across the table, his assistant put a hand over the mouthpiece of his telephone and leaned towards Peterson.

"It's the Associated Press in New York," he whispered. "They're hotter than a pistol about the blackout and threatening to call the President and every congressman in Washington if we don't crack loose with something."

"Why couldn't I have flunked Algebra Two," Peterson moaned. "No, I had to be a genius. Now look at me. A milkmaid." He looked at his watch. "Tell 'em we'll hold a press conference at 8:00 a.m. outside the ranch gate."

The assistant spoke briefly into the phone and again turned to Peterson. "They say they want to know now whether the milk and egg story is true. They say they haven't had anything but an official runaround and a lot of rumor."

"Tell them we neither deny nor confirm the story. Say we are investigating. We'll give them a formal statement in the morning," Peterson ordered.

He left the table and walked to the desk where Johnny was finishing his list of building supplies.

"What time do you usually get those eggs?" he asked.

"Well, as a rule, Hetty gets out and gathers them up about nine each morning. But they've probably been laid a couple of hours earlier.

"That's going to make us awfully late to produce anything for those babbling reporters," the scientist said.

"Come to think of it," Johnny said thoughtfully, "we could rig up a light in the chicken house and make the hens lay earlier. That way you could have some eggs about four or five o'clock in the morning."

Barney had been listening.

"And them eggs make a mighty fine breakfast of a morning," he volunteered cheerfully. Peterson glared at him and Johnny grinned.

"I think the doctor wants the golden kind," he said with a smile.

"Oh, them," Barney said with a snort of disgust. "They wouldn't make an omelet fit for a hog. You don't want to fuss with them, doc."

Under Johnny's direction, a crew of technicians ran a power line into the slightly-wrecked chicken house. There were loud squawks of indignation from the sleeping hens as the men threaded their way through the nests. The line was installed and the power applied. A one-hundred-fifty-watt bulb illuminated the interior of the chicken house to the discordant clucking and cackling of the puzzled birds.

Solomon, the big rooster, was perched on a crossbeam, head tucked under his wing. When the light flooded the shed he jerked awake and fastened a startled and unblinking stare at the strange sun. He scrambled hastily and guiltily to his feet and throwing out his great chest, crowed a shrieking hymn to Thomas A. Edison. Johnny chuckled as the technicians jumped at the sound. He left the hen house, went back to the house and to bed.

He set his alarm clock for 4:00 a.m. and dropped immediately into a deep and exhausted sleep.

MAKE MINE . . . HOMOGENIZED

When he and the sleepy-eyed Peterson went into the chicken house at 4:30, there were eleven of the golden eggs resting on the straw nests.

They turned the remainder of the normal eggs over to Hetty who whipped up a fast and enormous breakfast. While Peterson and Johnny were eating, a writing team of AEC public information men who had arrived during the night, were polishing a formal press release to be given to the waiting reporters at eight. The phones had been manned throughout the night. Peterson's bleary-eyed aide came into the kitchen and slumped into a chair at the table.

"Get yourself a cup of coffee, boy," Hetty ordered, "while I fix you something to eat. How you like your eggs?"

"Over easy, Mrs. Thompson and thanks," he said wearily. "I think I've got everything lined up, doctor. The eggs are all packed, ready to go in your car and the car will be ready in about ten minutes. They're still setting up down range but they should be all in order by the time you get there.

"The bio men and the others should be assembled in the main briefing room at range headquarters. I've ordered a double guard around the barn, to be maintained until the animal boys have finished their on-the-ground tests. And they're padding a device van to take Sally to the labs when they're ready.

"And . . . oh yeah, I almost forgot . . . the commissioner called about ten minutes ago and said to tell you that the Russians are going to make a formal protest to the U.N. this morning. They say we're trying to wipe out the People's Republic by contaminating their milk."

The sound of scuffling in the yard and loud yells of protest came through the back porch window. The door swung open and a spluttering and irate Barney was thrust into the room, still in the clutches of a pair of armed security policemen.

"Get your hands offn me," Barney roared as he struggled and squirmed impotently in their grip. "Doc, tell these pistol-packing bellhops to turn me loose."

"We caught him trying to get into the barn, sir," one of the officers told Peterson.

"Of course I was going into the barn," the indignant ranch hand screamed. "Where'd you think I would go to milk a cow?"

Peterson smiled. "It's all right, Fred. It's my fault. I should have told you Mr. Hatfield has free access."

The security men released Barney. He shook himself and glared at them.

"I'm terribly, sorry, Barney," Dr. Peterson said. "I forgot that you would be going down to milk the cows and I'm glad you reminded me. Do me a favor and milk Sally first, will you? I want to take that milk, or whatever it is, with us when we leave in a few minutes.

The sun was crawling up the side of the mountains when Johnny and Dr. Peterson swung out of the ranch yard between two armored scout cars for the sixty-mile trip down the range road. Dew glistened in the early rays of light and the clear, cool morning air held little hint of the heat sure to come by midmorning. There was a rush of photographers towards the gate as the little convoy left the ranch. A battery of cameras grabbed shots of the vehicles heading south.

It was the beginning of a day that changed the entire

foreign policy of the United States. It was also the day that started a host of the nation's finest nuclear physicists tottering towards pyschiatrists' couches.

In rapid order in the next few days, Peterson's crew reinforced by hundreds of fellow scientists, technicians and military men, learned what Johnny Culpepper already knew. They learned that (1) Sally's milk, diluted by as much as four hundred parts of pure water, made a better fuel than gasoline when ignited.

They also learned that (2) in reduced degrees of concentration, it became a substitute for any explosive of known chemical composition; (3) brought in contact with the compound inside one of the golden eggs, it produced an explosive starting at the kiloton level of one egg to two cups of milk and went up the scale but leveled off at a peak as the recipe was increased; (4) could be controlled by mixing jets to produce any desired stream of explosive power; and (5) they didn't have the wildest idea what was causing the reaction.

In that same order it brought (1) Standard Oil stock down to the value of wallpaper; (2) ditto for DuPont; (3) a new purge in the top level of the Supreme Soviet; (4) delight to rocketeers at Holloman Air Force Research Center, Cape Canaveral and Vandenburg Air Force Base; and (5) agonizing fits of hair-tearing to every chemist, biologist and physicist who had a part in the futile attempts to analyze the two ingredients of what the press had labeled "Thompson's Eggnog."

While white-coated veterinarians, agricultural experts and chemists prodded and poked Sally's Cloverdale Marathon III, others were giving a similar going-over to Hetty's chicken flock. Solomon's outraged screams of anger echoed across the desert as they subjected him to fowl indignities never before endured by a rooster.

Weeks passed and with each one new experiments disclosed new uses for the amazing Eggnog. While Sally placidly chewed her cuds and continued to give a steady five gallons of concentrated fury at each milking, Solomon's harem dutifully deposited from five to a dozen golden spheres of packaged power every day. At the same time, rocket research engineers completed their tests on the use of the Eggnog.

In the early hours of June 4th, a single-stage, two-egg, thirty-five-gallon Atlas rocket poised on the launching pads at Cape Canaveral. From the loud-speaker atop the massive blockhouse came the countdown.

"X minus twenty seconds. X minus ten seconds. Nine . . . eight . . . seven . . . six . . . five . . . four . . . three . . . two . . . FIRE!"

The control officer stabbed the firing button and deep within the Atlas a relay clicked, activating a solenoid that pushed open a valve. A thin stream of Sally's milk shot in from one side of the firing chamber to blend with a fine spray of egg batter coming from a jet in the opposite wall.

Spewing a solid tail of purple fire, the Atlas leaped like a wasp-stung heifer from the launching pads and thundered into space. The fuel orifices continued to expand to maximum pre-set opening. In ten seconds the nose cone turned from cherry-red to white heat and began sloughing its outer ceramic coating. At slightly more than forty-three thousand miles an hour, the great missile cleaved out of atmosphere into the void of space, leaving a shock wave that cracked houses and shattered glass for fifty miles from launching point.

A week later, America's newest rocket vessel, weighing more than thirty tons and christened *The Egg Nog*, was launched from the opposite coast at Vandenburg. Hastily modified to take the new fuel, the weight and space originally designed for the common garden variety of rocket fuel was filled with automatic camera and television equipment. In its stern stood a six-egg, one-hundred-gallon engine, while in the nose was a small, one-egg, fourteen-quart braking engine to slow it down for the return trip through the atmosphere.

Its destination—Mars!

A week later, *The Eggnog* braked down through the troposphere, skidded to a piddling two-thousand miles an hour through the stratosphere, automatically sprouted gliding wing stubs in the atmosphere and planed down to a spraying halt in the Pacific Ocean, fifty miles west of Ensenada in Baja, California. Aboard were man's first views of the red planet.

The world went mad with jubilation. From the capitals of the free nations congratulations poured into Washington. From Moscow came word of a one-hundred-ton spaceship to be launched in a few days, powered by a mixture of vodka and orange juice discovered by a bartender in Novorosk who was studying chemistry in night school. This announcement was followed twenty-four hours later by a story in *Pravda* proving conclusively that Sally's Cloverdale Marathon III was a direct descendant of Nikita's Mujik Droshky V, a prize Guernsey bull produced in the barns of the Sopolov People's Collective twenty-six years ago.

Late in August, Air Force Major Clifton Wadsworth Quartermain climbed out of the port of the two-hundred-ton, two dozen-egg, two-hundred-thirty-gallon space rocket *Icarus*, the first man into space and back. He had circled Venus and returned. No longer limited by fuel weight factors, scientists had been able to load enough shielding into the huge *Icarus* to protect a man from the deadly bombardment of the Van Allen radiation belts.

On September 15th, Sally's Cloverdale Marathon III, having been milked harder and faster than any Guernsey in history, went dry.

Less than half of the approximately twelve-hundred gallons of fuel she had produced during her hay days, remained on hand in the AEC storage vaults.

Three days later, Solomon, sprinting after one of his harem who was playing hard to get, bee-lined into the path of a security police jeep. There was an agonized squawk, a shower of feathers and mourning. A short time later, the number of golden eggs dropped daily until one morning, there were none. They never reappeared. The United States had stockpiled twenty-six dozen in an underground cave deep in the Rockies.

Man, who had burst like a butterfly into space, crawled back into his cocoon and pondered upon the stars from a worm's eye point of view.

Banging around in the back end of a common cattle truck, Sally's Cloverdale Marathon III came home to the Circle T in disgrace. In a corner of the truck, the late Solomon's harem cackled and voiced loud cries of misery as they huddled in the rude, slatted shipping coop. The truck turned off the county road and onto the dirt road leading to the main buildings. It rattled across the cattle guard and through the new unprotected and open gate in the barbed wire fence. Life had returned almost to normal at the Circle T.

But not for long.

Five days after Sally's ignominious dismissal from the armed forces, a staff car came racing up to the ranch. It skidded to a halt at the back-porch steps. Dr. Peterson jumped out and dashed up to the kitchen door.

"Well, for heaven's sake," Hetty cried. "Come on in, sonny. I ain't seen you for the longest spell."

Peterson entered and looked around.

"Where's Johnny, Mrs. Thompson?" he asked excitedly. "I've got some wonderful news."

"Now ain't that nice," Hetty exclaimed. "Your wife have a new baby or something? Johnny's down at the barn. I'll call him for you." She moved towards the door.

"Never mind," Peterson said, darting out the door, "I'll go down to the barn." He jumped from the porch and ran across the yard.

He found Johnny in the barn, rigging a new block and tackle for the hayloft. Barney was helping thread the new, manila line from a coil on the straw-littered floor.

"Johnny, we've found it," Peterson shouted jubilantly as he burst into the barn.

"Why, Doc, good to see you again," Johnny said. "Found what?"

"The secret of Sally's milk," Peterson cried. He looked wildly around the barn. "Where is she?"

"Who?"

"Sally, of course," the scientist yelped.

"Oh, she's down in the lower pasture with Queenie," Johnny replied.

"She's all right, isn't she?" Peterson asked anxiously.

"Oh, sure, she's fine, Doc. Why?"

"Listen," Peterson said hurriedly, "our people think they've stumbled on something. Now we still don't know what's in those eggs or in Sally's milk that make them react as they do. All we've been able to find is some strange isotope but we don't know how to reproduce it or synthesize it.

"But we do think we know what made Sally give that milk and made those hens start laying the gold eggs."

Johnny and Barney laid down their work and motioned the excited scientist to join them on a bench against the horse stalls.

"Do you remember the day Sally came fresh?" Peterson continued.

"Not exactly," Johnny replied, "but I could look it up in my journal. I keep a good record of things like new registered stock births."

"Never mind," Peterson said, "I've already checked. It was May 9th."

He paused and smiled triumphantly.

"I guess that's right if you say so," Johnny said. "But what about it?"

"And that was the same day that the hens laid the first golden egg too, wasn't it?" Peterson asked.

"Why it sure was, Doc," Barney chimed in. "I remember, cause Miz Thompson was so mad that the milk was bad and the eggs went wrong both in the same day."

"That's what we know. Now listen to this, Johnny," the scientist continued. "During the night of May 8th, we fired an entirely new kind of test shot on the range.

I can't tell you what it was, only to say that it was a special atomic device that even we didn't know too much about. That's why we fired it from a cave in the side of a hill down there.

"Since then, our people have been working on the pretty good assumption that something happened to that cow and those chickens not too long before they started giving the Eggnog ingredients. Someone remembered the experimental test shot, checked the date and then went out and had a look at the cave. We already had some earlier suspicions that this device produced a new type of beam ray. We took sightings from the cave, found them to be in a direct, unbroken line with the Circle T. We set up the device again and using a very small model, tried it out on some chick embryos. Sure enough, we got a mutation. But not the right kind.

"So we're going to recreate the entire situation right here, only this time, we're going to expose not only Sally but a dozen other Guernseys from as close to her blood line as we can get.

"And we already knew that you had a young rooster sired by Solomon."

"But, Doc," Johnny protested. "Sally had a calf early that morning. Isn't that going to make a difference?"

"Of course it is," Peterson exclaimed. "And she's going to have another one the same way. And so are all the other cows. You're the one that told me she had her calf by artificial insemination, didn't you?"

Johnny nodded.

"Well, then she's going to have another calf from the same bull and so will the other cows."

"Pore Sally," Barney said sorrowfully. "They're sure takin' the romance outta motherhood for you."

The next day the guards were back on the gate. By midafternoon twelve fine young Guernseys arrived, together with a corps of veterinarians, biologists and security police. By nightfall, Sally and her companions were all once again in a "delicate condition."

A mile from the ranch house, a dormitory was built for the veterinarians and biologists and a barracks thrown up for the security guards. A thirty-five thousand dollar, twelve-foot-high chain link fence, topped by barbed wire, was constructed around the pasture and armored cars patrolled the fence by day and kept guard over the pregnant bovines by night in the barn.

Through the fall, into the long winter and back to budding spring again, the host of experts and guards watched and cared for the new calf-bloated herd.

The fact that Sally had gone dry had been kept a carefully guarded national secret. To keep up the pretense and show to the world that America still controlled the only proven method of manned space travel, the Joint Chiefs of Staff voted to expend two hundred gallons of the precious, small store of milk on hand for another interplanetary junket, this time to inspect the rings around Saturn.

Piloting a smaller and more sophisticated but equally-well protected version of *Icarus*, Major Quartermain abandoned the fleshpots of earth and the adulation of his coast-to-coast collection of worshiping females to again hurtle into the unknown.

"It was strictly a milk run," Major Quartermain was quoted as saying as he emerged from his ship after an uneventful but propaganda-loaded trip.

MAKE MINE . . . HOMOGENIZED

By the middle of May, it was the consensus of the veterinarians that Delivery Day would be July 4th. Plans were drafted for the repeat atomic cave shot at 9:00 p.m., July 3rd. The pregnant herd was to be given labor-inducing shots at midnight, and, if all went well, deliveries would start within a few hours. Just to be sure that nothing would shield the cows from the rays of the explosion, they were put in a corral on the south side of the barn until 9:30 p.m., on the night of the firing.

Solomon's successor and a new bevy of hens were already roosting in the same old chicken house and egg production was normal.

On the night of July 3rd, at precisely 9:00 p.m., a sheet of light erupted from the Nevada hillside cave and the ground shook and rumbled for a few miles. It wasn't a powerful blast, nor had been the original shot. Sixty miles away, thirteen Guernsey cows munched at a rick of fresh hay and chewed contentedly in the moonlight.

At 3:11 a.m., the following morning the first calf arrived, followed in rapid order by a dozen more.

Sally's Cloverdale Marathon III dropped her calf at 4:08 a.m. on Independence Day.

At 7:00 a.m., she was milked and produced two and a half gallons of absolutely clear, odorless, tasteless and non-ignitable fluid. Eleven other Guernseys gave forth gushing, foaming, creamy rich gallon after gallon of Grade A milk.

The thirteenth cow filled two buckets with something that looked like weak cocoa and smelled like stale tea.

But when a white-smocked University of California

poultry specialist entered the chicken house later in the morning, he found nothing but normal, white fresh eggs in the nests. He finally arrived at the conclusion that Solomon's old harem had known for some time; whatever it was that Solomon had been gifted with, this new rooster just didn't have it.

A rush call went out for a dozen of the precious store of golden eggs to be sent to the testing labs down range.

Two hours later, Dr. Peterson, surrounded by fellow scientists, stood before a bank of closed circuit television monitors in the Frenchman's Flat headquarters building. The scene on the screens was the interior of a massive steel-and-concrete test building several miles up range. Resting on the floor of the building was an open, gallon-sized glass beaker filled with the new version of Sally's milk.

Poised directly above the opened beaker was a funnel-shaped vessel containing the contents of one golden egg.

Dr. Peterson reached for a small lever. By remote control, the lever would gradually open the bottom of the funnel. He squeezed gently, slowly applying pressure. An involuntary gasp arose from the spectators as a tiny trickle of egg fluid fell from the funnel towards the open beaker.

Instinctively, everyone in the room clamped their eyes shut in anticipation of a blast. A second later, Peterson peered cautiously at the screen. The beaker of milk had turned a cloudy pale blue. It neither fizzed nor exploded. It just sat.

He levered another drop from the funnel. The stringy, glutinous mass plopped into the beaker and the liquid swirled briefly and turned more opaque, taking on more of a bluish tinge.

A babble of voices broke through the room when it was apparent that no explosion was forthcoming.

Peterson slumped into a nearby chair and stared at the screen.

"Now what?" he moaned.

The "what" developed twelve hectic hours later after time lost initially in shaking, bouncing and beaming the new substance on the outside chance it might develop a latent tendency towards demolition.

Satisfied that whatever it was in the beaker wasn't explosive, the liquid was quickly poured off into sixteen small half-pint beakers and speeded to as many different laboratories for possible analysis.

"What about the other stuff?" Peterson was asked, referring to the brownish "milk" subsequently identified as coming from a dainty young cow known as Melody Buttercup Greenbrier IV.

"One thing at a time," replied Peterson. "Let's find out what we have here before we got involved in the second problem."

At 9:00 p.m., that night, Peterson was called to the radiation labs. He was met at the door by a glazed-eyed physicist who led him back to his office.

He motioned Peterson to a seat and then handed him a sheaf of photographic papers and other charts. Each of the photo sheets had a clear, white outline of a test beaker surrounded by a solid field of black. Two of the papers were all white.

"I don't believe it, Floyd," the physicist said, running his hands through his hair. "I've seen it, I've done it, I've tested it, proven it, and I still don't believe it."

Peterson riffled the sheaf of papers and waited expectantly.

"You don't believe what, Fred?" he asked.

The physicist leaned over and tapped the papers in Peterson's hands. "We've subjected that crazy stuff to every source and kind of high and low energy radiation we can produce here and that means just about everything short of triggering an H-device on it. We fired alphas, gammas, betas, the works, in wide dispersion, concentrated beam and just plain exposure.

"Not so much as one neutron of any of them went beyond the glass surrounding that forsaken slop.

"They curved around it, Floyd. They curved around it."

The physicist leaned his head on the desk. "Nothing should react like that," he sobbed. He struggled for composure as Peterson stared dazedly at the test sheets.

"That's not the whole story," the physicist continued. He walked to Peterson's side and extracted the two all-white sheets.

"This," he said brokenly, "represents a sheet of photographic paper dipped in that crud and then allowed to dry before being bombarded with radiation. And this," he waved the other sheet, "is a piece of photo paper in the center of a panel protected by another sheet of ordinary typing paper coated with that stuff."

Peterson looked up at him. "A radiation-proof liquid," he said in awed tones.

The other man nodded dumbly.

"Eight years of university," the physicist whispered

to himself. "Six years in summer schools. Four fellow-ships. Ten years in research.

"All shot to hell," he screamed, "by a stinking, hayburning cow."

Peterson patted him gently on the shoulder. "It's all right, Fred. Don't take it so hard. It could be worse."

"How?" he asked hollowly. "Have this stuff milked from a kangaroo?"

Back in his office, Peterson waved off a dozen calls while he gave orders for fresh quantities of the blue milk to be rushed to the Argonne laboratories for further radiation tests and confirmation of the Nevada results. He ordered a test set up for the brown fluid for the following morning and then took a call from the AEC commissioner.

"Yes, John," he said, "we've got something."

Operation Milkmaid was in full swing!

The following morning observers again clustered about the monitoring room as Peterson prepared to duplicate the tests, using a sample of Melody's brown-ish milk.

There was the same involuntary remote cringing as the first drop of egg fell towards the beaker, but this time, Peterson forced himself to watch. Again the gentle plop was heard through the amplifiers and nothing more. A similar clouding spread through the already murky fluid and when the entire contents of one egg had been added, the beaker took on a solid, brown and totally opaque appearance. The scientists watched the glass container for several minutes, anticipating another possible delayed blast.

When nothing occurred, Peterson nodded to an assistant at an adjoining console. The aide worked a series of levers and a remotely-controlled mechanical arm came into view on the screen. The claw of the arm descended over the beaker and clasping it gently, bounced it lightly on the cement bunker floor. The only sound was the muffled thunk of the glass container against the concrete.

The assistant wiggled his controls gently and the beaker jiggled back and forth, a few inches off the floor.

Peterson, who had been watching closely, called out. "Do that again."

The operator jostled the controls. "Look at that," Peterson exclaimed. "That stuff's hardened."

A quick movement confirmed this and then Peterson ordered the beaker raised five feet from the floor and slowly tipped. Over the container went as the claw rotated in its socket. The glass had turned almost 180° towards the floor when the entire mass of solidified glob slid out.

The watchers caught their breath as it fell to the hard floor. The glob hit the floor, bounced up a couple of inches, fell back, bounced again and then quivered to a stop. What was soon to be known as Melody's Mighty Material had been born.

The testing started. But there was a difference. By the time the brown chunk had been removed from the bunker it had solidified to the point that nothing would break or cut it. The surface yielded slightly to the heaviest cutting edge of a power saw and then sprang back, unmarked. A diamond drill spun ineffectually.

So the entire block started making the rounds of the various labs. It was with downright jubilation that radiation labs reported no properties of resistance for the stuff. One after the other, the test proved nothing until the physical properties unit came up with an idea.

"You can't cut it, break it or tear it," the technician told Peterson, as he hefted the chunk of lightweight enigma. "You can't burn it, shoot holes in it, or so much as mark the surface with any known acid. This stuff's tougher than steel and about fifty times lighter."

"O.K.," Peterson asked, "so what good is it?"

"You can mold it when you mix it," the technician said significantly.

"Hey, you're right," Peterson jumped up excitedly. "Why, a spacer cast out of this stuff and coated with Sally's paint would be light enough and shielded enough to work on regular missile fuels."

Working under crash priorities, the nation's three leading plastics plants turned out three, lightweight, molded, one-man space vehicles from the government-supplied Melody's Mix. A double coating of Sally's Paint then covered the hulls and a single stage liquid fuel rocket engine was hooked to the less-than-one-ton engineless hull.

Twenty-eight days after the milk first appeared, on a warm August evening, the first vehicle stood on the pads at Cape Canaveral, illuminated by towers of lights. Fuel crews had finished loading the tanks which would be jettisoned along with the engine at burn-out. Inside the rocket, Major Quartermain lounged uncomfortably and cramped in the take-off sling for a short but telling trip through the Van Allen radiation fields and back to Earth.

The take-off sling rested inside an escape capsule since the use of chemical fuel brought back many of the old uncertainties of launchings. On the return trip,

Quartermain would eject at sixty thousand feet and pull the capsule's huge parachute for a slow drop to the surface of the Atlantic where a recovery fleet was standing by. The light rocket hull would pop a separate chute and also drift down for recovery and analysis.

Inside the ship, Quartermain sniffed the air and curled his nose. "Let's get this thing on the road," he spoke into his throat mike. "Some of that Florida air must have seeped in here."

"Four minutes to final countdown," blockhouse control replied. "Turn on your blowers for a second."

Outside the ship, the fuel crews cleared their equipment away from the pad. The same ripe, heavy odor hung in the warm night air.

At 8:02 p.m., twenty-eight days after the new milks made their first appearance, Major Quartermain blasted off in a perfect launching.

At 8:03 p.m., the two other Melody Mix hulls standing on nearby pads, began to melt.

At 8:04 p.m., the still-roaring engine fell from the back end of Quartermain's rocket in a flaming arc back towards Earth. Fifteen seconds later, he hurtled his escape capsule out of the collapsing rocket hull. The parachute opened and the daring astronaut drifted towards the sea.

Simultaneously, in a dozen labs around the nation, blocks and molds of Melody's Mix made from that first batch of milk, collapsed into piles of putrid goo. Every day thereafter, newer blocks of the mix reached the twenty-eight-day limit and similarly broke down into malodorous blobs.

It was a month before the stinking, gooey mess that flowed over the launching pads at the Cape was cleaned up by crews wearing respirators and filter masks. It took considerably longer to get the nation's three top plastics firms back in operation as the fetid flow of unfinished rocket parts wrecked machinery and drove personnel from the area.

The glob that had been Quartermain's vehicle fell slowly back to Earth, disintegrating every minute until it reached the consistency of thin gruel. At this point, it was caught by a jet air stream and carried in a miasmic cloud halfway around the world until it finally floated down to coat the Russian city of Urmsk in a veil of vile odor. The United States disclaimed any knowledge of the cloud.

"LAS VEGAS, NEV., May 8 (AP)—The Atomic Energy Commission today announced it has squeezed the last drop from Operation Milkmaid.

"After a year of futile experimentation has failed to get anything more than good, Grade A milk from the world's two most famous cows, the AEC says it has closed down its field laboratory at the Circle T ranch.

"Dr. Floyd Peterson, who has been in charge of the attempt to again reproduce Sally's Milk, told newsmen that the famed Guernsey and her stablemate, Melody, no longer gave exotic and unidentifiable liquids that sent man zooming briefly to the stars.

" 'For a while, it looked like we had it in the bag,' Peterson said. 'You might say now, though, that the tests have been an udder failure.'

"Meanwhile, in Washington, AEC commissioner . . ."

THE LADY WHO SAILED *THE SOUL*

BY CORDWAINER SMITH (1913–1966)

GALAXY
APRIL

As Isaac points out below, "The Lady Who Sailed The Soul" *is a love story. Human love runs through the work of Cordwainer Smith (Paul M. A. Linebarger), whose careers as college professor, intelligence operative, and science fiction writer we have discussed at some length in earlier volumes of this series. For me,* The Best Of Cordwainer Smith *(1975) edited by J. J. Pierce, is one of the ten best sf books of the 1970s. (MHG)*

I am one of those who considers science fiction a mode of story telling that includes all *the genres, and is therefore much more than a genre itself. Think of all the different kinds of specialized fiction—love stories, war stories, mystery stories, adventure stories, sport stories, and so on, and so on, and so on.*

Any of them can be placed, and usually are, within a known society, past or present, in which case they are "straight" fiction.

THE LADY WHO SAILED *THE SOUL*

Any of them can also be placed within an invented society in which case they are either science fiction or fantasy. If the invented society is conceivable in terms of possible scientific advance, it is science fiction; otherwise it is fantasy. (That's three modes altogether.)

It just happens that "The Lady Who Sailed The Soul*" is a love story, set in the science fiction mode. (IA)*

1

The story ran—how did the story run? Everyone knew the reference to Helen America and Mr. Grey-no-more, but no one knew exactly how it happened. Their names were welded to the glittering timeless jewelry of romance. Sometimes they were compared to Heloise and Abelard, whose story had been found among books in a long-buried library. Other ages were to compare their life with the weird, ugly-lovely story of the Go-Captain Taliano and the Lady Dolores Oh.

Out of it all, two things stood forth—their love and the image of the great sails, tissue-metal wings with which the bodies of people finally fluttered out among the stars.

Mention him, and others knew her. Mention her, and they knew him. He was the first of the inbound sailors, and she was the lady who sailed *The Soul*.

It was lucky that people lost their pictures. The romantic hero was a very young-looking man, prematurely old and still quite sick when the romance came. And Helen America, she was a freak, but a nice one: a grim, solemn, sad, little brunette who had been born amid the laughter of humanity. She was not the tall, confident heroine of the actresses who later played her.

She was, however, a wonderful sailor. That much was true. And with her body and mind she loved Mr. Grey-no-more, showing a devotion which the ages can neither surpass nor forget. History may scrape off the patina of their names and appearances, but even history can do no more than brighten the love of Helen America and Mr. Grey-no-more.

Both of them, one must remember, were sailors.

2

The child was playing with a spieltier. She got tired of letting it be a chicken, so she reversed it into the fur-bearing position. When she extended the ears to the optimum development, the little animal looked odd indeed. A light breeze blew the animal-toy on its side, but the spieltier good-naturedly righted itself and munched contentedly on the carpet.

The little girl suddenly clapped her hands and broke forth with the question, "Mamma, what's a sailor?"

"There used to be sailors, darling, a long time ago. They were brave men who took the ships out to the stars, the very first ships that took people away from our sun. And they had big sails. I don't know how it worked, but somehow, the light pushed them, and it took them a quarter of a life to make a single one-way trip. People only lived a hundred and sixty years at that time, darling, and it was forty years each way, but we don't need sailors any more."

"Of course not," said the child, "we can go right away. You've taken me to Mars and you've taken me to New Earth as well, haven't you, Mamma? And we can go anywhere else soon, but that only takes one afternoon."

"That's planoforming, honey. But it was a long time

before the people knew how to planoform. And they could not travel the way we could, so they made great big sails. They made sails so big that they could not build them on Earth. They had to hang them out, halfway between Earth and Mars. And you know, a funny thing happened . . . Did you ever hear about the time the world froze?"

"No, Mamma, what was that?"

"Well, a long time ago, one of these sails drifted and people tried to save it because it took a lot of work to build it. But the sail was so large that it got between the Earth and the sun. And there was no more sunshine, just night all the time. And it got very cold on Earth. All the atomic power plants were busy, and all the air began to smell funny. And the people were worried and in a few days they pulled the sail back out of the way. And the sunshine came again."

"Mamma, were there ever any girl sailors?"

A curious expression crossed over the mother's face. "There was one. You'll hear about her later on when you are older. Her name was Helen America and she sailed The Soul *out to the stars. She was the only woman that ever did it. And that is a wonderful story."*

The mother dabbed at her eyes with a handkerchief.

The child said: "Mamma, tell me now. What's the story all about?"

At this point the mother became very firm and she said: "Honey, there are some things that you are not old enough to hear yet. But when you are a big girl, I'll tell you all about them."

The mother was an honest woman. She reflected a moment, and then she added, ". . . unless you read about it yourself first."

Helen America was to make her place in the history of mankind, but she started badly. The name itself was a misfortune.

No one ever knew who her father was. The officials agreed to keep the matter quiet.

Her mother was not in doubt. Her mother was the celebrated sheman Mona Muggeridge, a woman who had campaigned a hundred times for the lost cause of complete identity of the two genders. She had been a feminist beyond all limits, and when Mona Muggeridge, the one and only *Miss* Muggeridge, announced to the press that she was going to have a baby, that was first-class news.

Mona Muggeridge went further. She announced her firm conviction that fathers should not be identified. She proclaimed that no woman should have consecutive children with the same man, that women should be advised to pick different fathers for their children, so as to diversify and beautify the race. She capped it all by announcing that she, Miss Muggeridge, had selected the perfect father and would inevitably produce the only perfect child.

Miss Muggeridge, a bony, pompous blonde, stated that she would avoid the nonsense of marriage and family names, and that therefore the child, if a boy, would be called John America, and if a girl, Helen America.

Thus it happened that little Helen America was born with the correspondents in the press services waiting outside the delivery room. News-screens flashed the picture of a pretty three-kilogram baby. "It's a girl." "The perfect child." "Who's the dad?"

That was just the beginning. Mona Muggeridge was belligerent. She insisted, even after the baby had been photographed for the thousandth time, that this was the finest child ever born. She pointed to the child's perfections. She demonstrated all the foolish fondness of a doting mother, but felt that she, the great crusader, had discovered this fondness for the first time.

To say that this background was difficult for the child would be an understatement.

Helen America was a wonderful example of raw human material triumphing over its tormentors. By the time she was four years old, she spoke six languages, and was beginning to decipher some of the old Martian texts. At the age of five she was sent to school. Her fellow schoolchildren immediately developed a rhyme:

> *Helen, Helen*
> *Fat and dumb*
> *Doesn't know where*
> *Her daddy's from!*

Helen took all this and perhaps it was an accident of genetics that she grew to become a compact little person—a deadly serious little brunette. Challenged by lessons, haunted by publicity, she became careful and reserved about friendships and desperately lonely in an inner world.

When Helen America was sixteen her mother came to a bad end. Mona Muggeridge eloped with a man she announced to be the perfect husband for the perfect marriage hitherto overlooked by mankind. The perfect husband was a skilled machine polisher. He already had a wife and four children. He drank beer

and his interest in Miss Muggeridge seems to have
been a mixture of good-natured comradeship and a
sensible awareness of her motherly bankroll. The planetary yacht on which they eloped broke the regulations with an off-schedule flight. The bridegroom's
wife and children had alerted the police. The result
was a collision with a robotic barge which left both
bodies identifiable.

At sixteen Helen was already famous, and at seventeen already forgotten, and very much alone.

4

This was the age of sailors. The thousands of photo-
reconnaissance and measuring missiles had begun to
come back with their harvest from the stars. Planet
after planet swam into the ken of mankind. The new
worlds became known as the interstellar search missiles brought back photographs, samples of atmosphere,
measurements of gravity, cloud coverage, chemical
make-up and the like. Of the very numerous missiles
which returned from their two- or three-hundred-year
voyages, three brought back reports of New Earth,
an earth so much like Terra itself that it could be
settled.

The first sailors had gone out almost a hundred
years before. They had started with small sails not
over two thousand miles square. Gradually the size of
the sails increased. The technique of adiabatic packing
and the carrying of passengers in individual pods reduced the damage done to the human cargo. It was
great news when a sailor returned to Earth, a man
born and reared under the light of another star. He
was a man who had spent a month of agony and pain,

bringing a few sleep-frozen settlers, guiding the immense light-pushed sailing craft which had managed the trip through the great interstellar deeps in an objective time-period of forty years.

Mankind got to know the look of a sailor. There was a plantigrade walk to the way he put his body on the ground. There was a sharp, stiff, mechanical swing to his neck. The man was neither young nor old. He had been awake and conscious for forty years, thanks to the drug which made possible a kind of limited awareness. By the time the psychologists interrogated him, first for the proper authorities of the Instrumentality and later for the news releases, it was plain enough that he thought the forty years were about a month. He never volunteered to sail back, because he had actually aged forty years. He was a young man, a young man in his hopes and wishes, but a man who had burnt up a quarter of a human lifetime in a single agonizing experience.

At this time Helen America went to Cambridge. Lady Joan's College was the finest woman's college in the Atlantic world. Cambridge had reconstructed its protohistoric traditions and the neo-British had recaptured that fine edge of engineering which reconnected their traditions with the earliest antiquity.

Naturally enough the language was cosmopolite Earth and not archaic English, but the students were proud to live at a reconstructed university very much like the archaeological evidence showed it to have been before the period of darkness and troubles came upon the Earth. Helen shone a little in this renaissance.

The news-release services watched Helen in the cruelest possible fashion. They revived her name and the story of her mother. Then they forgot her again. She had put in for six professions, and her last choice was "sailor." It happened that she was the first woman to make the application—first because she was the only woman young enough to qualify who had also passed the scientific requirements.

Her picture was beside his on the screens before they ever met each other.

Actually, she was not anything like that at all. She had suffered so much in her childhood from *Helen, Helen, fat and dumb,* that she was competitive only on a coldly professional basis. She hated and loved and missed the tremendous mother whom she had lost, and she resolved so fiercely not to be like her mother that she became an embodied antithesis of Mona.

The mother had been horsy, blonde, big—the kind of woman who is a feminist because she is not very feminine. Helen never thought about her own femininity. She just worried about herself. Her face would have been round if it had been plump, but she was not plump. Black-haired, dark-eyed, broad-bodied but thin, she was a genetic demonstration of her unknown father. Her teachers often feared her. She was a pale, quiet girl, and she always knew her subject.

Her fellow students had joked about her for a few weeks and then most of them had banded together against the indecency of the press. When a news-frame came out with something ridiculous about the long-dead Mona, the whisper went through Lady Joan's:

"Keep Helen away . . . those people are at it again."

"Don't let Helen look at the frames now. She's the best person we have in the non-collateral sciences and we can't have her upset just before the tripos . . ."

THE LADY WHO SAILED *THE SOUL*

They protected her, and it was only by chance that she saw her own face in a news-frame. There was the face of a man beside her. He looked like a little old monkey, she thought. Then she read, "PERFECT GIRL WANTS TO BE SAILOR. SHOULD SAILOR HIMSELF DATE PERFECT GIRL?" Her cheeks burned with helpless, unavoidable embarrassment and rage, but she had grown too expert at being herself to do what she might have done in her teens—hate the man. She knew it wasn't his fault either. It wasn't even the fault of the silly pushing men and women from the news services. It was time, it was custom, it was man himself. But she had only to be herself, if she could ever find out what that really meant.

5

Their dates, when they came, had the properties of nightmares.

A news service sent a woman to tell her she had been awarded a week's holiday in New Madrid.

With the sailor from the stars.

Helen refused.

Then *he* refused too, and he was a little too prompt for her liking. She became curious about him.

Two weeks passed, and in the office of the news service a treasurer brought two slips of paper to the director. They were the vouchers for Helen America and Mr. Grey-no-more to obtain the utmost in preferential luxury at New Madrid. The treasurer said, "These have been issued and registered as gifts with the Instrumentality, sir. Should they be cancelled?" The executive had his fill of stories that day, and he felt humane. On an impulse he commanded the treasurer, "Tell you what. Give those tickets to the young people. No publicity. We'll keep out of it. If they don't want us, they don't have to have us. Push it along. That's all. Go."

The ticket went back out to Helen. She had made the highest record ever reported at the university, and she needed a rest. When the news-service woman gave her the ticket, she said,

"Is this a trick?"

Assured that it was not, she then asked,

"Is that man coming?"

She couldn't say "*the* sailor"—it sounded too much like the way people had always talked about herself—and she honestly didn't remember his other name at the moment.

The woman did not know.

"Do I have to see him?" said Helen.

"Of course not," said the woman. The gift was unconditional.

Helen laughed, almost grimly. "All right, I'll take it and say thanks. But one picturemaker, mind you, just one, and I walk out. Or I may walk out for no reason at all. Is that all right?"

It was.

Four days later Helen was in the pleasure world of New Madrid, and a master of the dances was presenting her to an odd, intense old man whose hair was black.

"Junior scientist Helen America—Sailor of the stars Mr. Grey-no-more."

He looked at them shrewdly and smiled a kindly, experienced smile. He added the empty phrase of his profession,

"I have had the honor and I withdraw."

They were alone together on the edge of the dining room. The sailor looked at her very sharply indeed, and then said:

"Who are you? Are you somebody I have already met? Should I remember you? There are too many people here on Earth. What do we do next? What are we supposed to do? Would you like to sit down?"

Helen said one "Yes" to all those questions and never dreamed that the single *yes* would be articulated by hundreds of great actresses, each one in the actress's own special way, across the centuries to come.

They did sit down.

How the rest of it happened, neither one was ever quite sure.

She had had to quiet him almost as though he were a hurt person in the House of Recovery. She explained the dishes to him and when he still could not choose, she gave the robot selections for him. She warned him, kindly enough, about manners when he forgot the simple ceremonies of eating which everyone knew, such as standing up to unfold the napkin or putting the scraps into the solvent tray and the silverware into the transfer.

At last he relaxed and did not look so old.

Momentarily forgetting the thousand times she had been asked silly questions herself, she asked him,

"Why did *you* become a sailor?"

He stared at her in open-eyed inquiry as though she had spoken to him in an unknown language and expected a reply. Finally he mumbled the answer,

"Are you—you, too—saying that—that I shouldn't have done it?"

Her hand went to her mouth in instinctive apology. "No, no, no. You see, I myself have put in to be a sailor."

He merely looked at her, his young-old eyes open with observativeness. He did not stare, but merely seemed to be trying to understand words, each one of which he could comprehend individually but which in sum amounted to sheer madness. She did not turn away from his look, odd though it was. Once again, she had the chance to note the indescribable peculiarity of this man who had managed enormous sails out in the blind empty black between untwinkling stars. He was young as a boy. The hair which gave him his name was glossy black. His beard must have been removed permanently, because his skin was that of a middle-aged woman—well-kept, pleasant, but showing the unmistakable wrinkles of age and betraying no sign of the normal stubble which the males in her culture preferred to leave on their faces. The skin had age without experience. The muscles had grown older, but they did not show *how* the person had grown.

Helen had learned to be an acute observer of people as her mother took up with one fanatic after another; she knew full well that people carry their secret biographies written in the muscles of their faces, and that a stranger passing on the street tells us (whether he wishes to or not) all his inmost intimacies. If we but look sharply enough, and in the right light, we know whether fear or hope or amusement has tallied the hours of his days, we divine the sources and outcome of his most secret sensuous pleasures, we catch the dim but persistent reflections of those other people who have left the imprints of their personalities on him in turn.

All this was absent from Mr. Grey-no-more: he had age but not the stigmata of age; he had growth without the normal markings of growth; he had lived without living, in a time and world in which most people stayed young while living too much.

He was the uttermost opposite of her mother that Helen had ever seen, and with a pang of undirected apprehension Helen realized that this man meant a great deal to her future life, whether she wished him to or not. She saw in him a young bachelor, prematurely old, a man whose love had been given to emptiness and horror, not to the tangible rewards and disappointments of human life. He had had all space for his mistress, and space had used him harshly. Still young, he was old; already old, he was young.

The mixture was one which she knew that she had never seen before, and which she suspected that no one else had ever seen, either. He had in the beginning of life the sorrow, compassion, and wisdom which most people find only at the end.

It was he who broke the silence. "You did say, didn't you, that you yourself had put in to be a sailor?"

Even to herself, her answer sounded silly and girlish. "I'm the first woman ever to qualify with the necessary scientific subjects while still young enough to pass the physical . . ."

"You must be an unusual girl," said he mildly. Helen realized, with a thrill, a sweet and bitterly real hope that this young-old man from the stars had never heard of the "perfect child" who had been laughed at in the moments of being born, the girl who had all

America for a father, who was famous and unusual and alone so terribly much so that she could not even imagine being ordinary, happy, decent, or simple.

She thought to herself, *It would take a wise freak who sails in from the stars to overlook who I am,* but to him she simply said, "It's no use talking about being 'unusual.' I'm tired of this Earth, and since I don't have to die to leave it, I think I would like to sail to the stars. I've got less to lose than you may think . . ." She started to tell him about Mona Muggeridge but she stopped in time.

The compassionate gray eyes were upon her, and at this point it was he, not she, who was in control of the situation. She looked at the eyes themselves. They had stayed open for forty years, in the blackness near to pitch-darkness of the tiny cabin. The dim dials had shone like blazing suns upon his tired retinas before he was able to turn his eyes away. From time to time he had looked out at the black nothing to see the silhouettes of his dials, almost-blackness against total blackness, as the miles of their sweep sucked up the push of light itself and accelerated him and his frozen cargo at almost immeasurable speeds across an ocean of unfathomable silence. Yet, what he had done, she had asked to do.

The stare of his gray eyes yielded to a smile of his lips. In that young-old face, masculine in structure and feminine in texture, the smile had a connotation of tremendous kindness. She felt singularly much like weeping when she saw him smile in that particular way at her. Was that what people learned between the stars? To care for other people very much indeed and to spring upon them only to reveal love and not devouring to their prey?

THE LADY WHO SAILED *THE SOUL*

In a measured voice he said, "I believe you. You're the first one that I have believed. All these people have said that they wanted to be sailors too, even when they looked at me. They could not know what it means, but they said it anyhow, and I hated them for saying it. You, though—you're different. Perhaps you will sail among the stars, but I hope that you will not."

As though waking from a dream, he looked around the luxurious room, with the gilt-and-enamel robot-waiters standing aside with negligent elegance. They were designed to be always present and never obtrusive: this was a difficult esthetic effect to achieve, but their designer had achieved it.

The rest of the evening moved with the inevitability of good music. He went with her to the forever-lonely beach which the architects of New Madrid had built beside the hotel. They talked a little, they looked at each other, and they made love with an affirmative certainty which seemed outside themselves. He was very tender, and he did not realize that in a genitally sophisticated society, he was the first lover she had ever wanted or had ever had. (How could the daughter of Mona Muggeridge want a lover or a mate or a child?)

On the next afternoon, she exercised the freedom of her times and asked him to marry her. They had gone back to their private beach, which, through miracles of ultra-fine mini-weather adjustments, brought a Polynesian afternoon to the high chilly plateau of central Spain.

She asked him, *she* did, to marry her, and he refused, as tenderly and as kindly as a man of sixty-five can refuse a girl of eighteen. She did not press him; they continued the bittersweet love affair.

They sat on the artificial sand of the artificial beach and dabbled their toes in the man-warmed water of the ocean. Then they lay down against an artificial sand dune which hid New Madrid from view.

"Tell me," Helen said, "can I ask again, why did you become a sailor?"

"Not so easily answered," he said. "Adventure, maybe. That, at least in part. And I wanted to see Earth. Couldn't afford to come in a pod. Now—well, I've enough to keep me the rest of my life. I can go back to New Earth as a passenger in a month instead of forty years—be frozen in no more time than the wink of an eye, put in my adiabatic pod, linked in to the next sailing ship, and wake up home again while some other fool does the sailing."

Helen nodded. She did not bother to tell him that she knew all this. She had been investigating sailing ships since meeting the sailor.

"Out where you sail among the stars," she said, "can you tell me—can you possibly tell me anything of what it's like out there?"

His face looked inward on his soul and afterward his voice came as from an immense distance.

"There are moments—or is it weeks—you can't really tell in the sail ship—when it seems—worthwhile. You feel . . . your nerve endings reach out until they touch the stars. You feel enormous, somehow." Gradually he came back to her. "It's trite to say, of course, but you're never the same afterward. I don't mean just the obvious physical thing, but—you find yourself—or maybe you lose yourself. That's why," he continued, gesturing toward New Madrid out of sight behind the sand dune, "I can't stand this. New Earth, well, it's like Earth must have been in the old days, I guess. There's something fresh about it. Here . . ."

"I know," said Helen America, and she did. The slightly decadent, slightly corrupt, too comfortable air of Earth must have had a stifling effect on the man from beyond the stars.

"There," he said, "you won't believe this, but sometimes the ocean's too cold to swim in. We have music that doesn't come from machines, and pleasures that come from inside our own bodies without being put there. I have to get back to New Earth."

Helen said nothing for a little while, concentrating on stilling the pain in her heart.

"I . . . I . . ." she began.

"I know," he said fiercely, almost savagely turning on her. "But I can't take you. I can't! You're too young, you've got a life to live and I've thrown away a quarter of mine. No, that's not right. I didn't throw it away. I wouldn't trade it back because it's given me something inside I never had before. And it's given me you."

"But if—" she started again to argue.

"No. Don't spoil it. I'm going next week to be frozen in my pod to wait for the next sail ship. I can't stand much more of this, and I might weaken. That would be a terrible mistake. But we have this time together now, and we have our separate lifetimes to remember in. Don't think of anything else. There's nothing, nothing we can do."

Helen did not tell him—then or ever—of the child she had started to hope for, the child they would now never have. Oh, she could have used the child. She could have tied him to her, for he was an honorable

man and would have married her had she told him.
But Helen's love, even then in her youth, was such
that she could not use this means. She wanted him to
come to her of his own free will, marrying her because
he could not live without her. To that marriage their
child would have been an additional blessing.

There was the other alternative, of course. She could
have borne the child without naming the father. But
she was no Mona Muggeridge. She knew too well the
terrors and insecurity and loneliness of being Helen
America ever to be responsible for the creation of
another. And for the course she had laid out there was
no place for a child. So she did the only thing she
could. At the end of their time in New Madrid, she let
him say a real goodbye. Wordless and without tears,
she left. Then she went up to an arctic city, a pleasure
city where such things are well-known and amidst
shame, worry and a driving sense of regret she ap-
pealed to a confidential medical service which elimi-
nated the unborn child. Then she went back to
Cambridge and confirmed her place as the first woman
to sail a ship to the stars.

6

The presiding lord of the Instrumentality at that
time was a man named Wait. Wait was not cruel but
he was never noted for tenderness of spirit or for a
high regard for the adventuresome proclivities of young
people. His aide said to him, "This girl wants to sail a
ship to New Earth. Are you going to let her?"

"Why not?" said Wait. "A person is a person. She
is well-bred, well-educated. If she fails, we will find

out something eighty years from now when the ship comes back. If she succeeds, it will shut up some of these women who have been complaining." The lord leaned over his desk: "If she qualifies, and if she goes, though, don't give her any convicts. Convicts are too good and too valuable as settlers to be sent along on a fool trip like that. You can send her on something of a gamble. Give her all religious fanatics. We have more than enough. Don't you have twenty or thirty thousand who are waiting?"

He said, "Yes, sir, twenty-six thousand two hundred. Not counting recent additions."

"Very well," said the lord of the Instrumentality. "Give her the whole lot of them and give her that new ship. Have we named it?"

"No, sir," said the aide.

"Name it then."

The aide looked blank.

A contemptuous wise smile crossed the face of the senior bureaucrat. He said, "Take that ship now and name it. Name it *The Soul* and let *The Soul* fly to the stars. And let Helen America be an angel if she wants to. Poor thing, she has not got much of a life to live on this Earth, not the way she was born, and the way she was brought up. And it's no use to try and reform her, to transform her personality, when it's a lively, rich personality. It does not do any good. We don't have to punish her for being herself. Let her go. Let her have it."

Wait sat up and stared at his aide and then repeated very firmly:

"Let her have it, *only if she qualifies*."

Helen America did qualify.

The doctors and the experts tried to warn her against it.

One technician said: "Don't you realize what this is going to mean? Forty years will pour out of your life in a single month. You leave here a girl. You will get there a woman of sixty. Well, you will probably still have a hundred years to live after that. And it's painful. You will have all these people, thousands and thousands of them. You will have some Earth cargo. There will be about thirty thousand pods strung on sixteen lines behind you. Then you will have the control cabin to live in. We will give you as many robots as you need, probably a dozen. You will have a mainsail and a foresail and you will have to keep the two of them."

"I know. I have read the book," said Helen America. "And I sail the ship with light, and if the infrared touches that sail—I go. If I get radio interference, I pull the sails in. And if the sails fail, I wait as long as I live."

The technician looked a little cross. "There is no call for you to get tragic about it. Tragedy is easy enough to contrive. And if you want to be tragic, you can be tragic without destroying thirty thousand other people or without wasting a large amount of Earth property. You can drown in water right here, or jump into a volcano like the Japanese in the old books. Tragedy is not the hard part. The hard part is when you don't quite succeed and you have to keep on fighting. When you must keep going on and on and on in the face of really hopeless odds, of real temptations to despair.

"Now this is the way that the foresail works. That sail will be twenty thousand miles at the wide part. It tapers down and the total length will be just under eighty thousand miles. It will be retracted or extended by small servo-robots. The servo-robots are radio-controlled. You had better use your radio sparingly, because after all these batteries, even though they are atomic, have to last forty years. They have got to keep you alive."

"Yes, sir," said Helen America very contritely.

"You've got to remember what your job is. You're going because you are cheap. You are going because a sailor takes a lot less weight than a machine. There is no all-purpose computer built that weighs as little as a hun-dred and fifty pounds. You do. You go simply because you are expendable. Anyone that goes out to the stars takes one chance in three of never getting there. But you are not going because you are a leader, you are going because you are young. You have a life to give and a life to spare. Because your nerves are good. You understand that?"

"Yes, sir, I knew that."

"Furthermore, you are going because you'll make the trip in forty years. If we sent automatic devices and have them manage the sails, they would get there—possibly. But it would take them from a hundred years to a hundred and twenty or more, and by that time the adiabatic pods would have spoiled, most of the human cargo would not be fit for revival and the leakage of heat, no matter how we face it, would be enough to ruin the entire expedition. So remember that the tragedy and the trouble you face is mostly work. Work, and that's all it is. That is your big job."

Helen smiled. She was a short girl with rich dark hair, brown eyes, and very pronounced eyebrows, but when Helen smiled she was almost a child again, and a rather charming one. She said: "My job is work. I understand that, sir."

8

In the preparation area, the make-ready was fast but not hurried. Twice the technicians urged her to take a holiday before she reported for final training. She did not accept their advice. She wanted to go forth; she knew that they knew she wanted to leave Earth forever, and she also knew they knew she was not merely her mother's daughter. She was trying, somehow, to be herself. She knew the world did not believe, but the world did not matter.

The third time they suggested a vacation, the suggestion was mandatory. She had a gloomy two months which she ended up enjoying a little bit on the wonderful islands of the Hesperides, islands which were raised when the weight of the Earthports caused a new group of small archipelagos to form below Bermuda.

She reported back, fit, healthy, and ready to go.

The senior medical officer was very blunt.

"Do you really know what we are going to do to you? We are going to make you live forty years out of your life in one month."

She nodded, white of face, and he went on, "Now to give you those forty years we've got to slow down your bodily processes. After all the sheer biological task of breathing forty years' worth of air in one month involves a factor of about five hundred to one. No lungs could stand it. Your body must circulate water. It must take in food. Most of this is going to be protein. There will be some kind of a hydrate. You'll need vitamins.

"Now, what we are going to do is to slow the brain down, very much indeed, so that the brain will be working at about that five-hundred-to-one ratio. We don't want you incapable of working. Somebody has got to manage the sails.

"Therefore, if you hesitate or you start to think, a thought or two is going to take several weeks. Meanwhile your body can be slowed down some. But the different parts can't be slowed down at the same rate. Water, for example, we brought down to about eighty to one. Food, to about three hundred to one.

"You won't have time to drink forty years' worth of water. We circulate it, get it through, purify it, and get it back in your system, unless you break your link-up.

"So what you face is a month of being absolutely wide awake, on an operating table and *being operated on without anesthetic,* while doing some of the hardest work that mankind has ever found.

"You'll have to take observations, you'll have to watch your lines with the pods of people and cargo behind you, you'll have to adjust the sails. If there is anybody surviving at destination point, they will come out and meet you.

"At least that happens most of the times.

"I am not going to assure you you will get the ship in. If they don't meet you, take an orbit beyond the farthest planet and either let yourself die or try to save yourself. You can't get thirty thousand people down on a planet singlehandedly.

"Meanwhile, though, you've got a real job. We are going to have to build these controls right into your body. We'll start by putting valves in your chest arteries. Then we go on, catheterizing your water. We are going to make an artificial colostomy that will go forward here just in front of your hip joint. Your water intake has a certain psychological value so that about one five-hundredth of your water we are going to leave you to drink out of a cup. The rest of it is going to go directly into your bloodstream. Again about a tenth of your food will go that way. You understand that?"

"You mean," said Helen, "I eat one-tenth, and the rest goes in intravenously?"

"That's right," said the medical technician. "We will pump it into you. The concentrates are there. The reconstitutor is there. Now these lines have a double connection. One set of connections runs into the maintenance machine. That will become the logistic support for your body. And these lines are the umbilical cord for a human being alone among the stars. They are your life.

"And now if they should break or if you should fall, you might faint for a year or two. If that happens, your local system takes over: that's the pack on your back.

"On Earth, it weighs as much as you do. You have already been drilled with the model pack. You know how easy it is to handle in space. That'll keep you going for a subjective period of about two hours. No one has ever worked out a clock yet that would match the human mind, so instead of giving you a clock we are giving you an odometer attached to your own pulse and we mark it off in grades. If you watch it in term of tens of thousands of pulse beats, you may get some information out of it.

"I don't know what kind of information, but you may find it helpful somehow." He looked at her sharply and then turned back to his tools, picking up a shining needle with a disk on the end.

"Now, let's get back to this. We are going to have to get right into your mind. That's chemical too."

Helen interrupted. "You said you were not going to operate on my head."

"Only the needle. That's the only way we can get to the mind. Slow it down enough so that you will have this subjective mind operating at a rate that will make the forty years pass in a month." He smiled grimly, but the grimness changed to momentary tenderness as he took in her brave obstinate stance, her girlish, admirable, pitiable determination.

"I won't argue it," she said. "This is as bad as a marriage and the stars are my bridegroom." The image of the sailor went across her mind, but she said nothing of him.

The technician went on. "Now, we have already built in psychotic elements. You can't even expect to remain sane. So you'd better not worry about it. You'll have to be insane to manage the sails and to survive utterly alone and be out there even a month. And the trouble is in that month you are going to know it's really forty years. There is not a mirror in the place but you'll probably find shiny surfaces to look at yourself.

"You won't look so good. You will see yourself aging, every time you slow down to look. I don't know what the problem is going to be on that score. It's been bad enough on men.

"Your hair problem is going to be easier than men's. The sailors we sent out, we simply had to kill all the hair roots. Otherwise the men would have been swamped in their own beards. And a tremendous amount of the nutrient would be wasted if it went into raising of hair on the face which no machine in the world could cut off fast enough to keep a man working. I think what we will do is inhibit hair on the top of your head. Whether it comes out in the same color or not is something you will find for yourself later. Did you ever meet the sailor that came in?"

The doctor knew she had met him. He did not know that it was the sailor from beyond the stars who called her. Helen managed to remain composed as she smiled at him to say: "Yes, you gave him new hair. Your technician planted a new scalp on his head, remember. Somebody on your staff did. The hair came out black and he got the nickname of Mr. Grey-no-more."

"If you are ready next Tuesday, we'll be ready too. Do you think you can make it by then, my lady?"

Helen felt odd seeing this old, serious man refer to her as "lady," but she knew he was paying respect to a profession and not just to an individual.

"Tuesday is time enough." She felt complimented that he was an old-fashioned enough person to know the ancient names of the days of the week and to use them. That was a sign that he had not only learned the essentials at the University but that he had picked up the elegant inconsequentialities as well.

Two weeks later was twenty-one years later by the chronometers in the cabin. Helen turned for the ten-thousand-times-ten-thousandth time to scan the sails.

Her back ached with a violent throb.

She could feel the steady roar of her heart like a fast vibrator as it ticked against the time-span of her awareness. She could look down at the meter on her wrist and see the hands on the watchlike dials indicate tens of thousands of pulses very slowly.

She heard the steady whistle of air in her throat as her lungs seemed shuddering with sheer speed.

And she felt the throbbing pain of a large tube feeding an immense quantity of mushy water directly into the artery of her neck.

On her abdomen, she felt as if someone had built a fire. The evacuation tube operated automatically but it burnt as if a coal had been held to her skin and a catheter, which connected her bladder to another tube, stung as savagely as the prod of a scalding-hot needle. Her head ached and her vision blurred.

But she could still see the instruments and she still could watch the sails. Now and then she could glimpse, faint as a tracery of dust, the immense skein of people and cargo that lay behind them.

She could not sit down. It hurt too much.

The only way that she could be comfortable for resting was to lean against the instrument panel, her lower ribs against the panel, her tired forehead against the meters.

Once she rested that way and realized that it was two and a half months before she got up. She knew that rest had no meaning and she could see her face moving, a distorted image of her own face growing old in the reflections from the glass face of the "apparent weight" dial. She could look at her arms with blurring vision, note the skin tightening, loosening and tightening again, as changes in temperatures affected it.

She looked out one more time at the sails and decided to take in the foresail. Wearily she dragged herself over the control panel with a servo-robot. She selected the right control and opened it for a week or so. She waited there, her heart buzzing, her throat whistling air, her fingernails breaking off gently as they grew. Finally she checked to see if it really had been the right one, pushed again, and nothing happened.

She pushed a third time. There was no response.

Now she went back to the master panel, re-read, checked the light direction, found a certain amount of infrared pressure which she should have been picking up. The sails had very gradually risen to something not far from the speed of light itself because they moved fast with the one side dulled; the pods behind, sealed against time and eternity, swam obediently in an almost perfect weightlessness.

She scanned; her reading had been correct.

The sail *was* wrong.

She went back to the emergency panel and pressed. Nothing happened.

She broke out a repair robot and sent it out to effect repairs, punching the papers as rapidly as she could to give instructions. The robot went out and an instant (three days) later it replied. The panel on the repair robot rang forth, "Does not conform."

THE LADY WHO SAILED *THE SOUL*

She sent a second repair robot. That had no effect either.

She sent a third, the last. Three bright lights, "Does not conform," stared at her. She moved the servo-robots to the other side of the sails and pulled hard.

The sail was still not at the right angle.

She stood there wearied and lost in space, and she prayed: "Not for me, God, I am running away from a life that I did not want. But for this ship's souls and for the poor foolish people that I am taking who are brave enough to want to worship their own way and need the light of another star, I ask you, God, help me now." She thought she had prayed very fervently and she hoped that she would get an answer to her prayer.

It did not work out that way. She was bewildered, alone.

There was no sun. There was nothing, except the tiny cabin and herself more alone than any woman had ever been before. She sensed the thrill and ripple of her muscles as they went through days of adjustment while her mind noticed only the matter of minutes. She leaned forward, forced herself not to relax and finally she remembered that one of the official busy-bodies had included a weapon.

What she would use a weapon for she did not know.

It pointed. It had a range of two hundred thousand miles. The target could be selected automatically.

She got down on her knees trailing the abdominal tube and the feeding tube and the catheter tubes and the helmet wires, each one running back to the panel. She crawled underneath the panel for the servo-robots and she pulled out a written manual. She finally found the right frequency for the weapon's controls. She set the weapon up and went to the window.

At the last moment she thought, "Perhaps the fools are going to make me shoot the window out. It ought to have been designed to shoot through the window without hurting it. That's the way they should have done it."

She wondered about the matter for a week or two.

Just before she fired it she turned and there, next to her, stood her sailor, the sailor from the stars, Mr. Grey-no-more. He said: "It won't work that way."

He stood clear and handsome, the way she had seen him in New Madrid. He had no tubes, he did not tremble, she could see the normal rise and fall of his chest as he took one breath every hour or so. One part of her mind knew that he was a hallucination. Another part of her mind believed that he was real. She was mad and she was very happy to be mad at this time and she let the hallucination give her advice. She reset the gun so that it would fire through the cabin wall and it fired a low charge at the repair mechanism out beyond the distorted and immovable sail.

The low charge did the trick. The interference had been something beyond all technical anticipation. The weapon had cleaned out the forever-unidentifiable obstruction, leaving the servo-robots free to attack their tasks like a tribe of maddened ants. They worked again. They had had defenses built in against the minor impediments of space. All of them scurried and skipped about.

With a sense of bewilderment close to religion, she

perceived the wind of starlight blowing against the immense sails. The sails snapped into position. She got a momentary touch of gravity as she sensed a little weight. *The Soul* was back on her course.

10

"It's a girl," they said to him on New Earth. "It's a girl. She must have been eighteen herself."

Mr. Grey-no-more did not believe it.

But he went to the hospital and there in the hospital he saw Helen America.

"Here I am, sailor," said she. "I sailed too." Her face was white as chalk, her expression was that of a girl of about twenty. Her body was that of a well-preserved woman of sixty.

As for him, he had not changed again, since he had returned home inside a pod.

He looked at her. His eyes narrowed and then in a sudden reversal of roles, it was he who was kneeling beside her bed and covering her hands with his tears.

Half-coherently, he babbled at her: "I ran away from you because I loved you so. I came back here where you would never follow, or if you did follow, you'd still be a young woman, and I'd still be too old. But you have sailed *The Soul* in here and you wanted me."

The nurse of New Earth did not know about the rules which should be applied to the sailors from the stars. Very quietly she went out of the room, smiling in tenderness and human pity at the love which she had seen. But she was a practical woman and she had a sense of her own advancement. She called a friend of hers at the news service and said: "I think I have got the biggest romance in history. If you get here soon enough you can get the first telling of the story of Helen America and Mr. Grey-no-more. They just met like that. I guess they'd seen each other somewhere. They just met like that and fell in love."

The nurse did not know that they had forsworn a love on Earth. The nurse did not know that Helen America had made a lonely trip with an icy purpose and the nurse did not know that the crazy image of Mr. Grey-no-more, the sailor himself, had stood beside Helen twenty years out from nothing-at-all in the depth and blackness of space between the stars.

11

The little girl had grown up, had married, and now had a little girl of her own. The mother was unchanged, but the spieltier was very, very old. It had outlived all its marvelous tricks of adaptability, and for some years had stayed frozen in the role of a yellow-haired, blue-eyed girl doll. Out of sentimental sense of the fitness of things, she had dressed the spieltier in a bright blue jumper with matching panties. The little animal crept softly across the floor on its tiny human hands, using its knees for hind feet. The mock-human face looked up blindly and squeaked for milk.

The young mother said, "Mom, you ought to get rid of that thing. It's all used up and it looks horrible with your nice period furniture."

"I thought you loved it," said the older woman.

"Of course," said the daughter. "It was cute, when I was a child. But I'm not a child any more, and it doesn't even work."

THE LADY WHO SAILED *THE SOUL*

The spieltier had struggled to its feet and clutched its mistress' ankle. The older woman took it away gently, and put down a saucer of milk and a cup the size of a thimble. The spieltier tried to curtsey, as it had been motivated to do at the beginning, slipped, fell, and whimpered. The mother righted it and the little old animal-toy began dipping milk with its thimble and sucking the milk into its tiny toothless old mouth.

"You remember, Mom—" said the younger woman and stopped.

"Remember what, dear?"

"You told me about Helen America and Mr. Grey-no-more when that was brand new."

"Yes, darling, maybe I did."

"You didn't tell me everything," said the younger woman accusingly.

"Of course not. You were a child."

"But it was awful. Those messy people, and the horrible way sailors live. I don't see how you idealized it and called it a romance—"

"But it was. It is," insisted the other.

"Romance, my foot," said the daughter. "It's as bad as you and the worn-out spieltier." She pointed at the tiny, living, aged doll who had fallen asleep beside its milk. "I think it's horrible. You ought to get rid of it. And the world ought to get rid of sailors."

"Don't be harsh, darling," said the mother.

"Don't be a sentimental old slob," said the daughter.

"Perhaps we are," said the mother with a loving sort of laugh. Unobtrusively she put the sleeping spieltier on a padded chair where it would not be stepped on or hurt.

12

Outsiders never knew the real end of the story.

More than a century after their wedding, Helen lay dying: she was dying happily, because her beloved sailor was beside her. She believed that if they could conquer space, they might conquer death as well.

Her loving, happy, weary dying mind blurred over and she picked up an argument they hadn't touched upon for decades.

"You did *so* come to *The Soul*," she said. "You did so stand beside me when I was lost and did not know how to handle the weapon."

"If I came then, darling, I'll come again, wherever you are. You're my darling, my heart, my own true love. You're my bravest of ladies, my boldest of people. You're my own. You sailed for me. You're my lady who sailed *The Soul*."

His voice broke, but his features stayed calm. He had never before seen anyone die so confident and so happy.

I REMEMBER BABYLON

BY ARTHUR C. CLARKE (1917–   )

PLAYBOY
MAY

"I Remember Babylon" is one of several science fiction stories in this volume that first appeared in the "men's magazines" of the day, and proves that these publications didn't always stress sexual content over ideas.

Although Arthur C. Clarke doesn't really need an introduction, it might be time to summarize his major awards in the field—Nebulas for "A Meeting With Medusa" in 1972; Rendezvous With Rama *in 1973; and* The Fountains Of Paradise *in 1979. Hugos for "The Star" in 1956;* Rendezvous With Rama *in 1974; and* The Fountains Of Paradise *in 1980. And of course, the Grand Master award of the Science Fiction Writers of America in 1985.*

And he's still going strong. (MHG)

This story is not entirely fictitious. Arthur Clarke did dream up communication satellites in 1945 and did publish an article on it. What's more, he had every right to assume that this would increase the flow of informa-

tion over the television sets. However, this story was printed in 1960 before the first communication satellites were really in operation and science fiction predictions can be wrong. Arthur was wrong this time, thank goodness. At least, so far. (IA)

My name is Arthur C. Clarke, and I wish I had no connection with the whole sordid business, but as the moral—repeat, moral—integrity of the United States is involved, I must first establish my credentials. Only thus will you understand how, with the aid of the late Dr. Alfred Kinsey, I have unwittingly triggered an avalanche that may sweep away much of Western civilization.

Back in 1945, while a radar officer in the Royal Air Force, I had the only original idea of my life. Twelve years before the first Sputnik started beeping, it occurred to me that an artificial satellite would be a wonderful place for a television transmitter, since a station several thousand miles in altitude could broadcast to half the globe. I wrote up the idea the week after Hiroshima, proposing a network of relay satellites 22,000 miles above the equator; at this height, they'd take exactly one day to complete a revolution and so would remain fixed over the same spot on the Earth.

The piece appeared in the October 1945 issue of *Wireless World*; not expecting that celestial mechanics would be commercialized in my lifetime, I made no attempt to patent the idea and doubt if I could have done so, anyway. (If I'm wrong, I'd prefer not to know.) But I kept plugging it in my books, and today the idea of communications satellites is so commonplace that no one knows its origin.

I REMEMBER BABYLON

I did make a plaintive attempt to put the record straight when approached by the House of Representatives Committee on Astronautics and Space Exploration; you'll find my evidence on page 32 of its report, *The Next Ten Years in Space.* And as you'll see in a moment, my concluding words had an irony I never appreciated at the time: "Living as I do in the Far East, I am constantly reminded of the struggle between the Western world and the U.S.S.R. for the uncommitted millions of Asia. . . . When line-of-sight TV transmissions become possible from satellites directly overhead, the propaganda effect may be decisive. . . ."

I still stand by those words, but there were angles I hadn't thought of—and which, unfortunately, other people have.

It all began during one of those official receptions which are such a feature of social life in Eastern capitals. They're even more common in the West, of course, but in Colombo there's little competing entertainment. At least once a week, if you are anybody, you get an invitation to cocktails at an embassy or legation, the British Council, the U.S. Operations Mission, L'Alliance Française or one of the countless alphabetical agencies the UN has begotten.

At first, being more at home beneath the Indian Ocean than in diplomatic circles, my partner and I were nobodies and were left alone. But after Mike godfathered Dave Brubeck's tour of Ceylon, people started to take notice of us—still more so when he married one of the island's best-known beauties. So now our consumption of cocktails and canapés is limited chiefly by reluctance to abandon our comfortable sarongs for such Western absurdities as trousers, dinner jackets and ties.

It was the first time we'd been to the Soviet embassy, which was throwing a party for a group of Russian oceanographers who'd just come into port. Beneath the inevitable paintings of Lenin and Stalin, a couple of hundred guests of all colors, religions and languages were milling around, chatting with friends or single-mindedly demolishing the vodka and caviar. I'd been separated from Mike and Elizabeth, but could see them at the other side of the room. Mike was doing his "There was I at fifty fathoms" bit to a fascinated audience, while Elizabeth watched him quizzically, and more people watched Elizabeth.

Ever since I lost an eardrum while pearl diving on the Great Barrier Reef, I've been at a considerable disadvantage at functions of this kind; the surface noise is about six db too much for me to cope with. And this is no small handicap when being introduced to people with names like Dharmasirawardene, Tissaverasinghe, Goonetilleke and Jayawickrame. When I'm not raiding the buffet, therefore, I usually look for a pool of relative quiet where there's a chance of following more than 50 percent of any conversation in which I may get involved. I was standing in the acoustic shadow of a large ornamental pillar, surveying the scene in my detached, or Somerset Maugham, manner, when I noticed that someone was looking at me with that "Haven't we met before?" expression.

I'll describe him with some care, because there must be many people who can identify him. He was in the mid-30s, and I guessed he was American; he had that well-scrubbed, crew-cut, man-about-Rockefeller-Center look that used to be a hallmark until the younger Russian diplomats and technical advisors started imitating it so successfully. He was about six feet in height, with shrewd brown eyes and black hair, prematurely gray at the sides. Though I was fairly certain we'd never met before, his face reminded me of someone. It took me a couple of days to work it out: remember John Garfield? That's who it was, as near as makes no difference.

When a stranger catches my eye at a party, my standard operating procedure goes into action automatically. If he seems a pleasant enough person but I don't feel like introductions at the moment, I give him the Neutral Scan, letting my eyes sweep past him without a flicker of recognition, yet without positive unfriendliness. If he looks a creep, he receives the coup d'oeil, which consists of a long, disbelieving stare followed by an unhurried view of the back of my neck; in extreme cases, an expression of revulsion may be switched on for a few milliseconds. The message usually gets across.

But this character seemed interesting, and I was getting bored; so I gave him the Affable Nod. A few minutes later he drifted through the crowd and I aimed my good ear toward him.

"Hello," he said (yes, he *was* American), "my name's Gene Hartford. I'm sure we've met somewhere."

"Quite likely," I answered. "I've spent a good deal of time in the States. I'm Arthur Clarke."

Usually that produces a blank stare, but sometimes it doesn't. I could almost see the IBM cards flickering behind those hard brown eyes and was flattered by the brevity of his access time.

"The science writer?"

"Correct."

"Well, this is fantastic." He seemed genuinely astonished. "Now I know where I've seen you. I was in the studio once when you were on the Dave Garroway show."

(This lead may be worth following up, though I doubt it; and I'm sure that "Gene Hartford" was phony—it was too smoothly synthetic.)

"So you're in TV?" I said. "What are you doing here—collecting material or just on vacation?"

He gave me the frank, friendly smile of a man who has plenty to hide.

"Oh, I'm keeping my eyes open. But this really is amazing; I read your *Exploration of Space* when it came out back in, ah——"

"Nineteen fifty-two; the Book-of-the-Month Club's never been quite the same since."

All this time I had been sizing him up, and though there was something about him I didn't like, I was unable to pin it down. In any case, I was prepared to make substantial allowances for someone who had read my books and was also in TV; Mike and I are always on the lookout for markets for our underwater movies. But that, to put it mildly, was not Hartford's line of business.

"Look," he said eagerly, "I've a big network deal cooking that will interest you—in fact, *you* helped to give me the idea."

This sounded promising, and my coefficient of cupidity jumped several points.

"I'm glad to hear it. What's the general theme?"

"I can't talk about it here, but could we meet at my hotel, around three tomorrow?"

"Let me check my diary; yes, that's OK."

There are only two hotels in Colombo patronized by Americans, and I guessed right first time. He was at the Mount Lavinia, and though you may not know it, you've seen the place where we had our private chat. Around the middle of *The Bridge on the River Kwai*, there's a brief scene at a military hospital, where Jack Hawkins meets a nurse and asks her where he can find Bill Holden. We have a soft spot for this episode, because Mike was one of the convalescent naval officers in the background. If you look smartly, you'll see him on the extreme right, beard in full profile, signing Sam Spiegel's name to his sixth round of bar chits. As the picture turned out, Sam could afford it.

It was here, on this diminutive plateau high above the miles of palm-fringed beach, that Gene Hartford started to unload—and my simple hopes of financial advantage started to evaporate. What his exact motives were, if indeed he knew them himself, I'm still uncertain. Surprise at meeting me and a twisted feeling of gratitude (which I would gladly have done without) undoubtedly played a part, and for all his air of confidence he must have been a bitter, lonely man who desperately needed approval and friendship.

He got neither from me. I have always had a sneaking sympathy for Benedict Arnold, as must anyone who knows the full facts of the case. But Arnold merely betrayed his country; no one before Hartford ever tried to seduce it.

What dissolved my dream of dollars was the news that Hartford's connection with American TV had been severed, somewhat violently, in the early Fifties. It was clear that he'd been bounced out of Madison Avenue for Party-lining, and it was equally clear that his was one case where no grave injustice had been done. Though he talked with a certain controlled fury of his fight against asinine censorship, and wept for a brilliant—but unnamed—cultural series he'd had kicked off the air, by this time I was beginning to smell so many rats that my replies were distinctly guarded. Yet, as my pecuniary interest in Mr. Hartford diminished, so my personal curiosity increased. Who *was* behind him? Surely not the BBC. . . .

He got around to it at last, when he'd worked the self-pity out of his system.

"I've some news that will make you sit up," he said smugly. "The American networks are soon going to have some real competition. And it will be done just the way you predicted; the people who sent a TV transmitter behind the Moon can put a much bigger one in orbit round the Earth."

"Good for them," I said cautiously. "I'm all in favor of healthy competition. When's the launching date?"

"Any moment now. The first transmitter will be parked due south of New Orleans—on the equator, of course. That puts it way out in the open Pacific; it won't be over anyone's territory, so there'll be no political complications on that score. Yet it will be sitting up there in the sky in full view of everybody from Seattle to Key West. Think of it—the only TV station the whole United States can tune into! Yes, even Hawaii! There won't be any way of jamming it; for the first time, there'll be a clear channel into every American home. And J. Edgar's boy scouts can't do a thing to block it."

So that's your little racket, I thought; at least you're being frank. Long ago I learned not to argue with Marxists and Flat-Earthers, but if Hartford was telling the truth, I wanted to pump him for all he was worth.

"Before you get too enthusiastic," I said, "there are a few points you may have overlooked."

"Such as?"

"This will work both ways. Everyone knows that the air force, NASA, Bell Labs, I.T.&T. and a few dozen other agencies are working on the same project. Whatever Russia does to the States in the propaganda line, she'll get back with compound interest."

Hartford grinned mirthlessly.

"Really, Clarke!" he said (I was glad he hadn't first-named me). "I'm a little disappointed. Surely you know that the States is years behind in pay-load capacity! And do you imagine that the old T.3 is Russia's last word?"

It was at this moment that I began to take him very seriously. He was perfectly right. The T.3 could inject at least five times the pay load of any American missile into that critical 22,000-mile orbit—the only one that would deliver a satellite apparently fixed above the Earth. And by the time the U.S. could match that performance, heaven knows where the Russians would be. Yes, heaven certainly *would* know. . . .

"All right," I conceded. "But why should fifty million American homes start switching channels just as soon as they can tune into Moscow? I admire the Russian people, but their entertainment is worse than their politics. After the Bolshoi, what have you? And for me, a little ballet goes a long, long way."

Once again I was treated to that peculiarly humorless smile. Hartford had been saving up his Sunday punch, and now he let me have it.

"You were the one who brought in the Russians," he said. "They're involved, sure—but only as contractors. The independent agency I'm working for is hiring their services."

"That," I remarked dryly, "must be some agency."

"It is, just about the biggest. Even though the States tries to pretend it doesn't exist."

"Oh," I said rather stupidly, "so *that's* your sponsor."

I'd heard those rumors that the U.S.S.R. was going to launch satellites for the Chinese; now it began to look as if the rumors fell far short of the truth. But how far short, I'd still no conception.

"You are so right," continued Hartford, obviously enjoying himself, "about Russian entertainment. After the initial novelty, the Nielsen rating would drop to zero. But not with the programs I'm planning. My job is to find material that will put everyone else out of business when it goes on the air. You think it can't be done? Finish that drink and come up to my room. I've a highbrow movie about ecclesiastical art that I'd like to show you."

Well, he wasn't crazy, though for a few minutes I wondered. I could think of few titles more carefully calculated to make the viewer switch channels than the one that flashed on the screen: ASPECTS OF 13TH CENTURY TANTRIC SCULPTURE.

"Don't be alarmed," Hartford chuckled above the whir of the projector. "That title saves me having trouble with inquisitive customs inspectors. It's perfectly accurate, but we'll change it to something with a bigger box-office appeal when the time comes."

A couple of hundred feet later, after some innocuous architectural long shots, I saw what he meant. . . .

You may know that there are certain temples in India covered with superbly executed carvings of a kind that we in the West scarcely associate with religion. To say that they are frank is a laughable understatement; they leave nothing to the imagination—*any* imagination. Yet at the same time they are genuine works of art. And so was Hartford's movie.

It had been shot, in case you're interested, at the Temple of the Sun, Konarak. "An awkward place to reach," Hartford told me, "but decidedly worth the trouble." I've since looked it up; it's on the Orissa coast, about 25 miles northeast of Puri. The reference books are pretty mealymouthed; some apologize for the "obvious" impossibility of providing illustrations, but Percy Brown's *Indian Architecture* minces no words. The carvings, it says primly, are of "a shamelessly erotic character that have no parallel in any known building." A sweeping claim, but I can believe it after seeing that movie.

Camerawork and editing were brilliant, the ancient stones coming to life beneath the roving lens. There were breath-taking time-lapse shots as the rising sun chased the shadows from bodies intertwined in ecstasy; sudden startling close-ups of scenes which at first the mind refused to recognize; soft-focus studies of stone shaped by a master's hand in all the fantasies and aberrations of love; restless zooms and pans whose meaning eluded the eye until they froze into patterns of timeless desire, eternal fulfillment. The music—mostly percussion, with a thin, high thread of sound from some stringed instrument that I could not identify— perfectly fitted the tempo of the cutting. At one moment it would be languorously slow, like the opening bars of Debussy's *L'Après-midi*; then the drums would swiftly work themselves up to a frenzied, almost unendurable climax. The art of the ancient sculptors and the skill of the modern cameraman had combined across the centuries to create a poem of rapture, an orgasm on celluloid which I would defy any man to watch unmoved.

There was a long silence when the screen flooded with light and the lascivious music ebbed into exhaustion.

"My God!" I said when I had recovered some of my composure. "Are you going to telecast *that?*"

Hartford laughed.

"Believe me," he answered, "that's nothing; it just happens to be the only reel I can carry around safely. We're prepared to defend it any day on grounds of genuine art, historic interest, religious tolerance—oh, we've thought of all the angles. But it doesn't really matter; no one can stop us. For the first time in history, any form of censorship's become utterly impossible. There's simply no way of enforcing it; the customer can get what he wants, right in his own home. Lock the door, switch on the TV set to our—dare I call it our blue network?—and settle back. Friends and family will never know."

"Very clever," I said, "but don't you think such a diet will soon pall?"

"Of course; variety is the spice of life. We'll have plenty of conventional entertainment; let *me* worry about that. And every so often we'll have information programs—I hate that word *propaganda*—to tell the cloistered American public what's really happening in the world. Our special features will just be the bait."

"Mind if I have some fresh air?" I said. "It's getting stuffy in here."

Hartford drew the curtains and let daylight back into the room. Below us lay that long curve of beach, with the outrigger fishing boats drawn up beneath the palms and the little waves falling in foam at the end of their weary march from Africa. One of the loveliest sights in the world, but I couldn't focus on it now. I was still seeing those writhing stone limbs, those faces frozen with passions which the centuries could not slake.

That slick voice continued behind my back.

"You'd be astonished if you knew just how much material there is. Remember, we've absolutely no taboos. If you can film it, we can telecast it."

He walked over to his bureau and picked up a heavy, dog-eared volume.

"This has been my bible," he said, "or my Sears, Roebuck, if you prefer. Without it, I'd never have sold the series to my sponsors. They're great believers in science, and they swallowed the whole thing, down to the last decimal point. Recognize it?"

I nodded; whenever I enter a room, I always monitor my host's literary tastes.

"Dr. Kinsey, I presume."

"I guess I'm the only man who's read it from cover to cover and not just looked up his own vital statistics. You see, it's the only piece of market research in its field. Until something better comes along, we're making the most of it. It tells us what the customer wants, and we're going to supply it."

"*All* of it? Some people have odd tastes."

"That's the beauty of the movie you just saw—it appeals to just about every taste."

"You can say that again," I muttered.

He saw that I was beginning to get bored; there are some kinds of single-mindedness that I find depressing. But I had done Hartford an injustice, as he hastened to prove.

"Please don't think," he said anxiously, "that sex is our only weapon. Exposé is almost as good. Ever see the job Ed Murrow did on the late sainted Joe McCarthy? That was milk and water compared with the profiles we're planning in *Washington Confidential*.

"And there's our *Can You Take It?* series, designed to separate the men from the milksops. We'll issue so many advance warnings that every redblooded American will feel he has to watch the show. It will start innocently enough, on ground nicely prepared by Hemingway. You'll see some bullfighting sequences that will really lift you out of your seat—or send you running to the bathroom—because they show all the little details you never get in those cleaned-up Hollywood movies.

"We'll follow that with some really unique material that cost us exactly nothing. Do you remember the photographic evidence the Nuremberg war trials turned up? You've never seen it, because it wasn't publishable. There were quite a few amateur photographers in the concentration camps who made the most of opportunities they'd never get again. Some of them were hanged on the testimony of their own cameras, but their work wasn't wasted. It will lead nicely into our series *Torture Through the Ages*—very scholarly and thorough, yet with a remarkably wide appeal. . . .

"And there are dozens of other angles, but by now you'll have the general picture. The Avenue thinks it knows all about Hidden Persuasion—believe me, it doesn't. The world's best *practical* psychologists are in the East these days. Remember Korea and brainwashing? We've learned a lot since then. There's no need for violence anymore; people enjoy being brainwashed, if you set about it the right way."

"And you," I said, "are going to brainwash the United States. Quite an order."

"Exactly—and the country will love it, despite all the screams from Congress and the churches. Not to mention the networks, of course. They'll make the biggest fuss of all when they find they can't compete with us."

Hartford glanced at his watch and gave a whistle of alarm.

"Time to start packing," he said. "I've got to be at that unpronounceable airport of yours by six. There's no chance, I suppose, that you can fly over to Macao and see us sometime?"

"Not a hope, but I've got a pretty good idea of the picture now. And incidentally, aren't you afraid that I'll spill the beans?"

"Why should I be? The more publicity you can give us, the better. Although our advertising campaign doesn't go into top gear for a few months yet, I feel you've earned this advance notice. As I said, your books helped to give me the idea."

His gratitude was quite genuine, by God; it left me completely speechless.

"Nothing can stop us," he declared—and for the first time the fanaticism that lurked behind that smooth, cynical façade was not altogether under control. "History is on our side. We'll be using America's own decadence as a weapon against her, and it's a weapon for which there's no defense. The air force won't attempt space piracy by shooting down a satellite nowhere near American territory. The FCC can't even protest to a country that doesn't exist in the eyes of the State Department. If you've any other suggestions, I'd be most interested to hear them."

I had none then and I have none now. Perhaps these words may give some brief warning before the first teasing advertisements appear in the trade papers, and may start stirrings of elephantine alarm among the networks. But will it make any difference? Hartford did not think so, and he may be right.

"History is on our side." I cannot get those words out of my head. Land of Lincoln and Franklin and Melville, I love you and I wish you well. But into my heart blows a cold wind from the past, for I remember Babylon.

CHIEF

BY HENRY SLESAR (1927–   )

PLAYBOY
JUNE

Henry Slesar is a vastly underrated writer of mystery, science fiction, horror, and fantasy short stories. An advertising executive in New York since 1949, he must be one of the most prolific writers since the end of World War II. Although he has only published some five novels and four story collections, his bibliography numbers many hundreds of short stories, a very large number of television and motion picture screenplays (he wrote dozens of episodes of Alfred Hitchcock Presents, *many based on his own short stories), at least thirty-nine radio plays for* CBS Radio Mystery Theatre, *and was head writer on the* The Edge Of Night *television soap for more than ten years! And much of this output is excellent work for which he should be much better known in both the sf and mystery fields.*

Among his best stories are those with twist endings. He is also a master of the short-short, one of the most difficult types of stories to do well. (MHG)

Henry Slesar

* * *

We can't very well have a headnote that's longer than the story, so let me just say that there are many ways to warn against a nuclear war. (IA)

Mboyna, chieftain of the Aolori tribe, showed no fear as the longboat approached the island. But it was more than the obligation of his rank which kept his face impassive; he alone of his tribesmen had seen white men before, when he was a child of the village half a century ago.

As the boat landed, one of the whites, a scholarly man with a short silver beard, came toward him, his hand raised in a gesture of friendship. His speech was halting, but he spoke in the tongue of Mboyna's fathers. "We come in peace," he said. "We have come a great distance to find you. I am Morgan, and these are my companions, Hendricks and Carew; we are men of science."

"Then speak!" Mboyna said in a hostile growl, wishing to show no weakness before his tribe.

"There has been a great war," Morgan said, looking uneasily at the warriors who crowded about their chief. "The white men beyond the waters have hurled great lightning at each other. They have poisoned the air, the sea and the flesh of men with their weapons. But it was our belief that there were outposts in the world which war had not touched with its deadly fingers. Your island is one of these, great chief, and we come to abide with you. But first, there is one thing we must do, and we beg your patience."

From the store of supplies in their longboat, the white men removed strange metal boxes with tiny windows. They advanced hesitatingly toward the chief and his tribesmen, pointing the curious devices in their direction. Some of them cowered, others raised their spears in warning. "Do not fear," Morgan said. "It is only a plaything of our science. See how they make no sound as their eyes scan you? But watch." The white men pointed the boxes at themselves, and the devices began clicking frantically.

"Great magic," the tribesmen whispered, their faces awed. "Great magic," Mboyna repeated reverently, bowing before the white gods and the proof of their godhood, the clicking boxes. With deference, they guided the white men to their village, and after the appropriate ceremony, they were beheaded, cleaned and served at the evening meal.

For three days and nights, they celebrated their cleverness with dancing and bright fires; for now, they too were gods. The little boxes had begun to click magically for them, also.

MIND PARTNER

BY CHRISTOPHER ANVIL

GALAXY SCIENCE FICTION
AUGUST

"Christopher Anvil" (Harry C. Crosby) specialized in taking social trends and processes to their logical and often funny conclusions. He also liked to take on the ideas of social thinkers, and such wonderful stories as "A Rose by Other Name," "Positive Feedback," and the present selection are among the best social science fiction of the late 1950s and early 1960s. Although he has written over two hundred stories, there is still no collection available—a situation that some intelligent publisher should rectify.

Although he was a favorite of John W. Campbell, Jr., and published many of his best stories in Astounding/ Analog, *"Mind Partner," which for my money is the best thing he ever wrote, appeared in Horace Gold's* Galaxy, *an editor and market I wish he had favored with more stories. (MHG)*

Such is the danger and menace of drugs to contemporary American society, that it is tempting to consider it

MIND PARTNER

an entirely modern phenomenon, unheard of in the simple and virtuous days of our parents and grandparents.

It is not so. Human beings have always managed to find materials that gave them highs. Alcohol, tobacco, mesquite and many other things (including cocaine) were discovered by primitive societies. Remember, too, that the "Assassins" of the Crusaders era, were so named because they got high on hashish. And Sherlock Holmes was a cocaine addict in the 1880s and 1890s.

Naturally, science fiction concerned itself with drugs even before our society became completely devoured by the menace. Christopher Anvil, back in 1960, was considering an ultimate drug in terms that sound extremely contemporary. (IA)

Jim Calder studied the miniature mansion and grounds that sat, carefully detailed, on the table.

"If you slip," said Walters, standing at Jim's elbow, "the whole gang will disappear like startled fish. There'll be another thousand addicts, and we'll have the whole thing to do over again."

Jim ran his hand up the shuttered, four-story replica tower that stood at one corner of the mansion. "I'm to knock at the front door and say, 'May I speak to Miss Cynthia?' "

Walters nodded. "You'll be taken inside, you'll stay overnight, and the next morning you will come out a door at the rear and drive away. You will come directly here, be hospitalized and examined, and tell us everything you can remember. A certified check in five figures will be deposited in your account. How high the five figures will be depends on how much your information is worth to us."

Christopher Anvil

"Five figures," said Jim.

Walters took out a cigar and sat down on the edge of his desk. "That's right—10,000 to 99,999."

Jim said, "It's the size of the check that makes me hesitate. Am I likely to come out of there in a box?"

"No." Walters stripped the cellophane wrapper off his cigar, lit it, and sat frowning. At last he let out a long puff of smoke and looked up. "We've hit this setup twice before in the last three years. A city of moderate size, a quietly retired elderly person in a well-to-do part of town, a house so situated that people can come and go without causing comment." Walters glanced at the model of mansion and grounds on the table. "Each time, when we were sure where the trouble was coming from, we've raided the place. We caught addicts, but otherwise the house was empty."

"Fingerprints?"

"The first time, yes, but we couldn't trace them anywhere. The second time, the house burned down before we could find out."

"What about the addicts, then?"

"They don't talk. They—" Walters started to say something, then shook his head. "We're offering you a bonus because we don't know what the drug is. These people are addicted to something, but *what?* They don't accept reality. There are none of the usual withdrawal symptoms. A number of them have been hospitalized for three years and have shown no improvement. We don't *think* this will happen to you— one exposure to it shouldn't make you an addict—but we don't *know*. We have a lot of angry relatives of these people backing us. That's why we can afford to pay you what we think the risk is worth."

Jim scowled. "Before I make up my mind, I'd better see one of these addicts."

Walters drew thoughtfully on his cigar, then nodded and picked up the phone.

Behind the doctor and Walters and two white-coated attendants, Jim went into the room at the hospital. The attendants stood against the wall. Jim and Walters stood near the door and watched.

A blonde girl sat on the cot, her head in her hands.

"Janice," said the doctor softly. "Will you talk to us for just a moment?"

The girl sat unmoving, her head in her hands, and stared at the floor.

The doctor dropped to a half-kneeling position beside the cot. "We want to talk to you, Janice. We need your help. Now, I am going to talk to you until you show me you hear me. You do hear me, don't you, Janice?"

The girl didn't move.

The doctor repeated her name again and again.

Finally she raised her head and looked through him. In a flat, ugly voice, she said, "Leave me alone. I know what you're trying to do."

"We want to ask you just a few questions, Janice."

The girl didn't answer. The doctor started to say something else, but she cut him off.

"Go away," she said bitterly. "You don't fool me. You don't even exist. You're nothing." She had a pretty face, but as her eyes narrowed and her lips drew slightly away from her teeth and she leaned forward on the cot, bringing her hands up, she had a look that tingled the hair on the back of Jim's neck.

The two attendants moved warily away from the wall.

The doctor stayed where he was and talked in a low, soothing monotone.

The girl's eyes gradually unfocused, and she was looking through the doctor as if he weren't there. She put her head hard back into her hands and stared at the floor.

The doctor slowly came to his feet and stepped back.

"That's it," he told Jim and Walters.

On the way back, Walters drove, and Jim sat beside him on the front seat. It was just starting to get dark outside. Abruptly Walters asked, "What did you think of it?"

Jim moved uneasily. "Are they all like that?"

"No. That's just one pattern. An example of another pattern is the man who bought a revolver, shot the storekeeper who sold it to him, shot the other customer in the store, put the gun in his belt, went behind the counter and took out a shotgun, shot a policeman who came in the front door, went outside and took a shot at the lights on a theater marquee; he studied the broken lights for a moment, then leaned the shotgun against the storefront, pulled out the revolver, blew out the right rear tires of three cars parked at the curb, stood looking from one of the cars to another and said, 'I just can't be sure, that's all.' "

Walters slowed slightly as they came onto a straight stretch of highway and glanced at Jim. "Another policeman shot the man, and that ended that. We traced that one back to the *second* place we closed up, the place that burned down before we could make a complete search."

"Were these places all run by the same people?"

"Apparently. When we checked the dates, we found that the second place didn't open till after the first was closed, and the third place till the second was closed. They've all operated in the same way. But the few descriptions we've had of the people who work there don't check."

Jim scowled and glanced out the window. "What generally happens when people go there? Do they stay overnight, or what?"

"The first time, they go to the front door, and come out the next morning. After that, they generally rent one of the row of garages on the Jayne Street side of the property, and come back at intervals, driving in after dark and staying till the next night. They lose interest in their usual affairs, and gradually begin to seem remote to the people around them. Finally they use up their savings, or otherwise come to the end of the money they can spend. Then they do like the girl we saw tonight, or like the man in the gun store, or else they follow some other incomprehensible pattern. By the time we find the place and close it up, there are seven hundred to twelve hundred addicts within a fifty-mile radius of the town. They all fall off their rockers inside the same two- to three-week period, and for a month after that, the police and the hospitals get quite a workout."

"Don't they have any of the drug around?"

"That's just it. They must get it all at the place. They use it there. They don't bring any out."

"And when you close the place up—"

"The gang evaporates like a sliver of dry ice. They

don't leave any drug or other evidence behind. This time we've got a precise model of their layout. We should be able to plan a perfect capture. But if we just close in on them, I'm afraid the same thing will happen all over again."

"Okay," said Jim. "I'm your man. But if I don't come out the next morning, I want you to come in after me."

"We will," said Walters.

Jim spent a good part of the evening thinking about the girl he'd seen at the hospital, and the gun-store addict Walters had described. He paced the floor, scowling, and several times reached for the phone to call Walters and say, "No." A hybrid combination of duty and the thought of a five-figure check stopped him.

Finally, unable to stay put, he went out into the warm, dark evening, got in his car and drove around town. On impulse, he swung down Jayne Street and passed the dark row of rented garages Walters had mentioned. A car was carefully backing out as he passed. He turned at the next corner and saw the big, old-fashioned house moonlit among the trees on its own grounds. A faint sensation of wrongness bothered him, and he pulled to the curb to study the house.

Seen through the trees, the house was tall and steep-roofed. It reached far back on its land, surrounded by close-trimmed lawn and shadowy shrubs. The windows were tall and narrow, some of them closed by louvered shutters. Pale light shone out through the narrow openings of the shutters.

Unable to place the sensation of wrongness, Jim swung the car away from the curb and drove home.

He parked his car, and, feeling tired and ready for sleep, walked up the dark drive, climbed the steps to the porch, and fished in his pocket for his keycase. He felt for the right key in the darkness, and moved back onto the steps to get a little more light. It was almost as dark there as on the porch. Puzzled, he glanced up at the sky.

The stars were out, with a heavy mass of clouds in the distance, and a few small clouds sliding by overhead. The edge of one of the small clouds lit up faintly, and as it passed, a pale crescent moon hung in the sky. Jim looked around. Save for the light in the windows, the houses all bulked dark.

Jim went down the steps to his car and drove swiftly back along Jayne Street. He turned, drove a short distance up the side street, and parked.

This time, the outside of the huge house was dark. Bright light shone out the shutters onto the lawn and shrubbery. But the house was a dark bulk against the sky.

Jim swung the car out from the curb and drove home slowly.

The next morning, he went early to Walters' office and studied the model that sat on the table near the desk. The model, painstakingly constructed from enlarged photographs, showed nothing that looked like a camouflaged arrangement for softly floodlighting the walls of the house and the grounds. Jim studied the location of the trees, looked at the house from a number of angles, noticed the broken slats in different shutters on the fourth floor of the tower, but saw nothing else he hadn't seen before.

He called up Walters, who was home having breakfast, and without mentioning details asked, "Is this model on your table complete?"

Walters' voice said, "It's complete up to three o'clock the day before yesterday. We check it regularly."

Jim thanked him and hung up, unsatisfied. He knelt down and put his eye in the position of a man in the street in front of the house. He noticed that certain parts of the trees were blocked off from view by the mansion. Some of these parts could be photographed from a light plane flying overhead, but other positions would be hidden by foliage. Jim told himself that floodlights *must* be hidden high in the trees, in such a way that they could simulate moonlight.

In that case, the question was—why?

Jim studied the model. He was bothered by much the same sensation as that of a man examining the random parts of a jigsaw puzzle. The first few pieces fitted together, the shapes and colors matched, but they didn't seem to add up to anything he had ever seen before.

As he drove out to the house, the day was cool and clear.

The house itself, by daylight, seemed to combine grace, size, and a sort of starched aloofness. It was painted a pale lavender, with a very dark, steeply slanting roof. Tall arching trees rose above it, shading parts of the roof, the grounds, and the shrubs. The lawn was closely trimmed, and bordered by a low spike-topped black-iron fence.

Jim pulled in to the curb in front of the house, got out, opened a low wrought-iron gate in the fence, and started up the walk. He glanced up at the trees, saw nothing of floodlights, then looked at the house.

The house had a gracious, neat, well-groomed appearance. All the windowpanes shone, all the shades were even, all the curtains neatly hung, all the trim bright and the shutters straight. Jim, close to the house, raised his eyes to the tower. All the shutters there were perfect and even and straight.

The sense of wrongness that had bothered him the day before was back again. He paused in his stride, frowning.

The front door opened and a plump, gray-haired woman in a light-blue maid's uniform stood in the doorway. With her left hand, she smoothed her white apron.

"My," she said, smiling, "isn't it a nice day?" She stepped back and with her left hand opened the door wider. "Come in." Her right hand remained at her side, half-hidden by the ruffles of her apron.

Jim's mouth felt dry. "May I," he said, "speak to Miss Cynthia?"

"Of course you may," said the woman. She shut the door behind him.

They were in a small vestibule opening into a high-ceilinged hallway. Down the hall, Jim could see an open staircase to the second floor, and several wide doorways with heavy dark draperies.

"Go straight ahead and up the stairs," said the woman in a pleasant voice. "Turn left at the head of the stairs. Miss Cynthia is in the second room on the right."

Jim took one step. There was a sudden sharp pressure on his skull, a flash of white light, and a piercing pain and a pressure in his right arm—a sensation like that of an injection. Then there was nothing but blackness.

Gradually he became aware that he was lying on a

bed, with a single cover over him. He opened his eyes to see that he was in an airy room with a light drapery blowing in at the window. He started to sit up and his head throbbed. The walls of the room leaned out and came back. For an instant, he saw the room like a photographic negative, the white woodwork black and the dark furniture nearly white. He lay carefully back on the pillow and the room returned to normal.

He heard the quick tap of high heels in the hallway and a door opened beside him. He turned his head. The room seemed to spin in circles around him. He shut his eyes.

When he opened his eyes again, a tall, dark-haired woman was watching him with a faint hint of a smile. "How do you feel?"

"Not good," said Jim.

"It's too bad we have to do it this way, but some people lose their nerve. Others come with the thought that we have a profitable business and they would like to have a part of it. We have to bring these people around to our way of thinking."

"What's your way of thinking?"

She looked at him seriously. "What we have to offer is worth far more than any ordinary pattern of life. We can't let it fall into the wrong hands."

"What is it that you have to offer?'"

She smiled again. "I can't tell you as well as you can experience it."

"That may be. But a man going into a strange country likes to have a road map."

"That's very nicely put," she said, "but you won't be going into any strange country. What we offer you is nothing but your reasonable desires in life."

"Is that all?"

"It's enough."

"Is there any danger of addiction?"

"After you taste steak, is there any danger of your wanting more? After you hold perfect beauty in your arms, is there any danger you might want to do so again? The superior is always addicting."

He looked at her for a moment. "And how about my affairs? Will they suffer?"

"That depends on you."

"What if I go from here straight to the police station?"

"You won't. Once we are betrayed, you can never come back. We won't be here. You wouldn't want that."

"Do you give me anything to take out? Can I buy—"

"No," she said. "You can't take anything out but your memories. You'll find they will be enough."

As she said this, Jim had a clear mental picture of the girl sitting on the cot in the hospital, staring at the floor. He felt a sudden intense desire to get out. He started to sit up, and the room darkened and spun around him.

He felt the woman's cool hands ease him back into place.

"Now," she said, "do you have any more questions?"

"No," said Jim.

"Then," she said briskly, "we can get down to business. The charge for your first series of three visits is one thousand dollars per visit."

"What about the next visits?"

"Must we discuss that now?"

"I'd like to know."

"The charge for each succeeding series of three is doubled."

"How often do I come back?"

"We don't allow anyone to return oftener than once every two weeks. That is for your own protection."

Jim did a little mental arithmetic, and estimated that by the middle of the year a man would have to pay sixteen thousand dollars a visit, and by the end of the year it would be costing him a quarter of a million each time he came to the place.

"Why," he asked, "does the cost increase?"

"Because, I've been told to tell those who ask, your body acquires a tolerance and we have to overcome it. If we have to use twice as much of the active ingredient in our treatment, it seems fair for us to charge twice as much."

"I see." Jim cautiously eased himself up a little. "And suppose that I decide right now not to pay anything at all."

She shook her head impatiently. "You're on a one-way street. The only way you can go is forward."

"That remains to be seen."

"Then you'll see."

She stepped to a dresser against the wall, picked up an atomizer, turned the little silver nozzle toward him, squeezed the white rubber bulb, and set the atomizer back on the dresser. She opened the door and went out. Jim felt a mist of fine droplets falling on his face. He tried to inhale very gently to see if it had an odor. His muscles wouldn't respond.

He lay very still for a moment and felt the droplets falling one by one. They seemed to explode and tingle as they touched his skin. He lay still a moment more, braced himself to make one lunge out of the bed, then tried it.

He lay flat on his back on the bed. A droplet tingled and exploded on his cheek.

He was beginning to feel a strong need for breath.

He braced himself once more, simply to move side-wise off the pillow. Once there, he could get further aside in stages, out of the range of the droplets. He kept thinking, "Just a moment now—steady—just a moment—just— Now!"

And nothing happened.

He lay flat on his back on the bed. A droplet tingled and exploded on his cheek.

The need for air was becoming unbearable.

Jim's head was throbbing and the room went dark with many tiny spots of light. He tried to suck in air and he couldn't. He tried to breathe out, but his chest and lungs didn't move. He could hear the pound of his heart growing fast and loud.

He couldn't move.

At the window, the light drapery fluttered and blew in and fell back.

He lay flat on the bed and felt a droplet tingle and explode on his cheek.

His skull was throbbing. His heart writhed and hammered in his chest. The room was going dark.

Then something gave way and his lungs were dragging in painful gasps of fresh air. He sobbed like a runner at the end of a race. After a long time, a feeling of peace and tiredness came over him.

The door opened.

He looked up. The woman was watching him sadly. "I'm sorry," she said. "Do you want to discuss payment?"

Jim nodded.

The woman sat down in a chair by the bed. "As I've explained, the initial series of three visits cost one thousand dollars each. We will accept a personal check or even an I.O.U. for the first payment. After that, you must have cash."

Jim made out a check for one thousand dollars.

The woman nodded, smiled, and folded the check into a small purse. She went out, came back with a glass of colorless liquid, shook a white powder into it, and handed it to him.

"Drink it all," she said. "A little bit can be excruciatingly painful."

Jim hesitated. He sat up a little and began to feel dizzy. He decided he had better do as she said, took the glass and drained it. It tasted exactly like sodium bicarbonate dissolved in water. He handed her the glass and she went to the door.

"The first experiences," she said, "are likely to be a little exuberant. Remember, your time sense will be distorted, as it is in a dream." She went out and shut the door softly.

Jim fervently wished he were somewhere else. He wondered what she had meant by the last comment. The thought came to him that if he could get out of this place, he could give Walters and the doctors a chance to see the drug in action.

He got up, and had the momentary sensation of doing two things at once. He seemed to lie motionless on the bed and to stand up at one and the same time. He wondered if the drug could have taken effect already. He lay down and got up again. This time he felt only a little dizzy. He went to the window and looked out. He was in a second-story window, and the first-floor rooms in this house had high ceilings. Moreover, he now discovered he was wearing a sort of hospital gown. He couldn't go into the street in that without causing a sensation, and he didn't know just when the drug would take effect.

He heard the soft click of the door opening and turned around. The woman who had talked to him came in and closed the door gently behind her. Jim watched in a daze as she turned languorously, and it occurred to him that no woman he had ever seen had moved quite like that, so the chances were that the drug had taken effect and he was imagining all this. He remembered that she had said the first experiences were likely to be a little exuberant, and his time sense distorted as in a dream.

Jim spent the night, if it was the night, uncertain as to what was real and what was due to the drug. But it was all vivid, and realistic events shaded into adventures he *knew* were imaginary, but that were so bright and satisfying that he didn't care if they were real or not. In these adventures, the colors were pure colors, and the sounds were clear sounds, and nothing was muddied or uncertain as in life.

It was so vivid and clear that when he found himself lying on the bed with the morning sun streaming in, he was astonished that he could remember not a single incident save the first, and that one not clearly.

He got up and found his clothes lying on a chair by the bed. He dressed rapidly, glanced around for the little atomizer and saw it was gone. He stepped out into the hall and there was a sudden sharp pressure on his skull, a flash of white light, and a feeling of limpness. He felt strong hands grip and carry him. He felt himself hurried down a flight of steps, along a corridor, then set down with his back against a wall.

The plump, gray-haired woman took a damp cloth and held it to his head. "You'll be all over that in a little while," she said. "I don't see why they have to do that."

"Neither do I," said Jim. He felt reasonably certain that she had done the same thing to him when he came in. He looked around, saw that they were in a small bare entry, and got cautiously to his feet. "Is my car still out front?"

"No," she said. "It's parked in back, in the drive."

"Thank you," he said. "Say good-by to Miss Cynthia for me."

The woman smiled. "You'll be back."

He was very much relieved to get outside the house. He walked back along the wide graveled drive, found his car, got in, and started it. When he reached the front of the house, he slowed the car to glance back. To his surprise, the two shutters on the third floor of the tower had broken slats. He thought this had some significance, but he was unable to remember what it was. He sat for a moment, puzzled, then decided that the important thing was to get to Walters. He swung the car out into the early morning traffic, and settled back with a feeling compounded of nine parts relief and one part puzzlement.

What puzzled him was that anyone should pay one thousand dollars for a second dose of that.

The doctors made a lightning examination, announced that he seemed physically sound, and then Walters questioned him. He described the experience in close detail, and Walters listened, nodding from time to time. At the end, Jim said, "I'll be *damned* if I can see why anyone should go back!"

"That *is* puzzling," said Walters. "It may be that they were all sensation-seekers, though that's a little odd, too. Whatever the reason, it's lucky you weren't affected."

"Maybe I'd better keep my fingers crossed," said Jim.

Walters laughed. "I'll bring your bankbook in to keep you happy." He went out, and a moment later the doctors were in again. It wasn't until the next morning that they were willing to let him go. Just as he was about to leave, one of them remarked to him, "I hope you never need a blood transfusion in a hurry."

"Why so?" Jim asked.

"You have one of the rarest combinations I've ever seen." He held out an envelope. "Walters said to give you this."

Jim opened it. It was a duplicate deposit slip for a sum as high as five figures could go.

Jim went out to a day that wasn't sunny, but looked just as good to him as if it had been.

After careful thought, Jim decided to use the money to open a detective agency of his own. Walters, who caught the dope gang trying to escape through an unused steam tunnel, gave Jim his blessing, and the offer of a job if things went wrong.

Fortunately, things went very well. Jim's agency prospered. In time, he found the right girl, they married, and had two boys and a girl. The older boy became a doctor, and the girl married a likable fast-rising young lawyer. The younger boy had a series of unpleasant scrapes and seemed bound on wrecking his life. Jim, who was by this time very well to do, at last offered the boy a job in his agency, and was astonished to see him take hold.

The years fled past much faster than Jim would have liked. Still, when the end came near, he had the pleasure of knowing that his life's work would be in the capable hands of his own son.

He breathed his last breath in satisfaction.

And woke up lying on a bed in a room where a light drapery blew back at the window and the morning sun shone in, and his clothes were folded on a chair by his bed.

Jim sat up very carefully. He held his hand in front of his face and turned it over slowly. It was not the hand of an old man. He got up and looked in a mirror, then sat down on the edge of the bed. He was young, all right. The question was, was this an old man's nightmare, or was the happy life he had just lived a dope addict's dream?

He remembered the woman who had doped him saying, "What we offer you is nothing but your reasonable desires in life."

Then it had all been a dream.

But a dream should go away, and this remained clear in his memory.

He dressed, went out in the hall, felt a sudden pressure on his skull, a flash of white light, and a feeling of limpness.

He came to in the small entry, and the plump, gray-haired woman carefully held a damp cool cloth to his head.

"Thanks," he said. "Is my car out back?"

"Yes," she said, and he went out.

As he drove away from the house he glanced back and noticed the two broken shutters on the third floor of the tower. The memory of his dream about this same event—leaving the place—jarred him. It seemed that those broken shutters meant something, but he was unable to remember what. He trod viciously on the gas pedal, throwing a spray of gravel on the carefully tailored lawn as he swung into the street.

He *still* did not see why anyone should go back there with anything less than a shotgun.

He told Walters the whole story, including the details of his "life," that he remembered so clearly.

"You'll get over it," Walters finally said, when Jim was ready to leave the hospital. "It's a devil of a thing to have happen, but there's an achievement in it you can be proud of."

"You name it," said Jim bitterly.

"You've saved a lot of other people from this same thing. The doctors have analyzed the traces of drug still in your blood. They think they can neutralize it. Then we are going to put a few sturdy men inside that house, and while they're assumed to be under the influence, we'll raid the place."

The tactic worked, but Jim watched the trial with a cynical eye. He couldn't convince himself that it was true. He might, for all he knew, be lying in a second-floor room of the house on a bed, while these people, who seemed to be on trial, actually were going freely about their business.

This inability to accept what he saw as real at last forced Jim to resign his job. Using the generous bonus Walters had given him, he took up painting. As he told Walters on one of his rare visits, "It may or may not be that what I'm doing is real, but at least there's the satisfaction of the work itself."

"You're not losing any money on it," said Walters shrewdly.

"I know," said Jim, "and that makes me acutely uneasy."

On his 82nd birthday, Jim was widely regarded as

the "Grand Old Man" of painting. His hands and feet felt cold that day, and he fell into an uneasy, shallow-breathing doze. He woke with a start and a choking cough. For an instant everything around him had an unnatural clarity; then it all went dark and he felt himself falling.

He awoke in a bed in a room where a light drapery fluttered at the window, and the morning sun shone into the room.

This time, Jim entertained no doubts as to whether or not this was real. He got up angrily and smashed his fist into the wall with all his might.

The shock and pain jolted him to his heels.

He went out the same way as before, but he had to drive one-handed, gritting his teeth all the way.

The worst of it was that the doctors weren't able to make that hand exactly right afterward. Even if the last "life" had been a dream—even if this one was—he wanted to paint. But every time he tried to, he felt so clumsy that he gave up in despair.

Walters, dissatisfied, gave Jim the minimum possible payment. The gang escaped. Jim eventually lost his job, and in the end he eked out his life at poorly paid odd jobs.

The only consolation he felt was that his life was so miserable that it must be true.

He went to bed sick one night and woke up the next morning on a bed in a room where a light drapery fluttered at the window and the early morning sun shone brightly in.

This happened to him twice more.

The next time after that, he lay still on the bed and stared at the ceiling. The incidents and details of five lives danced in his mind like jabbering monkeys. He pressed his palms to his forehead and wished he could forget it all.

The door opened softly and the tall, dark-haired woman was watching him with a faint smile. "I told you," she said, "that you couldn't take anything away but memories."

He looked up at her sickly. "That seems like a long, long while ago."

She nodded and sat down. "Your time sense is distorted as in a dream."

"I wish," he said drearily, looking at her, "that I could just forget it all. I don't see why anyone would come back for more of that."

She leaned forward to grip the edge of the mattress, shaking with laughter. She sat up again. "Whew!" she said, looking at him and forcing her face to be straight. "Nobody comes back for *more*. That is the unique quality of this drug. People come back to forget they ever had it."

He sat up. "I can forget that?"

"Oh, yes. *Don't* get so excited! That's what you really paid your thousand dollars for. The forgetfulness drug lingers in your bloodstream for two to three weeks. Then memory returns and you're due for another visit." Jim looked at her narrowly. "Does my body become tolerant of this drug? Does it take twice as much after three visits, four times as much after six visits, eight times as much after nine visits?"

"No."

"Then you lied to me."

She looked at him oddly. "What would you have expected of me? But I didn't lie to you. I merely said that that was what I was told to tell those who asked."

"Then what's the point of it?" Jim asked.

"What's the point of bank robbery?" She frowned at him. "You ask a lot of questions. Aren't you lucky I know the answers? Ordinarily you wouldn't get around to this till you'd stewed for a few weeks. But you seem precocious, so I'll tell you."

"That's nice," he said.

"The main reason for the impossible rates is so you can't pay off in money."

"How does that help you?"

"Because," she said, "every time you bring us a new patron, you get three free visits yourself."

"Ah," he said.

"It needn't be so terribly unpleasant, coming here."

"What happens if, despite everything, some sorehead actually goes and tells the police about this?"

"We move."

"Suppose they catch you?"

"They won't. Or, at least, it isn't likely."

"But you'll leave?"

"Yes."

"What happens to me?"

"Don't you see? We'll *have* to leave. Someone will have betrayed us. We couldn't stay because it might happen again. It isn't right from your viewpoint, but we can't take chances."

For a few moments they didn't talk, and the details of Jim's previous "lives" came pouring in on him. He sat up suddenly. "Where's that forgetfulness drug?"

She went outside and came back with a glass of colorless liquid. She poured in a faintly pink powder and handed it to him. He drank it quickly and it tasted like bicarbonate of soda dissolved in water.

He looked at her. "This isn't the same thing all over again, is it?"

"Don't worry," she said. "You'll forget."

The room began to go dark. He leaned back. The last thing he was conscious of was her cool hand on his forehead, then the faint click as she opened the door to go out.

He sat up. He dressed, drove quickly to Walters and told him all he could remember. Walters immediately organized his raid. Jim saw the place closed up with no one caught.

After two weeks and four days, the memories flooded back. His life turned into a nightmare. At every turn, the loves, hates, and tiny details of six separate lives poured in on him. He tried drugs in an attempt to forget, and sank from misery to hopeless despair. He ended up in a shooting scrap as Public Enemy Number Four.

And then he awoke and found himself in a bed in a room with a light drapery blowing in at the window, and the early morning sun shining brightly in.

"Merciful God!" he said.

The door clicked shut.

Jim sprang to the door and looked out in the carpeted hall. There was the flash of a woman's skirt; then a tall narrow door down the hallway closed to shut off his view.

He drew back into the room and shut the door. The house was quiet. In the distance, on the street, he could hear the faint sound of a passing car.

He swallowed hard. He glanced at the window. It had been, he reasoned, early morning when he had talked to the woman last. It was early morning now. He recalled that before she went out she said, "You'll forget." He had then lived his last miserable "life"

—and awakened to hear the click as the door came shut behind her.

That had all taken less than five seconds of actual time.

He found his clothes on a nearby chair and started to dress. As he did so, he realized for the first time that the memories of his "lives" were no longer clear to him. They were fading away, almost as the memories of a dream do after a man wakes and gets up. *Almost* as the memories of a dream, but not quite. Jim found that if he thought of them, they gradually became clear again.

He tried to forget and turned his attention to the tree he could see through the window. He looked at the curve of its boughs, and at a black-and-yellow bird balancing on a branch in the breeze.

The memories faded away, and he began to plan what to do. No sooner did he do this than he remembered with a shock that he had said to Walters, "If I don't come out next morning, I want you to come in after me."

And Walters had said, "We will."

So that must have been just last night.

Jim finished dressing, took a deep breath, and held out his hand. It looked steady. He opened the door, stepped out into the hall, and an instant too late remembered what had happened six times before.

When he opened his eyes, the plump, gray-haired woman was holding a damp cloth to his forehead and clucking sympathetically.

Jim got carefully to his feet, and walked down the drive to his car. He slid into the driver's seat, started the engine, and sat still a moment, thinking. Then he released the parking brake, and pressed lightly on the gas pedal. The car slid smoothly ahead, the gravel of the drive crunching under its tires. He glanced up as the car reached the end of the drive, and looked back at the tower. Every slat in the shutters was perfect. Jim frowned, trying to remember something. Then he glanced up and down the street, and swung out into the light early morning traffic.

He wasted no time getting to Walters.

He was greeted with an all-encompassing inspection that traveled from Jim's head to his feet. Walters looked tense. He took a cigar from a box on his desk and put it in his mouth unlit.

"I've spent half the night telling myself there are some things you can't ask a man to do for money. But we *had* to do it. Are you all right?"

"At the moment."

"There are doctors and medical technicians in the next room. Do you want to see them now or later?"

"Right now."

In the next hour, Jim took off his clothes, stood up, lay down, looked into bright lights, winced as a sharp hollow needle was forced into his arm, gave up samples of bodily excretions, sat back as electrodes were strapped to his skin, and at last was reassured that he would be all right. He dressed, and found himself back in Walters' office.

Walters looked at him sympathetically.

"How do you feel?"

"Starved."

"I'll have breakfast sent in." He snapped on his intercom, gave the order, then leaned back. He picked up his still unlit cigar, lit it, puffed hard, and said, "What happened?"

Jim told him, starting with the evening before, and ending when he swung his car out into traffic this morning.

Walters listened with a gathering frown, drawing occasionally on the cigar.

A breakfast of scrambled eggs and Canadian bacon was brought in. Walters got up, and looked out the window, staring down absently at the traffic moving past in the street below. Jim ate with single-minded concentration, and finally pushed his plate back and looked up.

Walters ground his cigar butt in the ashtray and lit a fresh cigar. "This is a serious business. You say you remembered the details of each of those six lives *clearly?*"

"Worse than that. I remembered the emotions and the attachments. In the first life, for instance, I had my own business." Jim paused and thought back. The memories gradually became clear again. "One of my men, for instance, was named Hart. He stood about five-seven, slender, with black hair, cut short when I first met him. Hart was a born actor. He could play any part. It wasn't his face. His expression hardly seemed to change. But his manner changed. He could stride into a hotel and the bellboys would jump for his bags and the desk clerk spring to attention. He stood out. He was important. Or he could slouch in the front door, hesitate, look around, blink, start to ask one of the bellboys something, lose his nerve, stiffen his shoulders, shamble over to the desk, and get unmercifully snubbed. Obviously, he was less than nobody. Or, again, he could quietly come in the front door, stroll across the lobby, fade out of sight somewhere, and hardly a person would notice or remember him. Whatever part he played, he lived it. That was what made him so valuable."

Walters had taken the cigar out of his mouth, and listened intently. "You mean this Hart—this imaginary man—is real to you? In three dimensions?"

"That's it. Not only that, I like him. There were other, stronger attachments. I had a family."

"Which seems real?"

Jim nodded. "I realize as I say these things that I sound like a lunatic."

"No." Walters shook his head sympathetically. "It all begins to make sense. Now I see why the girl at the hospital said to the doctor, 'You aren't real.' Does it *hurt* to talk about these 'lives'?"

Jim hesitated. "Not as long as we keep away from the personal details. But it hurt like nothing I can describe to have all six of these sets of memories running around in my head at once."

"I can imagine. All right, let's track down some of these memories and see how far the details go."

Jim nodded. "Okay."

Walters got out a bound notebook and pen. "We'll start with your business. What firm name did you use?"

"Calder Associates."

"Why?"

"It sounded dignified, looked good on a business card or letterhead, and wasn't specific."

"What was your address?"

"Four North Street. Earlier, it was 126 Main."

"How many men did you have working with you?"

"To begin with, just Hart, and another man by the name of Dean. At the end, there were twenty-seven."

"What were their names?"

Jim called them off one by one, without hesitation. Walters blinked. "Say that over again a little more slowly."

Jim repeated the list.

"All right," said Walters. "Describe these men."

Jim described them. He gave more and more details as Walters pressed for them, and by lunch time, Walters had a large section of the notebook filled.

The two men ate, and Walters spent the rest of the afternoon quizzing Jim on his first "life." Then they had steak and French fries sent up to the office. Walters ate in silence for a moment, then said, "Do you realize that you haven't stumbled once?"

Jim looked up in surprise. "What do you mean?"

Walters said, "Quiz me on the names of every man who ever worked for me. I won't remember all of them. Not by a long shot. You remember every last detail of this dream life with a total recall that beats anything I've ever seen."

"That's the trouble. That's why it's pleasant to forget."

Walters asked suddenly, "Did you ever paint? *Actually,* I mean. I ask because you say you were an outstanding painter in one of these 'lives.' "

"When I was a boy, I painted some. I wanted to be an artist."

"Can you come out to my place tonight? I'd like to see whether you can really handle the brushes."

Jim nodded. "Yes, I'd like to try that."

They drove out together, and Walters got out a dusty paint set in a wooden case, set up a folding easel, and put a large canvas on it.

Jim stood still a moment, thinking back. Then he began to paint. He lost himself in the work, as he always had, all through the years, and what he was painting now he had painted before. Had painted it, and sold it for a good price, too. And it was worth it. He could still see the model in his mind as he painted with swift precise strokes.

He stepped back.

"My Lady in Blue" was a cheerful girl of seventeen. She smiled out from the canvas as if at any moment she might laugh or wave.

Jim glanced around. For an instant the room seemed strange. Then he remembered where he was.

Walters looked at the painting for a long moment, then looked at Jim, and swallowed. He carefully took the painting from the easel and replaced it with another blank canvas. He went across the room and got a large floor-type ashtray, a wrought-iron affair with a galloping horse for the handle.

"Paint this."

Jim looked at it. He stepped up to the canvas, hesitated. He raised the brush—and stopped. He didn't know where to begin. He frowned and carefully thought back to his first lessons. "Let's see." He glanced up. "Do you have any tracing paper?"

"Just a minute," said Walters.

Jim tacked the paper over the canvas and methodically drew the ashtray on the paper. He had a hard time, but at last looked at the paper triumphantly. "Now, do you have any transfer paper?"

Walters frowned. "I've got carbon paper."

"All right."

Walters got it. Jim put a sheet under his tracing paper, tacked it up again, and carefully went over the drawing with a pencil. He untacked the paper, then methodically began to paint. At length, weary and perspiring, he stepped back.

Walters looked at it. Jim blinked and looked again. Walters said, "A trifle off-center, isn't it?"

There was no doubt about it, the ashtray stood too far toward the upper right-hand corner of the canvas.

Walters pointed at the other painting. "Over there we have a masterpiece that you dashed off freehand. Here we have, so to speak, a piece of good, sound mechanical drawing that isn't properly placed on the canvas. This took you longer to do than the other. How come?"

"I had done the other before."

"And you remember the motions of your hand? Is that it?" He put another canvas up. "Do it again."

Jim frowned. He stepped forward, thought a moment, and began to paint. He lost himself in a perfection of concentration. In time, he stepped back.

Walters looked at it. He swallowed hard, glanced back and forth from this painting to the one Jim had done at first. He lifted the painting carefully from the easel and placed it beside the other.

They looked identical.

The sun was just lighting the horizon as they drove back to the office. Walters said, "I'm going in there and sleep on the cot. Can you get back around three this afternoon?"

"Sure."

Jim drove home, slept, ate, and was back again by three.

"This is a devil of a puzzle," said Walters, leaning back at his desk and blowing out a cloud of smoke. "I've had half a dozen experts squint at one of those paintings. I've been offered five thousand, even though they don't know the artist's name. Then I showed them the other painting and they almost fell through the floor. It isn't possible, but each stroke appears identical. How do you feel?"

"Better. And I've remembered something. Let's look at your model."

They went to the big model of the mansion, and Jim touched the upper story of the tower. "Have some of the boys sketch this. Then compare the sketches with photographs."

Soon they were looking at sketches and photographs side by side. The sketches showed the tower shutters perfect. The photographs showed several slats of the shutters broken.

Walters questioned the men, who insisted the shutters were perfect. After they left, Jim said, "Everyone who sketched that place wasn't drugged. And the cameras certainly weren't drugged."

Walters said, "Let's take a look." They drove out past the mansion, and the shutters looked perfect. A new photograph showed the same broken slats.

Back at the office, Walters said, "Just what are we up against here?"

Jim said, "I can think of two possibilities."

"Let's hear them."

"Often you can do the same thing several different ways. A man, for instance, can go from one coastal town to another on foot, riding a horse, by car, by plane, or in a speedboat."

"Granted."

"A hundred years ago, the list would have been shorter."

Walters nodded thoughtfully. "I follow you. Go on."

"Whoever sees those shutters as perfect is, for the time being, in an abnormal mental state. How did he get there? We've assumed drugs were used. But just as there are new ways of going from one city to another, so there may be new ways of passing from one mental state to another. Take subliminal advertising, for instance, where the words, 'THIRSTY,' 'THIRSTY,' 'BEER,' may be flashed on the screen too fast to be consciously seen."

"It's illegal."

"Suppose someone found out how to do it undetected, and decided to try it out on a small scale. What about nearly imperceptible *verbal* clues instead of visual ones?"

Walters' eyes narrowed. "We'll analyze every sound coming out of that place and check for any kind of suspicious sensory stimulus whatever. What's your other idea?"

"Well, go back to your travel analogy. Going from one place to another, any number of animals can outrun, outfly, and out-swim a man. Let Man work on the problem long enough, and roll up to the starting line in his rocket-plane, and the result will be different. But until Man has time to concentrate enough thought and effort, the nonhuman creature has an excellent chance to beat him. There are better fliers, better swimmers, better fighters, better—"

Walters frowned. "Better *suggestionists?* Like the snake that's said to weave hypnotically?"

"Yes, and the wasp that stings the trapdoor spider, when other wasps are fought off."

"Hmm. Maybe. But I incline to the subliminal advertising theory myself." He looked at the mansion. "Where would they keep the device?"

"Why not the tower?"

Walters nodded. "It's an easy place to guard, and to shut off from visitors."

Jim said, "It might explain those shutters. They might not care to risk painters and repairmen up there."

Walters knocked the ash off his cigar. "But how do we get in there to find out?"

They studied the model. Walters said, "Say we send in a 'building inspector.' They'll knock him out, hallucinate a complete series of incidents in his mind, and send him out totally ignorant. If we try to raid the place in a group, they'll vanish with the help of that machine. But there must be *some* way."

Jim said thoughtfully, "Those trees overhang the room."

"They do, don't they?"

The two men studied the trees and the tower.

Jim touched one of the arching limbs. "What if we lowered a rope from here?"

Walters tied an eraser on a string and fastened the string to a limb. The eraser hung by the uppermost tower window. Walters scowled, snapped on the intercom, and asked for several of his men. Then he turned to Jim. "We'll see what Cullen thinks. He's done some jobs like this."

Cullen had sharp eyes and a mobile face that grew unhappy as he listened to Walters. Finally, he shook his head. "No, thanks. Ask me to go up a wall, or the side of a building. But not down out of a tree branch on the end of a rope."

He gave the eraser a little flip with his finger. It swung in circles, hit the wall, and bounced away.

"Say I'm actually up there. It's night. The rope swings. The limb bobs up and down. The tree sways.

All to a different rhythm. I'm spinning around on the end of this rope. One second this shutter is one side of me. The next second it's on the other side and five feet away. A job is a job, but this is one I don't want."

Walters turned to Jim after Cullen went out. "That settles that."

Jim looked at the tree limb. Two or three weeks from today, he told himself, the memories would come flooding back. The people who had done it would get away, and do it again. And he would have those memories.

Jim glanced at Walters stubbornly. "I am going to climb that tree."

The night was still, with a dark overcast sky as Jim felt the rough bark against the insides of his arms. He hitched up the belt that circled the tree, then pulled up one foot, then another as he sank the climbing irons in higher up. He could hear Cullen's advice: "Practice, study the model, do each step over and over in your head. Then, when you're actually doing it and when things get tight, *hold your mind on what to do next.* Do that. *Then* think of the next step."

Jim was doing this as the dark lawn dropped steadily away. He felt the tree trunk grow gradually more slender, then begin to widen. He worked his way carefully above the limb, refastened the belt, and felt a puff of warm air touch his face and neck, like a leftover from the warm day. Somewhere, a radio was playing.

He climbed, aware now of the rustling around him of leaves.

The trunk widened again, and he knew he was at

the place where the trunk separated into the limbs that arched out to form the crown of the tree.

He pulled himself up carefully, and took his eyes from the tree for a moment to look toward the mansion. He saw the slanting tile roof of an entirely different house, light shining down from a dormer window. He glanced around, to see the looming steep-roofed tower of the mansion in the opposite direction. He realized he must have partially circled the tree and lost his sense of direction.

He swallowed and crouched in the cleft between the limbs till he was sure he knew which limb arched over the tower. He fastened the belt and started slowly up. As he climbed, the limb arched, to become more and more nearly horizontal. At the same time, the limb became more slender. It began to respond to his movements, swaying slightly as he climbed. Now he was balancing on it, the steep roof of the tower shining faintly ahead of him. He remembered that he had to take off the climbing irons, lest they foul in the rope later on. As he twisted to do this, his hands trembled. He forced his breath to come steadily. He looked ahead to the steep, slanting roof of the tower.

The limb was already almost level. If he crawled further, it would sag under him. He would be climbing head down. He glanced back, and his heart began to pound. To go back, he would have to inch backwards along the narrow limb.

Cullen's words came to him: "When things get tight, *hold your mind on what to do next.* Do that. *Then* think of the next step."

He inched ahead. The limb began to sag.

There was a rustling of leaves.

The limb swayed. It fell, and rose, beneath him.

He clung to it, breathing hard.

He inched further. The leaves rustled. The limb pressed up, then fell away. He shut his eyes, his forehead tight against the bark, and crept ahead. After a time, he seemed to feel himself tip to one side. His eyes opened.

The tower was almost beneath him.

With his left arm, he clung tightly to the limb. With his right, he felt carefully for the rope tied to his belt. He worked one end of the rope forward and carefully looped it around the limb. He tied the knot that he had practiced over and over, then tested it, and felt it hold.

A breeze stirred the leaves. The limb began to sway.

The dark lawn below seemed to reach up and he felt himself already falling. He clung hard to the limb and felt his body tremble all over. Then he knew he had to go through the rest of his plan without hesitation, lest he lose his nerve completely.

He sucked in a deep breath, swung over the limb, let go with one hand, caught the rope, then caught it with the other hand, looped the rope around one ankle, and started to slide down.

The rope swung. The limb dipped, then lifted. The tree seemed to sway slightly.

Jim clung, his left foot clamping the loop of the rope passed over his right ankle. The swaying, dipping, and whirling began to die down. His hands felt weak and tired.

He slid gradually down the rope. Then the shutter was right beside him. He reached out, put his hand through the break in the slats, and lifted the iron catch. The hinges of the shutters screeched as he pulled them open.

A dead black oblong hung before him.

He reached out, and felt no sash in the opening. He climbed higher on the rope, pushed away from the building, and as he swung back, stepped across, caught the frame, and dropped inside.

The shutters screeched as he pulled them shut, but the house remained quiet. He stood still for a long moment, then unsnapped a case on his belt, and took out a little polarizing flashlight. He carefully thumbed the stud that turned the front lens. A dim beam faintly lit the room.

There was a glint of metal, then another. Shiny parallel lines ran from the ceiling to floor in front of him. There was an odd faint odor.

The house was quiet. A shift of the wind brought the distant sound of recorded music.

Carefully, Jim eased the stud of the flashlight further around, so the light grew a trifle brighter.

The vertical lines looked like bars.

He stepped forward and peered into the darkness.

Behind the bars, something stirred.

Jim reached back, unbuttoned the flap of his hip pocket and gripped the cool metal of his gun.

Something moved behind the bars. It reached out, bunched itself, reached out. Something large and dark slid up the bars.

Jim raised the gun.

A hissing voice said quietly, "You are from some sort of law-enforcement agency? Good."

Jim slid his thumb toward the stub of the light, so he could see more clearly. But the faint hissing voice went on, "Don't. It will do no good to see me."

Jim's hand tightened on the gun at the same instant that his mind asked a question.

The voice said, "Who am I? Why am I here? If I tell you, it will strain your mind to believe me. Let me show you."

The room seemed to pivot, then swung around him faster and faster. A voice spoke to him from all sides; then something lifted him up, and at an angle.

He stared at the dial, rapped it with his finger. The needle didn't move from its pin. He glanced at the blue-green planet on the screen. Photon pressure was zero, and there was nothing to do but try to land on chemical rockets. As he strapped himself into the acceleration chair, he began to really appreciate the size of his bad luck.

Any solo space pilot, he told himself, should be a good mechanic. And an individual planetary explorer should be his own pilot, to save funds. Moreover, anyone planning to explore Ludt VI, with its high gravity and pressure, and its terrific psychic stress, should be strong and healthy.

These requirements made Ludt VI almost the exclusive preserve of big organizations with teams of specialists. They sent out heavily equipped expeditions, caught a reasonable quota of spat, trained them on the way home, and sold the hideous creatures at magnificent prices to the proprietors of every dream parlor in the system. From this huge income, they paid their slightly less huge costs, and made a safe moderate profit on their investment. With a small expedition, it was different.

A small expedition faced risk, and a one-man expedition was riskiest of all. But if it succeeded, the trained spat brought the same huge price, and there were no big-ship bills for fuel, specialists, power equipment, and insurance. This, he thought, had almost been a successful trip. There were three nearly trained spat back in his sleeping compartment.

But, though he was a competent trainer, a skilled explorer, a passable pilot, and in good physical condition, he was no mechanic. He didn't know how to fix what had gone wrong.

He sat back and watched the rim of the world below swing up in the deep blue sky.

There was a gray fuzziness. Jim was standing in the dark, seeing the bars shining faintly before him.

The black knot still clung to the bars.

Somewhere in the old mansion, a phone began to ring.

Jim said, in a low voice, "You were the pilot?"

"No. I was the spat. The others died in the crash. Some of your race found me and we made a—an agreement. But it has worked out differently here than I expected. The experiences I stimulate in your minds are enjoyable to you and to me. Yet either the structure of your brains is different from that of the pilot, or you lack training in mind control. You cannot wipe away these experiences afterward, and though I can do it for you easily, it is only temporary."

A door opened and shut downstairs. There was a sound of feet on the staircase.

The hissing began again. "You must go and bring help."

Jim thought of the rope and the trees. His hand tightened on the gun and he made no move toward the window.

The hissing sound said, "I see your difficulty. I will help you."

There was the crack of a rifle, then several shots

outside. Jim swung the shutter open, felt a faint dizziness, and looked down on a warm sunlit lawn some thirty feet below.

A hissing voice said, "Take hold the rope. Now carefully step out. Loop the rope with your foot."

Somewhere in Jim's mind, as he did this, there was an uneasiness. He wondered at it as he climbed up the rope to the bar overhead, swung up onto the bar, slipped and nearly lost his grip. He could see the bar was steady and solid, and he wondered as it seemed to move under him. The green lawn was such a short distance down that there clearly was little danger, and he wondered why his breath came fast as he swung around on the bar, slid down to a sort of resting place where he put on climbing irons before starting down again. Always on the way down, the whistling voice told him that it was just a few feet more, just a few feet, as bit by bit he made his way down, and suddenly heard shots, shouts, and a repeated scream.

Jim stepped off onto the soft lawn, stumbled, and knelt to take off the climbing irons. His heart pounded like a trip-hammer. He realized there was a blaze of spotlights around him. He saw lights coming on in the mansion, and memory returned in a rush. He drew in a deep shaky breath, glanced at the tree, then saw a little knot of people near the base of the tower. He walked over, recognized Walters in the glow of the lights and saw a still figure on the ground.

Walters said, "I shouldn't have let him try it. Cover his face, Cullen."

Cullen bent to draw a coat up over the head of the motionless figure, which was twisted sidewise.

Jim looked down.

He saw his own face.

He was aware of darkness and of something hard beneath him. Voices came muffled from somewhere nearby. He heard the sound of a phone set in its cradle, the slam of a door, the scrape of glass on glass. He breathed and recognized a choking smell of cigar smoke.

Jim sat up.

Nearby was the model of the mansion. Jim swung carefully to his feet, made his way across the room, and opened the door to the next office. He blinked in the bright light, then saw Walters look up and grin. "One more night like this and I retire. How do you feel?"

"I ache all over and I'm dizzy. How did I get here?"

"I was afraid your going in there might misfire and touch off their escape, so I had the place surrounded. We saw you go in, there was about a five-minute pause, and the shutters seemed to come open. A figure came out. Then there was the crack of a rifle from the dormer window of a house across the street. I sent some men into that house, and the rest of us closed in on the mansion. We used the spotlights on our cars to light the place. We'd just found what we thought was your body—with a broken neck—when there was a thud behind us. There you were, and the other body was gone.

"Right then, I thought it was going to be the same as usual. But this time we nailed several men and women in quite a state of confusion. Some of them have fingerprints that match those from the first place we raided. We don't have the equipment yet, because that tower staircase was boarded up tight . . . What's wrong?"

Jim told his own version, adding, "Since that shot came *before* I opened the shutters, the 'figure' you saw go up the rope must have been an illusion, to fool whoever had the gun across the street. And since I heard someone running up the stairs a few minutes before you came in, I don't see how the stairs can be boarded up."

Walters sat up straight. "*Another* illusion!"

Jim said, "It would be nice to know if there's any limit to those illusions."

Walters said, "This afternoon, we tried looking at those shutters through field glasses. Beyond about four hundred feet, you could see the broken slats. So there's a limit. But if there's no equipment, this is uncanny, 'spat' or no 'spat.' "

Jim shook his head. "I don't know. You can use the same electromagnetic laws and similar components to make all kinds of devices—radios, television sets, electronic computers. What you make depends mainly on how you put the parts together. It may be that in the different conditions on some other planet, types of nerve components similar to those we use for thought might be used to create dangerous illusions in the minds of other creatures."

"That still leaves us with a problem. What do we do with this thing?"

"I got the impression it was like a merchant who has to sell his wares to live. Let me go back and see if we can make an agreement with it."

"I'll go with you."

Jim shook his head. "One of us has to stay beyond that four-hundred-foot limit."

*   *   *

MIND PARTNER

The stairs were narrow leading up into the tower. Jim found weary men amidst plaster and bits of board at a solid barricade on the staircase. He scowled at it, then shouted up the stairs, "I want to talk to you!"

There was a sort of twist in the fabric of things. Jim found himself staring at the wall beside the stairs, its plaster gone and bits of board torn loose. The staircase itself was open. He started up.

Behind him, a man still staring at the wall said, "Did you see that? He went *around* somehow."

The back of Jim's neck prickled. He reached a tall door, opened it, turned, and he stood where he had been before.

There was a faint hissing. "I am glad you came back. I can't keep this up forever."

"We want to make an agreement with you. Otherwise, we'll have to use force."

"There is no need of that. I ask only food, water, and a chance to use my faculties. And I would be very happy if the atmospheric pressure around me could be increased. Falling pressure tires me so that it is hard for me to keep self-control."

Jim thought of the first night, when there had been the appearance of light on mansion and grounds, but heavy clouds and only a thin moon in the sky.

The hissing voice said, "It had stormed, with a sharp fall in atmospheric pressure. I was exhausted and created a wrong illusion. Can you provide what I need?"

"The food, water, and pressure chamber, yes. I don't know about the opportunity to 'use your faculties.'"

"There is a painting in the world now that wasn't there before. You and I did that."

"What are you driving at?"

"I can't increase skill where there has been no practice, no earnest thought or desire. I can't help combine facts or memories where none have been stored. But within these limits I can help you and others to a degree of concentration few men of your world know."

"Could you teach us to concentrate this way on our own?"

"I don't know. We would have to try it. Meanwhile, I have been here long enough to have learned that your race has used horses to extend their powers of movement, dogs to increase their ability to trail by scent, cows and goats to convert indigestible grass and leaves into foodstuffs. These all were your partners in the physical world. It seems to me that I am much the same, but in the mental world."

Jim hesitated. "Meanwhile, you can help us to forget these dream lives?"

"Easily. But, as I say, the effect is not permanent."

Jim nodded. "I'll see what we can do."

He went to tell Walters, who listened closely, then picked up the phone.

Early the next morning, Jim climbed the steps to the high narrow door of the tower, put on dark glasses and went in. Right behind him came a corporal with a creepie-peepie TV transmitter. From outside came the windmill roar of helicopters, and, high up, the rumble of jets.

The corporal opened the shutter and spoke quietly into the microphone. A hissing voice spoke in Jim's mind. "I am ready."

Jim said, "This entire place is being watched by television. If there is any important difference between what observers here report and what the cameras show, this place and everything in it will be destroyed a few seconds later."

"I understand," said the hissing voice. Then it told him how to loosen one of the bars, and Jim loosened it and stood back.

There was the sound of footsteps on the staircase. A large heavy box with one end hinged and open was thrust in the doorway.

On the floor, something bunched and unbunched, and moved past into the box. Jim closed the box and snapped shut the padlock. Men lifted it and started down the staircase. Jim and the corporal followed. As they went out the front door, heavy planks were thrown across to a waiting truck. Sweating men in khaki carried the box up the planks into the truck. Then the rear doors swung shut, the engine roared, and the truck moved away.

Jim thought of the truck's destination, a pressure tank in a concrete blockhouse under a big steel shed out in the desert.

He looked around and saw Walters, who smiled at him and held out a slim envelope. "Good work," said Walters. "And I imagine some hundreds of ex-addicts reclaimed from mental hospitals are going to echo those sentiments."

Jim thanked him, and Walters led him to the car, saying, "Now what you need is sleep, and plenty of it."

"And how!"

Once home, Jim fell into an exhausted sleep, and had a nightmare. In the nightmare, he dreamed that he woke up, and found himself in a bed in a room where a light curtain blew in at the window, and the morning sun shone brightly in.

He sat up, and looked around carefully at the furniture, and felt the solid wall of the room as he asked himself a question that he knew would bother him again.

Which was the nightmare?

Then he remembered his fear as he climbed the tree, and Cullen's advice: "When things get tight, *hold your mind on what to do next.* Do that. *Then* think of the next step."

He thought a moment, then lay back and smiled. He might not be absolutely certain this was real. But even if it wasn't, he felt sure he would win in the end.

No nightmare could last forever.

THE HANDLER

BY DAMON KNIGHT (1922–   )

ROGUE
AUGUST

We have talked about the science fiction of Damon Knight in earlier volumes in this series. We have also praised his organizational contributions to the field, his seminal role as a critic within it, and his contributions as a teacher of sf writers, so allow me to mention a couple of his nonfiction books that are major contributions to literary history. One is Charles Fort, Prophet Of The Unexplained *(1970) the story of the man who gathered together unexplained "events" and gave a generation of young sf writers and writers-to-be an excellent source book of story ideas; and (this is the full title)* The Futurians: The Story Of The Science Fiction "Family" Of The 30's That Produced Today's Top Sf Writers And Editors *(1977), an account of a remarkable group of men who became what the title says they became. (MHG)*

I can't help but sigh over what American politics has degenerated into, in this television age. We have people running for president who are chiefly concerned with smiles and hair and waves of the hand. And behind them we have people who really run the campaign, dictate strategy, think up negative TV spots.

Neither can do it alone. The upfront guy may lack brains and this would show itself painfully if he weren't being constantly manipulated. The guy in the back may lack charisma and would get nowhere without the image that the front man can project.

Why does this occur to me now? Well, read "The Handler" which was written two decades before the time of Reagan and Bush. (IA)

When the big man came in, there was a movement in the room like bird dogs pointing. The piano player quit pounding, the two singing drunks shut up, all the beautiful people with cocktails in their hands stopped talking and laughing.

"Pete!" the nearest woman shrilled, and he walked straight into the room, arms around two girls, hugging them tight. "How's my sweetheart? Susy, you look good enough to eat, but I had it for lunch. George, you pirate—" he let go both girls, grabbed a bald blushing little man and thumped him on the arm— "you were great, sweetheart, I mean it, really great. NOW HEAR THIS!" he shouted, over all the voices that were clamoring Pete this, Pete that.

Somebody put a martini in his hand and he stood holding it, bronzed and tall in his dinner jacket, teeth gleaming white as his shirt cuffs. "We had a show!" he told them.

A shriek of agreement went up, a babble of did we have a *show* my God Pete listen a *show*—

He held up his hand. "It was a good show!"

THE HANDLER

Another shriek and babble.

"The sponsor kinda liked it—he just signed for another one in the fall!"

A shriek, a roar, people clapping, jumping up and down. The big man tried to say something else, but gave up, grinning, while men and women crowded up to him. They were all trying to shake his hand, talk in his ear, put their arms around him.

"I love ya *all!*" he shouted. "Now what do you say, let's live a little!"

The murmuring started again as people sorted themselves out. There was a clinking from the bar, "Jesus, Pete," a skinny pop-eyed little guy was saying, crouching in adoration, "when you dropped that fishbowl I thought I'd pee myself, honest to God— "

The big man let out a bark of happy laughter. "Yeah, I can still see the look on your face. And the fish, flopping all over the stage. So what can I do, I get down there on my knees—" the big man did so, bending over and staring at imaginary fish on the floor. "And I say, 'Well, fellows, back to the drawing board!' "

Screams of laughter as the big man stood up. The party was arranging itself around him in arcs of concentric circles, with people in the back standing on sofas and the piano bench so they could see. Somebody yelled, "Sing the goldfish song, Pete!"

Shouts of approval, please-do-Pete, the goldfish song.

"Okay, okay." Grinning, the big man sat on the arm of a chair and raised his glass. "And a vun, and a doo—vere's de moosic?" A scuffle at the piano bench. Somebody banged out a few chords. The big man made a comic face and sang, "Ohhh—how I wish . . .

I was a little fish . . . and when I want some quail . . . I'd flap my little tail."

Laughter, the girls laughing louder than anybody and their red mouths farther open. One flushed blonde had her hand on the big man's knee, and another was sitting close behind him.

"But seriously—" the big man shouted. More laughter.

"No, seriously," he said in a vibrant voice as the room quieted, "I want to tell you in all seriousness I couldn't have done it alone. And incidentally I see we have some foreigners, litvaks and other members of the press here tonight, so I want to introduce all the important people. First of all, George here, the three-fingered band leader—and there isn't a guy in the world could have done what he did this afternoon— George, I love ya." He hugged the blushing little bald man.

"Next my real sweetheart, Ruthie, where are ya? Honey, you were the greatest, really perfect—I mean it, baby—" He kissed a dark girl in a red dress who cried a little and hid her face on his broad shoulder. "And Frank—" he reached down and grabbed the skinny pop-eyed guy by the sleeve. "What can I tell you? A sweetheart?" The skinny guy was blinking, all choked up; the big man thumped him on the back. "Sol and Ernie and Mack, my writers, Shakespeare should have been so lucky—" One by one, they came up to shake the big man's hand as he called their names; the women kissed him and cried. "My stand-in," the big man was calling out, and "my caddy," and "Now," he said, as the room quieted a little, people flushed and sore-throated with enthusiasm, "I want you to meet my handler."

THE HANDLER

The room fell silent. The big man looked thoughtful and startled, as if he had had a sudden pain. Then he stopped moving. He sat without breathing or blinking his eyes. After a moment there was a jerky motion behind him. The girl who was sitting on the arm of the chair got up and moved away. The big man's dinner jacket split open in the back, and a little man climbed out. He had a perspiring brown face under a shock of black hair. He was a very small man, almost a dwarf, stoop-shouldered and round-backed in a sweaty brown singlet and shorts. He climbed out of the cavity in the big man's body, and closed the dinner jacket carefully. The big man sat motionless and his face was doughy.

The little man got down, wetting his lips nervously. Hello, Harry, a few people said. "Hello," Harry called, waving his hand. He was about forty, with a big nose and big soft brown eyes. His voice was cracked and uncertain. "Well, we sure put on a show, didn't we?"

Sure did, Harry, they said politely. He wiped his brow with the back of his hand. "Hot in there," he explained, with an apologetic grin. Yes I guess it must be, Harry, they said. People around the outskirts of the crowd were beginning to turn away, form conversational groups; the hum of talk rose higher. "Say, Tim, I wonder if I could have something to drink," the little man said. "I don't like to leave him—you know—" He gestured toward the silent big man.

"Sure, Harry, what'll it be?"

"Oh—you know—a glass of beer?"

Tim brought him a beer in a pilsener glass and he drank it thirstily, his brown eyes darting nervously from side to side. A lot of people were sitting down now; one or two were at the door leaving.

"Well," the little man said to a passing girl, "Ruthie,

that was quite a moment there, when the fishbowl busted, wasn't it?"

"Huh? Excuse me, honey, I didn't hear you." She bent nearer.

"Oh—well, it don't matter. Nothing."

She patted him on the shoulder once, and took her hand away. "Well excuse me, sweetie, I have to catch Robbins before he leaves." She went on toward the door.

The little man put his beer glass down and sat, twisting his knobby hands together. The bald man and the pop-eyed man were the only ones still sitting near him. An anxious smile flickered on his lips; he glanced at one face, then another. "Well," he began, "that's one show under our belts, huh, fellows, but I guess we got to start, you know, thinking about—"

"Listen, Harry," said the bald man seriously, leaning forward to touch him on the wrist, "why don't you get back inside?"

The little man looked at him for a moment with sad hound-dog eyes, then ducked his head, embarrassed. He stood up uncertainly, swallowed and said, "Well—" He climbed up on the chair behind the big man, opened the back of the dinner jacket and put his legs in one at a time. A few people were watching him, unsmiling. "Thought I'd take it easy a while," he said weakly, "but I guess—" He reached in and gripped something with both hands, then swung himself inside. His brown, uncertain face disappeared.

The big man blinked suddenly and stood up. "Well *hey* there," he called, "what's a matter with this party anyway? Let's see some life, some action—" Faces were lighting up around him. People began to move in closer. "What I mean, let me hear that beat!"

THE HANDLER

The big man began clapping his hands rhythmically. The piano took it up. Other people began to clap. "What I mean, are we alive here or just waiting for the wagon to pick us up? How's that again, can't hear you!" A roar of pleasure as he cupped his hand to his ear. "Well come on, let me hear it!" A louder roar. Pete, Pete; a gabble of voices. "I got nothing against Harry," said the bald man earnestly in the middle of the noise, "I mean for a square he's a nice guy." "Know what you mean," said the pop-eyed man, "I mean like he doesn't *mean* it." "Sure," said the bald man, "but Jesus that sweaty undershirt and all . . ." The pop-eyed man shrugged. "What are you gonna do?" Then they both burst out laughing as the big man made a comic face, tongue lolling, eyes crossed. Pete, Pete, Pete; the room was really jumping; it was a great party, and everything was all right, far into the night.

THE VOICES OF TIME

BY J. G. BALLARD (1930–   )

NEW WORLDS (GREAT BRITAIN)
OCTOBER

J. G. Ballard has long been one my favorite writers, but I must admit that I still prefer the Ballard who wrote The Wind From Nowhere, The Drowned World, The Burning World, *and* The Crystal World, *and most especially the stories contained in the collections* The Voices of Time *(1962),* Billenium *(1962),* Passport To Eternity *(1963), and* The Terminal Beach *(1964).*

"The Voices of Time" is a wonderful example of the Ballard of this period at his very best—beautiful prose under full control, taking on a subject few writers could handle—the effect on time of the Second Law of Thermodynamics. (MHG)

There's a certain modernism that has attempted to re-move the shackles that have bound intellectual activity in the past.

Thus, modern art has abandoned representationalism and we no longer expect artists to paint pictures that

*look like photographs. We seek impressions and moods
rather than bland realism.*

*In the same way, modern music abandons the sim-
plicity of "tunes we can whistle" and involves itself with
more intricate and even abstract combinations of sounds.
Even modern science abandoned the simple rules that
have governed our views of the Universe prior to
this century and began to play with relativity and
quantum theory which defy "common sense" and which
even bring the fundamental system of causality into
question.*

*It is not surprising, then, that modern literature can
shake free of simple plotting of beginning-middle-end,
and no longer feels it necessary to "tell a story" in the
old-fashioned way. It, too, can labor to express a mood
or build an emotion and to do it wildly. I can't do it
myself and I never try, but Ballard can and does. (IA)*

I

Later Powers often thought of Whitby, and the strange
grooves the biologist had cut, apparently at random,
all over the floor of the empty swimming pool. An
inch deep and twenty feet long, interlocking to form
an elaborate ideogram like a Chinese character, they
had taken him all summer to complete, and he had
obviously thought about little else, working away tirelessly through the long desert afternoons. Powers had
watched him from his office window at the far end of
the Neurology wing, carefully marking out his pegs
and string, carrying away the cement chips in a small
canvas bucket. After Whitby's suicide no one had
bothered about the grooves, but Powers often borrowed the supervisor's key and let himself into the

disused pool, and would look down at the labyrinth of moldering gulleys, half-filled with water leaking in from the chlorinator, an enigma now past any solution.

Initially, however, Powers was too preoccupied with completing his work at the Clinic and planning his own final withdrawal. After the first frantic weeks of panic he had managed to accept an uneasy compromise that allowed him to view his predicament with the detached fatalism he had previously reserved for his patients. Fortunately he was moving down the physical and mental gradients simultaneously—lethargy and inertia blunted his anxieties, a slackening metabolism made it necessary to concentrate to produce a connected thought-train. In fact, the lengthening intervals of dreamless sleep were almost restful. He found himself beginning to look forward to them, made no effort to wake earlier than was essential.

At first he had kept an alarm clock by his bed, tried to compress as much activity as he could into the narrowing hours of consciousness, sorting out his library, driving over to Whitby's laboratory every morning to examine the latest batch of X-ray plates, every minute and hour rationed like the last drops of water in a canteen.

Anderson, fortunately, had unwittingly made him realize the pointlessness of this course.

After Powers had resigned from the Clinic he still continued to drive in once a week for his checkup, now little more than a formality. On what what turned out to be the last occasion Anderson had perfunctorily taken his blood count, noting Powers' slacker facial muscles, fading pupil reflexes, the unshaven cheeks.

He smiled sympathetically at Powers across the desk,

wondering what to say to him. Once he had put on a show of encouragement with the more intelligent patients, even tried to provide some sort of explanation. But Powers was too difficult to reach—neurosurgeon extraordinary, a man always out on the periphery, only at ease working with unfamiliar materials. To himself he thought: *I'm sorry, Robert. What can I say—"Even the sun is growing cooler—"?* He watched Powers drum his fingers restlessly on the enamel desk top, his eyes glancing at the spinal level charts hung around the office. Despite his unkempt appearance—he had been wearing the same unironed shirt and dirty white plimsoles a week ago—Powers looked composed and self-possessed, like a Conrad beachcomber more or less reconciled to his own weaknesses.

"What are you doing with yourself, Robert?" he asked. "Are you still going over to Whitby's lab?"

"As much as I can. It takes me half an hour to cross the lake, and I keep on sleeping through the alarm clock. I may leave my place and move in there permanently."

Anderson frowned. "Is there much point? As far as I could make out Whitby's work was pretty speculative—" He broke off, realizing the implied criticism of Powers' own disastrous work at the Clinic, but Powers seemed to ignore this, was examining the pattern of shadows on the ceiling. "Anyway, wouldn't it be better to stay where you are, among your own things, read through Toynbee and Spengler again?"

Powers laughed shortly. "That's the last thing I want to do. I want to *forget* Toynbee and Spengler, not try to remember them. In fact, Paul, I'd like to forget everything. I don't know whether I've got enough time, though. How much can you forget in three months?"

"Everything, I suppose, if you want to. But don't try to race the clock."

Powers nodded quietly, repeating his last remark to himself. Racing the clock was exactly what he had been doing. As he stood up and said goodbye to Anderson he suddenly decided to throw away his alarm clock, escape from his futile obsession with time. To remind himself he unfastened his wristwatch and scrambled the setting, then slipped it into his pocket. Making his way out to the car park he reflected on the freedom this simple act gave him. He would explore the lateral byways now, the side doors, as it were, in the corridors of time. Three months could be an eternity.

He picked his car out of the line and strolled over to it, shielding his eyes from the heavy sunlight beating down across the parabolic sweep of the lecture theater roof. He was about to climb in when he saw that someone had traced with a finger across the dust caked over the windshield:

$$96,688,365,498,721$$

Looking over his shoulder, he recognized the white Packard parked next to him, peered inside, and saw a lean-faced young man with blond sun-bleached hair and a high cerebrotonic forehead watching him behind dark glasses. Sitting beside him at the wheel was a raven-haired girl whom he had often seen around the psychology department. She had intelligent but somehow rather oblique eyes, and Powers remembered that the younger doctors called her "the girl from Mars."

"Hello, Kaldren," Powers said to the young man. "Still following me around?"

Kaldren nodded. "Most of the time, Doctor." He sized Powers up shrewdly. "We haven't seen very much of you recently, as a matter of fact. Anderson said you'd resigned, and we noticed your laboratory was closed."

Powers shrugged. "I felt I needed a rest. As you'll understand, there's a good deal that needs rethinking."

Kaldren frowned half-mockingly. "Sorry to hear that, Doctor. But don't let these temporary setbacks depress you." He noticed the girl watching Powers with interest. "Coma's a fan of yours. I gave her your papers from *American Journal of Psychiatry,* and she's read through the whole file."

The girl smiled pleasantly at Powers, for a moment dispelling the hostility between the two men. When Powers nodded to her she leaned across Kaldren and said: "Actually I've just finished Noguchi's autobiography—the great Japanese doctor who discovered the spirochete. Somehow you remind me of him—there's so much of yourself in all the patients you worked on."

Powers smiled wanly at her, then his eyes turned and locked involuntarily on Kaldren's. They stared at each other somberly for a moment, and a small tic in Kaldren's right cheek began to flicker irritatingly. He flexed his facial muscles, after a few seconds mastered it with an effort, obviously annoyed that Powers should have witnessed this brief embarrassment.

"How did the clinic go today?" Powers asked. "Have you had any more . . . headaches?"

Kaldren's mouth snapped shut, he looked suddenly irritable. "Whose care am I in, doctor? Yours or Anderson's? Is that the sort of question you should be asking now?"

Powers gestured deprecatingly. "Perhaps not." He cleared his throat; the heat was ebbing the blood from his head and he felt tired and eager to get away from them. He turned toward his car, then realized that Kaldren would probably follow, either try to crowd him into the ditch or block the road and make Powers sit in his dust all the way back to the lake. Kaldren was capable of any madness.

"Well, I've got to go and collect something," he said, adding in a firmer voice: "Get in touch with me, though, if you can't reach Anderson."

He waved and walked off behind the line of cars. Reflected in the windows he could see Kaldren looking back and watching him closely.

He entered the Neurology wing, paused thankfully in the cool foyer, nodding to the two nurses and the armed guard at the reception desk. For some reason the terminals sleeping in the adjacent dormitory block attracted hordes of would-be sightseers, most of them cranks with some magical antinarcoma remedy, or merely the idly curious, but a good number of quite normal people, many of whom had traveled thousands of miles, impelled towards the Clinic by some strange instinct, like animals migrating to a preview of their racial graveyards.

He walked along the corridor to the supervisor's office overlooking the recreation deck, borrowed the key, and made his way out through the tennis courts and calisthenics rigs to the enclosed swimming pool at the far end. It had been disused for months, and only

Powers' visits kept the lock free. Stepping through, he closed it behind him and walked past the peeling wooden stands to the deep end.

Putting a foot up on the diving board, he looked down at Whitby's ideogram. Damp leaves and bits of paper obscured it, but the outlines were just distinguishable. It covered almost the entire floor of the pool and at first glance appeared to represent a huge solar disc, with four radiating diamond-shaped arms, a crude Jungian mandala.

Wondering what had prompted Whitby to carve the device before his death, Powers noticed something moving through the debris in the center of the disc. A black, horny-shelled animal about a foot long was nosing about in the slush, heaving itself on tired legs. Its shell was articulated, and vaguely resembled an armadillo's. Reaching the edge of the disc, it stopped and hesitated, then slowly backed away into the center again, apparently unwilling or unable to cross the narrow groove.

Powers looked around, then stepped into one of the changing stalls and pulled a small wooden clothes locker off its rusty wall bracket. Carrying it under one arm, he climbed down the chromium ladder into the pool and walked carefully across the slithery floor toward the animal. As he approached it sidled away from him, but he trapped it easily, using the lid to lever it into the box.

The animal was heavy, at least the weight of a brick. Powers tapped its massive olive-black carapace with his knuckle, noting the triangular warty head jutting out below its rim like a turtle's, the thickened pads beneath the first digits of the pentadactyl forelimbs.

He watched the three-lidded eyes blinking at him anxiously from the bottom of the box.

"Expecting some really hot weather?" he murmured. "That lead umbrella you're carrying around should keep you cool."

He closed the lid, climbed out of the pool, and made his way back to the supervisor's office, then carried the box out to his car.

". . . Kaldren continues to reproach me [*Powers wrote in his diary*]. For some reason he seems unwilling to accept his isolation, is elaborating a series of private rituals to replace the missing hours of sleep. Perhaps I should tell him of my own approaching zero, but he'd probably regard this as the final unbearable insult, that I should have in excess what he so desperately yearns for. God knows what might happen. Fortunately the nightmarish visions appear to have receded for the time being . . ."

Pushing the diary away, Powers leaned forward across the desk and stared out through the window at the white floor of the lake bed stretching toward the hills along the horizon. Three miles away, on the far shore, he could see the circular bowl of the radio-telescope revolving slowly in the clear afternoon air, as Kaldren tirelessly trapped the sky, sluicing in millions of cubic parsecs of sterile ether, like the nomads who trapped the sea along the shores of the Persian Gulf.

Behind him the airconditioner murmured quietly, cooling the pale blue walls half-hidden in the dim light. Outside the air was bright and oppressive, the heat waves rippling up from the clumps of gold-tinted cacti below the Clinic blurring the sharp terraces of the twenty-story Neurology block. There, in the silent dormitories behind the sealed shutters, the terminals slept their long dreamless sleep. There were not over five hundred of them in the Clinic, the vanguard of a vast somnambulist army massing for its last march. Only five years had elapsed since the first narcoma syndrome had been recognized, but already huge government hospitals in the east were being readied for intakes in the thousands, as more and more cases came to light.

Powers felt suddenly tired, and glanced at his wrist, wondering how long he had to eight o'clock, his bedtime for the next week or so. Already he missed the dusk, soon would wake to his last dawn.

His watch was in his hip pocket. He remembered his decision not to use his timepieces, and sat back and stared at the bookshelves beside the desk. There were rows of green-covered AEC publications he had removed from Whitby's library, papers in which the biologist described his work out in the Pacific after the H-tests. Many of them Powers knew almost by heart, read a hundred times in an effort to grasp Whitby's last conclusions. Toynbee would certainly be easier to forget.

His eyes dimmed momentarily, as the tall black wall in the rear of his mind cast its great shadow over his brain. He reached for the diary thinking of the girl in Kaldren's car—Coma he had called her, another of his insane jokes—and her reference to Noguchi. Actually the comparison should have been made with Whitby, not himself; the monsters in the lab were nothing more than fragmented mirrors of Whitby's mind, like the grotesque radio-shielded frog he had found that morning in the swimming pool.

Thinking of the girl Coma, and the heartening smile she had given him, he wrote:

> Woke 6:33 am. Last session with Anderson. He made it plain he's seen enough of me, and from now on I'm better alone. To sleep 8:00? (These countdowns terrify me.)

He paused, then added:

> *Goodbye, Eniwetok.*

II

He saw the girl again the next day at Whitby's laboratory. He had driven over after breakfast with the new specimen, eager to get it into a vivarium before it died. The only previous armored mutant he had come across had nearly broken his neck. Speeding along the lake road a month or so earlier he had struck it with the offside front wheel, expecting the small creature to flatten instantly. Instead its hard lead-packed shell had remained rigid, even though the organism within it had been pulped, had flung the car heavily into the ditch. He had gone back for the shell, later weighed it at the laboratory, found it contained over 600 grams of lead.

Quite a number of plants and animals were building up heavy metals as radiological shields. In the hills behind the beach house a couple of old-time propectors were renovating the derelict gold-panning equipment abandoned over eighty years ago. They had noticed the bright yellow tints of the cacti, run an analysis, and found that the plants were assimilating gold in extractable quantities, although the soil concentrations were unworkable. Oak Ridge was at last paying a dividend!!

Waking that morning just after 6:45—ten minutes later than the previous day (he had switched on the radio, heard one of the regular morning programs as he climbed out of bed)—he had eaten a light unwanted breakfast, then spent an hour packing away some of the books in his library, crating them up and taping on address labels to his brother.

He reached Whitby's laboratory half an hour later. This was housed in a 100-foot wide geodesic dome built beside his chalet on the west shore of the lake about a mile from Kaldren's summer house. The chalet had been closed after Whitby's suicide, and many of the experimental plants and animals had died before Powers had managed to receive permission to use the laboratory.

As he turned into the driveway he saw the girl standing on the apex of the yellow-ribbed dome, her slim figure silhouetted against the sky. She waved to him, then began to step down across the glass polyhedrons and jumped nimbly into the driveway beside the car.

"Hello," she said, giving him a welcoming smile. "I came over to see your zoo. Kaldren said you wouldn't let me in if he came so I made him stay behind."

She waited for Powers to say something while he searched for his keys, then volunteered: "If you like, I can wash your shirt."

Powers grinned at her, peered down ruefully at his dust-stained sleeves. "Not a bad idea. I thought I was beginning to look a little uncared-for." He unlocked the door, took Coma's arm. "I don't know why Kaldren told you that—he's welcome here any time he likes."

"What have you got in there?" Coma asked, pointing at the wooden box he was carrying as they walked between the gear-laden benches.

"A distant cousin of ours I found. Interesting little chap. I'll introduce you in a moment."

Sliding partitions divided the dome into four chambers. Two of them were storerooms, filled with spare tanks, apparatus, cartons of animal food, and test rigs. They crossed the third section, almost filled by a powerful X-ray projector, a giant 250-mega-amp G.E. Maxitron, angled onto a revolving table, concrete shielding blocks lying around ready for use like huge building bricks.

The fourth chamber contained Powers' zoo, the vivaria jammed together along the benches and in the sinks, big colored cardboard charts and memos pinned onto the draft hoods above them, a tangle of rubber tubing and power leads trailing across the floor. As they walked past the lines of tanks dim forms shifted behind the frosted glass, and at the far end of the aisle there was a sudden scurrying in a large-scale cage by Powers' desk.

Putting the box down on his chair, he picked a packet of peanuts off the desk and went over to the cage. A small black-haired chimpanzee wearing a dented jet pilot's helmet swarmed deftly up the bars to him, chirped happily, and then jumped down to a miniature control panel against the rear wall of the cage. Rapidly it flicked a series of buttons and toggles, and a succession of colored lights lit up like a juke box and jangled out a two-second blast of music.

"Good boy," Powers said encouragingly, patting the chimp's back and shoveling the peanuts into its hands. "You're getting much too clever for that one, aren't you?"

The chimp tossed the peanuts into the back of its throat with the smooth easy motions of a conjuror, jabbering at Powers in a singsong voice.

Coma laughed and took some of the nuts from Powers. "He's sweet. I think he's talking to you."

Powers nodded. "Quite right, he is. Actually he's got a two-hundred-word vocabulary, but his voice box scrambles it all up." He opened a small refrigerator by the desk, took out half a packet of sliced bread, and passed a couple of pieces to the chimp. It picked an electric toaster off the floor and placed it in the middle of a low wobbling table in the center of the cage, whipped the pieces into the slots. Powers pressed a tab on the switchboard beside the cage and the toaster began to crackle softly.

"He's one of the brightest we've had here, about as intelligent as a five-year-old child, though much more self-sufficient in a lot of ways." The two pieces of toast jumped out of their slots and the chimp caught them neatly, nonchalantly patting its helmet each time, then ambled off into a small ramshackle kennel and relaxed back with one arm out of a window, sliding the toast into its mouth.

"He built that house himself," Powers went on, switching off the toaster. "Not a bad effort, really." He pointed to a yellow polythene bucket by the front door of the kennel, from which a battered-looking geranium protruded. "Tends that plant, cleans up the cage, pours out an endless stream of wisecracks. Pleasant fellow all round."

Coma was smiling broadly to herself. "Why the space helmet, though?"

Powers hesitated. "Oh, it—er—it's for his own protection. Sometimes he gets rather bad headaches. His predecessors all—" He broke off and turned away. "Let's have a look at some of the other inmates."

He moved down the line of tanks, beckoning Coma with him. "We'll start at the beginning." He lifted the glass lid off one of the tanks, and Coma peered down into a shallow bath of water, where a small round organism with slender tendrils was nestling in a rockery of shells and pebbles.

"Sea anemone. Or was. Simple coelenterate with an open-ended body cavity." He pointed down to a thickened ridge of tissue around the base. "It's sealed up the cavity, converted the channel into a rudimentary notochord. Later the tendrils will knot themselves into a ganglion, but already they're sensitive to color. Look." He borrowed the violet handkerchief in Coma's breast pocket and spread it across the tank. The tendrils flexed and stiffened, began to weave slowly, as if they were trying to focus.

"The strange thing is that they're completely insensitive to white light. Normally the tendrils register shifting pressure gradients, like the tympanic diaphragms in your ears. Now it's almost as if they can *hear* primary colors, suggests it's readapting itself for a non-aquatic existence in a static world of violent color contrasts."

Coma shook her head, puzzled. "Why, though?"

"Hold on a moment. Let me put you in the picture

first." They moved along the bench to a series of drum-shaped cages made of wire mosquito netting. Above the first was a large white cardboard screen bearing a blown-up microphoto of a tall pagodalike chain, topped by the legend: *"Drosophila: 15 roentgens/min."*

Powers tapped a small perspex window in the drum. "Fruitfly. Its huge chromosomes make it a useful test vehicle." He bent down, pointed to a gray V-shaped honeycomb suspended from the roof. A few flies emerged from entrances, moving about busily. "Usually it's solitary, a nomadic scavenger. Now it forms itself into well-knit social groups, has begun to secrete a thin sweet lymph something like honey."

"What's this?" Coma asked, touching the screen.

"Diagram of a key gene in the operation." He traced a spray of arrows leading from a link in the chain. The arrows were labeled: *"Lymph gland"* and subdivided *"sphincter muscles, epithelium, templates."*

"It's rather like the perforated sheet music of a player piano," Powers commented, "or a computer punch tape. Knock out one link with an X-ray beam, lose a characteristic, change the score."

Coma was peering through the window of the next cage and pulling an unpleasant face. Over her shoulder Powers saw she was watching an enormous spiderlike insect, as big as a hand, its dark hairy legs as thick as fingers. The compound eyes had been built up so that they resembled giant rubies.

"He looks unfriendly," she said. "What's that sort of rope ladder he's spinning?" As she moved a finger to her mouth the spider came to life, retreated into the cage, and began spewing out a complex skein of interlinked gray thread which it slung in long loops from the roof of the cage.

"A web," Powers told her. "Except that it consists of nervous tissue. The ladders form an external neural plexus, an inflatable brain as it were, that he can pump up to whatever size the situation calls for. A sensible arrangement, really; far better than our own."

Coma backed away. "Gruesome. I wouldn't like to go into his parlor."

"Oh, he's not as frightening as he looks. Those huge eyes staring at you are blind. Or, rather, their optical sensitivity has shifted down the band; the retinas will only register gamma radiation. Your wristwatch has luminous hands. When you moved it across the window he started thinking. World War IV should really bring him into his element."

They strolled back to Powers' desk. He put a coffee pan over a bunsen and pushed a chair across to Coma. Then he opened the box, lifted out the armored frog, and put it down on a sheet of blotting paper.

"Recognize him? Your old childhood friend, the common frog. He's built himself quite a solid little air raid shelter." He carried the animal across to a sink, turned on the tap, and let the water play softly over its shell. Wiping his hands on his shirt, he came back to the desk.

Coma brushed her long hair off her forehead, watched him curiously.

"Well, what's the secret?"

Powers lit a cigarette. "There's no secret. Teratologists have been breeding monsters for years. Have you ever heard of the 'silent pair'?"

She shook her head.

Powers stared moodily at the cigarette for a moment, riding the kick the first one of the day always gave him. "The so-called 'silent pair' is one of modern genetics' oldest problems, the apparently baffling mystery of the two inactive genes which occur in a small percentage of all living organisms, and appear to have no intelligible role in their structure or development. For a long while now biologists have been trying to activate them, but the difficulty is partly in identifying the silent genes in the fertilized germ cells of parents known to contain them, and partly in focusing a narrow enough X-ray beam which will do no damage to the remainder of the chromosome. However, after about ten years' work Dr. Whitby successfully developed a whole-body irradiation technique based on his observation of radiobiological damage at Eniwetok."

Powers paused for a moment. "He had noticed that there appeared to be more biological damage after the tests—that is, a greater transport of energy—than could be accounted for by direct radiation. What was happening was that the protein lattices in the genes were building up energy in the way that any vibrating membrane accumulates energy when it resonates—you remember the analogy of the bridge collapsing under the soldiers marching in step—and it occurred to him that if he could first identify the critical resonance frequency of the lattices in any particular silent gene he could then radiate the entire living organism, and not simply its germ cells, with a low field that would act selectively on the silent gene and cause no damage to the remainder of the chromosomes, whose lattices would resonate critically only at other specific frequencies."

Powers gestured around the laboratory with his cigarette. "You see some of the fruits of this 'resonance transfer' technique around you."

Coma nodded: "They've had their silent genes activated?"

"Yes, all of them. These are only a few of the thousands of specimens who have passed through here, and, as you've seen, the results are pretty dramatic."

He reached up and pulled across a section of the sun curtain. They were sitting just under the lip of the dome, and the mounting sunlight had begun to irritate him.

In the comparative darkness Coma noticed a stroboscope winking slowly in one of the tanks at the end of the bench behind her. She stood up and went over to it, examining a tall sunflower with a thickened stem and greatly enlarged receptacle. Packed around the flower, so that only its head protruded, was a chimney of gray-white stones, neatly cemented together and labeled: *"Cretaceous Chalk: 60,000,000 years."*

Beside it on the bench were three other chimneys, these labeled: *"Devonian Sandstone: 290,000,000 years," "Asphalt: 20 years," "Polyvinylchloride: 6 months."*

"Can you see those moist white discs on the sepals?" Powers pointed out. "In some way they regulate the plant's metabolism. It literally *sees* time. The older the surrounding environment, the more sluggish its metabolism. With the asphalt chimney it will complete its annual cycle in a week, with the PVC one in a couple of hours."

"Sees time," Coma repeated, wonderingly. She looked up at Powers, chewing her lower lip reflectively. "It's fantastic. Are these the creatures of the future, doctor?"

"I don't know," Powers admitted. "But if they are their world must be a monstrous, surrealist one."

*　　*　　*

He went back to the desk, pulled two cups from a drawer, and poured out the coffee, switching off the bunsen. "Some people have speculated that organisms possessing the silent pair of genes are the forerunners of a massive move up the evolutionary slope, that the silent genes are a sort of code, a divine message that we inferior organisms are carrying for our more highly developed descendants. It may well be true—perhaps we've broken the code too soon."

"Why do you say that?"

"Well, as Whitby's death indicates, the experiments in this laboratory have all come to a rather unhappy conclusion. Without exception the organisms we've irradiated have entered a final phase of totally disorganized growth, producing dozens of specialized sensory organs whose function we can't even guess. The results are catastrophic—the anemone will literally explode, the Drosophila cannibalize themselves, and so on. Whether the future implicit in these plants and animals is ever intended to take place, or whether we're merely extrapolating—I don't know. Sometimes I think, though, that the new sensory organs developed are parodies of their real intentions. The specimens you've seen today are all in an early stage of their secondary growth cycles. Later on they begin to look distinctly bizarre."

Coma nodded. "A zoo isn't complete without its keeper," she commented. "What about Man?"

Powers shrugged. "About one in every 100,000—the usual average—contains the silent pair. You might have them—or I. No one has volunteered yet to undergo whole-body irradiation. Apart from the fact that it would be classified as suicide, if the experiments here are any guide the experience would be savage and violent.''

He sipped at the thin coffee, feeling tired and somehow bored. Recapitulating the laboratory's work had exhausted him.

The girl leaned forward. "You look awfully pale," she said solicitiously. "Don't you sleep well?"

Powers managed a brief smile. "Too well," he admitted. "It's no longer a problem with me."

"I wish I could say that about Kaldren. I don't think he sleeps anywhere near enough. I hear him pacing around all night." She added, "Still, I suppose it's better than being a terminal. Tell me, Doctor, wouldn't it be worth trying this radiation technique on the sleepers at the Clinic? It might wake them up before the end. A few of them must possess the silent genes."

"They *all* do," Powers told her. "The two phenomena are very closely linked, as a matter of fact." He stopped, fatigue dulling his brain, and wondered whether to ask the girl to leave. Then he climbed off the desk and reached behind it, picked up a tape recorder.

Switching it on, he zeroed the tape and adjusted the speaker volume.

"Whitby and I often talked this over. Toward the end I took it all down. He was a great biologist, so let's hear it in his own words. It's absolutely the heart of the matter."

He flipped the table on, adding, "I've played it over to myself a thousand times, so I'm afraid the quality is poor."

An older man's voice, sharp and slightly irritable, sounded out above a low buzz of distortion, but Coma could hear it clearly.

THE VOICES OF TIME

(Whitby) . . . for heaven's sake, Robert, look at those FAO statistics. Despite an annual increase of five percent in acreage sown over the past fifteen years, world wheat crops have continued to decline by a factor of about two percent. The same story repeats itself ad nauseam. Cereals and root crops, dairy yields, ruminant fertility—are all down. Couple these with a mass of parallel symptoms, anything you care to pick from altered migratory routes to longer hibernation periods, and the overall pattern is incontrovertible.

(Powers) Population figures for Europe and North American show no decline, though.

(Whitby) Of course not, as I keep pointing out. It will take a century for such a fractional drop in fertility to have any effect in areas where extensive birth control provides an artificial reservoir. One must look at the countries of the Far East, and particularly at those where infant mortality has remained at a steady level. The population of Sumatra, for example, has declined by over fifteen percent in the last twenty years. A fabulous decline! Do you realize that only two or three decades ago the Neo-Malthusians were talking about a 'world population explosion'? In fact, it's an implosion. Another factor is—

Here the tape had been cut and edited, and Whitby's voice, less querulous this time, picked up again.

. . . just as a matter of interest, tell me something: How long do you sleep each night?

(Powers) I don't know exactly; about eight hours, I suppose.

(Whitby) The proverbial eight hours. Ask anyone and they say automatically, 'eight hours.' As a matter of fact you sleep about ten and a half hours, like the majority of people. I've timed you on a number of occasions. I myself sleep eleven. Yet thirty years ago people did indeed sleep eight hours, and a century before that they slept six or seven. In Vasari's *Lives* one reads of Michelangelo sleeping for only four or five hours, painting all day at the age of eighty, and then working through the night over his anatomy table with a candle strapped to his forehead. Now he's regarded as a prodigy, but it was unremarkable then. How do you think the ancients, from Plato to Shakespeare, Aristotle to Aquinas, were able to cram so much work into their lives? Simply because they had an extra six or seven hours every day. Of course, a second disadvantage under which we labor is a lowered basal metabolic rate—another factor no one will explain.

(Powers) I suppose you could take the view that the lengthened sleep interval is a compensation device, a sort of mass neurotic attempt to escape from the terrifying pressures of urban life in the late twentieth century.

(Whitby) You could, but you'd be wrong. It's simply a matter of biochemistry. The ribonucleic acid templates which unravel the protein chains in all living organisms are wearing out, the dies

enscribing the protoplasmic signature have become
blunted. After all, they've been running now for
over a thousand million years. It's time to retool.
Just as an individual organism's life span is finite,
or the life of a yeast colony or a given species, so
the life of an entire biological kingdom is of fixed
duration. It's always been assumed that the evolutionary slope reaches forever upward, but in fact
the peak has already been reached, and the path-
way now leads downward to the common biological grave. It's a despairing and at present un-
acceptable vision of the future, but it's the only
one. Five thousand centuries from now our descendants, instead of being multibrained starmen,
will probably be naked prognathous idiots with
hair on their foreheads, grunting their way through
the remains of this Clinic like Neolithic men caught
in a macabre inversion of time. Believe me, I pity
them, as I pity myself. My total failure, my abso-
lute lack of any moral or biological right to existence, is implicit in every cell of my body . . .

The tape ended; the spool ran free and stopped.
Powers closed the machine, then massaged his face.
Coma sat quietly, watching him and listening to the
chimp playing with a box of puzzle dice.

"As far as Whitby could tell," Powers said, "the
silent genes represent a last desperate effort of the
biological kingdom to keep its head above the rising
waters. Its total life period is determined by the amount
of radiation emitted by the sun, and once this reaches
a certain point the sure-death line has been passed and
extinction is inevitable. To compensate for this, alarms
have been built in which alter the form of the organ-

ism and adapt it to living in a hotter radiological climate. Soft-skinned organisms develop hard shells; these contain heavy metals as radiation screens. New organs of perception are developed too. According to Whitby, though, it's all wasted effort in the long run— but sometimes I wonder."

He smiled at Coma and shrugged. "Well, let's talk about something else. How long have you known Kaldren?"

"About three weeks. Feels like ten thousand years."

"How do you find him now? We've been rather out of touch lately."

Coma grinned. "I don't seem to see very much of him either. He makes me sleep all the time. Kaldren has many strange talents, but he lives just for himself. You mean a lot to him, Doctor. In fact, you're my one serious rival."

"I thought he couldn't stand the sight of me."

"Oh, that's just a sort of surface symptom. He really thinks of you continuously. That's why we spend all our time following you around." She eyed Powers shrewdly. "I think he feels guilty about something."

"Guilty?" Powers exclaimed. "*He* does? I thought I was supposed to be the guilty one."

"Why?" she pressed. She hesitated, then said, "You carried out some experimental surgical technique on him, didn't you?"

"Yes," Powers admitted. "It wasn't altogether a success, like so much of what I seem to be involved with. If Kaldren feels guilty, I suppose it's because he feels he must take some of the responsibility."

He looked down at the girl, her intelligent eyes watching him closely. "For one or two reasons it may be necessary for you to know. You said Kaldren paced around all night and didn't get enough sleep. Actually he doesn't get any sleep at all."

The girl nodded. "You . . ." She made a snapping gesture with her fingers.

". . . narcotomized him," Powers completed. "Surgically speaking, it was a great success; one might well share a Nobel for it. Normally the hypothalamus regulates the period of sleep, raising the threshold of consciousness in order to relax the venous capillaries in the brain and drain them of accumulating toxins. However, by sealing off some of the control loops the subject is unable to receive the sleep cue, and the capillaries drain while he remains conscious. All he feels is a temporary lethargy, but this passes within three or four hours. Physically speaking, Kaldren has had another twenty years added to his life. But the psyche seems to need sleep for its own private reasons, and consequently Kaldren has periodic storms that tear him apart. The whole thing was a tragic blunder."

Coma frowned pensively. "I guessed as much. Your papers in the neurosurgery journals referred to the patient as K. A touch of pure Kafka that came all too true."

"I may leave here for good, Coma," Powers said. "Make sure that Kaldren goes to his clinics. Some of the deep scar tissue will need to be cleaned away."

"I'll try. Sometimes I feel I'm just another of his insane terminal documents."

"What are those?"

"Haven't you heard? Kaldren's collection of final statements about *Homo sapiens*. The complete works of Freud, Beethoven's deaf quartets, transcripts of the

Nuremburg trials, an automatic novel, and so on." She broke off. "What's that you're drawing?"

"Where?"

She pointed to the desk blotter, and Powers looked down and realized he had been unconsciously sketching an elaborate doodle. Whitby's four-armed sun. "It's nothing," he said. Somehow, though, it had a strangely compelling force.

Coma stood up to leave. "You must come and see us, Doctor. Kaldren has so much he wants to show you. He's just got hold of an old copy of the last signals sent back by the Mercury Seven twenty years ago when they reached the moon, and can't think about anything else. You remember the strange messages they recorded before they died, full of poetic ramblings about the white gardens. Now that I think about it they behaved rather like the plants in your zoo here."

She put her hands in her pockets, then pulled something out. "By the way, Kaldren asked me to give you this."

It was an old index card from the observatory library. In the center had been typed the number:

96,688,365,498,720

"It's going to take a long time to reach zero at this rate," Powers remarked dryly. "I'll have quite a collection when we're finished."

After she had left he chucked the card into the waste bin and sat down at the desk, staring for an hour at the ideogram on the blotter.

Halfway back to his beach house the lake road

forked to the left through a narrow saddle that ran between the hills to an abandoned Air Force weapons range on one of the remoter salt lakes. At the nearer end were a number of small bunkers and camera towers, one or two metal shacks, and a low-roofed storage hangar. The white hills encircled the whole area, shutting it off from the world outside, and Powers liked to wander on foot down the gunnery aisles that had been marked down the two-mile length of the lake toward the concrete sight-screens at the far end. The abstract patterns made him feel like an ant on a bone-white chessboard, the rectangular screens at one end and the towers and bunkers at the other like opposing pieces.

His session with Coma had made Powers feel suddenly dissatisfied with the way he was spending his last months. *Goodbye, Eniwetok,* he had written, but in fact systematically forgetting everything was exactly the same as remembering it, a cataloguing in reverse, sorting out all the books in the mental library and putting them back in their right places upside down.

Powers climbed one of the camera towers, leaned on the rail, and looked out along the aisles toward the sight-screens. Ricocheting shells and rockets had chipped away large pieces of the circular concrete bands that ringed the target bulls, but the outlines of the huge 100-yard-wide discs, alternately painted blue and red, were still visible.

For half an hour he stared quietly at them, formless ideas shifting through his mind. Then without thinking, he abruptly left the rail and climbed down the companionway. The storage hangar was fifty yards away. He walked quickly across to it, stepped into the cool shadows, and peered around the rusting electric trolleys and empty flare drums. At the far end, behind a pile of lumber and bales of wire, were a stack of unopened cement bags, a mound of dirty sand, and an old mixer.

Half an hour later he had backed the Buick into the hangar and hooked the cement mixer, charged with sand, cement, and water scavenged from the drums lying around outside, onto the rear bumper, then loaded a dozen more bags into the car's trunk and rear seat. Finally he selected a few straight lengths of timber, jammed them through the window, and set off across the lake toward the central target bull.

For the next two hours he worked away steadily in the center of the great blue disc, mixing up the cement by hand, carrying it across to the crude wooden forms he had lashed together from the timber, smoothing it down so that it formed a six-inch-high wall around the perimeter of the bull. He worked without pause, stirring the cement with a tire lever, scooping it out with a hubcap prized off one of the wheels.

By the time he finished and drove off, leaving his equipment where it stood, he had completed a thirty-foot long section of wall.

IV

JUNE 7: Conscious, for the first time, of the brevity of each day. As long as I was awake for over twelve hours I still orientated my time around the meridian; morning and afternoon set their old rhythms. Now, with just over eleven hours of consciousness left, they form a continuous interval, like a length of tape measure. I can see exactly how much is left on the spool and can do little to affect the rate at which it unwinds. Spend the time slowly packing away the library; the crates are too heavy to move and lie where they are filled.

Cell count down to 400,000.

Woke 8:10. To sleep 7:15. (Appear to have lost my watch without realizing it; had to drive into town to buy another.)

JUNE 14: 9½ hours. Time races, flashing past like an expressway. However, the last week of a holiday always goes faster than the first. At the present rate there should be about four to five weeks left. This morning I tried to visualize what the last week or so—the final, 3, 2, 1, out—would be like, had a sudden chilling attack of pure fear, unlike anything I've ever felt before. Took me half an hour to steady myself enough for an intravenous.

Kaldren pursues me like my luminescent shadow, chalked up on the gateway '96,688,365,498,702.' Should confuse the mail man.

Woke 9:05. To sleep 6:36.

JUNE 19: 8¾ hours. Anderson rang up this morning. I nearly put the phone down on him, but managed to go through the pretense of making the final arrangements. He congratulated me on my stoicism, even used the word "heroic." Don't feel it. Despair erodes everything—courage, hope, self-discipline, all the better qualities. It's so damned difficult to sustain that impersonal attitude of passive acceptance implicit in the scientific tradition. I try to think of Galileo before the Inquisition, Freud surmounting the endless pain of his jaw cancer surgery.

Met Kaldren downtown, had a long discussion about the Mercury Seven. He's convinced that they refused to leave the moon deliberately, after the "reception party" waiting for them had put them in the cosmic picture. They were told by the mysterious emissaries from Orion that the exploration of deep space was pointless, that they were too late as the life of the universe is now virtually over!!! According to K. there are Air Force generals who take this nonsense seriously, but I suspect it's simply an obscure attempt on K.'s part to console me.

Must have the phone disconnected. Some contractor keeps calling me up about payment for fifty bags of cement he claims I collected ten days ago. Says he helped me load them onto a truck himself. I did drive Whitby's pickup into town but only to get some lead screening. What does he think I'd do with all that cement? Just the sort of irritating thing you don't expect to hang over your final exit. (Moral: don't try too hard to forget Eniwetok.)

Woke 9:40. To sleep 4:15.

JUNE 25: 7½ hours. Kaldren was snooping around the lab again today. Phoned me there; when I answered a recorded voice he'd rigged up rambled out a long string of numbers, like an insane super-Tim. These practical jokes of his get rather wearing. Fairly soon I'll have to go over and come to terms with him, much as I hate the prospect. Anyway, Miss Mars is a pleasure to look at.

One meal is enough now, topped up with a

glucose shot. Sleep is still "black," completely unrefreshing. Last night I took a 16-mm film of the first three hours, screened it this morning at the lab. The first true horror movie; I looked like a half-animated corpse.

Woke 10:25. To sleep 3:45.

JULY 3: 5¾ hours. Little done today. Deepening lethargy; dragged myself over to the lab, nearly left the road twice. Concentrated enough to feed the zoo and get the log up to date. Read through the operating manuals Whitby left for the last time, decided on a delivery rate of 40 roentgens/min., target distance of 350 cm. Everything is ready now.

Woke 11:05. To sleep 3:15.

Powers stretched, shifted his head slowly across the pillow, focusing on the shadows cast onto the ceiling by the blind. Then he looked down at his feet, saw Kaldren sitting on the end of the bed, watching him quietly.

"Hello, Doctor," he said, putting out his cigarette. "Late night? You look tired."

Powers heaved himself onto one elbow, glanced at his watch. It was just after eleven. For a moment his brain blurred, and he swung his legs around and sat on the edge of the bed, elbows on his knees, massaging some life into his face.

He noticed that the room was full of smoke. "What are you doing here?" he asked Kaldren.

"I came over to invite you to lunch." He indicated the bedside phone. "Your line was dead so I drove round. Hope you don't mind me climbing in. Rang the bell for about half an hour. I'm surprised you didn't hear it."

Powers nodded, then stood up and tried to smooth the creases out of his cotton slacks. He had gone to sleep without changing for over a week, and they were damp and stale.

As he started for the bathroom door Kaldren pointed to the camera tripod on the other side of the bed. "What's this? Going into the blue movie business, Doctor?"

Powers surveyed him dimly for a moment, glanced at the tripod without replying, and then noticed his open diary on the bedside table. Wondering whether Kaldren had read the last entries, he went back and picked it up, then stepped into the bathroom and closed the door behind him.

From the mirror cabinet he took out a syringe and an ampoule, after the shot leaned against the door waiting for the stimulant to pick up.

Kaldren was in the lounge when he returned to him, reading the labels on the crates lying about in the center of the floor.

"O.K., then," Powers told him, "I'll join you for lunch." He examined Kaldren carefully. He looked more subdued than usual; there was an air almost of deference about him.

"Good," Kaldren said. "By the way, are you leaving?"

"Does it matter?" Powers asked curtly. "I thought you were in Anderson's care?"

Kaldren shrugged. "Please yourself. Come round at about twelve," he suggested, adding pointedly, "That'll give you time to clean up and change. What's that all over your shirt? Looks like lime."

Powers peered down, brushed at the white streaks. After Kaldren had left he threw the clothes away, took a shower, and unpacked a clean suit from one of the trunks.

Until this liaison with Coma, Kaldren lived alone in the old abstract summer house on the north shore of the lake. This was a seven-story folly originally built by an eccentric millionaire mathematician in the form of a spiraling concrete ribbon that wound around itself like an insane serpent, serving walls, floors, and ceilings. Only Kaldren had solved the building, a geometric model of $\sqrt{-1}$, and consequently he had been able to take it off the agents' hands at a comparatively low rent. In the evenings Powers had often watched him from the laboratory, striding restlessly from one level to the next, swinging through the labyrinth of inclines and terraces to the rooftop, where his lean angular figure stood out like a gallows against the sky, his lonely eyes sifting out radio lanes for the next day's trapping.

Powers noticed him there when he drove up at noon, poised on a ledge 150 feet above, head raised theatrically to the sky.

Kaldren!" he shouted up suddenly into the silent air, half-hoping he might be jolted into losing his footing.

Kaldren broke out of his reverie and glanced down into the court. Grinning obliquely, he waved his right arm in a slow semicircle.

"Come up," he called, then turned back to the sky.

Powers leaned against the car. Once, a few months previously, he had accepted the same invitation, stepped through the entrance, and within three minutes lost himself helplessly in a second-floor cul de sac. Kaldren had taken half an hour to find him.

Powers waited while Kaldren swung down from his eyrie, vaulting through the wells and stairways, then rode up in the elevator with him to the penthouse suite.

They carried their cocktails through into a wide glass-roofed studio, the huge white ribbon of concrete uncoiling around them like toothpaste squeezed from an enormous tube. On the staged levels running parallel and across them rested pieces of gray abstract furniture, giant photographs on angled screens, carefully labeled exhibits laid out on low tables, all dominated by twenty-foot-high black letters on the rear wall which spelt out the single vast word:

YOU

Kaldren pointed to it. "What you might call the supraliminal approach." He gestured Powers in conspiratorially, finishing his drink in a gulp. "This is *my* laboratory, Doctor," he said with a note of pride. "Much more significant than yours, believe me."

Powers smiled wryly to himself and examined the first exhibit, an old ECG tape traversed by a series of faded inky wriggles. It was labeled, *"Einstein, A.; Alpha Waves. 1922."*

He followed Kaldren around, sipping slowly at his drink, enjoying the brief feeling of alertness the amphetamine provided. Within two hours it would fade, leave his brain feeling like a block of blotting paper.

Kaldren chattered away, explaining the significance of the so-called Terminal Documents. "They're end-prints, Powers, final statements, the products of total fragmentation. When I've got enough together I'll build a new world for myself out of them." He picked a thick paperbound volume off one of the tables, riffled through its pages. "Association tests of the Nuremburg Twelve. I have to include these . . ."

Powers strolled on absently without listening. Over in the corner were what appeared to be three ticker-tape machines, lengths of tape hanging from their mouths. He wondered whether Kaldren was misguided enough to be playing the stock market, which had been declining slowly for twenty years.

"Powers," he heard Kaldren say. "I was telling you about the Mercury Seven." He pointed to a collection of typewritten sheets tacked to a screen. "These are transcripts of their final signals radioed back from the recording monitors."

Powers examined the sheets cursorily, read a line at random.

". . . Blue . . . People . . . Recycle . . . Orion . . . Telemeters . . ."

Powers nodded noncommittally. "Interesting. What are the ticker tapes for over there?"

Kaldren grinned. "I've been waiting for months for you to ask me that. Have a look."

Powers went over and picked up one of the tapes. The machine was labeled, *"Auriga 225-G. Interval: 69 hours."*

The tape read:

$$96,688,365,498,695$$
$$96,688,365,498,694$$
$$96,688,365,498,693$$
$$96,688,365,498,692$$

Powers dropped the tape. "Looks rather familiar. What does the sequence represent?"

Kaldren shrugged. "No one knows."

"What do you mean? It must replicate something."

"Yes, it does. A diminishing mathematical progression. A countdown, if you like."

Powers picked up the tape on the right, tabbed, *"Aries 44R951. Interval: 49 days."*

Here the sequence ran:

876,567,988,347,779,877,654,434
876,567,988,347,779,877,654,433
876,567,988,347,779,877,654,432

Powers looked round. "How long does it take each signal to come through?"

"Only a few seconds. They're tremendously compressed laterally, of course. A computer at the observatory breaks them down. They were first picked up at Jodrell Bank about twenty years ago. Nobody bothers to listen to them now."

Powers turned to the last tape.

6,554
6,553
6,552
6,551

"Nearing the end of its run," he commented. He glanced at the label on the hood, which read: *"Unidentified radio source, Canes Venatici. Interval: 97 weeks."*

He showed the tape to Kaldren. "Soon be over."

Kaldren shook his head. He lifted a heavy directory-sized volume off a table, cradled it in his hands. His face had suddenly become somber and haunted. "I doubt it," he said. "Those are only the last four digits. The whole number contains over 50 million."

He handed the volume to Powers, who turned to the title page. *"Master Sequence of Serial Signal received by Jodrell Bank Radio-Observatory, University of Manchester, England, 0012:59 hours, 21-5-72. Source: NGC 9743, Canes Venatici."* He thumbed the thick stack of closely printed pages, millions of numerals, as Kaldren had said, running up and down across a thousand consecutive pages.

Powers shook his head, picked up the tape again, and stared at it thoughtfully.

"The computer only breaks down the last four digits," Kaldren explained. "The whole series comes over in each 15-second-long package, but it took IBM more than two years to unscramble one of them."

"Amazing," Powers commented. "But what is it?"

"A countdown, as you can see. NGC 9743, somewhere in Canes Venatici. The big spirals there are breaking up, and they're saying goodbye. God knows who they think we are but they're letting us know all the same, beaming it out on the hydrogen line for everyone in the universe to hear." He paused. "Some people have put other interpretations on them, but there's one piece of evidence that rules out everything else."

"Which is?"

Kaldren pointed to the last tape from Canes Venatici. "Simply that it's been estimated that by the time this series reaches zero the universe will have just ended."

Powers fingered the tape reflectively. "Thoughtful

of them to let us know what the real time is," he remarked.

"I agree, it is," Kaldren said quietly. "Applying the inverse square law that signal source is broadcasting at a strength of about three million megawatts raised to the hundredth power. About the size of the entire Local Group. Thoughtful is the word."

Suddenly he gripped Powers' arm, held it tightly, and peered into his eyes closely, his throat working with emotion.

"You're not alone, Powers, don't think you are. These are the voices of time, and they're all saying goodbye to you. Think of yourself in a wider context. Every particle in your body, every grain of sand, every galaxy carried the same signature. As you've just said, you know what the time is now, so what does the rest matter? There's no need to go on looking at the clock."

Powers took his hand, squeezed it firmly. "Thanks, Kaldren. I'm glad you understand." He walked over to the window, looked down across the white lake. The tension between himself and Kaldren had dissipated; he felt that all his obligations to him had at last been met. Now he wanted to leave as quickly as possible, forget him as he had forgotten the faces of the countless other patients whose exposed brains had passed between his fingers.

He went back to the ticker machines, tore the tapes from their slots, and stuffed them into his pockets. "I'll take these along to remind myself. Say goodbye to Coma for me, will you."

He moved toward the door, when he reached it looked back to see Kaldren standing in the shadow of the three giant letters on the far wall, his eyes staring listlessly at his feet.

THE VOICES OF TIME

As Powers drove away he noticed that Kaldren had gone up onto the roof, watched him in the driving mirror waving slowly until the car disappeared around a bend.

V

The outer circle was now almost complete. A narrow segment, an arc about ten feet long, was missing, but otherwise the low perimeter wall ran continuously six inches off the concrete floor around the outer lane of the target bull, enclosing the huge rebus within it. Three concentric circles, the largest a hundred yards in diameter, separated from each other by ten-foot intervals, formed the rim of the device, divided into four segments by the arms of an enormous cross radiating from its center, where a small round platform had been built a foot above the ground.

Powers worked swiftly, pouring sand and cement into the mixer, tipping in water until a rough paste formed, then carried it across to the wooden forms and tamped the mixture down into the narrow channel.

Within ten minutes he had finished, quickly dismantled the forms before the cement had set, and slung the timbers into the back seat of the car. Dusting his hands on his trousers, he went over to the mixer and pushed it fifty yards away into the long shadow of the surrounding hills.

Without pausing to survey the gigantic cipher on which he had labored patiently for so many afternoons, he climbed into the car and drove off on a wake of bone-white dust, splitting the pools of indigo shadow.

*　　*　　*

He reached the laboratory at three o'clock, jumped from the car as it lurched back on its brakes. Inside the entrance he first switched on the lights, then hurried round, pulling the sun curtains down and shackling them to the floor slots, effectively turning the dome into a steel tent.

In their tanks behind him the plants and animals stirred quietly, responding to the sudden flood of cold fluorescent light. Only the chimpanzee ignored him. It sat on the floor of its cage, neurotically jamming the puzzle dice into the polythene bucket, exploding in bursts of sudden rage when the pieces refused to fit.

Powers went over to it, noticing the shattered glass fiber reinforcing panels bursting from the dented helmet. Already the chimp's face and forehead were bleeding from self-inflicted blows. Powers picked up the remains of the geranium that had been hurled through the bars, attracted the chimp's attention with it, then tossed a black pellet he had taken from a capsule in the desk drawer. The chimp caught it with a quick flick of the wrist, for a few seconds juggled the pellet with a couple of dice as it concentrated on the puzzle, then pulled it out of the air and swallowed it in a gulp.

Without waiting, Powers slipped off his jacket and stepped toward the X-ray theater. He pulled back the high sliding doors to reveal the long glassy metallic snout of the Maxitron, then started to stack the lead screening shields against the rear wall.

A few minutes later the generator hummed into life.

The anemone stirred. Basking in the warm subliminal sea of radiation rising around it, prompted by countless pelagic memories, it reached tentatively across the tank, groping blindly toward the dim uterine sun. Its tendrils flexed, the thousands of dormant neural cells in their tips regrouping and multiplying, each harnessing the unlocked energies of its nucleus. Chains forged themselves, lattices tiered upward into multifaceted lenses, focused slowly on the vivid spectral outlines of the sounds dancing like phosphorescent waves around the darkened chamber of the dome.

Gradually an image formed, revealing an enormous black fountain that poured an endless stream of brilliant light over the circle of benches and tanks. Beside it a figure moved, adjusting the flow through its mouth. As it stepped across the floor its feet threw off vivid bursts of color, its hands racing along the benches conjured up a dazzling chiaroscura, balls of blue and violet light that exploded fleetingly in the darkness like miniature star-shells.

Photons murmured. Steadily, as it watched the glimmering screen of sounds around it, the anemone continued to expand. Its ganglia linked, heeding a new source of stimuli from the delicate diaphragms in the crown of its notochord. The silent outlines of the laboratory began to echo softly; waves of muted sound fell from the arc lights and echoed off the benches and furniture below. Etched in sound, their angular forms resonated with sharp persistent overtones. The plastic-ribbed chairs were a buzz of staccato discords, the square-sided desk a continuous double-featured tone.

Ignoring these sounds once they had been perceived, the anemone turned to the ceiling, which reverberated like a shield in the sounds pouring steadily from the fluorescent tubes. Streaming

*through a narrow skylight, its voice clear and strong,
interweaved by numberless overtones, the sun sang
. . .*

It was a few minutes before dawn when Powers left
the laboratory and stepped into his car. Behind him
the great dome lay silent in the darkness, the thin
shadows of the white moonlit hills falling across its
surface. Powers free-wheeled the car down the long
curving drive to the lake road below, listening to the
tires cutting across the blue gravel, then let out the
clutch and accelerated the engine.

As he drove along, the limestone hills half hidden in
the darkness on his left, he gradually became aware
that, although no longer looking at the hills, he was
still in some oblique way conscious of their forms and
outlines in the back of his mind. The sensation was
undefined but none the less certain, a strange almost
visual impression that emanated most strongly from
the deep clefts and ravines dividing one cliff face from
the next. For a few minutes Powers let it play upon
him, without trying to identify it, a dozen strange
images moving across his brain.

The road swung up around a group of chalets built
onto the lake shore, taking the car right under the lee
of the hills, and Powers suddenly felt the massive
weight of the escarpment rising up into the dark sky
like a cliff of luminous chalk, and realized the identity
of the impression now registering powerfully within his
mind. Not only could he see the escarpment, but he
was aware of its enormous age, felt distinctly the countless millions of years since it had first reared out of the
magma of the earth's crust. The ragged crests three
hundred feet above him, the dark gulleys and fissures,

the smooth boulders by the roadside at the foot of the cliff, all carried a distinct image of themselves across to him, a thousand voices that together told of the total time that had elapsed in the life of the escarpment, a psychic picture as defined and clear as the visual image brought to him by his eyes.

Involuntarily, Powers had slowed the car, and turning his eyes away from the hill face he felt a second wave of time sweep across the first. The image was broader but of shorter perspectives, radiating from the wide disc of the salt lake, breaking over the ancient limestone cliffs like shallow rollers dashing against a towering headland.

Closing his eyes, Powers lay back and steered the car along the interval between the two time fronts, feeling the images deepen and strengthen within his mind. The vast age of the landscape, the inaudible chorus of voices resonating from the lake and from the white hills, seemed to carry him back through time, down endless corridors to the first thresholds of the world.

He turned the car off the road along the track leading toward the target range. On either side of the culvert the cliff faces boomed and echoed with vast impenetrable time fields, like enormous opposed magnets. As he finally emerged between them onto the flat surface of the lake it seemed to Powers that he could feel the separate identity of each sand grain and salt crystal calling to him from the surrounding ring of hills.

He parked the car beside the mandala and walked slowly toward the outer concrete rim curving away into the shadows. Above him he could hear the stars, a million cosmic voices that crowded the sky from one horizon to the next, a true canopy of time. Like jostling radio beacons, their long aisles interlocking at countless angles, they plunged into the sky from the narrowest recesses of space. He saw the dim red disc of Sirius, heard its ancient voice, untold millions of years old, dwarfed by the huge spiral nebulae in Andromeda, a gigantic carousel of vanished universes, their voices almost as old as the cosmos itself. To Powers the sky seemed an endless babel, the time-song of a thousand galaxies overlaying each other in his mind. As he moved slowly toward the center of the mandala he craned up at the glittering traverse of the Milky Way, searching the confusion of clamoring nebulae and constellations.

Stepping into the inner circle of the Mandala, a few yards from the platform at its center, he realized that the tumult was beginning to fade, and that a single stronger voice had emerged and was dominating the others. He climbed onto the platform, raised his eyes to the darkened sky, moving through the constellations to the island galaxies beyond them, hearing the thin archaic voices reaching to him across the millennia. In his pockets he felt the paper tapes, and turned to find the distant diadem of Canes Venatici, heard its great voice mounting in his mind.

Like an endless river, so broad that its banks were below the horizons, it flowed steadily toward him, a vast course of time that spread outwards to fill the sky and the universe, enveloping everything within them. Moving slowly, the forward direction of its majestic current almost imperceptible, Powers knew that its source was the source of the cosmos itself. As it passed him, he felt its massive magnetic pull, let himself be drawn into it, borne gently on its powerful back. Quietly it carried him away, and he rotated slowly, facing the direction of the tide. Around him the outlines of the hills and the lake had faded, but the image of the mandala, like a cosmic clock, remained fixed before his eyes, illuminating the broad surface of the stream. Watching it constantly, he felt his body gradually dissolving, its physical dimensions melting into the vast continuum of the current, which bore him out into the center of the great channel sweeping him onward, beyond hope now but at rest, down the broadening reaches of the river of eternity.

As the shadows faded, retreating into the hill slopes, Kaldren stepped out of his car, walked hesitantly toward the concrete rim of the outer circle. Fifty yards away, at the center, Coma knelt beside Powers' body, her small hands pressed to his dead face. A gust of wind stirred the sand, dislodging a strip of tape that drifted toward Kaldren's feet. He bent down and picked it up, then rolled it carefully in his hands and slipped it into his pocket. The dawn air was cold, and he turned up the collar of his jacket, watching Coma impassively.

"It's six o'clock," he told her after a few minutes. "I'll go and get the police. You stay with him." He paused and then added, "Don't let them break the clock."

Coma turned and looked at him. "Aren't you coming back?"

"I don't know." Nodding to her, Kaldren swung on his heel and went over to the car.

He reached the lake road, five minutes later parked the car in the drive outside Whitby's laboratory.

The dome was in darkness, all its windows shuttered, but the generator still hummed in the X-ray theater. Kaldren stepped through the entrance and switched on the lights. In the theater he touched the grilles of the generator, felt the warm cylinder of the beryllium, end-window. The circular target table was revolving slowly, its setting a 1 r.p.m., a steel restraining chair shackled to it hastily. Grouped in a semicircle a few feet away were most of the tanks and cages, piled on top of each other haphazardly. In one of them an enormous squidlike plant had almost managed to climb from its vivarium. Its long translucent tendrils clung to the edges of the tank, but its body had burst into a jellified pool of globular mucilage. In another an enormous spider had trapped itself in its own web, hung helplessly in the center of a huge three-dimensional maze of phosphorescing thread, twitching spasmodically.

All the experimental plants and animals had died. The chimp lay on its back among the remains of the hutch, the helmet forward over its eyes. Kaldren watched it for a moment, then sat down on the desk and picked up the phone.

While he dialed the number he noticed a film reel lying on the blotter. For a moment he stared at the label, then slid the reel into his pocket beside the tape.

After he had spoken to the police he turned off the lights and went out to the car, drove off slowly down the drive.

When he reached the summer house the early sunlight was breaking across the ribbonlike balconies and terraces. He took the lift to the penthouse, made his way through into the museum. One by one he opened the shutters and let the sunlight play over the exhibits. Then he pulled a chair over to a side window, sat back, and stared up at the light pouring through into the room.

Two or three hours later he heard Coma outside, calling up to him. After half an hour she went away, but a little later a second voice appeared and shouted up at Kaldren. He left his chair and closed all the shutters overlooking the front courtyard, and eventually he was left undistrubed.

Kaldren returned to his seat and lay back quietly, his eyes gazing across the lines of exhibits. Half-asleep, periodically he leaned up and adjusted the flow of light through the shutter, thinking to himself, as he would do through the coming months, of Powers and his strange mandala, and of the seven and their journey to the white gardens of the moon, and the blue people who had come from Orion and spoken in poetry to them of ancient beautiful worlds beneath golden suns in the island galaxies, vanished forever now in the myriad deaths of the cosmos.

DAW

Don't Miss These Exciting DAW Anthologies